ILD
Christmas
2014

Unwrap these Presents

EDITED BY ASTRID OHLETZ AND R.G. EMANUELLE

Table of Contents

Introduction

Family, happiness, love, presents, joy, snow, and plenty of food—all things that come to mind when we think of Christmas, possibly the most wonderful time of the year for some of us.

However, Christmas is not a merry time for everyone. Some people have to spend it alone; some hate that time of the year and don't celebrate it; and others don't even have a home to spend Christmas in.

That is why we decided to donate all profits from this anthology to the ***Albert Kennedy Trust*** in the UK and the ***Ali Forney Center*** in New York City. Both organizations provide housing for homeless LGBTIQ youth. Those young people really need our help, and we can't think of a better way to support the cause than to do what we love—writing, editing, and publishing.

A huge thank-you goes out to the authors who submitted their stories to us. We have an amazing variety of Christmas stories and even one Hanukkah story.

Also, thank you to the army of editors that supported us:

Nikki Busch, Day Petersen, Glenda Poulter, Michelle Aguilar, Sandra Gerth, Andi Marquette, Julie Klein, Blu, Debra Doyle, Alissa McGowan, and Fletcher DeLancey.

Last but not least, thanks to the team at Streetlight Graphics, who once again created an amazing cover.

Enjoy the read!
Astrid Ohletz & R.G. Emanuelle

Red Christmas Truck

NIKKI BUSCH

Your shiny red truck
at midnight
Christmas Eve,
your fortress against festivities,
let me in;
let me show you how to celebrate away
the demons of dysfunction past.
Inside the cold depths of this silent metal Mass,
my hand catches yours,
removes it from its clenched grip on the steering wheel,
strokes away your refusal
to see Christmas in a new light,
with me,
just me
by your side.
I graze the inside of your wrist,
ignite the hearth within your heart.
Ah yes I knew it was in there,
just had to stoke it.
My fingers lap like errant embers
beneath your corduroy shirt,
searing your belly
and the surface of your bra.
Plunging deeper,
I discover your hidden gift,
moist and waiting for delivery;
the only present I demand,
and you give it.
Plentifully.
Christmas Eve
in your shiny red truck,
we revel in the heat
and hum
of a hungry holy love.

Red and Green and Gray

JOVE BELLE

DUST BILLOWS UP WHEN CHARLIE drops the last box on the hand truck. She fans the air, but stifles a cough because Liz is watching her. There's something about the way Liz's eyes follow her that makes her feel vulnerable, and that's never a good way to feel in here.

As a little girl, Charlie always cast herself as the hero in the movie of her life. As an adult, she discovered that reality wasn't nearly as shiny as it is on the big screen. With a couple of bad decisions and the bang of a gavel, she was officially declared the bad guy. Now, instead of Hollywood sets, she has drab prison grey as a backdrop.

"That's the last one." Charlie feels stupid as soon as she says it because there aren't any boxes left on the shelf marked "CHRISTMAS" and Liz can see that for herself.

"Obviously." Liz rolls her eyes and flips her hair back. She's got dark eyeliner swooping out from her eyelids like wings, courtesy of some contraband liquid eyeliner. If Charlie ever tried that, she'd poke her own eye out with the wand and end up with a black smear over the side of her face.

"Come on, Blanca." Liz walks away, leaving the boxes behind.

Charlie kicks the hand truck forward and then does an awkward fast walk to catch up with Liz. It's not like they're friends or anything, but for whatever reason, they were put on this work assignment together and it's just better if they don't get separated.

"Hold up," Charlie yells after chasing Liz for half a block. Liz isn't even walking fast. She has that "I'm too cool to be bothered" gliding walk that all the Latina girls seem to share, yet she's always ahead of Charlie.

Liz glares, but stops and waits anyway. "Hurry up."

When they pass Liz's block, the Latinas yell and whoop and say things in Spanish that Charlie doesn't understand. Except *lesbiana*. She definitely knows that word.

Liz grabs her crotch and lurches her hips forward as she flips them off. They all know Liz isn't a lesbian, but maybe spending time with Charlie is a problem for her.

"Sorry," Charlie mumbles, almost under her breath, and feels stupid because of it. She doesn't need to apologize for being gay. She never did on the outside. It's weird—half the women in here are hooking up, but only a handful admit to being anything but completely straight. As far as she knows, though, Liz hasn't hooked up with anyone.

"Why? It's not your fault they're being stupid *putas*." Liz's words are rough and she doesn't look at Charlie when she says them. Still, it feels like Liz is defending her and Charlie likes that.

"Right." She shakes her head. When she'd arrived, they gave her a list of rules, both written from guards and understood from the other inmates. She's been trying to sort through them ever since. She's pretty sure that Liz shouldn't be calling her people *putas*, especially not to Charlie, but she's not going to point it out.

"Whatever. Let's just get this shit done."

They don't talk again until they reach the common area. There's a card game in the corner and it looks like her friend Mary might be winning. It's hard to tell because of the way they protect the markers from view. Winnings could just as quickly be confiscated by the guards as collected by the winner.

Other than the card game and a couple women watching TV, the room is empty. Charlie parks the stack of boxes next to the wall, out of the way in case other people come in. Liz opens the top box and pulls out a stack of paper decorations. There's a menorah, a reindeer, and a picture of a black woman in traditional African robes lighting a candle. The rest of the decorations are for an amalgam of holidays, but the majority are faded red and green.

When she was a kid, Charlie used to dream of decorating for Christmas with fancy decorations that they stored in the attic. Except the apartment her mom rented didn't have an attic and her mom thought decorations were a waste of money. The Department of Corrections seems to agree.

"Does it bother you?" Liz holds up a string of paper garland that looks as if a kindergartener glued it together.

Charlie shrugs. "It's ugly, but I don't really care. I just want to get this done." The condition of the decorations doesn't matter so long as they finish on time.

"No, not that." Liz tapes the ends of the garland on either side of the window that leads to the observation room where the guards hang out between patrols. The window gives them a clear view of the area while being protected by the grating between the layers of glass. The garland droops pathetically in the middle. "When they call you that, does it bother you?"

"Oh." Charlie doesn't know how to answer. She and Liz aren't friends, yet the question deserves an honest answer. But it's loaded, the kind of thing that can be used against her. She stares at Liz and tries to figure out her motivation for asking. Liz never looks her way, but picks another sad decoration from the box instead. Charlie decides to go for it. "No, why would it?"

"Because they're being bitches."

"Sure, but it's true." She shrugged and taped a round decoration to the wall. She thinks maybe it's supposed to look like a glass ornament for a tree, but she can't be sure. Not that it really matters. Nothing about these decorations from 1983 is going to make people feel festive, anyway.

"Hmm...since when doesn't the truth hurt?" Liz says it quietly enough so that Charlie thinks she wasn't meant to hear, so she doesn't respond.

Charlie works with an eye on the clock. She's not sure if she's allowed to leave at three or if she has to stay until the decorating is done. It's twenty minutes away, so she works a little faster, just in case.

Liz purposefully blocks her, standing with one hand on her hip and a crooked half-smile on her face. "What's your hurry, Turbo?"

"Nothing." Charlie checks the time again. "I just have a thing."

It's more than a thing, but she doesn't like to talk about it because most of the other women in here would think she's being pretentious. It's easier to leave it alone.

"A thing?" Liz looks skeptical, but she steps to the side. "What kind of thing."

This time, Charlie takes the box with her. They've cleared three of the five, but she doesn't want to take the chance that Liz will stop her again. "It's just...reading."

That was the simplest explanation. Hopefully, Liz would accept it.

"What's that even mean? Just reading? You going to the library?"

"No, the visitors' room." Charlie pulls about a thousand cotton balls from the bottom of the next box and half of them fall on the floor. What the hell is this mess even supposed to be? She looks closer and sees that they're glued together in little stacks. Snowmen. Liz stops what she's doing and helps Charlie pick up the ones from the floor. They spread them over the top of a bookshelf like a tiny snow army. Except that they are gray with age, so it looks more like a dust bunny migration.

"Who goes to the visitors' room to read? What aren't you telling me?"

Charlie sighs. She's not going to get away with not telling Liz the details. "They asked for volunteers in one of my classes." Her English composition class to be specific, but Liz wouldn't care about that. "We read letters to Santa."

"That's it? You just read the letters? That's dumb." Liz went back to the decorations. One more box to go.

"No, we write back."

"What? Let me understand this. Little Joaquin writes to Santa, asking for a tricycle or whatever shit, and he gets a letter back from an inmate? Ain't that something? His parents would shit for sure."

Charlie had thought about that and decided she didn't care. She likes the idea of Christmas. She especially likes that she might be helping a kid to believe in Santa for just a little longer. If she'd gotten a letter from Santa when she was a kid...well, that would have been something. It would have been better than anything her mom ever gave her, including the time she got the art set with the case that doubled as an easel. That only had two colors of paint missing and half the tablet was unused.

"I like it." She speaks softly, not really wanting to argue with Liz, but unable to not say something.

"Yeah?" Liz looks at her for a moment, her face blank. Charlie thinks if she'd ever managed to perfect a look like that, she might not have ended up in here in the first place. "How come they didn't ask the rest of us?"

Charlie hangs up a reindeer. Someone had drawn an oversized penis on the animal and she debates putting it back in the box. She decides the other women will enjoy the artwork, so she leaves it up.

"I don't know. They said they wanted students."

"Shit. I could be a student."

Charlie almost asks Liz if she can read, but stops herself in time. Plenty of the women in here can't. That doesn't mean they won't kick her ass for asking. Instead, she nods and says, "Yes, you could be."

"That's right." Liz nods like she's decided something important.

"Why don't you?" There are a few Latinas in her classes, but they are older. None of the girls Liz's age signed up.

"That's for punks." Liz's answer is immediate, but the look on her face says maybe she doesn't believe the words.

"Maybe." Charlie doesn't agree, but Liz looks like she's rethinking her answer anyway. Maybe if she gives her some space, Liz will change her mind on her own.

They work in silence for a few moments, then Liz asks, "You learn anything good?"

"I think so."

"But what's the point. Nobody gonna hire a convict." Liz draws out the word "convict" into two hard syllables.

Charlie doesn't know if that's true, but that isn't the point, anyway. "So what? I'm supposed to be dumb because that's what people think?"

"Nobody thinks you're dumb." Liz regards her seriously, then ducks her head. It looks like she might be blushing, but Charlie can't be sure. She's a little stunned to hear that Liz thinks about her at all.

"Thanks."

"So, these letters…what do they say?"

Charlie considers the letters, how most of them are from spoiled kids asking for toys that don't really matter. Those kids get a form letter back from Santa. "Most of them are crap. Rich kids telling instead of asking."

Liz purses her lips together and makes a noise that sounds a little bit like a disappointed sprinkler. "Then why read them?"

"Because, some of them…they're kids like I used to be. Hoping for something they'll never get."

Liz nods, slow and thoughtful. She has the last decoration in her hands and the clock has just reached three o'clock. "Maybe I could read some, too?"

Charlie takes the faded paper Santa from Liz and tapes it to the window. She tries to position it so that it will look like the guard in the chair has a Santa head. She's pretty sure they'll make her move it, but she thinks it's funny, anyway.

She stacks the empty boxes on the hand truck and says, "We need to hurry, then."

This time, Liz takes the hand truck from her and pushes it all the way to the storage room. She doesn't stop to talk to the other Latinas when they pass her block. "Ignore them bitches."

When they get back to the storeroom, they realize that someone locked it while they were gone. Liz taps her foot impatiently and Charlie smiles because who would ever have thought that Liz would want to read Dear Santa letters from a bunch of five-year-olds. But here she is puffing about being late because some asshole locked them out.

Charlie sees one of the guards who doesn't give her the creeps and she fast-walks to catch up with him. They're not supposed to run and the consequences vary depending on the guard's mood. She thinks this guard might be gay because as far as she knows, he's never hit on any of the women. Maybe he's just a decent guy, but she doubts it. Still, she likes that she's never walked in on him getting a blowjob from one of the inmates.

She finally catches him. Liz rolls her eyes as he searches through his key ring, grumbling the entire time about being interrupted. It takes a long time, but not as long as it would if she or Liz asked him to hurry. He waits until they put everything inside the room and relocks the door. Thank God for that or someone might steal all the busted-ass decorations.

"God, that took forever." Liz walks fast, and not that sliding, cool gait of hers, either. She looks like she's in a hurry and that makes Charlie smile again. "Hurry up, Blanca." Liz checks to make sure Charlie is with her.

"Charlie."

"Huh?"

"My name is Charlie, not Blanca." She knows enough Spanish to know what Liz is calling her, but she figures since their bonding over Santa, she'll take the chance and try to teach Liz her real name.

Liz makes an annoyed face, pursing her mouth and furrowing her brows. "I know your name."

That surprises Charlie. She'd noticed Liz, of course, but who wouldn't? Liz looks like an angry, East Los version of Penelope Cruz. But this is the second time Liz has said something to make Charlie think Liz has noticed her. She wants to ask about it but isn't sure how. Instead, she asks, "Then why do you call me Blanca?"

It's a stupid question. The Latinas call all the white women Blanca. It's just the way things are. Liz looks at her sideways, but doesn't stop walking. They're almost to the visitors' room. The look on Liz's face, as if she thinks Charlie is a special kind of dumb, makes her wish she hadn't asked.

"Forget I said that." Charlie shakes her head and hates the way the words come out as an uncertain mumble.

"No, you're right. I can call you Charlie. Just... bitches will give you shit if I do."

That sounds backwards to Charlie. She's pretty sure they'll give Liz a hard time, not her. "But they won't say anything to you?"

"Please. Nobody messes with me." Liz speaks with that false machismo that women develop after a few years inside. Or maybe it's not false for Liz, but so far it is for Charlie. She's only been here for six months, so maybe by the time she finishes her two-to-five years the machismo will be real. She hopes not. That overconfident "fuck you all" doesn't really match the rest of her personality. Still, maybe Liz is right and nobody messes with her. Or maybe she's decided she's willing to take it. Either way, Charlie isn't going to argue.

Charlie shrugs and smiles at Liz. She doesn't know what else to say and it doesn't matter anyway. They are at the visitors' room. She holds the door open and likes the way Liz smiles a little in return.

Liz pauses in the doorway. "Are you sure it's okay for me to be here?"

Charlie sees the coordinator, a volunteer with a tight bun who likes to be called Mrs. Gregson, and waves at her. Mrs. Gregson nods and starts toward them. "We're about to find out," Charlie replies.

Liz twirls her hair and shifts from foot to foot. Charlie almost puts her hand on Liz's arm to reassure her, but stops short of actual touching.

"Charlotte, it's good of you to join us today." Mrs. Gregson always speaks with stilted formality, but she isn't being snide. She's glad to see Charlie.

"I brought reinforcements." This time Charlie does touch Liz, nudging her forward. "This is my friend Liz."

She feels Liz tense at the word "friend," but Charlie doesn't elaborate. It's an introduction Mrs. Gregson will understand.

"That's lovely, dear. Nice to meet you, Liz. Is that short for Elizabeth?"

Liz nods and shakes Mrs. Gregson's hand and even chokes out a "Nice to meet you, too."

Charlie leads Liz to an empty table with a box of letters on it. Next to the box is a stack of form response letters, some blank paper with North Pole letterhead, a cup of pens, and a box of envelopes.

"We just pick one and go for it?" Liz grabs the top letter and sits down. She looks a little skeptical.

"Sure." Charlie selects her own letter and pulls it out to show Liz. It's pretty standard, some kid asking for expensive toys. "When they're like this, I just send back a form letter."

She tri-folds the letter and stuffs it in the envelope. They have to handwrite the address on the front, but she enjoys the practice. Her letters are still a little bumpy. She hopes the kids believe it was written by an elf or something.

"What's this other paper for?"

"In case you read one you want to write back to."

"That happens?"

"Not very often."

Liz opens a handful of letters. All of them get a form letter in return.

They work for an hour before Charlie reads one that makes her want to cry. It's from a little girl whose brother is sick. Her dad died last winter and her mom said they might have to move in with her aunt soon. She doesn't ask for anything, but wishes Santa a Merry Christmas and hopes her brother gets better soon.

She offers the letter to Liz. "Read this one."

While Liz is reading, Charlie thinks about what she wants to say. If she were the real Santa, she'd take the toys those other brats ask for and give them all to this kid and her brother.

"What are you going to tell her?"

Charlie shrugs. "I dunno. I'll thank her for writing and tell her that Santa loves her. And maybe tell her to give her mom and her brother a hug."

It wasn't much different from the form letter, but Charlie felt good about writing the words herself, like maybe the kid will think it's more special this way. She shows it to Liz when she's finished, something she's never done before. If Mrs. Gregson is ever near her when she comes across a letter like that, she shuffles it to the bottom of the pile until Mrs. Gregson leaves. Yet she feels okay letting Liz read what she wrote.

Liz hands it back. "Everyone thinks you're smart."

Charlie signs the letter "Santa" with big letters, like she imagines a man responsible for the happiness of all the children in the world would do, then folds it carefully and puts it in the envelope.

When she finishes, she notices Liz is still looking at her. She doesn't know why Liz said that about her being smart, but apparently she wants a response. "What? They only think that because I'm quiet."

"Is that why you really wanted to do this? Because you're still learning?"

"Oh, that." Charlie tried very hard to form her letters properly. What gave her away? "Yeah, I like the practice, but that's not why I'm doing this."

"Then why?"

"It just makes me feel good." She watches Liz, expecting her to scoff or roll her eyes, which is what she would do if any of her friends were here.

Instead Liz smiles and says, "Yeah, me too."

Their hands touch when they reach into the box at the same time. It feels nice, but Charlie pulls away.

"Why don't you have a girlfriend?" Liz doesn't look up from her letter.

"I do. Or, at least I did." Charlie's girlfriend, Amanda, hasn't been to see her in six weeks. They haven't talked on the phone in three. How long before she should officially move Amanda into the "ex" category?

"What's that even mean?" Liz asks.

"We're not communicating very well these days." Charlie doubts Liz cares about Amanda.

"She giving you a hard time? Want me to talk to her for you?" Liz asks with a straight face and Charlie thinks it's adorable. She can almost picture Liz walking up the steps to Amanda's house, her entire gang of fiercely made-up Latina girlfriends behind her.

Charlie shakes her head, forces herself not to smile. "She's not answering my calls. Doubt she'll answer yours."

"Oh, she's on the outside?"

"That's right."

"That's no excuse. Bitch is crazy to not treat you right. You should dump her."

"Maybe I will." She's been planning to do just that for over a week, but can't do anything until Amanda picks up the phone.

"Then what? Got someone new lined up?"

Charlie almost asks if Liz is volunteering, but doesn't because she's afraid of the answer. She kinda wants her to say yes and would be sad if she said no. On the other hand, she's terrified of what it would mean if she did say yes. Relationships are hard enough without prison rules to navigate.

"What about you?" Charlie changes the subject instead of answering.

Liz pauses long enough to grab a new letter. They're making good progress, the two of them. "My boyfriend," she shrugs slowly, "he's okay, ya know? But he...he's not a long-term thing."

"I'm sorry." She's really glad that she didn't make the crack about Liz volunteering to be her girlfriend. As a general rule, she doesn't play with straight girls. It's just too complicated.

"Don't be. I just got him to get my mom off my back. She thinks if I don't have a man, I must be gay."

"Are you?" Charlie ducks her head and looks around to see if anyone else is listening. Liz is being cool, but if anything is going to get her popped in the mouth, that question will do it.

"I dunno. Maybe. But you can't tell nobody that."

Charlie sits up straight, squirming a little. "So, why tell me?"

Liz shrugs one shoulder, shakes her head, and bites her bottom lip. She's definitely flirting. Charlie is almost sure of it. She feels her face flush with heat, so she looks at the letter in her hands and clamps her mouth shut to keep herself from saying something stupid.

"All right, everyone. That's time for today. Bring your addressed envelopes up here." Mrs. Gregson's cheerful announcement breaks whatever moment that's building between her and Liz. Charlie's pretty sure it's a good thing, but she's a little sad they didn't get to finish the conversation.

Liz walks to the front with her, their shoulders touching occasionally. Charlie apologizes the first time because it's not polite to bump into people. By the third time, she figures it's on purpose, so she just smiles and watches Liz from the corner of her eye.

They drop their letters into the outgoing box and Mrs. Gregson asks if they'll be back the next day. Charlie glances at Liz when she says, "I will be."

When Liz agrees she'll come again, too, Charlie's stomach does a giddy, flip-flop butterfly thing. She ducks her head and tries not to smile, but she can't help herself.

As they're walking back to the cellblocks, Liz says, "It's movie night." She leaves the statement open, as if there will be more words to follow that don't quite make it out of her mouth.

Charlie nods. She doesn't always go to movie night. Yes, it's something to do, but it's crowded and not everyone showers regularly. She likes to practice her reading in her bunk instead.

"Are you going?" Liz asks.

"I don't know. You?"

"'Course. I could save you a seat. If you want."

Charlie can't imagine sitting with Liz. One white girl in the middle of the Latinas would cause people to talk. "Really?"

"Yeah, like in the back, away from the others. You know?" Liz's shoulder touches hers again.

Charlie stops walking completely. She wants to look at Liz, to make sure she understands what's happening. "Serious?"

Liz chews her lip again. "If you want."

She wants. She had no idea how much she wanted until right this very minute, but she definitely wants.

"Okay."

"Great." Liz smiles. It's not the first time Charlie's seen that happen but it feels like it. She almost takes Liz's hand, then remembers where they are and how they're not allowed to touch.

When they reach Liz's block, she turns off without really saying anything, but she's still smiling. Charlie realizes her cheeks ache because she's been smiling, too. She rubs her face as she passes the common area. The decorations look a little brighter now.

She touches the Santa head as she passes by on the way to her own cellblock. Maybe she's the bad guy instead of the good guy, like she always wanted to be, but maybe that's okay. Maybe she and Liz can be bad guys together for a while.

The Miracle of the Lights

CINDY RIZZO

On the second night of Chanukah, I constructed a makeshift menorah out of an empty glass bottle and two tightly rolled pieces of paper crammed into the opening. Bending the papers away from one another, so that the whole contraption looked like the letter Y, I lit the ends and quickly said the blessings in a quiet corner of the park in Union Square.

I had been in this city four days—four cold and icy days—and I still had not found Tova.

She had left our village of Am Masada a few months ago, two days after Yom Kippur. The wedding they had planned for her and the boy she'd glimpsed only once in the presence of her parents, was to be held at the end of the holidays. They had mailed the invitations over the summer and were ready to move into the whirlwind of wedding preparation on the day Tova left.

On that morning, as I lay in bed twisting the sheets around my restless body, I heard faint scratching at my window. Because I was the eldest daughter with four brothers, I had my own bedroom, though it is generous to call where I slept a room. It was more like a large closet, but it was mine and I guarded the space jealously. No brothers were permitted to enter.

The scratching was Tova's signal. I uncoiled myself from the bedding and leaped over to the window. It was mid-October and mornings in the Catskill Mountains were already very chilly.

When I raised the window, Tova's head poked through the opening. I reached for her and she fell into my arms.

"Did I wake you, Chavalah?" she whispered into my ear.

I shook my head no. "I was twisting and turning all night." My body hiccupped with a quiet laugh. "Look at the bed."

Tova turned her head and saw the messy tangle of white sheets and blanket. She sighed. "I know this is hard for you. But you understand why I have to go. They are fitting me for a dress this afternoon. It's getting too difficult to pretend that I'm going through with this."

"I know," I said as I held her tighter. "But thinking of you out there where you don't know a soul and thinking of me here without you, it's…it's too much."

She handed me a small white bag. "I got us phones so we can stay in touch. I entered my number in yours. Hide it somewhere. I was only able to put ten dollars on it so we can't speak too often or too long. But at least we can remain in contact. I will call you every week right after Shabbos. Keep it on vibrate, so no one else can hear. I can't leave a message, so if you don't answer, I will call the next week."

"I'll make sure I can answer."

I raised my head and looked at her, committing to memory her dark brown hair, pulled back in a ponytail, covered by a gray wool cap I hadn't seen before. A sprinkle of pale, brown freckles spilled over both sides of the bridge of her nose. Her eyes, the color of black coffee, stared back, resolute but sad.

I glanced down and saw she was wearing faded green khaki pants tucked into her snow boots. We were only permitted to wear skirts and dresses tailored to the appropriate length below our knees.

"Where did you get these clothes?"

"From the donation box next to the library. I can move more freely in these than I can in my regular clothes. Plus they are warmer."

I nodded and then looked down at the floor. "I don't know when I will see you again," I said as a tear escaped. I gulped, trying to stop myself from crying. It felt too self-indulgent in these last few minutes we had together.

Tova lifted my chin, her expression serious, the hint of a challenge in her voice. "I don't know either, but Chava, you will soon be facing the same choice. There will be a boy chosen for you and a wedding will be planned. You turn eighteen before Chanukah comes."

I put my arms around her waist and drew myself into her embrace. She held me and we stayed quiet for a few minutes. Even through the fabric of her heavy wool coat I felt the rapid beating of her heart against the side of my head. I wanted to pull her to my bed, remove the layers of cloth separating us, and touch her the way we had learned from one another last summer and the way we'd continued to touch each other when we found a stolen hour. Those moments were rare, and I knew this was not the time or the place.

"I love you," Tova said and then kissed the top of my head. "I always will."

"I love you. And I always will."

These were the words we regularly repeated to one another like vows. I lifted my head from her chest and her lips reached mine. For a few seconds, I was able to forget she was leaving, forget I would soon have my own decision to make, a decision I would have to make without Tova.

I caressed the back of her neck and moved my mouth to that place below her ear that always made her moan with pleasure. She pulled away.

"There isn't time." I heard the regret in her voice. "I need to go. There will soon be men in the street heading to the morning minyan."

I couldn't let her leave. What kind of life would there be for either of us without the other. I grabbed the fabric of her coat at the shoulder and pulled her back to me. "No!"

"Shh, shh. I know. I know. It's not easy for me either." She put her hand on my arm and I released my hold. "Remember what we discussed. I will find us a safe place and you will come to me if you decide to leave here. They cannot keep you at home after you turn eighteen."

There was one more hug and then she slipped back out the window and was gone.

The wind off the Hudson River seemed to move right through my winter coat as if it wasn't there at all. The cough I'd developed a few days after I arrived was getting worse, stronger and more frequent, wracking my body and leaving my muscles sore.

My heart ached as I imagined Mama, Papa, and my brothers gathered around the menorah, lighting the candles and singing the blessings. The thought of potato latkes melting in my mouth with the taste of applesauce on my lips, made me weak with hunger.

I walked west until I reached the Christopher Street pier. Throughout I kept careful watch for Tova and for kids who spent their days and nights on the streets, so I could ask them if they'd seen her. I had one photograph of us from last summer at the week-long camp for Hasidic girls. That was the summer when everything began, when our lifelong friendship became something more. We stood together in white and blue camp T-shirts and our long skirts, sunburnt faces turned slightly toward one another. It would not have been too difficult for someone to notice the look on our faces and figure out that we loved one another. Because of that, the picture had lived in the far reaches of my wallet. Now I kept it in my pocket. It was too dangerous to take my wallet out on the street.

I followed Tova here a few days after I turned eighteen and three Shabboses after our weekly calls suddenly stopped. At first, she had kept her promise to call every week, and while I worried about her all the time, at least these short conversations let me know that she was well. I could hear the whooshing of the wind through the phone as she stood on a pier in New York City that was the meeting spot for kids who had no place else to go. "Safety in numbers," she had tried to reassure me.

Then the calls stopped and when I tried the number she'd put in my phone, it just rang and rang. I tried on different days. I let it ring a hundred times. But she never answered.

I decided to leave home because I couldn't be disloyal to Tova. If I did nothing, I would be abandoning her when she could possibly need me most. If I went to my parents, I would be ensuring her return home and the awful fate from which she had run. She would be forced to marry so that her family could minimize the shame that had already befallen them. Her disappearance had cast a shadow of scandal that would make it more difficult for her parents to find suitable matches for her brothers and sisters.

I really didn't want to leave, at least not yet. Mama had not said a word to me about getting married. I hadn't been confronted with some unknown boy standing awkwardly in our living room. Instead Mama and Papa were all wrapped up in my twin brothers' bar mitzvahs, which were to take place in February. After such a big event and the need to rest afterward, I might have been able to hold out through Pesach and leave when the weather was warmer.

Besides, the truth was, except for Tova and the prospect of marrying, I was pretty satisfied with my life in Am Masada. I liked the way we were governed by strict adherence to the calendar of solemn and joyous holidays that kept our peoples' connection to Hashem alive in our hearts. Most of all, I loved singing with Papa, whose position as the hazzan for our community had earned him great respect and admiration.

In school we learned that it is forbidden for a man to hear a woman sing. But one day, when I was folding laundry, I forgot myself and began to sing, not realizing Papa was in the next room. When I looked up and saw him standing in the doorway, I stopped in mid-verse. My hand flew to my mouth.

"Papa, I'm so sorry. I didn't realize..."

He waved my apology away. "I know that, shayna. I couldn't help but listen. You have a beautiful voice. Like a songbird kissed by an angel. Put down that laundry and come with me. Despite what some in our community believe, it is not forbidden for a father to hear his daughter sing."

And that was how it started. He and I would sing in his study when nobody else was home. He even taught me how to read the cantillation markings for chanting Torah so that I would know when my voice should rise or fall and when to draw out the end of a word.

"Ah, Chava, if girls could be cantors, you... Well, let's just hope one of your brothers has half the voice you do."

"See," said Tova as we took one of our long Shabbos morning walks, "you can never use this gift you've been given if you stay here. Just like I can never study science or philosophy. The only thing we will be able to do is have babies."

"There's nothing wrong with babies," I said. "I would like to be a mother one day." I looked down at the rutted, dirt road at my feet. "Except I don't want a husband. I want the fathers to leave so we can raise our children together."

She looked at me, an amused expression on her face. "I'm sure the Rebbe would give us his blessing." She laughed and I couldn't help but do so as well, picturing the bearded patriarch of our village bent over his holy books trying to find some loophole in the ancient laws.

I grabbed onto the railing on the pier as another spell of coughing jerked my body in all directions and left me dizzy and exhausted. As the coughing subsided, I turned and saw three large boys towering over me. I didn't recognize any of them from my nightly walks around the area.

"Hey babe," the biggest one said. "Want something for that awful cough?" His tone was calm but I couldn't help but notice the smirk on his face.

"I-I have no money." My wallet was empty, but I'd pinned twenty dollars to my underwear.

"Won't cost a thing." He held his hand out. Two light blue pills rested in his palm.

"What is that?"

"Cough medicine. Actually it'll cure anything for a while. Helps keep your troubles away. You'll feel, hmmm, ecstatic." He smirked again and I heard laughter from his two companions.

"No thank you." I knew he was offering me something much stronger and more dangerous than cough medicine.

I turned away toward the railing and felt a hand on my shoulder pulling me back.

"You'll take these and then you'll come with us."

My breathing quickened and I felt my heart beating fast. Then my body went into another spasm of coughing.

The same boy grabbed me with both hands. "You're no good to us with that cough. Take the pills!"

I squirmed to break his hold, but the other two stepped closer. I screamed, "No! Stop! Leave me alone!" I tried to struggle to be free of them, but they were on me in seconds. One of them forced open my mouth while the hand with the pills moved closer.

Then suddenly that hand jerked back and away from me.

"Now what manner of animal do we have here? You girls wanna venture a guess?" There was laughter again; this time it didn't come from the boys but from four even taller strangers standing behind them. I looked up and saw a quartet of fancy hairstyles: long dark braids with multicolored beads; blonde hair piled on top of a head; tight, red curls; and long, sleek black hair. These were women. Very tall women. One had the boy with the pills by the waist.

"I'd say we got ourselves three examples of hetero-erectus," said the blonde, her voice straining from the effort of holding back the boy.

"I don't know, girl," said the long-haired one, "not much erectus goin' on here. I'd say Nee-andro-thal." Her friends giggled. "Ummm, hmmm," they said.

"Now why don't you boys go back to Jersey or whatever hick town you come from and leave these kids alone?"

As soon as those words were out of Long Hair's mouth, they were all at each other, grabbing, pushing. Terrified I'd get pulled into this fight, I leaned back onto the railing trying to slip away.

"Okay, stop it all right now or someone gets really hurt."

I looked over and saw a flash of silver. The woman with the long hair was holding a knife. The boys began to back off.

"That's right. Now go take a long walk off this pier." She waved the knife at them. "I said get going!"

The four women and I watched as the boys moved away. "Fuck you tranny," one of them called out. "Fuckin' freak," said another.

Every minute or so, Long Hair called out, "C'mon keep going." Then she folded the knife, put it in her purse, and turned to me.

"Are you hurt, honey?"

I shook my head and looked at them. Something seemed different but I couldn't figure out what it was.

"I'm Esmerelda," said Long Hair. "And these are my girls, Clarice, Mariella, and Janelle. What's your name, baby?"

I shook my head again. Since I'd arrived, I'd told no one my name. Instead, I showed them the picture of Tova. "Have you seen her?"

None of them had.

"That your girlfriend?" asked one of them.

I took a deep breath, closed my eyes, and nodded. Then I started coughing again.

"Okay now, baby, we need to get you some place warm and take care of that cough," said Esmerelda.

She reached back in her purse and gave me a plastic card. There was a picture of her and the words "Street Team Coordinator, LGBT Youth Services in the Village."

"This is a place you can go, sweetheart, to get out of the cold. It's safe. No one will hurt you there." She looked at me, her arms folded over her chest.

"And since you don't want to tell us your name, I'm going to call you Ariel, from The Little Mermaid. You got that long reddish hair and light eyes. And we found you by the water."

I again looked at the four of them with questions on my face, trying to figure out what seemed different.

"Oh, Ariel honey," said the blonde, "if you could only see the way you're looking at us." She smiled. "You never seen transgender girls before?"

Transgender. It wasn't a word I knew.

"C'mon. We'll tell you all about it on the way to the Center," said Esmerelda as she took my hand.

I remained still, trying to decide if it would be safe to go with them. They had saved me from the awful boys, but the image of the knife, its metal reflecting light from the street lamps on the pier, made me hesitate. Then I started to cough again and felt warm arms surround me and the soft reassurance of a hand rubbing the middle of my back.

"It's okay, baby. We'll get you better."

I decided to take the chance.

We entered a large room with long tables arranged in rows. Kids were everywhere. Some were hunched over plates. Others were standing in bunches laughing. Adults were walking around with trays of food. The sound was deafening and reminded me of times when I'd gone with Mama to pick up my brothers at school.

"Now you sit right down here while I go see about finding you something to eat." Esmerelda put her hands on my shoulders as I lowered myself onto a chair. "The girls will be right here with you."

"Where you from, honey?" It was the blonde, Janelle. "I come from Florida and these winters up here are workin' my last nerve."

I couldn't risk telling anyone about Am Masada. "I need to find the girl in the picture," was all I said.

"Well look around. She could be right here."

I scanned the room trying to focus through the chaos. Two girls stood in a corner together kissing. I opened my mouth in surprise that they would do such a thing in front of so many people. Tova and I had always been so careful.

"Okay Ariel, this will be good for what ails you. Hot vegetable soup and chicken fingers, plus a piece of chocolate cake."

I looked at the tray of food set down in front of me and frowned. I couldn't eat any of it.

"I can't," I said pointing to the food. "It's treyf."

Esmerelda looked confused. "You don't like the tray? Here..." She removed the bowl and plates and put them all on the table as she whisked away the tray.

"No. Treyf, treyf. Unclean. I can't eat this."

They all began talking to me at once. "Hold on," said Esmerelda, her hands raised in front of her. "Let me get Tracy. She's volunteering tonight. Maybe she can figure out what's going on."

A few minutes later she returned with someone tall and thin, with blonde hair tied back. Her long legs were covered in tight-fitting blue jeans. She crouched down beside me, and I could see the most beautiful green eyes. She was like a princess. I thought of Queen Esther.

"Hey, Ariel," she said softly, her voice was melodic, it's cadence rising and falling in pitch. "Why can't you eat the food, baby?"

"It's not clean."

"Why do you say that?"

"It's treyf. I cannot eat treyf."

"Is this food different from what you're used to?"

I nodded.

"What do you eat at home?" Her voice was soft and comforting. I felt a pang in my heart for my family and for Tova.

"Kashrut."

"And what is that?"

How to make them understand? And even if I did, what would it matter?

The princess stood and turned. She waved her arm in front her and then pointed toward me. "Robin! Baby, come here."

This person she called Robin approached. She had wavy brown hair that seemed to go in all directions. Her features were soft and welcoming.

"Ariel, this is my partner, Robin."

Partner, what did she mean? Were they like Tova and me?

Robin sat down in the chair next to me.

"Tell Robin what you told me about the food."

"I cannot eat it. It's unclean."

"How is it unclean?"

"It's treyf, not kashrut. Do you understand?"

She nodded. "You're an Orthodox Jew."

"Hasidic."

Again she nodded. Warm relief spread through my chest. "Did your parents kick you out?"

I shook my head. "No. I left to find her." I showed her Tova's picture.

She put her hand on my arm.

"You love her, like me and Tracy?" She pointed to the princess.

"Yes," I whispered.

"So Ariel, I'm Jewish, too."

I breathed out. This could be a good thing or not. On the one hand she seemed to understand. On the other hand, she could call Mama and Papa before I had the chance to find Tova.

"But I observe differently than you do."

"What do you mean?" I asked.

"I don't follow the same rules as you, but I know enough to be helpful. You see, there's more than one way to be a Jew. I can explain all that later, but I just want you to know for now, Ariel, that you're safe with me and with all of us here."

"It's Chava. My name is Chava."

She smiled. "Chava, it means 'life' in English, right?"

I smiled back.

"Okay, now to get you some food. Will you eat a banana or an orange that hasn't been peeled or cut?"

"I can, yes." I began to cough again.

"Great, you need the vitamin C with that cough. I'm going out to find you a kosher meal and some cough medicine. Do you know that it's Chanukah?"

"Yes, I lit two flames and said the blessings." I wanted her to know that I hadn't abandoned the commandment.

"Well let's see what we can do to make the rest of the holiday a bit more joyous for you while we continue to look for your girlfriend. Can you tell me her name?"

"It's Tova."

"Tova and Chava. Together you translate as 'good life.' That's a hopeful omen."

She stood and left the big, noisy room. Esmerelda brought me some hot water and a whole lemon, along with an orange and a banana. I squeezed the juice from the lemon into the water and drank.

Five nights later I still could not find Tova. I was staying with Robin and Tracy in their beautiful apartment with a view of the river. They brought me food I could eat and each night we lit candles and said the blessings. There were even latkes, though they came from the kosher store and didn't taste as good as Mama's.

On the eighth night they were taking me to their shul for a special Chanukah celebration.

"Rabbi Goldfarb would like to talk to you before services," said Robin.

My eyes grew wide. "No, I cannot speak to a rabbi. He will send me back!"

"*She* may be able to help you find Tova. We've looked in all the places where homeless kids hang out. The rabbi can help us look in other places."

"She? A woman rabbi?" I began to laugh.

"Now Chava, we talked about how there's not just one way to be an observant Jew. There are many rabbis who are women, cantors too."

The hazzan can be a woman! My mind filled with possibilities for myself. "Does your shul have a woman hazzan?"

"The cantor?"

I nodded.

"Yes. And there's a man as well."

"Like Papa."

"Your father is a cantor?"

I looked down at the floor, afraid I'd said too much.

"I'm not surprised now that I've heard how beautifully you sing the Chanukah blessings."

She was shorter than I pictured her, with light brown, curly hair and dressed in a charcoal blazer with matching pants. On her head was a small, multicolored yarmulke, held in place with a bobby pin. Married women must cover their heads, but never with a yarmulke. I stared at her trying to make sense of it all.

She welcomed me to Congregation Shaare Avodah, the Gates of Love, an unusual name for a shul. Her voice was warm and gentle.

We talked about what I'd been doing since I left home. How I'd walked the streets, sleeping and eating when I could, as I looked everywhere for Tova.

"There are communities of Orthodox gay men and lesbians here in New York City. She may have found them. I'm going to ask around."

I agreed to let her use her phone to take a picture of my photograph of Tova. For the first time since the beginning of Chanukah, I began to feel hopeful.

As we left the rabbi's office to take our seats for the service, I looked around for the women's section. But instead of heading toward the back of the sanctuary, I was guided to the very front row where chairs had been reserved for Robin, Tracy, and me as if we were honored guests. A man sat down next to Tracy.

Men and women sitting side by side in shul? I turned around and was amazed to see the rows behind me filling up with everyone all mixed together. I had so much to learn about the different ways there were to be a Jew.

The service was familiar and at the same time completely strange. I recognized some of the prayers and their melodies, but they had a piano and a chorus that sang with the hazzan at times. It felt like I'd been transported to some new Jewish planet.

The rabbi had asked me to accept an honor. Accompanied by Robin and Tracy, I was to come up to the bimah, light the Chanukah candles, and sing the blessings. At home, women and girls were not permitted to go anywhere near the bimah so I was nervous about standing up in front of all these people.

As the rabbi entered, wearing a beautifully embroidered tallis, the yarmulke still placed at the top of her head, the congregation quieted.

"Tonight we have someone special here who I am inviting to begin our celebration by lighting the Chanukah candles. As you know, this congregation has been engaged in campaigns to end the epidemic of homelessness that particularly affects LGBT youth. Well, right before this service, I met with one of these young people, a teenage girl who comes from a Hasidic family. She left her community recently to search for her girlfriend who'd run away to avoid an arranged marriage. Please welcome her as we all stand for the lighting of the candles."

When I accepted her invitation to sing the blessings, I asked her not to use my name, in case there was anyone who might connect me back to Am Masada. I stood and walked slowly to the front, Robin and Tracy on either side of me. I lit the shamash, the center candle, and then used it to light the others that surrounded it. I sang the first blessing in a loud, clear voice that echoed off the vaulted ceiling. When I paused and took a breath to start the second blessing, I heard my name piercing the silence, getting louder with each repetition.

"Chava! Chava! Chava!"

I turned, the shamash still in my hand, and saw someone running down the center aisle coming toward me. At first, all I could see was dark brown hair flying forward, and then her face became visible. It was Tova! I quickly put the candle back and ran to meet her.

"Tova!"

Our arms grasping one another in a tight hug, we stood together not speaking for a good number of seconds. Then the rabbi spoke.

"For anyone who doubts the existence of modern-day Chanukah miracles, I suggest you observe what is happening right now at Shaare Avodah as we commemorate our peoples' miracle from ancient times."

"I'm sorry I lost the phone," Tova whispered in my ear. "Someone tried to take it from me on the pier, and it dropped into the water."

"Where have you been?" I whispered back. "We've looked everywhere."

"With Shuli and Sarah, two Orthodox women who are together like us. They found me in the subway station, and when I told them where I was from, they took me home with them."

"Do you want to go somewhere to be alone?" It was Robin standing next to us.

"No, I want to finish the blessing, with Tova."

The rabbi looked down at us and smiled. "Ready to continue?"

I nodded and gave Tova the shamash so she could light the candles while I sang the second blessing.

"One more thing, before you are seated," Rabbi Goldfarb said to the congregation." We usually recite this blessing only on the first night, but I think it's more than appropriate that we all recite the prayer that thanks God for helping us to reach this day."

I smiled up at her as she used her arms to invite the entire congregation to join us.

When we finished, I turned to Tova, the lights from the nine lit candles were shining brightly in her eyes.

"I love you. I always will," I said.

She wiped away a tear that was forming. "I love you and I always will. Happy Chanukah, Chava."

"Happy Chanukah. Tova Chava, a good life."

GLOSSARY

Bar Mitzvah (Bat Mitzvah for girls): coming of age ritual when a boy turns thirteen

Bimah: a raised platform with a reading desk where those leading the service stand

Hashem: a name for God used by religious Jews outside of the context of prayer

Hasidism: a traditional, mystical-based sect of Judaism; communities adhere to strict, fundamentalist practices

Hazzan: or cantor; a non-rabbinic clergy trained in vocal arts who leads a congregation in prayer

Kashrut: or kosher; the laws that define what foods can be eaten by religious Jews

Latkes: potato pancakes; a traditional food for Chanukah

Minyan: a group of at least ten people (men only in this context) assembled for prayer

Pesach: the holiday of Passover, commemorating the ancient Jews' flight from Egypt

Rebbe: or rabbi; the religious leader of the congregation

Shabbos: the weekly Sabbath that begins at sundown on Friday and ends at sundown on Saturday

Shayna: term of endearment meaning beautiful

Shul: or synagogue; the house of worship

Tallis: a Jewish prayer shawl

Torah: the first five books of the Hebrew Bible

Treyf: not kosher

Yarmulke: the round head covering worn by religious Jewish men and by observant, progressive Jewish women

A Christmas Epiphany

WENDY TEMPLE

CLAIRE SHAW SAT AT THE kitchen table sipping an espresso while casually flicking through *The Scotsman* newspaper. The sweet scent of fruit and spice mingled with the heavy coffee aroma; Christmas carols played in the background.

The light, airy ambiance of the kitchen belied the bleak, damp scene outside. Thick rain spattered off the windows, the ominous dark sky blurred by the water running down the outside of the glass. Inside, Claire was shielded from the elements.

A ping from the oven timer nudged her to her feet. Moving with a fluid grace, she opened the oven door. The blast of heat dissipated rapidly to reveal twelve identically shaped mince pies. Bubbling with sweet hot filling, the golden brown Christmas pastries, all in a row, presented themselves like soldiers awaiting inspection. They were perfect, exactly the way she intended them to be.

Leaving the pies to cool, she cleaned up the kitchen. Humming along to the Christmas carols, Claire went through her mental checklist. The decorating was complete, food was prepared, that only left the handful of small packages on the kitchen table waiting to be wrapped. She wiped her hands on a dishtowel and sat down to complete her final task, wrapping each item with care and precision. She loved Christmas.

Ding-dong! Bang! Bang! Bang!
Ding-dong! Ding-dong!
Thump! Thump! Thump!

Startled, she shot to her feet, Christmas wrapping forgotten. Whoever was assaulting the front door certainly wanted her attention. She hastily made her way from the kitchen along the hall, then opened the patterned glass door into the foyer.

Ding-dong! Ding-dong! Thump! Thump! Thump!

"I'm coming!"

Claire looked through the peephole of the heavy wooden door and saw Margo Blair-Scott Q.C. standing on the other side, staring straight at her. Beginning to panic, Claire hastily opened the front door to the prominent lawyer. "Margo? Is everything okay? Zoe?"

"Zoe is fine." Margo stormed past Claire into the foyer, her long wool coat billowing behind her, much like her black silk gown in a courtroom.

Claire scanned the gravel driveway expecting to see her daughter, but Margo's sporty Mercedes, parked right in front of the house, was empty. Turning back for an explanation, she watched as Margo shook the rain from her coat before hanging it on a peg. Obviously she was staying. Claire closed the door with a sigh, shutting out the patter of the falling rain, cloaking the pair in silence.

"Who is home?" Margo asked, her tone abrupt, eyes searching the hall.

Claire's forehead wrinkled. "I'm alone."

Hands on hips, Margo turned her full attention to Claire and ground out through gritted teeth, "The girls are sleeping together!"

Claire barely managed to refrain from rolling her eyes. Margo clearly hadn't lost her flair for the dramatic. Claire was sure the woman must be a sight to behold for the impressionable young lawyers, but she was too long in the tooth to be affected by Margo's histrionics, so she waited patiently for the courtroom dramatics to subside.

When she was satisfied that she had Margo's attention, Claire answered, "I have no idea of the sleeping arrangements at your house, but they do share a bed when they stay over here."

"Don't be obtuse. You know *exactly* what I mean." A long bony finger poked the air for emphasis.

Claire sighed. "Margo, how can you be sure?"

"I heard them!" The thunderous reply echoed in the tiled hall.

"Perhaps you shouldn't snoop around."

The lawyer's eyes narrowed. "You knew! You knew about this and told me nothing." Margo paced in the hall. "How long? How long have you known?"

Claire waited for the tantrum to subside before answering in a soothing tone, "I didn't know, but I suspected."

Margo stopped abruptly. Tendrils of blonde hair escaped from the loose bun, softening the lawyers flushed features. "Why didn't you tell me?" Margo accused, anger and frustration lacing her reply.

"Because I knew you would overreact, like this." Claire waved a hand towards Margo to underscore her point and leaving the other woman open mouthed. Sensing an opportunity to defuse the tension, Claire changed tack. "Would you like some coffee?" She gently touched Margo's shoulder as she walked past her to the kitchen.

Shaking her head, Margo followed Claire. "I'll have tea, please."

Claire filled the kettle at the kitchen sink before turning to face Margo, who sat stiffly in a high backed chair, her hands clasped on the table in front of her. The lawyer looked out of place amongst the baking and unfinished wrapping as she sat taking in her surroundings. Claire knew those sharp grey orbs saw everything, absorbing the important and dismissing the irrelevant in seconds. She watched as they slowly scanned her own body before meeting her gaze. Claire remembered that look well—unapologetically bold, with a hint of challenge.

"This is very festive."

"I enjoy it."

"Baking, too," Margo tilted her head towards the pies. "You are a veritable paragon of domesticity."

Turning from Margo to fetch the tea tray, Claire closed her eyes, ignoring the sarcasm and verbal sparring. She would not be baited. With a polite smile plastered on her face, Claire placed the tray on the kitchen table then poured tea into fine china cups decorated with delicate pink roses.

"Milk? Sugar?" Claire indicated the containers on the tray.

"Milk, please."

Margo watched as Claire added milk to both cups. "You could have had a full-time career and had someone in to do all this." She swept an arm over the table.

"I could have, but I enjoy lecturing part-time. It has allowed me to spend more time with the children over the years." Claire placed a cup and saucer in front of Margo, then took the seat opposite.

"Thank you." Margo sipped her tea. Her stomach rumbled loudly, and she glanced down before returning her gaze to Claire. "I skipped breakfast."

Claire gestured at the cooling mince pies. "Please, help yourself." She watched Margo gingerly pick up one of the warm pastries and examine it thoroughly before cautiously biting into it.

The look of surprise that crossed the lawyer's features was almost comical in its transformational powers as Margo's eyes went wide, then closed. "My God, Claire, this is delicious," she mumbled around a mouthful of flaky crust and fruit, her hand covering her mouth.

"Thank you." Claire's smile turned genuine. She was pleased to see Margo enjoying something as simple as a Christmas mince pie.

As Margo ate, her tongue poked out to lick the crumbs from her red lips. When the pie was finished, she used a napkin to primly dab the corners of her mouth. "That was heavenly. Thank you."

Margo sat back in the kitchen chair, sipping her tea, some of the earlier tension evaporating from her slim frame. She picked up a small, neatly wrapped gift and read the tag. Holding it up, she said, "How is the grand old bag? Coming for Christmas dinner?"

Claire recognized the wrapping on the gift that was for her mother-in-law. Having Roger's mother for dinner was always a polite strain. The veneer of tolerance that emanated from the older woman tested Claire's patience to its limits. Constant criticism, nothing overt, but the "you will never be good enough," lurked below the surface of the carefully crafted barbs cast her way.

"Oh, you didn't go to Jenners" meant the gift wasn't quite right. Claire's response was a polite feigned indifference, and everyone would act as if they hadn't noticed.

"She's lonely," she replied as she placed her empty cup on the saucer.

Margo rolled her eyes. "Everyone knows she is insufferable, only you would find a way to excuse her. She was like that before her husband died, and I suspect she is a lot worse now that he isn't here to listen to her complaining."

"Roger and the children are the only family she has."

"So you put up with her antics for the sake of everyone else?"

"Something like that."

Margo rested her elbows on the table. "Well you certainly play the role of daughter-in-law to perfection."

Claire chose to ignore the comment, and the challenge in Margo's eye. She rose from the table and collected the teacups to put into the sink, giving them both a moment to collect their thoughts. Hearing the scraping of a chair along the tile floor, she turned from the sink.

Shaking her head in frustration as she pushed her empty chair back under the table, Margo asked, "Can we move rooms? This place is stifling."

Claire wasn't surprised by the request, Margo was being distracted by the ambiance in the kitchen, and Margo Blair-Scott Q.C. did not tolerate distractions well. She lost focus when her thought processes were disrupted. Claire knew that better than anyone. She had been the cause of Margo's lack of focus on more than one occasion.

Margo's heels echoed on the patterned tiled floor as Claire led her past the large drawing room to a door further along the wide hallway. Claire knew Margo would prefer this room to the one decorated for Christmas morning.

Standing to the side, she invited Margo in. Her stomach fluttered with anticipation as she caught the familiar scent of jasmine wafting from the Q.C. as she passed. The scent triggered memories long buried under layers of self-protection and expectation. Claire's eyes closed as a warm sensation washed through her. Inhaling deeply, a smile sprung to her lips, her shoulders relaxing as she exhaled.

"Claire?"

Claire's eyes shot open. The sound of Margo's voice catapulted her back to the moment, her hand unconsciously rubbing away the knot in her stomach.

She entered the office and closed the door behind her, the clicking of the latch signalling a privacy they had both avoided for many years. They had bumped into each other numerous times at functions and parties, dropping their daughters off at school or each other's home, politely skirting around each other, but an invisible connection bound them together across distance and time. Casual glances in a crowded room full of memories only they shared, and yet not a meaningful word spoken. Cultivated conversation in the company of others oblivious to the undercurrent swirling around them. So many words left unspoken, so many opportunities not taken.

Claire watched as sharp grey eyes assessed the room in one sweep, taking in her sanctuary with laser-like precision before turning to meet her own eyes. The look held a familiarity that transported Claire back to a time when they were younger, a time when they were free to explore and have fun before the crushing weight of expectations snuffed out the last vestiges of freedom. The weight still hung heavy between them, the tension still creaking after all these years.

Regarding Margo warily, like prey would a deadly predator, Claire stepped further into the room. She dared not take her eyes off the other woman. This was dangerous territory.

Margo picked up a foot high nude female bronze, and Claire shuddered as long, slim fingers traced the curves of the smooth metal, and a memory of those fingers caressing her skin shot to the surface.

Claire's breath rasped in her chest as she watched, transfixed by the cool hand moving slowly up her bare leg towards the juncture of her thighs. Muscles quivering, gasping as the hand reached its goal. Encountering the slick, wet arousal, two long fingers entered her swiftly.

Claire's vision swam as arousal flooded through her. Biting down on the inside of her cheek to prevent a gasp escaping, she squeezed her eyes shut and hoped Margo would not realise her predicament.

"This is a beautiful piece." Eyes dark with desire held Claire's as Margo caressed the cool bronze with her fingertips. She blinked, breaking eye contact as she turned from Claire to replace the statue. Clearing her throat, breaking the spell, she said, "Anyway, about the girls." The veneer slammed back in place, instantly shutting out the memories.

Claire motioned towards a dark leather sofa. "Shall we?"

Sitting in the corner of the sofa facing Claire, Margo crossed her legs and stretched one arm along the back.

She appeared relaxed, but Claire was not taken in by the deceptively calm pose.

"So, how do we put a stop to this nonsense with the girls?"

Claire shook her head. "We don't."

"You can't seriously be thinking of letting it continue."

"We should leave them alone."

Lips pursed, Margo's long fingers drummed impatiently on the back of the sofa. "How long have you known?"

With effort, Claire managed to keep her feelings under wraps as she sat at the opposite end of the sofa, one leg tucked casually behind the other, hands clasped loosely in her lap. She remained silent as she considered her reply. She wasn't surprised that it had taken Margo so long to spot the attraction that had been developing between their daughters. The Q.C. tended to be wrapped up in her career.

"As I said, I couldn't be certain anything was going on, but I first considered the possibility that they might be intimate during this past summer."

The drumming fingers stilled. "Why wasn't I made aware of this?"

Claire was being cross-examined, but she was not intimidated. "Until you arrived here today, I only suspected something might be developing between them. Unlike you, I did not go searching for proof. Why has it taken you this long to see it?" Turning the tables, Claire was now on the offensive.

"You should have told me. We could have put a stop to this before it gained traction."

"Why?"

Margo leaned forward as her voice became louder. "What do you mean 'why?' Are you saying you are happy about your daughter being a lesbian?"

Claire rolled her eyes. "They're seventeen. They don't know *what* they are, but I intend to leave them alone to find out. All I want is for my daughter to be happy."

"Are you saying you are not happy?"

The challenge in Margo's eyes was Claire's undoing. She did not want this conversation to become personal, but it was a path they were destined to travel at some time, no matter how long they avoided doing so.

"I'm content with my life. I love my children, my marriage is...adequate." Claire returned the question. "What about you?"

"Don't, Claire."

"Why? Because it will force you to face the truth?"

"You don't know what you are talking about." Margo turned her face away from Claire, her fingers pressing hard into her thigh.

"Don't I?" Claire's asked softly. "Have you ever been in love?"

Margo shook her head, but would not turn around. "I won't have this conversation."

"Look at me."

The quiet command forced Margo to slowly turn her head until her eyes met Claire's.

Eyes full of unshed tears as her chin trembled, Claire ached to comfort her, but she needed to hear Margo's answer. "Have you ever been in love?"

"Don't, Claire, please." Her voice was hoarse, and Margo closed her eyes and swallowed hard as a lone tear slowly trickled down a face etched in pain. Her chin dropped as a hand clutched at her sweater.

"Look at me." When Margo opened her eyes, Claire's heart ached at the sadness in their depths. Time seemed to stand still as Claire waited for her reply.

"Only once," Margo choked out as she exhaled a shuddering breath.

Nodding, Claire replied, "Me too."

"God damn you!" Margo swiped at a tear as she abruptly rose from the sofa and stormed over to the window, looking out at the dull grey canvas, arms hugging her body protectively. "And damn this bloody rain."

Claire had never seen Margo so vulnerable. Cautiously, not wanting to startle her, she joined the other woman at the window. “I prefer snow,” Claire whispered.

Claire heard Margo gasp as she laid a hand on her shoulder. A sigh escaped Margo’s lips when Claire’s hand slipped around the trim waist to cover the Q.C’s. Enjoying the warmth and the physical contact, they stood together absorbing the sensation of one another for the first time in over twenty-five years. Claire had missed the familiar softness of a woman’s body.

When Claire spoke, her lips were centimetres from Margo’s ear. “You were an only child. The weight of expectation on you was greater than most.” She gently rocked from side to side, movement intended to offer Margo some comfort.

The lawyer exhaled, her head shaking slowly. “You haven’t changed a bit, you know. Still offering kind words and understanding with no expectation of anything in return. Still my selfless Claire.”

That aspect of her nature was the principal reason Claire had chosen not to enter the courtroom. Teaching law in its purest form really had been the best career choice for her. “Perhaps.”

Margo sighed. “It’s true that I was expected to marry a man that my father approved of and have children with him. I was under a lot of pressure to do just that, and, I wanted to make my father proud by emulating his success. He didn’t have a son, so it fell to me to be both successful and keep the family line going.” Margo took a long breath.

The words were spoken so quietly, Claire had to concentrate on them, straining to hear each and every one, not wanting to miss a single syllable of Margo’s admission. Sensing there was more, Claire stood completely still, holding her breath as she waited for Margo to continue. It was the first time that Margo was speaking openly and honestly regarding the decision she’d made that drastically changed both of their lives.

"I have outperformed my father in both the bedroom and the courtroom. I have three children, and I am well on my way to becoming a judge, which means I have a fantastic shot at making it all the way to the Supreme Court. I want that for myself."

Margo turned to face her, taking both of Claire's hands in her own. "I have only been in love once, and it scared me to death. It has always been you, Claire, but loving you terrified me. It was all consuming, and I wasn't in control. That's why I cut you out of my life. I was unable to continue with just a friendship. I ran screaming into the arms of safe, tolerant Richard, who doesn't ask questions." Swallowing, Margo choked out the final words. "I'm sorry I was a coward."

Gazing deeply into Margo's tear filled grey eyes, Claire found the truth for the first time. Her heart beat faster as she absorbed the words. All these years, Claire had thought she wasn't enough, that Margo had simply walked away from her, walked away from what they'd shared. Hearing that Margo had been in love with her and had run away from that love was a revelation. Her chest ached, the tightness making breathing more difficult. The declaration was too little, too late.

The pain Claire had lived through was real. Margo abandoning her was a confidence-crushing blow that shaped her career and led her into Roger's arms. No apology could change any of that. The love she had for her children had helped erase the pain over the years. Given the choice, because of her children, she would not change any of the events. Margo's honesty, while refreshing, ultimately made little difference to her. Claire stood silently looking down at their joined hands as she absorbed the new information. Her shoulders slumped as the energy drained from her.

"Are you angry?"

Was she angry? Slowly shaking her head, Claire realised she had no anger left for Margo. It had fizzled out over the years without Claire noticing. Even this new revelation was unable stir it up.

"No, I'm not angry. A little sad, perhaps, but not angry." She raised her head to look at Margo. "You cut me out of your life so thoroughly, I always thought it was easy for you to walk away. It was a difficult time for me after the break up."

Claire thought back to that time. She rarely did, preferring that it remain a dark, distant memory. After their breakup, she had lost herself for a few months. Margo hadn't been around to witness the desolation and devastation caused by her leaving. Everyone had gone their separate ways after graduation from university, and Claire had headed home to her parents' house. No one else had been aware of the weight loss, the gaunt, pale complexion, and the crippling depression that overtook her for almost six months. To everyone but her parents, she had gone travelling.

Her stomach still roiled at the memory, leaving a sour taste in her mouth. It was a darkness she never wanted to step inside again. A shudder ran up her spine as she thought of the possibility of returning there.

"You ran right into Roger's arms."

Claire nodded. "It felt good to be wanted after the hurt." Her voice was raw, the words raspy.

"Why not another woman?"

Claire held Margo's gaze for a few moments, considering her answer. As always, the truth won out. "Because you were the only woman I ever wanted."

"There haven't been any others?" Margo's words were laced with surprise.

Claire shook her head. "No, no others."

Wide eyed, Margo asked, "You have been faithful to Roger all these years?" Disbelief and wonder were evident in her question.

Claire murmured, "I had children to raise."

They stood in silence comforting each other, Margo's thumbs idly caressing the backs of Claire's hands. Over two decades of distance evaporated with each passing moment.

"Zoe will be off to university after the summer."

Claire's stomach fluttered. Was Margo suggesting that they pick up after all these years? The parted lips, the step closer...she recognised the signs. She shook her head. "Margo, I couldn't..."

Margo dropped Claire's hands as if they were hot embers. "No, of course not. That would be absurd." Margo stepped back from Claire, putting some physical distance between them. She took a deep breath. "I ask about you, you know."

Yesterday that statement would have surprised Claire, but not now, not after Margo's unusually truthful confession. It had been a rare exhibition of vulnerability, but the walls were going back up as Margo idly perused the knick-knacks on the antique writing desk.

"I hear good things about your lectures from former students." Margo briefly glanced over her shoulder at Claire before returning her attention to the desk.

Claire's head tilted to one side, a smile ghosting across her lips. "I hear interesting things about you, too."

Margo turned on her heel to face Claire, her knuckles white as she gripped a photo frame. "You can't believe all the gossip from the gutters around Advocate's Close."

The venom in the Q.C.'s voice didn't surprise Claire; Margo had always possessed the ability to switch from one emotion to another in an instant. Unsettling to many, it worked wonders in a courtroom, keeping opposing counsel and defendants off balance and Margo on the front foot.

"Actually, I was referring to the rumour that you may soon become a Sheriff."

Margo's posture relaxed, her tone softening. "Ah yes, the Judicial Appointments Board has made the recommendation."

Claire knew this would be the next step for Margo on her way to her ultimate goal—a judgeship in Scotland's supreme courts and the grand title of The Right Honourable Lady Blair-Scott. "Congratulations."

"Thank you." Margo replaced the framed photograph that sat proudly on Claire's desk. "He's a very handsome young man."

"He is more grown up every time I see him," Claire responded, her voice tinged with sadness.

"Is he coming home for Christmas?" Margo's voice conveyed a hint of empathy.

"He arrives this evening, then on Boxing Day he flies out to Val-d'Isere to meet up with friends. He does love to ski."

"You don't see much of him?"

"Not nearly enough. He's enjoying university life to the fullest, rarely making the journey back from York. I shouldn't complain, but I do miss him."

"One down, one to go. What will you do with yourself when Zoe leaves for university after the summer?"

Claire's chest fell as she released a long breath. There was the question she had been refusing to consider for the last few months. With both her children away from home, that left her and Roger to rattle around in a house that only found them together in the bedroom. Most of the time when they were both home, they were in their respective offices. They hadn't been intimate in months, and even then it was never of Claire's initiating.

"You need some passion in your life." Margo took a step towards Claire, her voice becoming more animated. "Have an affair. There must be plenty of students who would jump at the chance."

Claire's eyes grew wide. "Good God, Margo, I would never be intimate with a student. It's thoroughly inappropriate."

Margo shrugged, seemingly unconcerned by Claire's admonishment. "Of course it is, but that doesn't stop it from going on all the time."

Claire folded her arms across her chest. "Not with me."

Throwing a dismissive hand in the air, Margo continued, "You need something in your life or it's just going to fizzle out into mind numbing obscurity. Get laid, have an affair, go skydiving. You need to find an outlet for all that passion burning inside you."

Margo shuddered, and Claire knew she was thinking about their first time together.

A dark night in the Swiss Alps, tension that had been building between the two of them for months. The excuses they both made, feigning fatigue after a day on the slopes, both aware of what they wanted. Margo tasting Claire for the first time as her cries of passion filled the wooden structure while their friends partied in the main room below.

Lightheaded, Claire took a deep breath; aware she had been silent, caught up in the memory. Arousal pulsed as strongly as the heartbeat that pounded in her chest.

"You said that you are content with your life?" Margo rasped. "Content is just not good enough for the woman I remember."

"I shall take that under advisement."

Running a trembling hand through her hair, Claire swallowed hard. She wanted to change the subject. Anything would be better than having her life put under a microscope, especially one in the hands of someone as sharply focussed as Margo. "Where are the girls?"

Margo rolled her eyes. "Christmas shopping. I can't imagine anything I would like to do less than that. I hate Christmas. It was tolerable when the children were young. At least they showed delight when unwrapping their gifts. But teenagers, they appreciate very little and are utterly self-absorbed. The only things that really make them happy are a blank cheque and being able to stay out late."

Claire couldn't argue with that. Matthew was always calling home to ask that money be put into his bank account, and Zoe was always pushing to stay out late. "You make a valid point."

Margo dismissed the endorsement with a swat of an elegant hand. "Of course I do."

Claire smiled at her response. Margo had always been full of confidence splashed with a fair dollop of arrogance. Once her mind was made up, it was almost impossible to change it. No one believed in Margo more than Margo herself, and she didn't need anyone else to believe in her. It was both utterly beguiling and infuriating. For a young Claire, it had been intoxicating. In full flow, Margo was magnificent.

"What? Do you find me amusing?" A shapely eyebrow raised in challenge.

"No. I was remembering what it was about you that I found so attractive."

"Oh, I see. My charm, I assume." Margo smiled.

Claire enjoyed the rare glint of humour from her old friend. Margo had never felt comfortable being funny, especially when the humour was directed at herself. A full smile blossomed on Claire's generous lips. There were parts of Margo she would always miss.

Standing staring openly at each other, a moment of understanding passed between the pair, an acknowledgement of something that went deeper. It was not a spark, rather more a memory of what once was.

Breaking the connection, Margo glanced at her watch. "I should get going, I have a Christmas hamper to collect and the traffic is terrible. May I use your bathroom?"

From the corner of her eye, Claire glimpsed Margo, hands in the pockets of her slacks, leaning in the open doorway of the drawing room, observing her as she made adjustments to the Christmas tree decorations.

"It's perfect," Margo said as she stepped into the room.

Claire stepped back from the tree, folded her arms over her chest and reviewed her work. She glanced over her shoulder. "Thank you." Turning back to the tree, she added, "We haven't come to an agreement about the girls."

Margo's breath shot out through her nose. "Fine. I'll leave them alone, for now."

Arms still folded, Claire turned to face her. "No."

"No?"

"Promise me you will not interfere in any way."

Frowning, Margo shook her head. "But—"

Claire cut off any objection. "They are seventeen. The chances are they will go to separate universities, and this will fizzle out."

"What if it doesn't?"

Claire shrugged. "Then it doesn't. The girls carry on without any interference."

"So, you are asking me to do nothing?" Margo asked, her disbelief obvious.

"Yes."

"This can't be what you want for Zoe!"

Anticipating the outburst, Claire had planned her next argument while Margo had been planning a quick exit. "It's not about what you or I want."

Margo began to pace in front of the large fireplace. "What about marriage, grandchildren?" Her hands emphasised each point, years of practice behind each gesture.

"They are not excluded from having either."

Coming to an abrupt stop, Margo dropped her courtroom façade. "Don't be flippant, Claire! You know exactly what I mean."

In calm, modulated tones, Claire replied, "I do. You are worried about yourself and your reputation. You need to get over it and stop being concerned with what other people think."

"That doesn't concern you?"

Claire shook her head, a patient smile gracing her elegant features. "No, Margo, not in the least. If my daughter is a lesbian and someone has an issue with that, the problem lies with them. I hope for your sake you can find a way to reconcile that within yourself. Christ knows you have slept with half the female faculty."

Margo's head snapped up. "That is a gross exaggeration."

"The numbers aren't important, my point remains the same."

"Which is?"

"You're a lesbian."

"So are you!"

"I know." The look of intensity in Claire's eyes made the lawyer take a step back. "And if our daughters turn out to be lesbians, I do not want them living behind a veneer of acceptability concocted out of fear about what people might think about you!"

Eyes wide, startled by the rare flash of anger from her former lover, Margo stepped back, a hand going to her chest. The venom in Claire's voice was like a physical slap in the face.

Driven by anger at the past and present, Claire stepped forward, pressing her advantage. "Leave. Them. Alone."

Margo swiftly closed the gap between them and pressed her lips against Claire's. A hand wrapped itself into the soft hair at the back of Claire's neck and pulled her impossibly closer to Margo.

Claire gasped, eyes wide, shocked by the sudden turn of events. As soft lips nibbled at her own, something stirred within her, a longing so deep it dislodged years of contentment in an instant, replacing it with need and a yearning for something long denied her.

Moaning as a warm tongue caressed her lips, demanding entrance, Claire ached inside. Her heart beat quickly as passion long kept at bay bubbled to the surface, released like vintage champagne uncorked after years of storage. She needed more. Deepening the kiss, she pressed Margo back against the wall. Claire's hands moved under Margo's sweater, and she slipped her leg between Margo's thighs. Hot arousal coursed through her as Margo's fingers dug into her shoulders. Claire grasped Margo's buttocks, pulling her closer as she ground against a strong thigh.

Margo groaned.

Initially overwhelmed by the emotional onslaught, Claire's desire was replaced by a soothing, healing balm. The realisation that she did crave passion and love, but not from the woman kissing her so thoroughly, galvanised something inside her. Claire deliberately eased away from their kiss, leaving Margo chasing a ghost from another time. Nothing

Margo tried to do could erase the hurt and abandonment she'd inflicted so many years ago.

A groan from Margo was her only objection as they each stood wrapped in the other's arms. Claire saw her thoughts mirrored in Margo's eyes. This was the final good-bye.

Margo buried her face against Claire's cotton clad shoulder.

"Margo, I..."

Raising her head, Margo placed a finger on Claire's lips. "I understand."

Staring at each other, they shared a long, sad smile until finally Margo nodded and stepped back.

"Will you walk me out?"

"Of course."

Margo swirled her long black coat around her shoulders and effortlessly slipped her arms into the sleeves. Straightening, she raised her chin, indicating she was ready to depart.

At the main door, Claire reached for the latch, only to have Margo grasp her hand. Turning back, Claire was surprised to see moisture in the keen grey eyes.

"It will always be you." Margo kissed Claire on the cheek and waited for the door to be opened.

As she stepped outside, Margo held her arms out, laughing as she tilted her head to the darkening skies, her breath crystallising in the cold air. Turning to Claire, she looked like the girl she had been when they had fallen for each other so many years ago.

"You may get your wish to have snow for Christmas."

Claire smiled, nodding. "I just might." And as Margo walked away, Claire watched until she disappeared in a flurry of snowflakes.

A New Christmas Carol

EVE FRANCIS

MOVING IN DECEMBER SUCKED. CAROLINE now knew that first hand. She hadn't wanted to purchase a new house during the busy summer season—it would have been too chaotic. Daniel, her son, was in a lot of soccer tournaments, and she wanted to be there for him. The divorce from Jay was still being processed. So, what was the rush, anyway? She and Jay split amicably, so they could stand being around one another during awkward morning coffees while they discussed the state of their finances. Caroline continued to live in the guest room and it wouldn't be *that* big of a deal.

But once the divorce was finalized, Jay started dating a woman named Natalie, and Caroline knew she needed to go. She packed her things and put them in storage, but she wasn't able to find a suitable house until late November. Because of a busy season at work, she couldn't move until mid-December. And now, in the aftermath of one of the heaviest snowfalls of the year, she was stuck warming her hands over a mug of instant coffee in her new kitchen. She had spent most of the morning lifting heavy boxes in the sub-zero temperature when the movers didn't move fast enough.

The cold was only half of Caroline's worries. She couldn't use cardboard boxes to pack since she couldn't set them down on the wet ground without the cardboard turning to mush and splitting at the slightest touch. The plastic coverings for her couch and mattress barely covered anything, and now water marked most of the exposed surfaces. The team of movers she hired were ornery and stressed, probably since it was so close to Christmas with only one shopping day left. They had shoved her stuff into the far side of the living room, and left it there. Now they waited with their truck idling and Christmas music blaring.

And still, the men expected a tip. Caroline wanted to be nice and cheery because it *was* Christmas, but all she could hear was the incessant "ba-da-da-dum" of the "Drummer Boy" from the van's speakers. Her blood slowly boiled as she approached the vehicle.

"Is that it?" she asked, her mug of coffee still in her hands. She peered in the back of the truck, inspecting it slowly. There was lots of dust, water spots, and a few plastic bags, but nothing else. Everything she owned was now in her living room.

"Yes, ma'am. Please sign here. We have other things to do today."

Caroline pressed her lips together. She took the pen and scribbled her name.

"You have my credit card number, yes? The one I made the reservation with?"

The tall man nodded. "Yes, ma'am."

Caroline flinched at the sound of the word "ma'am". She wasn't that old, was she? Almost forty in another few months. But that was another calendar year away and she didn't like to be prematurely reminded.

"Well, then. I guess that's it. Thanks again. See you around."

"Ma'am," the man called after her.

Caroline turned, raising a thin, brown eyebrow. "Yes?"

The mover flinched, as if he could detect the sudden anger in her expression. *He must see this every day*, Caroline thought. The widow or the divorcee moving out of a nice house and into another one, close enough to see the kids—but far enough away to not cause problems. He didn't have to make anything worse. Caroline also knew that if she just *tipped* him, then maybe he would go away. But a job well done deserved a reward. And this job, as the water stains on her couch proved, was not exactly in tip-top shape.

"Nothing," the mover said. "Have a Merry Christmas. Or happy holidays."

Caroline felt her stomach do another flip-flop. "Yes" she said. "You too, I suppose."

Caroline watched as the moving van drove down the street and turned the corner from her new kitchen window. When she sighed, she swore she could hear it echo off the empty walls. *What good is Christmas if it is the first time you're away from the ones you love?* She was glad she didn't have a calendar yet and no time to put up Christmas decorations.

Caroline had never been away from Daniel for longer than two nights. And never during the holidays. *But that is how it is now, right?* Daniel would celebrate Christmas with Jay this year. Then she and Jay would take turns having their son for the holidays, like a never-ending game of Ping-Pong. She knew this side of divorce would be hard, but necessary. She couldn't get proverbial cold feet now, even if she was really, really cold in her new place.

Caroline found the furnace and cranked the heat up. She unpacked the smaller boxes first, before she grew tired. She flopped down on her couch and took a break with another cup of coffee.

There *was* something good about the Christmas season, she remembered. Everyone had their holidays soon, and there would be enough alcohol—from Christmas parties and visiting relatives—to stock a ship. Just what she needed to dull these Christmas blues.

Caroline picked up her cell phone and began to plan a party.

Trisha arrived first. "I bring tidings of good joy," she said and then furrowed her brow. "Comfort and joy? Figgy pudding? I have no idea how that song goes."

"Ugh. I don't want to hear any Christmas carols or anything about Christmas whatsoever. But thank you for coming." Caroline opened her door, one of few on the block without a wreath. "Don't mind the mess. I'm still moving in. That's why you're here, right? Unpacking and a housewarming party."

"Hah," Trisha said. She shucked her coat off and opened the closet. Her smile fell from her face as she realized there were no hangers out yet. "I see you really were serious about helping you unpack."

"What are friends for?" Caroline sighed. "I have some alcohol out, if that helps."

"Getting drunk and moving furniture? I'm in."

"Hopefully not in that order," Melanie said. She slipped inside while Caroline held the door. She presented a plate of cookies in one hand and a bottle of rum in the other. Her smile faded as soon as Caroline narrowed her eyes.

"What?" Melanie asked. "It's just gingerbread. Vegan gingerbread at that. One of the kids at Matt's school is like scary-allergic to eggs, so I made these. No good?"

"It's a Christmas cookie," Caroline said. "I strictly forbid it."

"So put me on the naughty list. I like gingerbread." Melanie smiled. "Now are you going to get me a drink? I'm still freezing and could use some cheer to warm me up."

Caroline stepped out of the way just as Trisha returned with coat hangers. There were another couple minutes of shuffling and handing off alcohol, coats, and cookies as the women got ready and organized. By the time everyone sat down at the small table inside the kitchen, there was another knock at the door.

"Hello, Adriana," Caroline said. "Fashionably late as ever."

Adriana's red-painted lips pressed into a gleeful smile. "But I have alcohol and I have food."

"Christmas food?"

"Does Kutya count? I didn't think it would count. I mean, it's a Ukrainian thing. It's got like... no resonance in the US. So how are you going to know it's festive?"

Caroline signed again. "Because you just told me."

Adriana winked at her friend. "Well, then I guess you'll have to deal."

Caroline took the plate as Adriana hung up her coat. Inside the kitchen, she added the Kutya to her friends' pile of Christmas treats.

"I also have a fruitcake in the car," Trisha said cautiously. "But I figured it wasn't a good idea to bring it in."

"Let it freeze," Adriana said. "It's fruit cake anyway, so what's it good for?"

"I could use a doorstop..." Caroline remarked.

"What you really *could* use is help unpacking a few more boxes," Trisha teased.

Caroline nodded. There was some more chatter as wine was passed around and Caroline made a quick cheese and cracker platter, since there was no other food she'd rather eat. Even if the Ukrainian dish did look tempting, just knowing that it was to celebrate Christmas made her stomach turn.

"You're really boycotting this whole thing, aren't you?" Melanie asked.

"Yes. Let's pretend Christmas doesn't exist, okay? Okay. Good. Glad we had this discussion." She popped a cracker in her mouth and nodded. "This is a housewarming party, anyway, and since this is my house, I will throw you out if you speak of holidays and good cheer."

"Regular Scrooge," Adriana said. "It's quite becoming for you."

Caroline rolled her eyes.

"It can't be that bad, can it?" Melanie asked.

"Yes, it can."

"I understand," Trisha said, her voice suddenly sympathetic. She had been divorced twice in her short thirty-five years, but they were uncomplicated affairs with no kids involved. "But you can't wallow in your despair or loneliness or whatever. I mean, there's Skype, right? Daniel's going to say hello that way. And he's only like, half an hour away. Even in the most deadly snowstorm, there's hope, Caroline."

"Yes, I know," Caroline said, sipping her wine. "We'll definitely have Skype."

"Well, there you go. All settled. And he's coming for New Years?"

"Yes."

"Then you're fine. You're only worried about living alone again."

"I am not," Caroline said.

"We'll keep you together for Christmas—with this *housewarming* party—and before you know it, you'll be with Daniel again."

Caroline nodded. She wanted to mope more, but Trisha wouldn't understand. Neither would Melanie or Adriana for that matter. They were still in the first five years of their marriages, one with kids and the other without. The breakdown hadn't happened yet.

Well, there's also the fact that Trisha, Melanie, and Adriana aren't lesbians. So their marriages weren't stressed and they could enjoy sex with their husbands for a little while longer. Caroline hadn't been given that option anymore.

"Have you been writing?" Adriana pulled a stool over to the kitchen island and looked at Caroline as though they were the only ones present. "I know you wanted to work on a few things for... gifts... over the...Can I mention Christmas presents? Or is that forbidden too?"

"Let's just call it 'Light Holiday' and be done with it," Melanie suggested.

"Light Holiday?"

"Yeah. If you study the different groups that have holidays around this time, you'll see that most of the holidays focus on light in some way. It's all the same story, just told from different points of view."

"I like that," Caroline said. "That way you don't have to go with the same decorations if you don't want to. You can pick and choose your celebration."

"Speaking of which," Adriana said. "Isn't that kind of what you want to write?"

Caroline blushed.

A few months earlier, when all the friends were together, Caroline revealed she wanted to write a novel once the divorce process was complete. She had grown tired of the celebrated authors, the winners of Pulitzers and grants, always being men. Usually white men, who only seemed to whine about nothing to Caroline.

"It's boring. I mean, I understand the need to do complain and talk about the human condition or whatever you want to call it. But do white men really need to have anymore epiphanies? Haven't they got it all out yet?"

"So what are you suggesting?" Adriana had asked. "Writing *On The Road* from the perspective of the Mexican women they never named?"

"Yes," Caroline had said. "Or writing any story that we all know and love, but flipping it. Like fairy tales, Shakespeare, or even some Dickens, since all of the copyright have passed on those. Can you imagine if *Great Expectations* had been told from Havisham's point of view? Or if Pip had been gay?"

Melanie rolled her eyes. "Always with the gayness, always with the lesbian women hidden in history."

"That's the point, though. They're always *hidden*. It's always Gertrude Stein reading Hemingway's books and telling him what works. And yet, we don't pay near enough attention to her or Alice B. Toklas. I want to bring them out and put them on the center stage."

Trisha furrowed her brow. "While I support a distracting task like this, don't you think you're just trying to make up for lost time?"

Caroline hadn't known how to respond. Trisha was at least half-right; Caroline wanted to give voice to the silent lesbians in literature—because she knew that she was like them. And by telling a story from Havisham's point of view, Caroline could give herself hope that she wouldn't have to worry about turning into an old, crazy woman with regrets. If she gave Havisham life after marriage, then she could have life, too.

"We all live through books," Adriana said. "It's just that some books are easier to find than others."

"Right," Caroline said. "Thank you."

Now, inside her new kitchen with Adriana's eyes on her again, Caroline wasn't too sure what to say about her writing.

"I've been really busy lately with packing. But I have found some time for poetry."

"Poetry?" Trisha said. "Really? Like... haikus?"

"Or dirty limericks?" Melanie laughed.

"No," Caroline said. "But haikus are interesting. You can capture the silence of the moment with them. And I like that."

Caroline glanced at the boxes still packed in her living room. She counted out the syllables on her fingers as she spoke:

I hate Christmas time
Boxes make cardboard prisons
Now I need more wine.

Her friends laughed and applauded. She bent at the waist and laughed with them.

They poured more wine and clinked their glasses in a toast. Caroline smiled at her friends, made small talk about her upcoming PR campaign, and a bunch of other work related endeavors she and her friends often discussed. They were working women, with stellar careers—*but*, Caroline thought, *only some of us are really happy*. Caroline liked to believe she was happier now, but it was hard to tell. She felt as if her friends thought she was crazy when she said she was leaving Jay, because she wanted to date women and focus on writing again. It was like going back to high school again, restarting her life, when her friends knew that it was a foolish notion.

Maybe it was. Caroline was still so new to everything when it came to love. All she really knew was what she had read about in books—and those had been few and far between. Mary Oliver's poem "Wild Geese" was one piece of work about love that had stuck with her. The poem was about animals and human loneliness, and how the world didn't really care whether or not you suffered. But you had to move on.

Caroline had been having a particularly bad day when she first read the work. Her interest in women had always been there, but below the surface. While she could recall a crush or two on a woman, such as the budding poet in her high school creative writing class, the best friend and next door neighbor, one of her first bosses at her company, she had never really had words to articulate her desire. She was already married when shows like *Queer as Folk* or *The L Word* was on TV and she could see characters that were "like her." And really, while she watched those shows and understood her longing in a new way, she never *liked* those characters. They had been too self-centered, too pretentious, too focused on desire. Caroline didn't want to walk in a pride parade, not because she was ashamed of herself, but because she had always believed that love was not about herself. It was about *someone else*, about a *relationship*, and at the time, she had chosen to spend her life with a man. When their love became strained, Caroline focused on her son instead. Her longing for women was something she never really paid attention to, it was so much like breathing for her.

But when she read "Wild Geese" something changed. She thought it was beautiful, so she Googled the poet. When she read that Mary Oliver was gay and had spent her last years with her photographer lover, she suddenly realized the poem's message about suffering. The world didn't care if you were gay. But you, the reader and speaker in your own life, *should* care about what makes you happy. If you didn't grasp what you could, then the world would simply move on without you.

Caroline realized that morning how unhappy she really was.

Jay asked her if she was leaving him for a woman. But that was such a trope, such a cliché. She wanted to tell him she was leaving him for a poem, because that had been the best embodiment of love she had ever felt. Instead she had turned away and tried to come up with the best self-help, Dr.

Phil-like response she could think of. *I'm not happy, but maybe this way I can be.* Jay hadn't fought her on it, and for that, Caroline was grateful. The divorce was easy. Even when Jay brought home Natalie, a girl ten years younger than Caroline, she had been happy for him. *Love wasn't about you—it was always about other people.* And Caroline knew that this was what they both wanted. Even if it meant spending the first Christmas alone.

"Is that what this is about?" Trisha said, picking up a Christmas cookie and glancing at Caroline.

"What what is about?" Caroline asked, focusing on her friends again. "I'm sorry, I didn't hear."

"We ran into Natalie at the grocery store," Melanie explained.

"And I was wondering if she was why you're boycotting Christmas," Trisha added. "Are you upset Jay got a girl before you?"

"No, no," Caroline said. "It's never been about that."

"Then what is it about?" Trisha asked. "We don't really talk about it. You know you can, right?"

"I know. It's not as simple as falling in love with another person. It's more like, I suddenly saw my life from another angle, if that makes sense?"

"You didn't want to celebrate Christmas anymore," Adriana said. "But a different Light Holiday instead?"

"Yeah, sure," Caroline said. "I just realized I wasn't happy."

"And are you now?"

Caroline smirked. "I was until you brought forbidden food into my house."

Melanie laughed. "Fine, fine. I'll eat all the gingerbread, Adriana will eat the Kutya, and Trisha—"

"No," Trisha held up her hands. "I'm much too full!"

"Well, fine," Melanie said. "I'll eat it too. And then we'll be even, Caroline. No more Christmas food left to distract you."

"Except wine," Melanie said, holding up a bottle. She smiled as she topped off everyone's glasses and then raised her glass. "To your new place, Caroline."

Caroline held up her glass and nodded. "To my new place."

After everyone left, Caroline put away the leftovers. Most of the gingerbread cookies were gone, but she knew Daniel would finish them when he was here for New Years. She put the rest of the Kutya into the fridge before she was too tempted to eat it. As she looked around her kitchen, her stomach growled. *Another shopping trip is definitely in order.*

Caroline was halfway through making a shopping list before she realized she had included stuff that only her husband and son would eat. *Why on earth would I want Pop Tarts? Granola bars? No, not at all.* As she made another list, she struggled to remember what she liked to eat. The last time she made a shopping list for herself was in college.

Pizza. That was as far from festive as it could be. And really, she was living on her own again. Why not go back to the classics for a while?

She flipped open her laptop and Googled to find a local pizza place. As she filled out the online order form she came to a section that asked for "special instructions." After a few minutes of thought, she typed, "Write a poem in the box" and hit submit before she could change her mind.

Nothing happened. She tried again, but this time the browser froze. She glanced at the clock and sighed. *I wonder if it's too close to closing time for them to make me a pizza.* She picked up her phone and dialled in.

"Hello?" a woman answered.

"Hi, yes. Are you still open?"

"Barely," the woman said. "We close in fifteen minutes."

"Is that enough for a pizza? I would have called earlier, but the online form didn't work and—"

"Really?" the woman interrupted. "I'm sorry about that, hold on."

Caroline heard the woman yell at someone. Caroline heard a man answer but couldn't tell what was said. It was only a moment before the woman was back on the line.

"Sorry about that. We've been having trouble with the online system. But please give me your order."

"Okay, great. Thanks so much." Caroline went back to her screen. Half of what she had specified was frozen, but she listed off the toppings as the woman on the other end wrote it all down.

"Anything else?"

"Um..." Caroline looked at her screen. She tried to scroll down to the lower half of the section, before it suddenly all disappeared. "Oh. It just disappeared."

"Don't worry, we're almost done anyway. I think we just had the special instruction section. Did you put anything there?"

Caroline thought about her foolish request. *Write a poem on the box? How ridiculous.* This is what happened when machines stood in and took customer service requests—and when Caroline had had too much wine. She couldn't bring herself to utter the request aloud.

"Um, nope. That's it."

"Well, okay. We will have it to your place in no time. Sorry about the online form."

"Don't worry about it. I'll be here."

Caroline sighed as she hung up the phone. She sat down with another glass of wine and waited.

Outside, snow began to fall.

Kim Sauer, the assistant manager at the local Pizza Tavern, hung the office up phone with a bang. She knew her boss wouldn't want to make another pizza this close to closing—even if Kim convinced him that they had a certain obligation. Their online system *sucked* because Sal wouldn't update the software. So a lot of orders bounced and a lot of pizzas got lost in cyberspace. This wasn't the first customer call, though the woman on the phone had been a lot nicer than the college kids who usually ordered this late.

"You know, you lose business that way," Kim lectured Sal. "People want to order pizza and they want to do it from the privacy of their homes. They can't do that if the system keeps freezing."

"Well, that's what phones are for. This person figured out how to use a phone. No harm done."

"But some people don't like the phone, Sal. You have to make things *accessible* to people."

"That's why I have you, dear," he said with a wink. "You know how to make things easier for customers, so I let you get the phone. Anyone else who complains has to get used to it. This is the real world, after all. It doesn't bend to your whim."

Kim sighed. "So I'll make the pizza, then?"

Sal lifted his eyebrows and nodded. Kim was used to this by now. Using her cane for leverage, she got some of the dough from the freezer and turned on one of the big industrial stoves. She glanced down at her writing pad to make a note of the toppings when her phone buzzed with an email. She had synced her IOS to the staff computer and the ringtone let her know it was an email from the pizza server. She tied her black hair behind her head and glanced down. Order 62 stared back at her, with Caroline Braithwaite's name on the first line.

So it did go through. Maybe the system wasn't completely broken. Kim opened up the email and verified the order with what she had written down. The toppings were fine: double cheese, with green peppers, mushrooms, but no olives. Kim began to un-wrap the fresh toppings she had put away and pulled out the sauce again.

The space between the industrial ovens and the fridge was only two feet, maybe, but it was far enough for Kim. She could manage the walk without her cane on the best of days, but not much beyond it. And at nearly one in the morning, during the cold months of winter, it sometimes felt impossible. She grasped her cane as she moved around to gather her materials, relishing the fact that this was the last order. For sure this time. She didn't have to rush too much and she could go right home afterwards.

Kim knew Sal from a family friend. She grew up in this part of town, before she moved in with one of her girlfriends in San Francisco—and before the accident that made her walk with a cane. The night she was injured, Kim and her girlfriend had a bad fight (again), Kim went out and got drunk (again), and then she fell down a flight of stairs. Her knee shattered in the process, along with the relationship. Kim had stayed around to attend AA in San Francisco, but it hadn't helped. To Kim, AA was a room full of people who wanted to dwell on their problems, not look at the world and realize they were a tiny, tiny part in it all.

So she came back home. She got a job in a pizza place, though she was in her early thirties. It was kind of sad, she knew. But most people were getting used to starting their lives over again. In this economy, you had to take what you could get.

"Hey Tiny Kim," Sal said.

Kim jumped, lost in her thoughts. "Yeah?"

"You okay to lock up if I leave? The wife… she's already mad I'm working so close to Christmas, you know. It's just easier…"

"Go," Kim said.

Sal lingered. "You sure? You got a ride home?"

"Yes. I'm not a complete invalid. Now go before I beat you with my cane."

"There we go," Sal said, a chuckle in his voice. "I miss the old Kim when you get quiet."

"Uh-huh. And belligerence is the only way to solve it."

"You know it," Sal said. "And hey, Merry Christmas. Or whatever you wanna celebrate."

"Thanks," Kim said. She wiped a loose strand of hair back, getting flour on her face. "Merry Christmas to you, too."

Kim waved from the counter and waited until Sal was gone. She sighed. Christmas was hard. She agreed to take this shift so she didn't have to be alone tonight. She knew she wasn't going to drink—even if Christmas was the drinking season, worse than Easter to a diabetic, she still knew she'd resist the temptation. It didn't make much sense to celebrate good times when they had been few and far between.

She flicked on the radio. Sal hated the incessant chatter of weather reports, traffic copters, and 90s adult contemporary—or God forbid, Christmas songs, but Kim needed something to break up the dead air as she began to cook. She spread the sauce and the cheese as "God Rest Ye Merry Gentleman" finished.

"And that was..." The radio announcer repeated the title. "I hope you are all snug in your beds. The storm we were talking about earlier will hit us in the early morning hours. Small flurries have already begun. Be sure to take it easy on those roads—and sleep in, as much as you can."

Kim sighed. She didn't mind driving in a snowstorm, but getting up the front walkway of her building was going to be hell if they hadn't shovelled yet. She tried not to think about it and threw herself into her work. When she got to the special instructions on the online order form, she paused. *Write a poem in the box? How cute.* She hadn't thought about poetry, especially for this season, in a long time.

Wait. On the phone, Caroline had only given her first name. But on the online order, her full name was Caroline Braithwaite.

No way. Was this the same woman Kim had known in high school? Would she even still have the same last name now? From what Kim could recall, Caroline seemed like the white picket fence and married life type of woman. She was destined for much bigger things beyond this town, too.

But so were you, Kim realized. *And yet, sometime we end up where we began.*

Kim slid the pizza into the large stove as she thought of her high school years. She pictured Caroline with long dark curls, a small mouth, and an impeccable eye for scenery in her creative writing. *Could it be her? What's the harm if it is?*

Kim smiled. She knew the perfect way to test her hunch. Grabbing a box for the pizza, and a permanent marker, she began to write, the words coming to her like an old song.

There were three knocks on the door—*bam, bam, bam* with an even space between them. It sounded as though the delivery person was knocking in a pattern. Caroline thought of Marley's chains in *The Christmas Carol.* What if the spirits of past, present, and future were coming to visit her tonight? Caroline laughed at the thought.

"Hello," the pizza person said when Caroline opened the door. "Are you Caroline?"

"The one and only." Caroline smiled, and then noticed the snow outside. "You must be freezing. And it's so late. Here, come in."

The girl came inside. *But girl isn't quite right, is it?* This wasn't a teenager trying to earn a couple extra bucks so she could go to the mall or the movies. This was a woman—and an attractive one at that. Her black hair was in a ponytail draped over one shoulder, her cheeks slightly red from the chill. Her eyes were brown—a deep brown that was almost black and Caroline found herself getting lost in. Caroline shuddered, just slightly, as the chill from the night touched her.

"Sorry. Please make yourself at home. I'm sure it's late and you have other deliveries. I'll get your money."

"No," the woman said. "I mean I have no other deliveries. You're the last one for tonight."

"Either way, I'm sure you want to get back home."

The woman nodded half-heartedly. Caroline wished the woman had a nametag, but she wasn't wearing a uniform.

"Are you the owner?" Caroline asked as they moved into the kitchen.

"No. Assistant manager. But I know the owner. We're family friends from ages ago."

"So you're local?" Caroline asked.

"More or less. I used to live in San Francisco...and now I live here."

"Seems like a short story for such a big move," Caroline said. The woman shrugged as she took tentative steps into the kitchen. Caroline watched as the woman looked around the little house and the unpacked boxes. Caroline shook her head at the mess. Her friends hadn't helped unpack at all.

The only rooms up to Caroline's standards were the kitchen and bedroom.

"I know," Caroline said. "It's a disaster area. I just moved in. Just ignore it."

"No, it's fine."

The woman put the box down slowly. Caroline realized she carried a cane in her right hand and had been using her hip to balance the box. Not exactly the pizza girl fantasy that Caroline had first thought when she ordered the pizza. But this was nicer, almost. Caroline laid the money on the counter.

"This okay?"

"Yes. I can make change—"

"No. Keep it. You were nice to take my order this late."

"Not at all." The woman lingered, as if she was waiting for something else. She pocketed the money, before glancing at Caroline, and then looking away flustered. Caroline watched as her cheeks became a shade darker.

"This is your last delivery, I think you said?"

She nodded.

"Then can I offer you a drink? It's the one good thing about moving in the winter, everyone has booze for Christmas."

The woman smiled, but held up her free hand. "No, thank you. I wouldn't mind some water, though."

"Coming right up. You're certainly living on the edge for this holiday season."

As Caroline got the woman her drink, she felt a small ball of tension roll itself through her. What was she doing? It was late, she was still a little buzzed from the wine and her friends' ceaseless chatter, and it was Christmas—a Light Holiday. Not everyone boycotted Christmas. Caroline just needed to eat her pizza and go to bed and allow this poor woman to go home.

"Here you are," Caroline said.

The woman thanked her with a nod. She kept her hand on the cane, avoiding Caroline's eyes, as the silence stretched between them.

"Job hazard?" Caroline asked, referring to the cane. "Slip on the ice?"

"Oh. I had a spill, yeah. But it's old now. Last year around this time. Not many people ask me, actually. Most look away."

"I've seen a lot of spills. Nothing to be ashamed about, really."

The woman smiled again and her eyes became softer, sweeter than before. *Wow, she is pretty.* Caroline was about to open the pizza box when the woman stepped forward.

"I should go."

"No, it's okay. If it's your last order of the night, you should stay." Caroline motioned to a chair.

"I don't know..."

Caroline tilted her head to the side. In another light, the woman's face took on a different quality than she was used to. More than just pretty, the woman was...familiar.

"You...Have we met before?"

The woman laughed. "I was wondering if you'd remember me."

Caroline's heart dropped. She had used it as a bad pick-up line before, but now the woman's face took on a more definite shape. She was older now—and this was no longer the foolish girl-crush Caroline had had during their creative writing course. But it was *her*. It had to be. Before the woman could sit down, the words were already out of Caroline's mouth.

"Kim?"

"Yes. Though I kind of go by Tiny Kim now—like Tiny Tim—on account of the cane. I thought that was where you were going when you first mentioned it."

Caroline put a hand over her mouth. The memory came back in bits and pieces, like a haiku in her mind. In their creative writing class, Kim had stood at the front and recited a poem about falling in love with a woman. Her lips were red, her black hair short and cropped. She wore a collared shirt, un-tucked, and carefree, like the way she spoke about love. Kim had been much younger then, a freshman when most of the students were seniors. More than Mary Oliver,

Kim was why poetry represented Caroline's queerness, even twenty years later. That was why poetry, more than any other art, made her think of women and love.

"What happened to you?" Caroline asked. "We all thought you'd be out of there, winning Pulitzers prizes. No one wanted to read after you. It always felt like child's play."

Kim laughed, though the lines around her eyes creased with sadness. "Thanks. But you guys were good, too. I did try to do the whole poet thing. That's why I was in San Francisco. But things kind of...went off course. I fell for the whole illusion of the poet. The past and present ghosts of great men and women, drinking themselves to death. I thought that was part of art."

Caroline suddenly became aware of the drink in her hand and placed it down on the counter. "Does this bother you?"

Kim shook her head. "I don't drink anymore, but I can't stop people."

"Still..." Caroline replaced her drink with water. She got plates and napkins while listening to Kim tell what happened to her after high school. It seemed as if she had been dying to tell someone, especially someone who could remotely understand.

"The last drink I had was the night I got this." Kim held up her cane. "It was around Christmas and I fell down a flight of icy stairs outside a bar. I remember going in and out of consciousness at the bottom of the steps. I suppose it was my Christmas Epiphany, you know? The kind they always talk about in church or on Lifetime movies. I slipped on the ice and an angel appeared—only my angel was Anne Sexton's ghost. She told me I was crazy, and that she knew crazy, and that I should just go home."

"And so you're here now. Working... at a pizza place."

"Temporary for now. Turns out poetry doesn't have a lot of job openings." Kim smiled and leaned forward. "What about you? Last thing I saw, you were heading to your own kind of poetic greatness."

"Not really. I got a good job. A husband. A son." She sighed. "But now I'm divorced."

"Oh, I'm sorry."

"No, don't be. It's for the better. I... I love him, but I realized that I wasn't happy."

"I know the feeling," Kim said.

Their eyes met one another. Clear and hopeful. Caroline felt a lump rise up in her throat. She lifted the lid of the pizza box, thinking that food would help ease whatever tension she felt inside the room. But as the steam rose up, the words on the lid of the pizza box became clear. And another memory came rushing back to her as she read over the stanza.

Sit here and think about your life;
Your last night and your many firsts
Then make a wish and dream a little
Try and get what you deserve.

"It's not the whole poem," Kim said. "Not all of it would fit, so I had to pick and choose."

"I remember," Caroline said. This was the poem Caroline knew from high school. But it was so hard to capture, she worried that it was all a dream. "What was the rest of it? Just humor me for a while—a summary will do."

Kim smiled. "The poem was about a café in Paris that granted people's wishes. A woman walked in and wished for her best friend to fall in love with her. This part—what's written in the box—was the precursor to warn people about getting what they wanted. People like to think about their past and try to get it back. But wishes are rarely kind with our memories. They have to have more meaning than nostalgia."

"And the girl in the poem?" Caroline asked. "How did that turn out for her?"

"She made a different wish. But she still fell in love with someone. She was happy."

"Yeah?"

"Yes. I wanted to have a happy ending, for once."

Caroline's fingers traced over the words in the pizza box. She felt a sudden surge of hopefulness wash over her. She closed her eyes and then bit her lip. "Should I make a wish now? I mean, it's not exactly a café in Paris..."

"Sure," Kim said. "It's as good as anything, right?"

Their eyes met again. Caroline continued to look without worry or apprehension. She heard the steady thump of her heart and felt the slow ache of love moving through her, and allowed herself to dream a while.

Kim closed her eyes first. When Caroline followed, she repeated the poem like a prayer before she let her heart speak: *I wish for a better Christmas—a new Light Holiday*. She opened her eyes to see Kim still sitting in front of her. A light shined behind, like an aura. It was so sudden and beautiful that Caroline almost forgot to breathe.

"You good?" Kim asked.

"Yes," Caroline said. "Will you stay for pizza?"

"Definitely."

Caroline could tell from the way she smiled that that had been her wish. A small thing—just to stay for a meal. Caroline glanced past Kim as she handed her a slice, along with a napkin. She spotted her new window that looked out on her backyard, and noticed there was absolutely no grass to see. Snow fell down by the streetlamp, casting an amber glow.

"It's getting late, you know."

"It is," Kim said. "It'll be hard to drive, but I can make it."

"Even with that?" Caroline asked, pointing to the cane.

"Damn," Kim said playfully. "I wished for it to be gone."

"You should stay here."

"I should?"

Caroline nodded.

Kim took a bite of pizza, considering it slowly. "Was that your wish?"

"Not quite..." Caroline said. She leaned on the kitchen island, her hands linking around Kim's wrists. The touch was slow and tentative. Caroline was still new to approaching a woman. The pizza lay forgotten between them. Kim leaned forward also and held her hands. When their lips met, they were huddling over the pizza box, the poem looking up at them.

It wasn't perfect, Caroline knew. But it was definitely a proper start.

"Okay… hello? Hello? Can you hear me?"

"Yes, Mom, you have it. You're doing fine," Daniel said on the other end. He sat with his face in his hands, rolling his eyes.

"Well, then. Good morning, Happy Christmas."

"You seem in a better mood, Caroline," Jay said, passing by the screen in his robe. He paused and raised his eyebrows, genuinely interested.

"Yes, I'm in a much better state of mind. Christmas isn't so bad, apparently." Caroline looked behind her as Kim walked with her cane to the coffee pot. Caroline motioned with her head to get over here, but Kim held up a hand. *This is all about you*, Kim seemed to mouth.

They talked, the night, about poetry and their lives. The years between them disappeared, and along with Caroline's hatred of the season. While Kim was still sleeping early the next morning, Caroline crawled out of bed. She wrote the first poem that came to her; a picture of nature, with two women at the center. She decided that maybe she could rewrite *A Christmas Carol*, after she scared away all the ghosts of her pasts.

"Anyway, how are you, Daniel?" Caroline asked. "What did Santa bring you?"

"Come on, Mom. I know there is no such thing as Santa."

"Well, maybe not in human form. But there's a certain spirit to Christmas that I like. And I think that's as real as anything."

Daniel sighed. Kim blew a kiss to Caroline. Caroline reciprocated without a second thought.

"Who do you have with you, Mom?"

"No one."

"Come on, now. If I could figure out there's no Santa, then I know you have a girl there."

"Maybe..." Caroline said. She stretched out her arm and ushered Kim forward. Kim joined, her brown eyes wide and nervous. Caroline slid an arm around her and pulled her into the webcam. "Daniel and Jay, this is Kim. Kim, this is everyone else."

She waved and mumbled a greeting. Caroline kissed her on her cheek.

"Kim was just making us breakfast. And then we're going to open our presents. But first, tell me what you got, D. I'm riveted."

Caroline leaned into the screen, absorbing every last word her son told her about his holiday as Kim's arms snaked around her back. Everything, from the snow outside to the smell of Kim's perfume began to rearrange itself into another poem inside Caroline's mind. As soon as Caroline held it, she also let it go.

Throughout the morning, the snow continued to fall. As Kim and Caroline finished the phone call and had breakfast together, the world outside went on.

Mary Christmas

L.T. SMITH

For as long as I can remember, I have been in love with my best friend. It took me nearly sixteen years to realise that little fact about my life, and still it came as a shock. I just thought that's how friends felt about each other. In retrospect, wanting to be with her all of the time, wanting to cuddle her, kiss her cheek, hold her hand seemed a little too familiar for even the closest of friends. It was definitely a case of not seeing the wood for the trees, and then having the startling realisation that there was only one tree I wanted.

Mary Carpenter. That's her name, a simple name—not classy, not double-barrelled, not anything special. But her name belied how very special she was, and not just to me. There was just something about her that attracted people to her, something about her that made a person feel better knowing she existed in this world. Everyone loved Mary. Everyone. If I didn't know better, I would have said even my parents loved her more than they loved me. Not that I minded. It was the boys who hovered around her all the way through school that I hated. Those pimply-faced wankers would try to cop a feel of her at any opportunity.

That's where Mary and I met. School, I mean. Infant school. We bonded immediately, becoming firm friends within minutes. She poured sand into my hair from the sand pit and I punched her squarely in the face, and those things seemed to solidify our friendship, though we came out of the experience grainier and bloodier than when we started. Blood sisters from the beginning.

Life with her in it always seemed better, brighter, full of fun. Being with Mary filled me with such agonisingly wonderful emotions that I knew she would always be a part of my world. Either that, or I would shrivel up and die in a corner somewhere. Overly dramatic? Yes. But that's how it's always been, and would continue to be if I had anything to do with it.

Anyone would think I should have caught a clue in my teens, especially with all those hormones raging inside of me, screaming, 'Give it to me. Give it to me. I don't know what *it* is, but give it to me anyway.' But no.

I didn't even go down the 'experimenting with others of the same sex' path, as quite a few of my classmates seemed to do. My experimenting happened with lads. I should have realised then, but, once again, no. I was so far in the closet I couldn't even find my way past my t-shirts and to the doors, not that I was looking for them. I was oblivious to the fact I was a lesbian.

When Mary had a date, I would be happy for her. Well, happy in the way that included grinning and nodding stupidly whilst wondering why there was a feeling of emptiness creeping inside me. When she wanted to stay out late, I would lie and tell her parents she was staying over at my house, when I knew for a fact she was shacked up with some twat-faced, tit grabbing, arse-wipe of a boy, and they were probably doing unmentionables with the stickier parts of their developing bodies.

She never told me, though—never bragged about it, complained about it, or laughed about it. She was always the same, always my Mary.

I'm not surprised she had all the lads in a tizz. Mary Carpenter was a beauty. Her body was that of an athlete—firm, strong, toned. Whatever the season, Mary's skin appeared to always have a soft tan, and instead of this hiding her other features, it gloriously enhanced them.

Her eyes. God, those eyes. I could live and die a thousand times in them and still beg for more. Dark. Dark and intense, and able to absorb the world with just one look. Thick lashes framed those perfect orbs, making them even more striking. But that wasn't all. Her long dark hair shone when there was any kind of light, and even when there wasn't. Her lips appeared to have been crafted by a Heavenly Being rather than the result of genetics passed down to her from her parents.

Even though I had duly noted every one of Mary's attributes, I was still surprised to discover that my feelings for my best friend ran deeper than platonic love. The moment I first realised I was in love with her instead of the sisterly adoration I believed I felt will be forever engraved in my mind.

We were seated in Pizza Hut, wading through a 14-inch Hawaiian. Not the most romantic of places, but who said a person had to be sitting on a beach in Hawaii to get the gist of the tropics? I was picking pineapple off my half as if it was the spawn of Satan, and she was laughing at me.

'Why do you insist on getting pineapple on the pizza when you hate it?'

Her voice was soft, yet sultry. It was me recognising the 'sultry' part that made me realise that things were not as they usually were. My hand hovered over the pizza, mozzarella clinging to the piece of pineapple dangling from my fingers almost like a fucked up fruit version of a bungee jump.

Her face was animated; her parted lips exposing wonderfully straight white teeth. I sucked in an involuntary breath as the ache inside my chest intensified into sweet agony. A light seemed to glow behind her, illuminating her outline as if she was being signposted to me by God, 'This is she!' With her very own nimbus to seal the deal.

It was at that precise moment that I knew I was in love with Mary Carpenter, that miniscule moment in time when all my sad little life up to that point seemed to make sense to me. I remember the pull of the idiotic love-struck grin slowly sliding into place across my lips, remember sighing dreamily, leaning forward, my fruit and cheese combo dragging across the table.

'Are you okay, Louise?'

The sultry tone was gone, replaced by what I can only term as confusion, with maybe a little panic for good measure. The intense eyes were boring into mine, her body language and expression expectant yet guarded.

'Yeah. Sure. I just don't like pineapple.' What the fuck?

And I wondered why Mary Carpenter didn't want me the way I wanted her. Even at the precise moment I realised I was in love, I couldn't think of anything else to say apart from a reference to me not liking pineapple. That's the kind of sad fucker I was. Or should say 'am.'

It has been six years since I realised I was in love with Mary Carpenter. Six long years. Six years of wanting her, yearning for her, praying that she would one day look in my direction and realise I was what she wanted. And for those six years I had to stand to the side and watch her become more beautiful, witness the longing looks from all the men she met—and even some of the women. The green-eyed monster seemed to be forever present, but I told him, unceremoniously, to fuck off.

Not long after I realised I was in love with Mary, we went off to university. Separately. She went to Durham, and I stayed nearer home in Manchester. We stayed in touch. We were best friends, after all. We even made the time to meet when our schedules allowed. It was these times I loathed and loved. To be with her was a pleasurable pain. Don't get me wrong, being with her was glorious, but it was the knowledge that she would be gone again, living her life 130 miles away from me, that was the kick in the teeth.

Let me get one thing straight: I *wasn't* straight. Being in love with my best friend had awakened me to all the possibilities that life could hold. I wish I could say that in the six years I was waiting for Mary to notice me in a way that went beyond friendship, I was a saint, but, alas, I wasn't. I wasn't a tramp; I was just searching for someone who could ease the yearning I had for the one woman who was unobtainable.

In some ways, I still feel bad about all the women I'd been with. They wanted so much from me, and I couldn't give it. I wanted to. God, I wanted to. But how could I give my heart when it had already been lost when I was 19 years old? Maybe even way before that, but I was too stupid to realise it earlier. Relationships seemed to be built on empty foundations, and I counted the days until I could make an excuse and flee from what I termed the shackles of life with someone I didn't love, would never love, could never love.

Stupid, I know. Why would I give up a chance of happiness because of someone I knew I could never have? Simple. Because I knew I would never know true happiness unless I was with her. She was my all, my everything, my heart's desire. For me, Mary was the woman all other women had to aspire to be, and she didn't even know it.

Mary was oblivious to my pining. Surprising, considering I am the worst actress known to mankind. Her behaviour towards me never changed. When we saw each other, she was still filled with excitement, bubbly, wanting us to do the same things we had always done. But now I felt weird cuddling up with her on the sofa, watching old films. I felt like I was taking advantage of her whenever she slipped her arms around me, pulled me close, and told me how much she missed me when she was away. It was becoming more and more difficult to not be on edge all of the time I was with her. I was afraid the longing I felt for her might expose me; I might turn in her arms and kiss her when she was dozing behind me.

She didn't feel the same way about me. Mary was as straight as they came. So, I made excuses not to curl up with her, lean against her, or share the same bed when she stayed over at my house or me at hers. Eventually, she stopped trying to get me close. Maybe she did know about my feelings for her and was glad for the distance, or maybe we were just growing apart. Each of those scenarios made my heart ache every time I thought of her, which was nearly all of the time.

And I still ordered Hawaiian pizza, even when she wasn't with me. I would pick off each piece of fruit and pretend I was passing it to her, imagine our hands were touching as she accepted my fruity offering. But only when it was home delivery, I hasten to add. Waiters and actual dates would undoubtedly have given startled looks at my extended gift and my love-struck grin.

Fuck. I am probably funding the cultivation of this tropical plant in South America and supporting fair trade workers. *Ananas comosus* should be changed to "Sponsored by Louise Thomas—The Sad Little Shit." Sure. Funding fair trade workers is a good thing, but wasting my hard earned dosh on a fruit I didn't even eat wasn't.

So where does this leave me? Why am I focusing on my past life?

Maybe because it wasn't just in the past. It was all too real, all too present. Especially now that Christmas was winging its merry little way into the season like a fucking bad penny, and I was the host this year for the family luncheon—the luncheon that Mary Carpenter was attending with her boyfriend / man friend / partner / whatever the fuck "he" it was that she had been seeing for a few months. Patrick, or some other such arse holed name, was the man of the moment. I hadn't even met him, and I hated him already. Mary had talked about him when she called me, but not in a lot of detail. I hadn't seen hide nor hair of her since she had started seeing him. Maybe that's why I hated him. Maybe it was just because it wasn't me she was waxing lyrical about.

And the worst thing?

She had news. I knew it was bad news, even before I heard it. It didn't take a rocket scientist to work it out. Mary was getting married, and I was getting my heart broken. Not what I'd asked Santa for this year, not by a long shot.

At least I learned a life lesson: Never trust a fat guy in a red suit who is always laughing, especially if he has broken into my house and has a full sack of something dangling over his shoulder. I can guarantee that his bag wouldn't be full of festive cheer. More than likely, it would be full of weapons of torment in order to get me in shape for December 25th.

Knowing that Mary was going to be married would be a form of torture. I had no doubt that when she made her announcement, I would feel deprived of oxygen and have my pressure points pushed to the point of fainting, and my heart would definitely take the worst beating. Not to mention the intense interrogation techniques my sister and parents would put me through, as they had known for years that I felt more than friendship for Mary.

No. Christmas this year could go and fuck itself.

I slept quite well, considering I was like a kid with head lice all Christmas Eve. But I had to be up on Christmas morning to get "the bird" in the oven at the crack of the devil's arse o'clock. After that, I had too much time on my hands. I prepared all of the vegetables, set the table, did all the little odd bits and bobs that a person usually remembers at the last minute, and it was still not even nine in the morning.

It was a choice of twiddling my thumbs until they became sore, or a long soak in the bath. I picked both, as sitting in the bath and trying to relax wasn't happening. Every time I stretched out to lounge in the bubbles, Mary's face appeared in front of me. Usually I would have made the most of the opportunity to be naked and wet and conjuring her face, but not this time. Seeing her face blossom into one of her breath-taking smiles would usually have had me grabbing for the loofah, but today her smile always followed her saying, "I'm getting married, Lou. Can you believe it?"

No, I couldn't. I did, but I couldn't believe it. Wouldn't allow myself to believe it until it wasn't just an image of her saying it, but the real deal, and then I would probably still keep denying it.

In the end, I gave up. There was no point trying to relax when it was impossible to do so. I was clean, and that's all that mattered.

Thankfully, my sister Hannah and her brood of urchins came earlier than the one o'clock we'd agreed upon. Considering the clock in my bedroom claimed it was only 10:24 a.m., I was perfectly within my rights to keep them hanging about on the doorstep until I had put some clothes on. Her excuse for turfing up two and a half hours early was her "concern" about how much I had to do for the Christmas lunch. I knew she was lying through her teeth, especially when I noted the kids were as high as kites already, and she had probably only turned up early so she could dump the kids in front of my TV and leave me to sort them out. It didn't help matters when I spotted her husband, Pete, sloping off into the living room and clicking the door shut behind him. I stuck my middle fingers up in that general direction, thus alleviating some of the tension that was building inside me.

Hannah had barely enough time to take off her coat and bollock her kids before the doorbell went again. She looked at me sheepishly before shrugging and grinning stupidly. There was something afoot, something I just wasn't getting.

I opened the door, and wasn't surprised to see my parents standing there, grinning like idiots. I turned quickly to see Hannah mouthing something to them over my shoulder, just before her dip shit grin surfaced again. Anyone who hadn't met us would have known that Hannah was related to my parents just because of her grin. Not that having a grin like that was something to be proud of.

'What's going on?' The tone of my voice was commanding. Authoritative. The voice of a leader. I was impressed with my forcefulness, even lifting an eyebrow to reinforce my position as Alpha.

"Get out of the bloody way, Lou. It's freezing out here." My mum shoved past me to hug Hannah, and I knew they were whispering behind my back. Either that, or I was becoming paranoid.

"Hello, sweetheart. Merry Christmas." My dad was the same as always—loving, kind, and considerate of my temperamental emotions when I was in charge of feeding the horde. He wrapped his arms around me and gave me a hug, one that I returned with equal fervour. "Are you ready for your surprise?"

"Jim!" My mum's voice seemed to slice through my back and twat Dad around the face. He grimaced before blessing me with a wink. "Don't tell her…what…erm…"

"Her present! That's her surprise."

Hannah was in on it too, but for the life of me I couldn't put my finger on what "it" was. Had they won the lottery and were paying off my mortgage but wanted the whole family there to see me dance around the room and scream until I peed my pants?

I tilted my head, my eyes narrowing in accusation, but I knew it wouldn't get me anywhere. I was shite at getting information, even when reading it from a leaflet.

My mum came back to me and hugged me close, landing a kiss on my cheek, followed by another and another. She knew that always made me laugh like a kid; and she also knew it was a complete change of subject.

"Jim?" My mum spoke over my shoulder. "Get Hannah's boys to help you get the presents out of the car." After a slight pause, she added, "And Lou can help you too."

I pulled from her embrace and looked at her quizzically. "I'm Head Chef today, not Bellboy."

"You're a pain in the arse, that's what you are," came from behind me.

Trust Hannah to think she was a comedian. A crap comedian at that. One that would be sporting a festive black eye if she kept trying to press my buttons like she was playing with bubble wrap.

The words "fuck you" formed on my lips, but I knew I would have had to have my teeth surgically removed from halfway down my throat if I came out with that delightful epithet in front of my mother. So, I gritted my teeth, which were still in place, and went out into the cold December morning, Hannah's two lads dancing around like Ariel, the fairy sprite from Shakespeare's *The Tempest,* on uppers behind me.

It was going to be a long day.

It was quarter to one, and it appeared that an army of ants had received marching orders to create havoc in my pants. I couldn't sit still. My mother had taken over cooking duties, whilst Hannah and I became her sous chefs—taking orders from her like we were on the front line. My eyes constantly turned to the kitchen clock, and I had to mentally deduct an hour because I hadn't bothered putting the clock back over two months earlier at the end of British summertime. At least it kept me on top of my maths skills.

And the reason for behaving like I had ants in my pants?

"She"—and I don't mean Haggard's Queen Ayesha—would be here at any moment. I could feel her getting closer. Honestly. I always knew when Mary was on her way. It was as if my world became more vivid, as if it was filmed in Technicolor when she was in it. That, and the fact that Mary was never late. If anything, she would be early. I so wanted her to be early. So wanted her to be here with me, just me. Not Patrick. Not the man who was going to take her away from me and make her his wife.

"You got something in your eye, Lou?"

Hannah's face peered up at me, the blade of a huge knife glinting from the region of her hand.

I shook my head.

"So why are you standing there with your eyes tightly shut?"

My mum's voice drifted over from the other side of the kitchen, her attention on making her "secret recipe" gravy. "She's working out the clock again."

Ding dong!

I physically felt my heart drop, lift, drop, lift, shoot side to side, drop and lift in the matter of seconds. Nausea swept through me, and I thought I would hurl my breakfast across the room in a splendid rainbow of chunks. Then I remembered I hadn't eaten.

Ding dong!

The feeling that swept over me, maybe because of the cardiac dysrhythmia of moments before, created a coolness throughout my body and made my legs seem weak and useless.

"Are you going to get that?" Hannah waved the knife in the air in front of me. "Or do I have to do everything?"

Amazing how Christmas can make us all act like kids, isn't it?

Ding dong! Ding dong!

"Lou! Just answer the bloody door. My gravy's going lumpy."

I don't remember moving from the kitchen and into the hallway, but I must have. My hand was shaking as I lifted it to the latch; tunnelled vision made my fingers seem longer and misshapen.

Swallowing hard, I tentatively pulled the door open, all the while readying myself to meet Mary's future husband. I knew I had to smile, knew I had to be on my best behaviour even though I wanted to drag her inside and leave him to freeze to death on my front doorstep, maybe even shouting out a "fuck off" for good measure.

But when I saw her…when my eyes met hers…when it seemed, once again, that I had fallen straight into her, straight inside of her, nothing else mattered. Not Patrick, not that Mary didn't love or want me, nothing. It was enough. Just being near her was enough.

Maybe that was because it had to be enough.

Her smile was, as ever, radiant, her eyes filling with light that likely showed the happiness she was feeling at seeing me. I was her best friend, after all, and it had been over three months since we had last seen each other. Our phone calls had been hit and miss, too.

She didn't wait for a hello. Mary's arms wrapped around me and pulled me close, her face burying itself in my hair. The scent of her filled my nostrils as I breathed her in. It was her smell, hers and hers alone. I knew without a shadow of a doubt that I would be able to pick her out of a line-up, even if I was blindfolded.

I felt tears prick my eyes and had to swallow hard to suppress the emotion that was bubbling up inside me. Mary squeezed me harder, and I struggled to keep the sob back. Her hand stroked my hair, then stilled. She drew back and looked straight into me, her beautiful eyes sparkling with unshed tears, a sad smile pulling at the corners of her mouth.

Concern flooded through me. Why was she on the verge of crying? Had something happened with *him*? Had *he* hurt her? Told her *he* didn't want her after all? A tingle of anger spread up from the region of my chest and then dissipated with my next thoughts.

What if it was me? Had I done something? Exposed my longing for her in my look, my embrace?

I started to pull back, give her space, but she wouldn't let me. She kept holding on to me, her eyes becoming darker the longer I looked at her, the pupils taking over the colour and making them appear black.

"I've missed you so much, Lou. So much."

Mary's voice was soft, but sounded ragged. I couldn't understand why she seemed unhappy. This was the day she should have been skipping about and announcing to the heavens that she was so happy she could explode. This was the day she would be telling us all about the man she loved, the commitment she was about to make, the life she was about to embark on. This wasn't a day where she should be sad—unless the bastard had broken her heart just before Christmas.

No. Her appearance didn't support my theories. She didn't look as if she was nursing a rejection. Unlike me.

Instead of telling her how much I had missed her too, I changed the focus. I decided to put the "man of the moment" in the spotlight.

'Where's Patrick?'

Mary tilted her head and frowned. "Patrick?"

I bit my lip. I had to or else I would have called him a fine selection of names that couldn't be repeated to people with sensitive stomachs. "Yeah. *Pat*-rick. You know, your *boyfriend*?' I cringed at the obvious dislike in my tone, and tried to smile to distract her from my bitterness.

Mary's eyes widened. I felt her stiffen, too. Shit. I hadn't pulled it off. She had guessed I wasn't Patrick's number one fan. How could I be? Ever since she had met him I hadn't seen her, hadn't really heard from her either, apart from a quick call now and again.

"Oh! *That* Patrick! He, well…" A small laugh escaped her mouth. "Sorry. He'll be here in a little while." She grinned that grin I loved so much, and I felt my heart melt. "You're stuck with just me for now."

That was my ultimate wish. And it wouldn't be stuck. Definitely not stuck. It could be many verbs, but that one didn't even appear on the list. Such a shame that Patrick would be turning up after all.

As soon as the thought flitted through my head, guilt washed over me. I had to get used to the fact that Mary was not mine, would never be mine, never wanted to be mine. Alas, thinking those thoughts was a lot easier than accepting the sentiments behind them, as I still longed for her to be mine and me to be hers.

"Hello, love. Good to see you!"

My dad had broken free from Pete and the kids to greet the woman he considered his adopted daughter. I heard my mum shouting his name from the kitchen, but he ignored her as he pulled Mary into a hug. "Where's that strapping lad of yours? I was hoping to meet him today."

I wasn't. Any similarity between me and my dad stopped there.

My mum called him again and he waved his hand in front of us as if to dismiss her, his face crinkling briefly into a disinterested look followed by his traditional cheeky grin.

"I saw that." My mother had come looking for him, and judging by the expression on her face, I doubted he would get off lightly. "Hello, Mary love. Can I pinch him for a little while?" She smiled at Mary before giving my dad a death stare. "He needs to sort the turkey out."

"Why? Has it been misbehaving?"

Why didn't dads know when to give in?

My mum didn't answer. I doubted she could have, considering her lips were pressed so tightly against her teeth, nothing was going to get past them. Not even a snotty retort.

Her expression was enough to make Dad realise that he was on the threshold of the doghouse, Christmas Day or not, and he scuttled off to do her bidding, leaving just Mary and me, and an expectant atmosphere.

It was a good job that Mary always seemed to know what to do in all situations.

"Shall we?" She indicated we should follow my parents, and I realised that we were still standing in the hallway and the front door hadn't even been closed.

Sometimes I am even more of a knob than I thought.

Christmas lunch went surprisingly well, considering there were four women in the kitchen. The reason was probably because we all knew our rank: Mum, Hannah, Mary, then me. I was glad I was last. At least I only had to do the boring shite and not take charge of a 15 pound turkey. We had enough leftovers for the usual fare of turkey sandwiches, turkey salad, turkey hotpot, and my dad's speciality, "Is it really turkey?" That one, he usually ate on his own.

We hadn't opened presents beforehand, even though Hannah's lads had pestered the living shit out of anyone who would listen. Therefore, the afternoon was spent unwrapping gifts and oohing and ahhing in all the right places, even if it was the customary Christmas jumper with a cross-eyed reindeer on the front. Every year my parents bought us the same thing as a joke. It was a tradition. Hannah and I always got gloves, a hat, a scarf, and a diary. At least they had stopped with the chocolate selection boxes and colouring books, although Hannah's kids appreciated them. Then again, so did I when I was twelve. I wasn't one for writing a diary, as I never got past the second week in January, but Hannah still filled her pages with shit. I know this because I still read them when I got the chance, although she had never worked that out.

Amazingly, just before I was about to give Mary my present, my mum stood up and announced she was going to do the washing up. What was even more astounding was that Hannah volunteered to assist, something she would usually do only if dragged by her hair, screaming all the way. I looked towards Mary, who just grinned at me and shrugged.

Before I had the opportunity to ask if they wanted us to help, my mum cut me off. "You spend time with Mary, love. We've got this."

I opened my mouth to question why, but she waved me off. They had barely disappeared before Pete got up from the sofa, stretching and grimacing.

"I'm stuffed. I think I'll take the lads out for a walk. Get rid of some of that energy."

The kids looked up at him in surprise, the game console controllers gripped firmly in their hands. Pete was not known for pursuing any health or fitness regime. He broke a sweat changing channels.

"Coming, Jim?"

My dad's head whipped up, and he looked at Pete as if he had lost his marbles. My mother's voice answered for him from the kitchen.

"Yes. He is."

There is something unnerving about mothers and the acuity of their hearing, and not only for eavesdropping on the kids. Quite a lot of the time, the dads copped it too.

Within minutes, the men had bundled up and were on their way out of the door, leaving me alone with Mary Carpenter. I was beginning to wonder if my choice of Christmas gift for her was so bad that no one wanted to be around to witness my best friend's attempt at being gracious in her acceptance. Two tickets to see *A Midsummer Night's Dream* and a weekend stay in London didn't seem too shabby a present, although I had to swallow my gall at the knowledge that Mary would be sitting with Patrick watching the play. I didn't want to even consider what they would be doing in the hotel room after the show. That *performance* would forever be omitted from any thought I would ever have. There was no way I could cope with thinking of him touching her. No way could I bear ever thinking of anyone touching her but me. God only knew how I would cope when they got married.

"Looks like it's just the two of us."

Mary's voice was soft, her dark eyes sparkling, and I had to purposefully tear my eyes away.

"Here you go." My voice was a little squeaky, so I cleared my throat before continuing. "It's not much, but the thought was there."

I held out the envelope with the tickets and hotel booking confirmation and waited for her to take it. Her attention wavered from the gift to my face, my face to the gift. I waved it in front of her. "Are you going to take it or not?"

I released a small laugh to follow my question and ease my…erm…unease.

Mary tipped her head in affirmation, the grin spreading beautifully across her soft, exquisitely crafted red lips.

Just seeing her smile made my heart contract, and a sigh released itself into the air with no help from me. I was so in love with this woman, so in love. Everything about her just made me feel so much, made me feel so alive, as if I could understand the universe and my reason for being in it with just one glance from her in my direction.

A soft tug brought me back to the reality of the moment, and my eyes dropped to see Mary's fingers holding the tip of the envelope.

"Are you going to let go, or do I have to wrestle you for it?"

I think it was because I had been caught daydreaming that I laughed wildly, slapped her arm, and nearly knocked her off the sofa. Either that, or I was a complete twat. Maybe both.

I watched as Mary pulled the A4 sized packet towards her, her brows furrowing in contemplation as she examined it.

"What is it?"

"A bike. You may want to pump the tyres a little once you get it out."

Her girlish chuckle swam around in my smugness that was gloriously wafting in the air with the knowledge I had made that noise, that emotion, happen.

"Git."

I opened my mouth to answer, "your git," but caught myself just in time.

Mary pulled out the sheets of paper and scanned the details, her eyes widening as she did so. She pulled the tickets for the play to the front and read them carefully before looking at the hotel information again. I was beginning to squirm. What if she didn't like it?

"I...thought...erm...well, I thought you and...and *Patrick* might like a weekend away." Every single word stuck in my throat, but I felt, in some fucked up way, as if I had to justify my gift.

"Patrick?" Mary's eyes met mine, and I could see confusion dancing there. "Why Patrick?"

I couldn't argue with that. It was exactly what I'd thought as I had sealed the envelope. However, I did argue it. I had to defend my previous words, even though I didn't believe a single one of them.

"Well, who else would you take apart from the man in your life?" The same man who hadn't even shown his face yet. What was he doing? "Where is he today? Isn't he coming?"

My tone sounded a little bit curt, but I believed it was justified. If I was with Mary, if she was my woman, there would be no way I would leave her on her own on Christmas Day. All I would want to do would be to bask in the warmth of her smile. Everything else would take a back seat.

Fuck. What was the matter with me? Why was I so bloody romantic all of a sudden, so bloody mushy? Worse still, why was I challenging him being a part of Mary's life? Was it because I still hadn't met the man who occupied the place I wanted to be? Or was it because Mary still hadn't told me much about him, still hadn't told me her news?

Mary just stared at me, the tickets and booking details held out sideways, almost as if they had been forgotten. A small smile played at the corner of her mouth, and I thought it was because she was thinking of him.

"He had to pull a shift." Her voice sounded dreamy, as if she was summoning up a memory of a better time. "Now and again, he works at a seafood restaurant."

Who on earth had seafood for Christmas dinner in Manchester? Flipper?

Mary leaned forward and wrapped her arms about my neck. Initially I felt myself stiffen, but when I caught her scent, felt the warmness of her body against mine, I melted into her. Her breath tickled my ear and, embarrassingly, I felt my nipples harden against her chest and prayed the thickness of her jumper disguised it.

"Thank you, Lou." Each syllable landed on my ear like a kiss, and a shiver rippled down my spine. "I…love…love…love…" I held my breath expecting a miracle "…them."

Clamping my eyes closed, I swallowed the disappointment of the reality of the situation that made my heart ache so badly. I squeezed her tightly before allowing her to pull away. Instead of leaving the embrace, her lips gently brushed my cheek. Then again, this time just shy of my mouth.

The temptation to turn my head and capture her lips with mine was battling with my sense of reason; my teeth gritted together in a painful clenching. They were within my reach. Those lips, I mean. So close, so damned close. But they could have been hundreds of miles away for all the good it did me. Our lips, however much I wanted them to, would not press together in a kiss.

"Open your eyes, Lou." Her voice was tender, gentle, almost caressing. "I have something for you."

Slowly, my eyelids parted and I sucked in a breath. Mary's face was right in front of my own, her dark eyes glistening. All I had to do was lean forward less than six inches, and my longing for her would be exposed, my love for her would be exposed as I claimed her lips as mine. I didn't even consider that my eyes were actually exposing me already.

"Yes?"

My question, although only one word, stumbled from my mouth as if it was unsure of its direction. All I wanted for Christmas was Mary Carpenter. All I'd ever wanted was her. She was a lifetime of gifts, a lifetime of wanting, a lifetime that I wanted to be a lifetime of us.

"About Patrick..." It was as if a bucket of water had been dumped over my head. I tried to move away from her, but she gripped me tighter. "Listen, Lou. I have something to tell you."

Here it came. The news. The announcement. The happily fucking ever after.

"I have some news for you."

I wanted to die right there and then. Was this the reason everyone had scarpered? Did they all know for sure what Mary was going to tell us? My parents and sister had known about my feelings for Mary for years, but after they had guessed, I had sworn them to secrecy. I didn't want Mary to ever feel uncomfortable around me. I especially didn't want her to know how much I ached for her, longed for her, yearned for her touch, her kiss, her smile.

"Wouldn't it be better if you wait for your boyfriend to arrive?" My voice was cold, unaccepting.

She chuckled, and I felt my lips twitch into a thin, straight line.

"He won't be coming, Lou."

I would have expected there to be a hint of sadness at this revelation, but she seemed happy about it.

"Why not? Doesn't he want to spend Christmas with his future wife?"

Mary's eyes widened in surprise, and so did her mouth. "Future wife? Me? Patrick's future wife!"

I pursed my lips, my teeth softly gnashing together, then bit my lip in order to engage my brain. I was totally fucking confused now. It didn't take much for that to happen; even showing me a row of shovels and telling me to take my pick would do it.

"Your news. Your and Patrick's news."

Releasing her hold on me, Mary stood up. "Wait. Don't move."

The words barely left her mouth before she was gone, and I was left half perched on the sofa, wondering what had just happened.

I heard the front door open, felt the chill of the air whip around my legs. Where the hell was she going? But like a good girl, I continued to sit, continued to wait. I'd been waiting for her for years, a few minutes longer wouldn't hurt.

I heard the door slam shut and tried to act casual, tried to act like I wasn't on pins. I didn't even have time to cross one leg over the other before she was standing in front of me. With one fluid movement, Mary knelt down, wrapped gifts in her hands.

I stared at the packages before lifting my eyes to meet hers. She was flushed, her cheeks glowing from the fresh air and the mad dash she'd made. Her hair was windblown, strands dancing around the contours of her face. She was beautiful, and I felt my breath catch before it stuttered back into the air.

"Patrick is here."

Her voice was low, so low I had to keen my ears to hear her words. And then I wished I hadn't. If someone had thrust a hand down my throat, grabbed my heart, then squeezed it with superhuman strength before ripping it out through my throat and tossing it aside, I couldn't have felt the agony of the situation any worse. Patrick had turned up. Fucking Patrick. RatPrick Patrick.

My jaw clenched painfully as I turned to look over my shoulder at the doorway, fully expecting to see a devilishly handsome man standing there, a lopsided, shit-eating grin on his chiselled features. But there was no one there. The doorway was empty.

I stared, blinked, and then stared a while longer at nothing, fully believing I was not staring hard enough.

Something touched my knee, something that felt like a hand. The heat of it shot up through my thigh and blossomed throughout my lower body.

"No, Lou. Not there. Here."

Her voice was so close to me that it felt as if her mouth was right next to my ear. But it wasn't. She was still kneeling in the same position she'd been in before I'd looked towards the door, the presents still resting in her hands like an offering.

"What do you mean?"

Patrick wasn't next to her. There were only the two of us in the room. I think I would've noticed otherwise. I might be stupid at times, but my eyesight was pretty good, although I was beginning to doubt my sanity.

"Here."

She lifted the presents towards me, and I became more confused. Why was she trying to get me to open gifts when she had told me Patrick had arrived?

"But where's Patrick?"

Mary placed the presents on the floor and picked up the top one. Her hand absently stroked across the ribbon and straightened the tag, long fingers toying with the string that attached it to the brightly festive paper. She sighed, and her shoulders rose and fell dramatically. Mary tilted her head and stared at the gift, then lifted her chin and allowed those dark brown eyes to land on me and begin, or so it seemed, to read me like a book.

I opened my mouth to ask her again where her boyfriend was, but she leaned forward and placed two fingers on my lips, shaking her head as if to silence me.

"I feel a little bit stupid now." I was too focussed on stopping myself from kissing her fingers to do anything but let her continue. 'I…I have something to tell you, Lou. Something I've wanted to tell you for a very long time."

My bottom lip dropped as I attempted to respond, but I couldn't speak. Having her skin touching my lips, my parted lips, was nearly my undoing. It would have been so easy to kiss those perfect digits, to swipe my tongue over them and savour their texture, taste, the everything that was Mary Carpenter. But I didn't. Whatever happened between us, whatever it was she wanted to say, I would never do anything to jeopardise our friendship. I loved her. She was my all, my absolute. And if that meant forever living on the sidelines as others romanced her, then so be it.

"Just hear me out, okay?"

She leaned closer, her eyes darting to each of mine in quick succession, as if exacting my promise. I nodded, luxuriating in the sensation of my lips moving over her fingers.

"Promise?"

I nodded again.

Mary tentatively removed her fingers from my lips, and their absence left a chill behind. But not for long. Her thumb came back and brushed slowly along my bottom lip, her eyes watching the movement as if mesmerised by her caress.

"Do you know how special you are to me, Lou?" Her thumb slid down towards my chin, the skin coming alive at her touch. "How very special…" Her tone was wistful.

I felt as if I was being hypnotised. Her delectable thumb was stroking the base of my jaw, backwards and forwards,

forwards and backwards, her eyes watching the journey in rapt fascination.

"For years I have known how I felt about you. Years." The thumb stopped, dropped, and she leaned back onto her haunches. Dark eyes penetrated mine. "You are my best friend. My very best friend."

My head was shaking from side to side. Why was she reiterating our friendship? Was she trying to let me know she knew how I felt, but that she didn't feel the same way? And what about Patrick? I still had no idea what was going on.

With one fluid movement, she was on her feet, her back turned towards me. "Do you remember when we kids and we used to rush home from school to watch cartoons?"

Her voice sounded distant, even though she was only a matter of feet away. *What the fuck?*

Mary turned her head and looked at me over her shoulder. "Do you, Lou? Remember it?"

"Of course I do." My voice was hoarse, either from lack of use or something else that was building inside me.

Mary smiled at me before turning away. Her head dipped, and I wondered what was going through her mind.

"Do you remember when we were about eleven, and a new cartoon series started on Nickelodeon?"

I shook my head, and then remembered she couldn't see me. "No. And I don't understand what—"

"SpongeBob Squarepants."

Why on earth was she talking about fucking SpongeBob Squarepants at that precise moment? Or about cartoons in general? Couldn't she just tell me that she didn't think of me the way I felt about her? It would save a lot of time and keep me from feeling like a prize one dick head in the process.

"Look, Mary, I don't know why you're talking about."

"Can you remember where he lived? SpongeBob, I mean?"

I shook my head, as I had no idea where she was going with her references to a program I hadn't watched for years. Then it struck me, like a lightning bolt. Sharp and exact, and I gasped in understanding.

Mary turned to face me, her expression so open, so honest, so full of expectation. "Do you remember, Lou?"

"A pineapple. He lived in a pineapple…under the sea." I could barely get the words out, and I didn't understand why.

Mary turned back to me and dropped to her knees in front of me. She reached out and took my hand, then ran her thumb along the back of it. I stared at the movement, not truly believing I was seeing what I was seeing. Each stroke of her thumb assured me that I wasn't losing my mind. How could I be going mad when I felt every stroke, every movement as if it was the most intense thing I had ever felt? I couldn't dream up the delightful ripples that shot up my arm before exploding throughout the whole of my body, could I?

"You used to call me SpongeBob, remember? Because I love pineapple."

My heart was beating so fast, so hard, that I felt lightheaded. Mary brought my hand to her mouth and landed a soft kiss on my knuckles. I blinked, then blinked again. I hadn't dreamt it. I couldn't have. I felt her lips touch my skin, the thrill of it, the softness of her mouth as it made contact, even heard a small noise as she delivered the kiss.

"Can you remember what I used to call you?"

Her voice was soft, tender, so unbelievably, agonisingly Mary. My tears began to well. I could feel them choking me as they escaped from wherever they had been stored for so many years. It was as if I was ballooning, expanding, whilst shrinking at the same time. As I nodded, a tear tipped over my eyelid and began to track down my cheek. Mary gently wiped it away.

"Say it, Lou. Tell me the name."

A sob broke from my lips, and I shook my head to jolt myself from my inability to speak. Without thought, I cupped her face, my hands shaking as if they were holding something fragile. I wanted to look into her eyes as I said it, wanted to see that what I was hoping for wasn't just in my head.

I swallowed the lump in my throat and opened my mouth, but the word stuck. I shook my head and gulped back the emotion before stuttering out the name.

"Pa…Patrick."

The smile she gave me was blindingly brilliant, her head tilting sideways to press her cheek against my palm.

"Yes. Patrick. His starfish best friend is Patrick. Just like mine." She took one of my hands from her face and kissed my knuckles, her eyes closing for a moment as contact was made, then she looked up at me.

My heart. My poor, poor heart. Its cadence was frighteningly rapid, but it felt magnificent. Never in a million years had I ever thought this could happen. I'd dreamt of it, longed for it, cried myself to sleep for the want of it, but deep down I never believed it would happen.

Mary raised herself onto her knees so her eyes were level with mine, and my hand slipped onto her shoulder.

"So, you see, Lou. Patrick is here. The person I love is right here." She pulled my hand to her chest and placed it just beneath her breast. "Right here, too."

I squeezed my eyes tightly shut as I processed what she had said. Then, without actually thinking it through, I leaned into the space between us and pressed my lips against hers.

Soft. So bloody soft. Her lips felt better than I ever could have imagined. I just held mine against hers, didn't move them, didn't budge from the initial contact. I wanted to commit this moment to memory, capture it and store it in the folder inside my brain that was labelled "Perfection."

It was Mary who moved her lips first, Mary who increased the pressure and started to slowly capture my mouth. Our initial contact had been everything I had ever hoped it would be, but having Mary Carpenter kiss me was way beyond anything I had ever have conjured in my limited imagination.

The heat of her seeped into me, and mine into her. Slow, languishing movements of two mouths connecting for the first time. Her lips parted, encouraging me to stroke her bottom lip with my tongue. The taste of her was all consuming, and I felt the hunger rising within me.

I lurched forward, my body pressing against hers, her arms wrapping tightly around me and pulling me closer. My kiss was hard, demanding. It was as if the dam had burst, and now I could finally unleash it all, unleash my love for Mary Carpenter. Show her with a kiss what she meant to me. Show her that she was my all, my reason for being, and the woman I had always loved…would always love.

My fingers threaded through her hair, luxuriating in the feel of the silken strands that I had lusted after for years. Her tongue met mine and the charge of it spread through my body, hitting every region, every extremity. I don't know which of us moaned, but the sound of it filled my ears, the vibration pulsing through me, creating my moan that slipped inside her mouth.

Mary's hands were on my back, her arms holding me close, but I wanted to be closer. I wanted to be beneath her skin, wanted to be part of her as she had always been part of me.

But Mary pulled her mouth from mine, leaving me kissing air. Coolness touched my lips, and my eyes shot open in question. If it wasn't for her arms still holding me and her half hooded eyes, I would have started to panic, thinking I had misread the situation.

"I love you, Louise." Her expression was serious, her eyebrows dipping slightly, indicating she was thinking about something. Why did she look so expectant? So concerned?

Then it hit me. I can't believe I hadn't gushed it as soon as I realised what was going on, considering I had said it every day for six years, even if it was only to thin air or to her photograph.

I cupped her face and pulled her closer, making sure she was looking at me. I wanted her to know how I felt, to realise how very much she meant to me.

"I have loved you for the better part of my life, Mary. And I intend to love you for the rest of it."

Tears formed in her eyes. She blinked, and they broke free and slipped down her cheeks. I brushed them away. I moved nearer and kissed the tip of her nose before resting my forehead against hers.

It should have felt weird, looking at her from such a close range, but it didn't. It did make my eyes hurt, but I knew I could stand any amount of pain to be this close to her.

"I can't tell you how long I've waited to hear you say those words." Her voice drifted between us, and I could feel as well as hear each word. "You git."

Huh?

I leaned back a tad so I could look at her. "Did you just say what I think you just said?"

A crooked grin broke out on Mary's face. "What? Giiiiiit?" She dragged out the last word, making it sound comical.

I half closed my eyes and gave her a questioning look. "Yes. That." I licked my lips and enjoyed the way Mary watched my tongue. "Why are you calling me a git?" My tone came out playful, miraculously just how I wanted it to sound.

Mary shook her head in a futile attempt to look stern, making a tsking sound as she did so. "My beloved git, why have you not told me before that you loved me?"

I released an incredulous laugh. "What? Tell you that I loved you even though I truly believed you were straight?"

"Yes. You *assumed* I was straight. You never questioned it."

"Why would I question it?" I was getting confused. "You had more boyfriends than you knew what to do with." Though even one had been more than I could possibly bear.

She laughed that beautiful, womanly laugh of hers and cocked her head to the side. "And why do you think I had all of those boyfriends?"

I shrugged. "Because you wanted them?"

She laughed again, and I glared at her.

Mary leaned forward and kissed me, her lips touching mine so quickly that I didn't get the chance to respond.

"No." Her voice was sultry, her index finger coming up to touch my lips whilst her eyes followed. "It was because I wanted *you*. Not them. *You*."

"Me?"

Obviously I was unconvinced. Who wouldn't have been? To me, Mary was as straight as they came. Until she kissed me, that is. Kissed me. On the mouth. With tongue. Kissed me with those perfect lips. Kissed me and made my life brighter, happier, more fulfilled than I ever dreamed possible.

A stupid grin tried to break out, but I suppressed it and tried to focus. With the woman I loved sitting at my feet, looking adoringly at me, hiding my idiotic grin was no mean feat.

"Yes, you." She sighed. "I can't tell you how many times I wanted to admit it, just tell you I loved you, but..." She shifted slightly, and I followed her.

"But?"

She reached out and grasped my hand, rubbing her fingers against my palm. "But I didn't know you felt the same."

I opened my mouth to rebut her words, but she didn't give me the chance to speak.

"You stopped wanting to be close, didn't want to cuddle when we watched films." Mary sucked in a breath and held it for a moment before releasing it in a final rush of words. "And you stopped wanting to share a bed when we stayed over at each other's houses."

I snorted.

Mary tilted her head and looked straight into me. "What's the matter?"

"I didn't want to stop being close, Mary. I was just too scared that if you found out how I felt, you would hate me for wanting you the way I did." I lifted our joined hands and kissed her knuckles. "For wanting you the way I still do."

She pulled me towards her, and I went willingly, not thinking about the consequences. Mary was kneeling on the floor, and I was seated on the sofa. There was only one outcome of me moving forward. I landed squarely on top of her, her falling backwards and taking me with her.

Having Mary beneath me was like all my Christmas wishes pooled into one—past, present, and future. I luxuriated in our closeness, the feel of her firm body supporting my weight. Even the way she oofed seemed a welcome of my body as I landed on top of her, made it more real somehow. Dark brown eyes stared up at me, and I felt myself become lost in her all over again.

"You have the most amazing green eyes I have ever seen, Lou."

Each word slipped inside me and made me tingle in places I never knew existed. Her hands came up and tangled through my hair.

"And I love your hair. So soft…so unbelievably soft." The words began to drift near the end, and my eyelids fluttered. "Why did we wait so long for this…for us?"

I slowly shook my head. I wanted to ask her why she still waited when she knew I was gay, but I couldn't find any words. Answers to that question could come later, but for now I would allow my actions to speak for me.

I gently pressed my lips on hers and indulged in the absolute connection we shared. I didn't move, just held them against hers and filed this moment as the first in the collection of blissful memories I knew I would share with her as we moved on with our future together. It seemed that I kept on wanting to just to connect with her rather than pursue my wildest fantasies.

Mary was still too, as if she was doing exactly the same thing as I was. My heart was racing wildly, and I wasn't sure whether the beating I could feel ricocheting through me was just mine, or both of ours.

'So, when do we get… Lou?"

Considering our lips were otherwise engaged, it would have been impossible for the voice that invaded our perfect moment to belong to either of us. Even if we hadn't been kissing, the voice was too deep, too manly. Too much like my dad's.

I tried to struggle up, but ended up getting more tangled in the situation. I could see a pair of short legs standing to the side of my head, and my face burned with embarrassment.

"What are you doing, Aunty Lou?"

Alfie, Hannah's eldest had decided that standing next to us was not close enough, and he dipped his face to be on level with ours. I wouldn't have thought my face could go any redder, but it did.

"Hey, champ. Enjoy your walk?" Apparently Mary wasn't fazed by the invasion, and I was surprised at the calmness in her voice. She just snaked her hands around me and hugged me tighter. I wanted to bury my face against her neck and wait for everyone to bugger off so I could collect myself. I don't know why. It wasn't as if my family didn't know I was gay. But it is different being caught getting jiggy with it with the woman of your dreams by your dad and nephews, isn't it?

James decided that joining his brother by standing as close as he could possibly get and enjoying catching his aunt with her metaphorical pants down was more interesting than going on his Xbox One. "Are you getting married?"

The rumble of Mary's laugh reverberated through her chest and into mine, and I looked down at her. Her eyes were sparkling wildly, and I realized she loved how we had been caught. I couldn't help but join her, and soon the tears were streaming down our faces.

"What's going on?" My mother had come in. "About bloody time you two got it on."

What the hell? My mother was condoning me sprawling all over Mary Carpenter on my living room floor in front of her grandkids? This was turning into a family get together. All I needed was...

"Smile!"

I turned my face in the direction of Hannah's voice and experienced the blinding flash of a camera. I felt like a celebrity caught in the act, and fully expected to see it on Hannah's Facebook page in minutes.

"Lou?" Mary's voice was low and exceptionally calm. "Do you think we should tell everyone about us?"

I looked back at her, little orbs still dancing in front of my eyes courtesy of the camera flash. Through the spectacular luminous display, I caught the raised eyebrow and the expectant look from the woman I was covering.

What else did my family have to witness to understand that I was romantically involved with my best friend? "Are you serious?"

Mary nodded, but I glimpsed the beginning of a smile tugging at the corner of her mouth. It was as if I used her body as a trampoline, as I seemed to bounce to my feet with hardly a stumble. Hand extended, I waited for her fingers to slip across my palm before I tugged her to a standing position and securely wrapped my arm around her.

"I'd like to make an announcement." My eyes scanned the room and noted the expectant faces—apart from my dad, who just appeared confused. Nothing unusual in that, especially at family gatherings.

James was getting antsy. "I said, are you getting married?"

I think he was still at the stage where if you kissed someone it meant you had to get hitched, just in case a baby appeared. Considering he was nearly ten, that was a little disconcerting.

"Of course they are. They're in love."

Alfie, bless him, smacked James around the back of his head, making his brother grunt. Before an all-out scrap could ensue, Hannah dragged Alfie away to stand behind her, her hand firmly gripping his shoulder to make sure he didn't make a break for it and smack his brother in the face.

"Listen, son. This is history in the making."

Hannah nodded at me to continue with my announcement, but her words had got me thinking. There was something underlying her simple phrase, something in keeping with my sister's big sisterly sneakiness.

"What do you mean by 'history in the making?'" My question was innocent enough, but the blush that crept up Hannah's face made me realise that the events of today were a little more complex than I had realised.

Mary pulled me closer. "It's not Hannah's fault, love."

"What do you mean 'It's not her fault?'" Why was I suddenly having the urge to repeat snippets of people's conversations?

"Erm…well, let's put it this way. I didn't do this on my own today."

Mary's voice was quiet, almost as if she wanted me to miss what she'd said. Turning, I looked at her. As expected, Mary looked a tad guilty. For what, I had no clue.

"Didn't do what on your own? Kiss me?"

I think I've already mentioned that I am an idiot.

My mum spoke up. "Come off it, Lou. If it was left up to you, you would still be hankering after Mary when you're seventy. There's stubbornness, and then there's you."

I started to speak, but realised I couldn't deny her words. I opened my mouth, gurned a little, and then shut it again without uttering so much as a gurgle.

"And you, Mary Carpenter, are no better. From the time you were kids, anyone with eyes could tell you two were meant to be together."

My mum was on a roll now. God help us all. I felt Mary squirm, and I wanted to laugh.

"As a mother, I know. I could see it." She hooked a thumb at my dad. "Him, on the other hand, he wouldn't have a clue."

I fully expected my dad to ask where Patrick was, but he didn't. He just glared at my mum, then nodded and agreed.

"How many years have you both dodged the inevitable? Ten?" I wanted to say it had only been six years, but didn't think it was the right time to interrupt my mother on a rant. "However long it's been, it's gone on too long." My mum's attention landed on Mary, and I felt her stiffen. "That's why I called you. Told you to do something, or else you never would.'"

Called her? My mum had called Mary and told her to get her act together? What the hell?

"And if it hadn't been for Hannah, you'd probably still be dawdling about and looking for your arse with both hands."

Hannah too? Bloody hell. It was a family conspiracy—our very own version of *The Sopranos* but with less blood and fewer fuck words.

"But... I couldn't...didn't... What if..." At least Mary tried to speak. I stood next to her wallowing in my muteness.

My mum held her hand up to silence Mary, but not in way that was meant to be cutting or rude. It was my mum's way of letting us know she hadn't quite finished.

"You can't live your lives on ifs, buts, and maybes, Mary love. And you too, Louise." She moved closer to us, her smile gentle and reassuring. "Life is too precious to worry about rejection. What you should worry about is never doing anything with it, never speaking out, never showing your heart." Mum stopped in front of us and rested one hand on my arm and the other on Mary's. "And to live your lives hiding away your love is the biggest mistake you could make. You two belong together. Always have, always will."

Emotion surged up my throat, the aching of it terrifyingly wonderful. Then the tears came, but not from hurt or anger. The tears were of happiness, acceptance, and recognition of what I could have lost because I was too bloody frightened to speak my heart to the one person who held it. What my mother had said was so true. So bloody true. I'd been so afraid of losing Mary's friendship that I'd nearly lost her completely. I had been blinded by circumstance and expectation—my own—that I had thought that Mary could never feel anything but friendship for me. Even when I had told her I was gay, she'd been so understanding. It had been me who had freaked out when I...

Shit! Big fuck off light bulb over the head moment. Realisation shot into my mind as I recalled what I had done five years ago, the day I had confided my sexuality to my best friend. No wonder she had never told me how she felt.

"God! I am so sorry."

It was the day I had told Mary Carpenter that I was a lesbian, to keep someone else from telling her first. Even I'd realised it would have hurt her to find out second-hand. It was that same day that I had also said, "*Don't worry, Mary. I don't think of you that way. You're my friend. My best friend.*"

I thought she'd gone quiet because she was stunned by my revelation, and then she left not long after.

"When I told you I was gay, I only said what I said because I didn't want to freak you out. I loved you even then."

Mary slowly shook her head before releasing a deep sigh. "That's all in the past, Lou. Don't worry about it."

God. Her eyes were so dark, so intensely dark.

Hannah apparently decided that it was her turn to speak. "You should tell her, Mary."

I still hadn't forgotten her "history in the making" comment, but that could wait.

"I don't think..." Mary grimaced, the sentence unfinished.

Hannah moved over to the sofa and bent to retrieve the presents I had dropped when I had launched to grab the woman I loved. "Which one is it?"

She held three presents in her hands, her eyes darting to each tag as if they would reveal the contents. She stopped and looked over to us. "Give it to her and tell her. She needs to know this isn't a flash in the pan, a sudden epiphany."

I think that was the very first time in my life I had heard my sister use the word epiphany, and I knew for a fact it would be the last.

Mary sighed and moved forward to select one of the gifts. I watched, fascinated, as she deliberated before extending it to me.

I opened it tentatively, slowly pulling the Sellotape from each section of paper. I could hear James and Alfie discussing what on earth the gift could be, considering how both their mother and Mary seemed so obsessed by it.

As the paper separated, I felt tears welling again. I knew what it was before I peeled the covering away. My hands were holding a box. Inside the box were two figurines of two very well-known characters. At the base of the cellophane covering was a Post-it with "You and Me. Best friends forever" surrounded by little love hearts. SpongeBob and Patrick grinned back at me, their goofy smiles shooting directly to my heart and making it ache in that swelling-with-too-much-love kind of way.

"I told you Patrick was here."

My vision was becoming blurry, but the bright yellow and pink were unmistakable. I trailed my fingers over the faces of my cartoon heroes, paying special attention to their smiles. As if from a distance, I heard Hannah encourage Mary to continue.

"I, well, this isn't a new gift," she murmured.

My head shot up, my eyes fixing on hers. Mary chewed her lip, then sighed as if realising she had to continue now she'd started.

"I bought it five years ago. I…bought it to give to you… to help me tell you how I felt."

"So, why didn't you?"

"Because you told her just beforehand that you didn't think of her that way, you knob head."

Trust Hannah to not be able to keep her gob shut. Now was not the time to mention my oversized mouth and inability to recognise a special moment.

"Is this true?"

My question was aimed at Mary. She tilted her head, her eyes closing momentarily, then she straightened her shoulders and stared right into my eyes, and it felt as if I was having my soul examined.

"Yes. But it was for the best."

"I'm bored. Mum, can I—"

I heard Hannah shush Alfie and then whisper for him and James to go and find their dad, who was God knew where.

"How can it be for the best? We've wasted five years."

Mary's smile was so beautiful, so radiant, that I wanted to kiss her senseless without a care for my audience.

"We, my woman, have never wasted a moment. Every single day you have been in my life was a gift, the reason for me breathing. I have loved loving you, loved being in love with you whether you knew it or not." Her hand reached up, slender fingers stroking the side of my face. "And I will live and love every day from now on, with the wonderful knowledge that you love me back."

I didn't answer her. I couldn't. Words would have been redundant. They were mere air, after all. Throwing my arms around her, I kissed her, our lips melding together perfectly as if each had been made in the other's mirror image. Mary pulled me closer, our connection blindingly beautiful, perfectly synchronised.

I heard shuffling from behind me and knew my family was finally giving us the privacy we needed. I heard my dad's mumbled, "But what's happened? Is Patrick coming or what?" I smiled into Mary's mouth.

The kiss was perfect, just like her. My lips knew hers, and hers knew mine. It seemed as if our kiss was the promise of one soul to another, a promise to never forget the love we shared. To never forget the connection we had. To never forget to keep telling each other how we felt, how we loved each other and would continue to do so for the rest of our lives.

I have been in love with my best friend for as long as I can remember, and I will continue to love her for the rest of my life. Given the chance, I would continue to love her beyond even that.

She was my woman, my SpongeBob, my pineapple loving best friend whom I loved to distraction, loved with the completeness of my whole being, and would love which every breath I took for the rest of my life.

Mary Carpenter was my reason to breathe in and out every day. She was my Merry Christmas, Happy New Year, birthdays, and everything else. And the best bit was knowing she felt the same way, even though it had taken us years to pluck up the courage to admit it. We knew now, and that's all that really mattered.

For that knowledge, for that love, for *my* Mary Carpenter, I am truly thankful. These were Christmas gifts I definitely would not be returning this year, although I seriously doubted Hannah's gift of a jumper sporting a cross-eyed reindeer on the front would have a long life.

I might even trade it in for one sporting the character who lived in a pineapple under the sea. That seems like a better fashion statement after all, especially for a starfish.

Christmas Road Trip

JAE

MEGHAN WIPED HER HAND OVER the fogged-up window and stared at the unfamiliar white landscape passing by. How much longer was this going to take? She'd thought that it was a short trip, but this bus ride seemed to last forever. *Jeez, are we going via Timbuktu? And on a bus of all things!* In her imagination, this journey had always been very different.

Even though she hadn't seen a stop ahead, the bus came to a halt and opened its door.

Not again. They had stopped twice already since Meghan had gotten on the bus. If they continued at this pace, she'd spend eternity on this freaking bus.

A woman climbed aboard, her blonde hair matted by the helmet that was now dangling from her hand. Bicycle pants clung to her shapely thighs and calves. She walked along the rows of seats, looking for a place to sit, but most of their fellow travelers were staring off into space with dazed expressions on their faces or were trying to see out the window, so no one made eye contact.

Finally, the stranger reached Meghan's place at the back of the bus and gestured next to her. "Is this seat taken?"

So far, none of the other people getting on the bus had approached her, probably chased off by her foul mood.

But the blonde didn't seem to notice her scowl. She continued to look at her with a friendly smile, patiently waiting for her answer.

Meghan sighed, but she had never been able to resist a woman's smile. "No. You can take it." She moved a little to the side. At least she'd have something nice to look at now.

"Thanks." The blonde sat and offered her hand. "Kellie Gibson." Her grip was unexpectedly strong for such a slender woman, but her skin felt soft.

Nice. Meghan always appreciated a firm handshake and soft skin on a woman. "Meghan Webster."

Kellie's eyes widened. "I thought you looked familiar. Are you *the* Meghan Webster?"

Meghan had long since gotten used to people recognizing her wherever she went. "Yes. I'm the head coach of the US women's soccer team." She grimaced. "Well, I *was* the head coach. Now that incompetent bunch calling themselves the management team will probably have my equally incompetent assistant replace me." She smacked her fist against the fogged-up window, making the people in front of them turn in their seats and glower at her. Unimpressed, Meghan stared back.

"Oh, right. I heard my neighbors talk about it when I left my apartment earlier, but then I turned on my MP3 player, so I didn't hear if management made a decision yet." Kellie pointed at the earbuds shoved into the front of her shirt.

A pretty nice shirt, revealing a bit of cleavage, despite the winter weather outside.

Meghan gave her an appreciative glance out of the corner of her eye and smirked at herself. Well, at least some things apparently hadn't changed. Despite everything that had happened, here she was, ogling women. Well, one woman, but this one was so attractive that she'd keep Meghan looking for quite some time.

"I'm very sorry about what happened. You didn't deserve that." Kellie put her hand on Meghan's forearm.

For a moment, Meghan let the warm touch distract her from her misery. Then her morose mood returned, and she flicked a drop of condensation off the windowpane. "I so didn't need all this." She swept her arm in a gesture that encompassed the entire bus. "Especially not on Christmas Eve. That's just cruel."

"Yeah, that really spoils the Christmas cheer, doesn't it?" Kellie said with a little grin.

Meghan studied her. *She's taking this awfully well.*

The bus braked again, and more people got on. The seats all around them were quickly filling up.

"You'd think people would stay at home, safe and sound, on Christmas Eve," Meghan murmured. But then again, that hadn't helped her.

"No, lots of people are traveling to visit family. The streets were hel…uh, I mean, they were incredibly busy earlier."

Meghan couldn't care less. Christmas had never been her thing, and she was still cursing herself for agreeing to put up a Christmas tree this year. That would teach her for listening to her sisters.

"What about you?" Kellie peeked at Meghan's clothes. "Apparently, you weren't traveling to visit family for Christmas."

The bus started to move again.

Meghan shook her head. "No. My sisters and I get along better if there are at least two thousand miles between us. We stopped spending Christmas together when my parents died." She studied the woman next to her. "And you? Anyone who'll miss you when you're not there for Christmas?"

"My dad," Kellie said. For the first time, her ever-present smile faded. She turned her head and stared out the window.

Meghan didn't know what to do. She'd never been good at comforting others. Maybe that was part of why she'd been so successful as a coach. She hated having to console her players after losing a game, so she made sure they won most of them. Hesitantly, she reached over and put her hand on Kellie's arm.

Kellie put her hand on top of hers, turned her head, and looked into her eyes.

They rode in silence for a while.

Slowly, Kellie's smile returned.

Meghan gave her arm one last pat and withdrew.

As the bus traveled up yet another hill, she leaned her head against the back of the seat and closed her eyes. She tried to sleep, but that was an impossible endeavor now. Time seemed to drag. Only God knew when they'd finally arrive. Growling, she opened her eyes again, turned her head, and studied her traveling companion. "You never told me your story."

"My story?" Kellie looked back at her with her big, blue eyes.

"Yeah. What brings you to this hellhole?" Meghan indicated the bus.

Kellie's gaze darted around. "Sssh. Don't call it that. You don't want the driver and his boss to change their minds and decide to send you to a different destination, do you?"

Meghan bit her tongue. Nope. She certainly didn't want that. Her mother had always told her to watch her language. Maybe she should start to follow that advice. Swearing apparently wasn't appreciated around here. *Prudes.* "Okay, okay. But you still didn't answer my question. What brings you here?"

Was that a blush creeping up Kellie's cute face? "Ooh, I bet you've got some story to tell! Shoot!"

The man in the seat in front of her turned and gave her a narrowed-eyed stare.

Meghan ignored him, focusing only on Kellie, who was squirming in her seat.

"I think I'd better tell you later." Kellie peeked at the man in front of them. "Some people here might be a little... sensitive, so you'd better watch what you say."

Huffing, Meghan crossed her arms over her chest. "Oh, come on. It's not like there's much entertainment here. I'm bored to death already."

Again, the man in the seat before hers whirled around and glared at them. "If you can't stop making tasteless jokes and telling depressing stories, at least keep it down. The rest of us don't want to listen to that kind of thing."

Meghan rolled her eyes.

"I'll tell you later," Kellie said, her voice lowered to a whisper.

"All right. But no chickening out."

Kellie slid her finger in a cross pattern over her chest. "Cross my heart and hope to—"

The man in front of them jerked around and sent them a deathly glare.

Kellie held up both hands, palm out. "Okay, okay. We'll shut up. Sorry, sir."

As he turned back around, throwing one last warning glance at them over his shoulder, Kellie and Meghan looked at each other like two first graders being caught talking during class.

Meghan grinned, her mood improving.

As the bus traveled farther up the curvy street, Kellie pulled the earbuds from her shirt, directing Meghan's attention down toward her full, firm breasts.

Mmm, nice.

"Do you want them?" Kellie whispered close to Meghan's ear.

When tingles ran down Meghan's body, she grinned to herself. Who knew that was even still possible? She searched Kellie's face. Was she really offering what Meghan thought she was offering? "Uh, what?"

"The earbuds," Kellie said, a grin curling the corners of her mouth up. "I thought you might want to listen to some music. Maybe it'll help you relax and forget about this whole mess."

Couldn't hurt to give it a try. Meghan nodded and took the earbuds that Kellie held out. Their fingers brushed, again making Meghan tingle all over.

Their hands lingered against each other for a second before Kellie pulled back. Her expression was unreadable, not giving away whether she felt the chemistry between them too.

Meghan untangled the cord and put the earbuds into her ears.

At her nod, Kellie pressed play on her MP3 player.

Nothing happened. Only the muted sounds of the traveling bus filtered past the earbuds.

Meghan reached over to see if the cable had gotten lose, again letting her hand brush against Kellie's. She unplugged the cable and then put it back in.

Still only silence, no music.

She pulled the earbuds from her ears and handed them back.

"Too loud?" Kellie asked. She fumbled for the tiny volume wheel. "I'm sorry. I had it set pretty—"

"No, that's not it. It's not working."

Kellie shook the device. "Oh. It must have gotten damaged."

The bus drove up a steep incline, slowed, and came to a stop. The door swung open with a hiss.

Meghan expected to see more travelers climb aboard, but instead, the driver got up from his seat and announced, "Last stop. All out, please."

Instantly, silence descended as the travelers looked at each other, each hoping someone else would get up the nerve to leave the bus first. A few wiped at the condensation and tried to see out the windows, but no one moved from his or her seat. Finally, an old woman stood and made her way down the aisle. As soon as she'd stepped off the bus, others jumped up and followed her.

Despite her earlier impatience to arrive at their destination, Meghan now found herself hesitating.

Kellie put the MP3 player away and took a deep breath. "Then let's go."

Not sure what to expect, Meghan followed her. She wanted to reach out and take Kellie's hand but held herself back. They barely knew each other and would likely never see each other again once they got off the bus. The thought made her sad.

Kellie made her way down the aisle and then stepped outside.

Behind her, Meghan paused on the last step before squaring her shoulders and jumping down. Slowly, she looked around. Whatever she had expected to find, this wasn't it.

A lonely bus stop lay in front of them, fog wafting around it.

Meghan and Kellie exchanged glances.

Around them, the other travelers were whispering to each other, apparently not sure what to make of this either.

"Are we to wait here or what?" Meghan asked. She found herself whispering too.

"No idea. I've never made this trip before either." Kellie gave her a small smile.

Meghan had to laugh, but it sounded a bit hysterical. "I'd hope not."

A man with curly, gray hair got up from the bench in front of the bus stop. "Ah, the new group. Welcome. I'm Peter, your instructor. If you'd please follow me."

He led them along the deserted street, easily climbing the steep hill, even though he looked as if he were closer to seventy than to sixty.

Finally, they reached a nondescript building at the top of the hill.

"This is it?" Meghan whispered to Kellie.

Kellie shrugged. "Doesn't look like much, does it?"

To Meghan's surprise, the door of the building wasn't locked, and there was no gate.

Do they just let anyone in here?

The group followed Peter inside and up a winding staircase that seemed to go on forever. Upstairs, golden light danced over polished hardwood floors and sparkled on the crystal chandeliers hanging from the high ceilings. Peter opened a mahogany door and led them into a room that looked as if it were too large to fit into the house that hadn't seemed all that big from the outside. A giant oil painting of children playing on a flower-dotted meadow took up one wall.

"Please, take a seat." Peter gestured to a circle of chairs. "I know you had a long trip, so make yourselves comfortable.

I'll be right back to start your training, but there's something I have to take care of first. As you can imagine, Christmas is a busy time around here."

He hurried out, leaving behind his group.

Some of them started to pace while others looked around curiously. A woman wearing an apron lifted one corner of the oil painting away from the wall to see if there was anything behind it.

Meghan wanted to look out the window but realized there were none. The room didn't hold anything of interest either. *Figures. Can't give away all the company secrets to the newbies.* That's how she'd done it in soccer too. Never tell anyone your winning strategy if you weren't sure you could trust him or her. She pulled Kellie with her to the chairs and took a seat.

Kellie plopped down next to her and stowed her bicycle helmet under her chair.

"Why do you keep holding on to that thing?" Meghan asked. "I don't think you'll need it here."

A blush rose up Kellie's slender neck. "Sentimental reasons, probably. But you're right, of course. I think the mode of transportation around here is a little different."

Meghan chuckled. "I just bet it is. Which reminds me… You still haven't told me what brought you here."

Kellie slid to the edge of the seat, looking as if she wanted to jump up and escape. "Uh, it's not that interesting a story."

"Let me be the judge of that. Come on. I'll tell you mine and you tell me yours." Meghan winked at her.

Still, Kellie kept hesitating.

"Come on. This may be our only chance before they assign us God knows where and we never see each other again."

"All right." Kellie took a deep breath. "But if you laugh at me, I swear I'll—"

"Would I do something like that?"

"Oh, yeah. You look like someone who'd have a good laugh about my story."

Meghan regarded her with a steady gaze. "And that would be so bad after a day like this?"

Kellie sighed. "Guess not. It's just embarrassing."

Too cute. Meghan suppressed a smile, not wanting her to think she was laughing at her already. "Okay, I promise to do my best not to laugh. Now, will you tell me? Please?"

Kellie inhaled deeply. "I went on a bike ride earlier..."

"On Christmas Eve?"

"Why not? I'm single, so it's not like there's someone wanting to gaze at the Christmas tree lights with me."

The mention of Christmas tree lights made Meghan wince. Quickly, she shoved all thoughts of Christmas tree decorations away and focused on Kellie's story. *So she doesn't have a boyfriend. Or girlfriend. Not that it matters.* "Yeah, but it's the middle of winter. When I woke up this morning, it was barely twenty degrees in New York. Not exactly balmy weather for a bike ride."

"It's much warmer in Florida, so I ride like this all year. By the way, it's not like you're dressed for winter weather either." Kellie gestured at Meghan's favorite pair of pajamas.

Meghan slid her hands over the geckos on her pajama pants. "What can I say? I left in a hurry. So, what happened then? On your bike ride?"

Kellie stared at the tips of her cycling shoes. "I was riding down the street, rounding a corner, when—"

A murmur went through the crowd of waiting men and women.

Meghan turned her head.

Peter strode back into the room and took up position at the head of the half-open chair circle. He waved at them to gather and listen.

Meghan leaned over and whispered, "Don't think you're safe now. I want to hear the rest of your story."

"Later," Kellie whispered back.

They both leaned forward and focused their attention on Peter.

"Welcome again," he said and regarded each member of their group with a friendly smile. "I know most of you are not too happy about being here."

"Damn right," a man two chairs to Meghan's right said what she was only thinking.

"And some probably thought they'd end up somewhere else." Peter gave the man who'd spoken up a pointed glance, making him snap his mouth shut. "Some of you might even think they don't deserve to be here. But rest assured, you do. It's been a long-held tradition that whoever gets here on Christmas Eve or Christmas Day automatically becomes part of our special unit."

"Yeah, and probably gets a nice little uniform to go with that," Meghan whispered.

Kellie shushed her.

Peter paused in his speech and looked at Meghan. "Oh, you're right, dear. I forgot the uniforms. Be right back." Again, he marched out and left the group behind.

"Oh, boy." Meghan sank against the back of her seat. "I thought they'd be better organized here, but they're worse than my girls. At least one of them always forgets her uniform when she shows up for an important game."

Kellie chuckled. "I don't think our uniforms will look anything like the ones you're used to."

Meghan didn't think so either, but she didn't want to even imagine what Peter would bring back. "You were telling me about your bike ride."

"Meghan…"

"You were riding down the street, turning a corner, when…?" Meghan prompted.

Kellie ran both hands through her matted, blonde hair. "When a woman crossed the street in front of me."

"And you plowed right into her."

"No. I… Well, she had a…" Kellie paused and rubbed her flushed cheeks.

Meghan put one elbow on her knee and leaned toward her. "A dog? A herd of children trailing behind her? A machine gun? What? Come on, tell me before Peter gets back!"

Kellie looked down, making her hair fall around her face like a curtain. She peeked out from beneath her bangs and whispered, "A very nice rack."

Meghan sat up straight and grinned. So Kellie definitely played for her team—if there even were teams here. "And?"

"And I might have been a bit distracted..."

"You ogled her, admit it!"

Kellie blew out a breath. "Okay, yes, I ogled her. I also had my MP3 player on, so I didn't see or hear the garbage truck backing up right in front of me—and here I am." She indicated the circle of chairs.

Despite her promise not to, Meghan had to laugh. "We have that in common."

"What? Being dead?"

"Yeah, that too. But I meant ogling women. That's why I'm here too."

Kellie sat up straight. "Really? My neighbors left out that part of the story. What happened?"

"I was at home, watching a recruitment tape in the living room, when the lights on my Christmas tree began to flicker. I got up to fix them, craning my head to keep watching because one of the players I had my eye on...well, she had a really nice rack too."

They exchanged commiserating looks.

"What happened then?" Kellie asked.

"I put my hand on the string of lights and—zzzzzz! Electrocuted. On Christmas Eve. In my gecko pajamas."

Kellie reached over and patted her leg. "Ouch."

"Yeah. Not the most pleasant way to go; that's for sure. Not that I have a personal standard of comparison, mind you." By now, she could smile about it. "My friends always said women would be my death one day, but I never thought it would be literal."

Kellie laughed. "Well, at least we were both wearing clothes." She pointed at a naked guy with only a towel wrapped around his hips. Apparently, he had died in his birthday suit.

Peter returned with a stack of uniforms. He unfolded one of them and proudly held it up.

"You've got to be kidding me." Meghan groaned.

Their new uniform consisted of a belt cord, a pair of gladiator sandals, and a billowing, white dress that hid any hint of the wearer's curves.

"Well, at least we won't be ogling each other in that thing," Kellie whispered.

Speak for yourself.

"Where are the wings?" one of the women to their left asked.

Peter shook his head. "We don't give them to people who died in accidents. Too risky." He held up a list. "I'm going to assign you each a partner now, and then we'll head over to our guardian angel training center."

"Where the hell were our guardian angels when we needed them?" Meghan grumbled.

"Ssssh!" Eyes wide, Kellie pressed her finger to her lips. "You really have to stop saying the H word. I don't think they're too fond of that here. It's like you were playing for Western New York Flash but kept talking about the Portland Thorns."

Meghan grinned. "You're a soccer fan?" *Be still my heart.* Of course, it was no longer beating anyway.

"Sssssh!" Several people shushed her as Peter began to call out names.

Meghan held her breath. *Please, please, please, don't let me get partnered with died-in-the-shower guy over there.* He had more hair on his back than a gorilla. Even once he was covered by that ugly angel uniform, she didn't want to stare at his unshaven face for all eternity.

"Meghan Webster," Peter called.

Meghan slowly raised her hand and braced herself. "Here."

Every gaze zeroed in on her.

"Nice win in the last world cup," Peter said.

Meghan blinked. "You watch TV up here?"

Peter gave her a mysterious smile. "We don't have to. But you'll find out how all of that works soon enough. And to answer your earlier question about where your guardian angels were when you needed them..."

Oh, shit. He heard that? Or was he reading her mind? If people up here could do that, she was in trouble.

"We're a little understaffed at the moment. That's why we need to start your training right away. So, let's see who we've partnered you with." He trailed his index finger over the list. "There we are. Kellie Gibson."

Thank you, thank you, thank you, God. Maybe she could later tell him in person.

Meghan and Kellie beamed at each other.

Once everyone had changed into the new uniform, Peter led them downstairs.

Now in a much better mood, Meghan followed Kellie and the rest of the group over to the training center. Even though Meghan had liked her better in the tight bicycle pants and the revealing shirt, Kellie managed to look good even in the angel uniform. She caught a peek at muscular calves as she followed her down the stairs. *I wonder if guardian angels date.*

Well, she had eternity to find out.

Holiday Spirit

FLETCHER DELANCEY

Robin peered through the fat raindrops spattering her windshield and smiled. "Right on time. Thank you, National Weather Service."

She'd obsessively checked the NWS website for updates on the storm before leaving her house, and the last check had indicated that she would arrive in the coastal town of Florence, Oregon, about four hours before the storm did. This rain was the warm-up, the tap on the shoulder letting everyone know that the real show was coming soon. She couldn't wait.

Growing up in the high desert on the east side of the Cascade Mountains meant that she was well acquainted with thunderstorms and snowstorms. But the coastal winter storms were something altogether different: vast oceanic systems of howling winds and sideways rain that could cover the entire state if they made it all the way on land at full strength, which they never did. They expended their fury on the coast, occasionally coming inland as far as the Willamette Valley and toppling trees in the state's population centers. The *Oregonian* would print excited headlines about fifty-mile-per-hour gusts in Portland, but Robin knew that was small stuff. The little coastal towns regularly racked up gusts in the eighties and nineties, yet somehow those never made it into the state's biggest newspaper. If it didn't happen in the big cities, it didn't happen.

And it never happened on Robin's side of the Cascades. All her life she'd heard tales of those storms from Aunt Jackie, who made them seem like something from another planet.

"In the southeast, they'd call 'em hurricanes," Aunt Jackie would say. "On the upper East Coast they'd call 'em nor'easters. But we just call 'em winter storms." Then she'd tell the story about the year the local pizza parlor's roof peeled off and landed on her front lawn, or the one where flooding turned half the county into a virtual island for ten days. She'd talk about carrying a chainsaw in the back of her pickup so that she could cut trees out of the road when they fell and blocked her way, and how everyone still remembered the winter when the power only went out once.

Robin had grown up on Aunt Jackie's tales of life at the Oregon coast, and while she'd been there more times than she could count, she'd never seen a winter storm for herself. It was always something that she and Aunt Jackie were going to do together. Somehow they never got around to it.

The raindrops fell faster, and Robin flipped her wipers from intermittent to normal speed. The forested hills lining the Siuslaw River valley were now almost invisible behind the gray mists, lending an otherworldly look to a landscape that was already as different from the high desert as one could get.

"It doesn't smell right," Aunt Jackie had often said. "Too dry, too full of sage. Even when it rains here, it smells dry." She'd lived in the high desert for twenty years and still hadn't gotten used to it, always pining for the lush scent of her beloved coastal rain forest.

Robin rolled down her window a couple of inches, ignoring the rain that drove in, and took deep breaths. It *was* lush, bursting with the scent of rampant growth and equally rapid decay, of leaf mold and rotting logs and thick hemlocks and firs. She imagined Aunt Jackie in her passenger seat, sticking her nose out the other window and gulping in the air, and her eyes watered.

God, she missed her. It had already been a year, yet it felt like a week. If Aunt Jackie had never gotten over missing the coast in twenty years, how was Robin going to get over missing her in anything less?

"I wish you were here," she said as she rolled up her window. The sudden cessation of wind noise and rain was jarring and much too quiet. She could almost hear Aunt Jackie's voice, making her typical acerbic response. *If wishes were horses, you could saddle up and ride.*

"And if wishes were fishes, we'd all cast nets," she murmured.

Another curve in the road and the bridge came into view. She was crossing the North Fork Siuslaw, and Florence was just ahead. Already she could see the decorations attached to the power poles and street lamps. But it wasn't until she reached the big intersection and turned north on Highway 101 that the Christmas lights started in earnest. Shops and homes twinkled with lights in their windows and under their eaves, and an occasional inflatable reindeer was tied to a rooftop. It wasn't yet dark, but this was Christmas Eve after all. People tended to turn on their lights early.

Her hotel was another mile down the road, its large sign proclaiming NO VACANCY, and Robin congratulated herself on being smart enough to reserve ahead. Winters at the coast were quiet, except during Christmas and storms. Storm watching had become a tourist activity, and having one on the holiday practically guaranteed packed hotels.

She pulled in under the overhang, turning off her wipers when they began screeching on the now-dry windshield, and killed the engine. With the particular joy that came from being cooped up in a car too long, she stepped out, stretched, and inhaled deeply.

Ah, there it was, the sea smell. Under the scent of rain and wet pavement was the unmistakable tang of salt, seaweed, and beach. She breathed it in for several minutes, listening to the swish of cars going by on the highway and watching the rain dripping off the overhang. Then she headed into the lobby to check in.

"Excuse me?"

"I'm sorry, Ms. Marsten. Are you sure you didn't make a reservation at our Newport property by mistake?"

"I'm sure," Robin managed through gritted teeth. It just figured that they'd lose her reservation on Christmas fucking Eve. "I do know the difference between Florence and Newport."

The desk manager at least had the grace to look embarrassed. "I didn't mean to suggest otherwise. But I'm afraid we don't have any rooms tonight. I could check our Newport property—"

"Are you kidding? I do not want to drive for another hour. Can't you find me a room in Florence?"

"I'm sorry, but that's not...I'm not authorized to do that."

"So you've lost my reservation, and you won't help me find a different place to stay."

"I don't believe we've lost your reservation, Ms. Marsten. If you had a confirmation number..."

"Oh, for God's sake. Just tell me where I can start looking for another room."

He wrote down the names and numbers of two hotels on a business card, which she snatched out of his hand with little grace and no thanks. In a fine fury, she stomped out the door but stopped short when she saw her car.

A silver tabby cat was on her hood, resting contentedly with its front paws tucked under. It looked at her with big dark eyes, apparently quite happy with the engine heat and disinclined to move.

"You're going to have to get off," she told the cat. "I have to find a new hotel, because yours is full and your staff is incompetent."

The cat blinked at her and turned its head, the tag on its red collar flashing in the hotel lights.

Robin went back to the lobby door and pushed it open. "Hey," she called. "You need to come get your cat off my car."

The manager looked up from his computer. "We don't have a cat."

"Well, there's one on my car."

He shrugged. "It's not ours." With that he turned back to his computer screen, clearly dismissing the cat as somebody else's problem.

Robin let the door shut and faced the tabby. "I am never staying at this hotel again. What a jackass."

The cat's ears flicked back, then forward again. Its fur was wet, Robin realized. It must have been out in the rain for some time before finding this shelter.

She walked to her car and laid a hand on the hood. "Look, I know you're comfy, and it's shitty weather out there, but you belong to someone and that someone isn't me. You already have a place to stay, and I have to go find one. So…shoo." She patted the hood, hoping the sound and movement would scare the cat off.

It stretched out its neck to sniff at her.

"Shoo." She slapped the hood harder.

The cat got up, stretched, and walked over to sniff her hand.

"Really?" Robin couldn't help smiling at the sheer chutzpah. Her smile broadened when the cat nudged her hand with its head, and before she knew it, she was scratching its cheeks. The cat moved its head this way and that, giving her full access and purring so loudly that she could hear it over the sound of the rain.

"Okay, fine. Let's see what your tag says. If I'm going to be calling hotels, I guess I can call your owner first." She reached down, chuckling when the cat bumped her hand in an effort to get scratched. "Tag first. Petting later." Finally getting her fingers on the tag, she angled it toward the overhead light and saw a phone number. "Wait a minute. That's not a Florence prefix. How far are you from home?"

She flipped the tag over, looking for an address, and stared in disbelief. Then she dropped the tag and looked at the cat accusingly.

"You're kidding me."

The cat sat, curling its tail around its feet, and stared up at her.

"Your name is Jackie?"

At the sound of its name, the cat got up again and rubbed against her. Half the water on its fur transferred to Robin's sweater, but she hardly noticed. What were the odds that on the one-year anniversary of her aunt's death, she'd run into a cat with the same name?

"Okay. This is just a weird coincidence. But Aunt Jackie, just in case you're watching from wherever you are, don't worry. I'll take your little namesake home."

She pulled her phone from her pocket and tried to get the cat to hold still while she read off the number. It took several attempts, since Jackie was determined to be petted, but she finally succeeded by stroking the cat with the back of the hand holding the phone while grabbing the tag in the other. She punched in the number and lifted the phone to her ear, petting Jackie as she listened to the rings.

"Hello?" said a female voice.

"Hi. My name is Robin Marsten, and I think I have your cat. A silver tabby named Jackie?"

"Oh my God! You have Jackie? Where are you? Is she all right?"

"She's wet but otherwise fine, so far as I can tell. And she's very pushy about being petted."

A strangled sound came out of the phone, and when the woman next spoke, her voice sounded scratchy. "Thank God! I've been so worried. She's been gone for a week, I've looked everywhere, I thought she was—" She stopped with a gasp and cleared her throat. "Thank you so much for calling. Where did you find her?"

"At the Dunes Hotel in Florence."

"In *Florence*? How did she end up there? That's twenty miles!"

Well, that answered one question. Robin looked down at the cat, who lifted a paw and curled it as soon as they made eye contact. "I don't know, but I'd be happy to bring her back to you."

"I—" The woman took a shuddering breath. "I would appreciate that so very much. You're incredibly kind, and you have saved my Christmas. No, you've saved my whole year. Thank you so much."

She began listing off directions to her house, and every time she mentioned a landmark, Robin said "uh huh" until Jackie's owner finally said, "You must be a local. Do you live in Florence?"

"No, I live in Bend. But my aunt used to live here. Right around where you are, it sounds like. Her house was on the edge of the cliff, but she sold it twenty years ago and retired to live near my parents and me."

"Oh, then I'll just give you the address. It's 238 Seacrest Drive. It's a three-story—"

"A-frame house at the end of the street," Robin finished, shaking her head. "That was my aunt's house."

"Wow. That's kind of an unbelievable coincidence, isn't it?"

Robin petted Jackie the cat and said, "Not so unbelievable, actually."

It wasn't as hard getting Jackie into the car as Robin would have thought. She'd considered opening the door first, but didn't want to take the chance that Jackie might jump off and vanish while she was otherwise occupied. So she carefully picked up the cat and petted her while holding her against her shoulder. When this went well, she continued the petting as she slowly stepped to the door. Jackie purred and seemed quite relaxed, not batting an eye when Robin shifted to a one-handed hold. As quickly as she could, she opened the door and sat inside, tossing Jackie onto the passenger seat and yanking the door shut before the surprised cat could react.

"It's okay," she said, holding out her hand. "I'm taking you home."

Jackie sniffed her hand, rubbed her cheek on it, and then began exploring. Robin thought all hell might break loose once she started the engine, so it was probably best to let Jackie sniff everything beforehand. She didn't expect the cat to jump up onto the dashboard and spread herself out there.

"Uh...you sure you want to be there? You're going to see everything. I don't think cats are supposed to enjoy driving in cars."

Jackie began washing herself.

"Okay, then. I guess you know what you're doing." Robin started the car, watching for any adverse reaction.

Jackie lifted a front paw and cleaned it.

"Right." She let out the clutch, pulled through the hotel's overhang, and headed back into the rain.

It was a longer drive than usual to Aunt Jackie's street, because she didn't dare go around the sharp curves at her normal rate of speed. She was afraid of the cat sliding off her dashboard. For her part, Jackie occasionally stopped her bath long enough to gaze out the window at the darkening forest whipping by, but otherwise was focused on getting her fur back into top shape.

Robin passed one familiar landmark after another and had to swallow a lump in her throat when she turned into the gravel lane, which was now marked by a tasteful wooden sign for Sitka House Bed and Breakfast. No vacancy, of course, because that would have been too easy.

She'd never actually driven down this lane herself; it had always been her parents driving when they came to visit Aunt Jackie. She had been sixteen when her aunt sold the house, and deep down she'd always been a little angry at her for selling it so soon. Her adult side knew that the three-story house and large property had become too much for her aging aunt to care for, but her child side thought it was completely unfair that Aunt Jackie didn't wait for her to get old enough to buy it herself. Never mind that two decades later she still couldn't afford it. Property values had gone up a hell of a lot since then.

"I still think you should have held it for me in trust and let me inherit," Robin grumbled. "Why couldn't you be rich like other people's aunts?"

Jackie stopped her bath and rolled onto her stomach, looking straight out the windshield with apparent recognition.

"No, you send me a cat that gets to live in your house instead. I think you might have misread my wishes."

She came around a curve and automatically went to the side to avoid the huge pothole that had always been there, but the road surface was perfectly smooth. Interesting. That meant the current owners of the homes along this lane were working together to keep it graded and graveled. Aunt Jackie had often ranted that she was the only one who cared about it, but she couldn't afford to pay for its upkeep by herself.

When Robin pulled into the circular driveway at the end of the lane, she understood the state of the road. This, it turned out, was the Sitka House. Its current owner clearly had cash, because the house looked beautiful, so did the yard, and the circular drive was filled in with small, round river pebbles, not the sharp-edged, larger gravel of the road.

She turned off the engine and opened the door, but didn't even get one foot out before the cat tromped across her legs and leapt to the ground. By the time Robin managed to get herself out of the car and upright, Jackie was already trotting up the steps to the wide front porch. A sudden sweep of heavier rain sent Robin up the steps as well, seeking the protection of the porch roof.

The front door opened and she had a brief glimpse of a woman with plush curves and shoulder-length, dark blonde hair before the owner of Sitka House leaned down and scooped up her cat.

"Jackie! Oh thank God!"

She hugged the cat with her eyes closed and a huge smile on her face, but then her expression crumpled and she began to cry.

"How could you do that to me, you furry little twerp! I've been worried out of my mind." Her eyes opened, and she managed a watery smile at Robin. "I'm sorry; I'm not usually like this. Please come in."

Robin followed her into the foyer, which had been turned into a mudroom with shoe benches and hooks for coats. She was reluctant to move farther with her wet shoes, but didn't want to take them off when she wasn't planning to stay.

Jackie's owner walked a few steps into the living area, speaking to her cat in low tones and occasionally sniffling. After a minute, she put the cat down by a beautiful Christmas tree that had to be ten feet high and returned to the mudroom, her nose red but her face wreathed in a welcoming smile.

"Robin, wasn't it? I'm Evelyn." She held out a hand. "It is *so* good to meet you. I can't thank you enough for bringing Jackie back to me."

Her grip was firm. Robin smiled back, enjoying the brilliance of her blue eyes even through the leftover tears. Evelyn looked to be her own age, which was odd for a bed-and-breakfast owner. An inheritance, perhaps?

"No thanks necessary," she said. "Jackie sort of insisted on it."

Evelyn laughed. "Yes, she does that. She insisted on me adopting her, too. She just showed up last Christmas Eve, this bedraggled little adolescent cat that couldn't have been more than six months old, but she had the attitude of a CEO. Ever since then, she's run this place at least as much as I have. I can't get over how good she looks, and she's not even hungry!" She paused. "Is something wrong?"

Robin tore her gaze away from Jackie, who was sitting in the middle of the living area and carefully cleaning her hind leg, toes reaching for the ceiling. "Um. Did you say Christmas Eve? You've had her for a year?"

"Yes, why?"

Robin shook her head. "Just a strange coincidence. Anyway, I'm glad everything's turned out all right and that Jackie has such a good home. But I need to head back—"

"Oh no, you can't possibly leave yet. Surely you have time for coffee? Or tea? Or hot chocolate? I make very good cups of all three."

Robin hesitated. She was feeling slightly creeped out, but Evelyn seemed nice and really, it was all just happenstance, right?

"Please," Evelyn said. "You don't seem to understand what you've done for me. I'm so grateful, and it wouldn't feel right to just turn you back out into the rain after you came all this way. Stay for a while and let me make you something."

"Well, when you put it that way..."

"Oh good! Now I usually serve in the dining room, but you're practically family since Jackie adopted you, and besides, your aunt owned this house, so come into the kitchen." Evelyn didn't wait for a response, instead striding down the hallway and clearly expecting Robin to follow.

With one last wary glance at the cat, Robin toed off her shoes and headed down a hall she hadn't seen for twenty years.

Everything was so different. She'd often fantasized about seeing this house again, but in her dreams it looked just as it had when Aunt Jackie had lived here. Now the only things she recognized were the wood floors, the moldings, and the classic staircase. Either Evelyn or some previous owner had made substantial changes, and transforming the foyer into a mudroom was just the start. The old wallpaper had been stripped and replaced with a brighter pattern, but only on the bottom half of the walls. Then there was a line of molding stained to match the stairs, and above that the walls were painted a creamy yellow. Aunt Jackie's clutter of family photos and her own watercolors were gone, replaced with a few large and beautiful landscape paintings that Robin suspected cost as much as her mortgage payment. Recessed lighting had been installed in the ceiling, and there were even tiny lights flush with the stair steps, probably a safety feature for guests.

When she entered the kitchen, she saw at a glance that the cheap, dark cupboards were now white with glass fronts. It would never have occurred to her to put glass fronts on cupboards, but it worked here and made the kitchen look larger and more airy. Even the huge window looking out over the sea cliff had been changed for one of the modern double-paned types, something Aunt Jackie had always said she wanted to do but couldn't afford.

"What'll it be, then? Coffee, tea, or hot cocoa?" Evelyn turned with her hand on the new granite counter and looked at her expectantly.

"Actually, coffee sounds great."

"Perfect. In that case I'll join you. Hang on; I'm about to make a bit of noise." Evelyn bustled around, spooning some beans into a small grinder and holding down the top as it chewed them up. Robin was already impressed; she just scooped the instant stuff into a mug and called it good. Who had time to grind their own beans?

As Evelyn set a kettle to boil and brought cups and saucers to the light oak table by the window, Robin noted what appeared to be professional pans hanging from a rack and a set of spices that was easily ten times the size of her own. Evelyn must love to cook. Well, it made sense; she was running a bed-and-breakfast after all.

She turned to look at the door she'd just come through and stopped breathing.

"Ah, I see you've found the best part of the kitchen." Evelyn came up to stand beside her. "I found that in the attic when I bought the place, along with a whole pile of smaller watercolors. I used the smaller ones in the guest rooms, but this needed a special space. And because it's so long and narrow, it was perfect for going over a doorway. I'm sure you recognize the location."

"Yes," Robin managed. "That's Heceta Head."

"Right. All of the watercolors are of local landmarks, which made them perfect for the guest rooms. I never could find the artist, because she didn't sign her whole name, and none of the gallery owners around here recognized the style. But I named Jackie after her."

Robin swallowed against the tightness in her throat. "Her name was Jackie Linderhall. She left almost all of her watercolors behind because when she moved, it was to a much smaller house that didn't have room for all of her art, and my parents' house was already full of it. The couple who bought this house from her said they loved the paintings and would take any she'd leave behind, so she thought they were going to a good home." But somehow they'd ended up piled in the attic? That was so wrong.

Evelyn was staring at her. "Jackie Linderhall…was your aunt?"

The tears rose up without warning, and Robin couldn't hold them back. She nodded and turned away, wiping the tears off her cheeks, but they kept coming. A light touch on her shoulder was probably meant to help, but it just made things worse, and she clamped her jaw shut against the sob that was trying to escape.

"I'm guessing your loss is recent," Evelyn said softly.

"One year ago today," Robin rasped.

"I'm so sorry. What an awful time to lose a loved one, on Chr—" Evelyn stopped. "Oh. *Oh.* That's the strange coincidence."

Jackie the cat chose that moment to appear in the kitchen, making a beeline for Robin's legs and rubbing happily against them. Both women stared at her in silence.

"Would you like a dash of whisky in your coffee?" Evelyn asked at last.

"God, yes."

The coffee was fantastic. Evelyn's company was even better. She listened patiently while Robin spilled out story after story of her beloved aunt and the many times she'd been in this house as a child. They went through one refill each, and then their empty cups grew cold as the winds grew stronger, and still Robin talked while Evelyn listened. The storm was getting closer and Robin really should have been finding a place to stay, but she couldn't bring herself to care. Whatever magic had led her here was making her unwilling to leave, and the purring cat in her lap was probably part of it. She felt warm, safe, and suffused with a sense of belonging. Even if she could only be here for an hour or two, she'd take that for all it was worth. The idea of getting in her car and driving back down to Florence grew more unappealing with every passing minute.

At last Jackie jumped out of her lap and demanded food, after which Evelyn offered a tour of the house. Robin accepted immediately.

They started on the ground floor, with Evelyn pointing out the changes she'd made and describing how things had looked when she'd bought the house four years ago. From the sound of it, nothing much had changed until she came along, though the house had gone through at least one other owner before then.

Evelyn had very good taste, Robin had to admit. Everything she'd done had been an improvement, and in many cases it was what Aunt Jackie had always wanted to do. When she said as much, Evelyn's face glowed with pleasure, turning her rather plain features into something altogether beautiful.

They finished with the ground floor and went up the stairs, where Evelyn opened the door to what had been Aunt Jackie's studio. Now it was one of the guest rooms, clearly empty of any occupant. Come to think of it, Robin realized, the two downstairs guest rooms had also been empty, and there hadn't been any other cars in the driveway or the parking area off to the side.

"Wait," she said. "There's no one here. But your sign said no vacancy."

"Ah. That's just my little Christmas gift to myself. I don't accept guests over the holidays. I know I could probably pack the house, but it's not worth it. This is my time to relax and treat myself to some well-earned peace."

Robin looked around the room and tried to hide her disappointment. "Good for you. I think that's a great idea."

Evelyn frowned; she must have heard the lack of sincerity in her voice. But she recovered and finished the tour with class and courtesy, taking them back downstairs after showing off the last of the guest rooms. Her own rooms were up on the third floor, and Robin understood why she was not extending the tour that far.

They ended in the living room by the beautifully decorated Christmas tree, where Robin thanked her host for a lovely afternoon.

"No thanks necessary," Evelyn said. "You gave me the greatest gift I could ask for this Christmas. I hardly think a few drinks and a tour come close to the same value."

It was on the tip of Robin's tongue to ask if maybe she could rent a room and they'd call it even, but she caught herself in time. Evelyn surely had plans for tomorrow and family to spend the day with, just as Robin would if she hadn't informed her parents that she'd be at the coast this Christmas.

It was funny, though. She'd come to Florence to feel closer to her aunt on the anniversary of her death, and there was no place she felt closer than right here. But she had no reason to stay.

Evelyn waited as she put her shoes back on and then accompanied her onto the porch, where Robin drew back in dismay at the sight of the rain. It was falling much harder now, and in every direction as the wind whipped it into swirls. Of course her coat was inside her car. She was going to get soaked just running there.

"Well, this is getting nasty," Evelyn said. "I think the storm is going to hit full strength a little earlier than they said. Where are you staying, by the way? At the Dunes?"

Robin shivered as a gust blew cold spray straight under the porch roof and into their faces. "That's where I was supposed to stay. But they lost my reservation."

"On Christmas Eve? Oh, for heaven's sake. You know, that whole 'lost your reservation' thing is a crock. They didn't lose it. They never entered it in the database in the first place, or else they did but then forgot to save the record. That's the only way something like this can happen. So where are they putting you up instead?"

"They're not. The manager gave me the numbers of a couple of other hotels in Florence, and I was just going to call them when I found Jackie."

Evelyn stared at her wide-eyed, then shook her head. "Okay, that's not going to happen. You're staying here."

"But your Christmas—"

"Would be one I'd remember forever as the year I threw a Good Samaritan out in a storm because I wanted to keep to my own tradition. That's not going to happen either." She looked out at the wind and gave one nod. "Here's what *is* going to happen. You're going to put your car in my garage so it's safe from the storm. It's one thing to be parked on a nice big patch of asphalt when the winds hit ninety, and something else to be right under the trees. Then you're going to join me for dinner—which I warn you will be light, because I don't cook on Christmas—and maybe an after-dinner drink. And then you're going to sleep in my best room and enjoy this storm with a full view of the ocean."

"I..." Robin closed her mouth at the look on Evelyn's face and wondered why she was even trying to object. "I would be delighted."

"Better." Evelyn smiled. "I take it you remember where the garage is?"

"Around that side of the house, unless you moved it."

"No, it's still there. I'll go through and open it up for you." She looked askance at Robin's clothes. "Where is your coat?"

"In the car. It wasn't raining this hard when I got here."

Evelyn ducked back into the mudroom and reappeared an instant later with a raincoat. "Here, borrow mine. Otherwise you'd be soaked to the skin before you got your car door open."

It was a little large for her, but fine for the purpose. "Thank you."

"You're welcome. Now shoo."

Robin ran through the rain and broke speed records getting into her car, but still wasn't quick enough to keep out an astonishing amount of water that now dripped off the inside of her door. She blew out a breath and started the engine, then smiled. "'Shoo,' she says. Like I'm a cat. This is your idea of a joke, isn't it, Aunt Jackie?"

Her wheels crunched over the gravel as she drove slowly around the house, and even at that speed the wipers could hardly clear the water off the windshield. She was devoutly glad to not be driving back down the twisty cliffside highway through weather like this.

The warm light of the garage beckoned to her, and she rolled into the empty space next to a red Honda CRV. Evelyn stood near the back wall, motioning her forward and then holding up a hand. Robin stopped, set the brake, and stepped out. Puddles were already forming beneath her car.

"Wow," she said. "I didn't know that much water could fall out of the sky in such a short time."

Evelyn laughed. "Well, you said you wanted to experience a winter storm. You picked a good one."

Robin left her shoes and the dripping coat in the mini-mudroom space Evelyn had built by her inner garage door, then followed her back into the house and up the stairs, this time with her overnight bag on her shoulder. They went to the room directly over the dining area, the one that hadn't existed when Aunt Jackie had lived here. Or rather, it had, but then it was two tiny bedrooms that had been used for storage. Knocking out the wall between them had transformed the space, and even though that solution had never occurred to Aunt Jackie, Robin knew she would have loved it.

"Fresh towels are in the bathroom," Evelyn said, pointing to a door that would once have led into the hall. "The comforter is goose down, but if you're allergic, I can bring up a hypoallergenic one instead."

"No, I love down comforters. I live under one at home."

"Good. The notebook on the desk is full of information you won't need, since you know the area, but the wifi password is on the first page. And that's it, I think. I'll leave you here to get comfortable. Come to the kitchen whenever you're ready. Dinner is going to be reheated leftovers, so there's no prep time. I'll just pop it in when you join me." She bustled out the door, leaving Robin in the silence of a room that could have been anywhere, so unfamiliar was it.

Except for one thing. She walked up to the watercolor that hung over the desk and ran her finger along the frame, smiling at the stylized signature in the bottom right corner.

"She put your paintings back. You're still here, and everyone who comes to stay gets to know a little bit of you. There's something so right about that."

A ghostly touch brushed the back of her knee.

"Gaah!" The yelp that came out of her throat was embarrassingly high, as was the involuntary leap that propelled her into the edge of the desk. She bounced off and turned, her hand pressed against her hammering heart.

Jackie the cat crouched on the floor, ears back and eyes wide.

"Jesus Christ, you scared the shit out of me!" Robin began to laugh. "Looks like I scared you, too. Well, you deserved it. You should know better than to sneak up on a slightly freaked-out person. I'm halfway to thinking you're my aunt, you know."

She knelt and held out her hand, and Jackie's ears came back up. A moment later Robin was petting a purring, squirming cat. She checked the open door, saw no sign of Evelyn, and bent down to put her lips near Jackie's head.

"Are you?" she whispered.

Jackie gave no sign of understanding, merely bumping her head against a hand that was not petting her fast enough. Robin resumed proper petting speed, relieved and a little disappointed.

Evelyn chuckled when Robin appeared in her kitchen twenty minutes later, arms full of cat. "I see she couldn't resist your lure."

"Is an open bag a lure?" Robin set Jackie on the floor. "I came out of the bathroom and found her in my overnight bag."

"It's one of her favorite things, yes. But she has an uncanny ability to know when she's not wanted. People who don't like cats barely even see her. Those who do can hardly get rid of her." She opened the oven door and slid a covered casserole dish inside. "I hope you like pork loin and roasted winter vegetables."

"Are you kidding? I'd pay twelve dollars a plate to have it in Bend."

"My presentation might be not be up to restaurant standards, but it tasted great yesterday. Have a seat. I'm having red wine with dinner; is that good for you, or would you like something else?"

Robin looked at the table, artistically prepared with two place settings, and gave up on offering to help. "Red sounds perfect. How did you get so much done in twenty minutes?"

"I run a B&B. Lots of practice."

Dinner was a pleasant affair, with excellent food and easy conversation. Robin learned that Evelyn was just two years older than she, went to school at Stanford, had been part of a successful Internet startup in Silicon Valley—which explained the cash she'd poured into the house—and that most of her relatives were in the San Francisco area. Their tradition was for a big family event on Thanksgiving, while Christmas was a quieter holiday. For Evelyn, Christmas had become a mini-vacation, in which she accepted neither guests nor invitations. It was her time to be alone.

"And before you start feeling guilty," she said with apparent telepathy, "remember that until a few hours ago I thought I really *would* be alone this year. I was sure Jackie was dead. So having both her and her savior in my kitchen is a gift."

"Savior of cats," Robin mused. "Not something I'd expected to put on my CV, but who knows, maybe it'll give me an edge the next time I go job hunting."

"It certainly would with me."

Her tone of voice made Robin wonder if she should be reading something into that statement, but Evelyn was occupied with topping off their water glasses and gave no indication that she'd intended a double meaning. With a mental shrug, Robin set it aside and asked how she'd gotten from Silicon Valley to a house on the edge of an Oregon coastal cliff, whereupon she received an education in the huge pressures, ridiculous work hours, and burnout rates for Silicon Valley employees. She couldn't relate, having never had a job that took over her life that way, but could certainly see how calling all of her own shots in a quiet, rural environment would have appealed to Evelyn after that.

They conversed long after the last bite had been taken, and when Evelyn finally rose to clear the table, Robin insisted on being allowed to help with the washing up. It was an odd sort of déjà vu, standing at her aunt's kitchen sink and washing dishes, except of course the sink wasn't the same and neither were the cupboards or counters. She shot a glance at Evelyn, who was drying the casserole dish, and smiled to herself. Aunt Jackie would have liked her.

The kitchen was spic and span in no time, and Robin happily followed Evelyn's suggestion that they take the rest of the wine into the living room. She tried to focus on their conversation but couldn't keep her eyes off the large picture window, where the porch light illuminated the front yard and nearby forest. The storm wasn't supposed to hit full strength for another hour, but it looked as if things were really rocking out there as the trees lashed back and forth and the rain blew horizontally.

"I always thought Aunt Jackie was exaggerating about that," she said in wonder.

"About what?"

"Rain falling sideways. It really does."

"Oh, yes. Quite a pain when you're trying to put groceries in your car. There's no way to keep the water out. And if you park with your door facing the wind, sometimes you can't get it open. You have to wait for a moment between gusts. If you park the other way, you risk getting the door ripped right out of your hand." Evelyn pointed. "Look at the reflection of the room. Can you see it moving?"

Moving? What did she mean by that? The reflection wasn't—

A gust hit, and Robin gasped at the sight of the window bowing inward. "Holy shit! Is that normal?"

"It is. Don't worry; it won't break. Two years ago we had gusts up to a hundred and nine, and all of the windows held. Of course, if a tree limb comes flying in, I can't make any promises."

"This is amazing." Robin set her wineglass down and walked up to the window, resting her fingers on it as she watched the furious weather. "There is nothing like this on my side of the mountains. I mean, we get some awesome thunderstorms, but they blow in and out and they're very localized. This thing is beating up the entire coastline."

"And it will last all night."

"Which is more than my ex could manage." Robin clapped a hand over her mouth. "I didn't mean to say that. That was the wine, I swear."

Evelyn looked like she was trying hard not to crack up. "It's all right; we seem to have that in common."

"What, a mouth that moves without engaging the brain? I don't think you have that problem."

"No, an ex that didn't satisfy. Although you're right; I don't have the other problem." Evelyn lifted her glass in a toast and drank, a wickedly teasing smile on her lips.

Robin found that smile immensely attractive and was suddenly very curious about the gender of Evelyn's ex. She picked up the bottle, refilled their glasses, and sat back in her chair. "How does someone as forthright as you end up with an ex that doesn't satisfy? I'd have thought you'd give him the boot after the first time."

"Because it didn't happen the first time. Or the second, or the third. It started happening after we'd tangled up our lives together, and getting them separated again looked like too much work." Evelyn gave her another one of those smiles. "And I know you're fishing. You set off my gaydar in the kitchen, when you didn't want me to see you crying."

"Seriously? Wait a minute, you apologized for crying when we met. You said you weren't normally like that."

"I'm not. And if you had functioning gaydar, yours would have gone off then."

"My gaydar works perfectly well, thank you very much."

"Really? Then why did you ask me about my fictional male ex?"

"Because I was trying to be discreet!"

Evelyn laughed. "I've only known you for a couple of hours, but it seems to me that you trying to be discreet is like an elephant trying to tiptoe."

"You're hilarious. And since when is not wanting to be seen crying a surefire sign of lesbianism?"

"It's not, but it's often a pretty good indicator of a soft butch or chapstick lesbian."

"You're making this up."

"So you're not gay, then?"

"Of course I am!"

"Good to know."

"You—" Robin blew out a breath. "Why do I feel like a door just slammed somewhere behind me?"

"Because you're not seeing clearly. You should be feeling like a door just opened."

Exasperation initially kept Robin from realizing what had just been said, but then she caught on. She stared at Evelyn, a tingle going down her spine.

"I'm not very good at talking in circles," she said. "Could you just tell me—in a purely hypothetical situation, of course—whether or not you'd slap me if I came over there and tried to kiss you?"

Evelyn gave her a long, unreadable look. "Not."

"Not what?...oh." The smile that came onto her face was involuntary and could not be wiped off. "Well, in that case..."

She stood up and took a step toward Evelyn's chair. Her heel landed on something that wasn't the area rug, and an ear-splitting yowl made her jump half a foot in the air. When she came down she scrambled for balance, her heart pounding. "Gaah! Jackie!"

Evelyn had her head down and was pinching the bridge of her nose between forefinger and thumb, her shoulders shaking. For a moment Robin was torn between outrage at being laughed at and horror at having stepped on the cat right in front of her owner. Then the comedy of the situation sank in, and she had to laugh. "Okay, that moment is lost. I'm going to see if Jackie hates me."

She found Jackie sulking in the mudroom and carefully crouched down a respectful distance away. "I'm sorry, Jackie, really. Humans are stupid and Evelyn's right; I'm like an elephant. Are you okay?"

The air moved beside her and then Evelyn was there, kneeling on the floor. "Jackie, come here. She didn't mean it."

Jackie ignored Robin and ran straight up to Evelyn, accepting the caresses that were her due. Evelyn rubbed her cheeks and ran a hand down her tail. "Still intact, I see. Robin thinks she's an elephant because I said something that really wasn't very kind, and I probably ought to apologize. Do you think she understands that I was just playing with her?"

Robin wasn't sure whether she was expected to respond, but Evelyn kept talking.

"She doesn't know me very well yet, so she doesn't realize that I only tease people I like. And I like her quite a lot, so thank you for bringing her home. I'm still pretty upset with you for taking a week to hike down to Florence and find her, but if you feel that strongly about it, then she must be something special. Of course, I already knew that when she took the time to bring you home. And I've really enjoyed her company this evening. So you should forgive her, and I should apologize to her, and then maybe we can get back to the part where she was just about to kiss me."

Robin slipped a hand under her chin, gently bringing her head up, and took a moment to look into beautiful blue eyes. Then she closed the distance between them. Evelyn's lips were just as soft as they looked, and when a hand slipped around the back of her neck, she forgot the cat, forgot that they were kneeling on the mudroom floor, forgot the storm and everything else. There was only so much her brain could handle, and right now the feel of Evelyn's lips and wandering hands were taking up all of her mental powers.

When they finally separated, she rested their foreheads together and whispered, "Apology accepted. Though it wasn't really necessary."

"I think it was," Evelyn said. "But you accepted it very graciously."

"Maybe I could keep accepting it someplace more comfortable than the floor?"

Evelyn chuckled. "No, the apology is done. Anything else I might offer is going to be in a different category. But I don't want to do that on the floor, either." She pushed herself back and stood, holding out a hand and pulling Robin up with surprising strength.

"Wait," Robin said. "I'm not taking a step until I know where Jackie is."

"Good policy." They looked around and found Jackie sitting by the Christmas tree, batting at a loose ribbon.

"Is that why you have a shoes-off policy in your house? I thought it was to save the flooring, but now I think it might be to save Jackie."

"Initially it was the first, but if you're going to be around in the future, it will definitely be the second."

"You just can't resist, can you?"

Evelyn shook her head. "No, not really. But if it helps, I'm hoping you'll be around in the future."

"I'd like to be."

"It's a long drive from Bend."

"It was a long drive when my aunt lived here, too. We still visited about once a month."

"You came once a month, and yet you've never seen a winter storm?"

"Well, I exaggerated a little. We came once a month most of the year. But not in the winters. Though we did come for Christmas once, when I was about eight. I remember being very excited about playing in the snow on the beach, because I thought it would be so cool to have snow and sand together. Imagine my dismay when Aunt Jackie told me it almost never snows here. I was crushed."

"Poor you. No snow and no storms." Evelyn looked distant for a moment, then met Robin's eyes with purpose in her own. "Come on. We're going outside."

"We're what?" Clearly Evelyn had drunk a bit too much wine; it was nasty out there. Robin was all for watching it from the comfort and warmth of the living room, but… "Aren't those gusts up to about seventy by now?"

Evelyn held up a finger and strode down the hall into the kitchen. She was back almost before the door had finished closing. "Seventy-eight is the highest so far. I have a little weather station," she added when Robin raised her eybrows. "There's an anemometer on the roof."

"Must be a tough one to hang on in these storms. So tell me again why you want to go out in winds that are approaching eighty? Not to mention the rain that falls sideways."

"Because I want to show you something. And don't ask me to explain, because it won't make any sense. Just...come with me." She held out a hand.

Well, why not? The rest of the day had been completely outside Robin's experience, so she might as well be consistent. She took Evelyn's hand and let herself be led out to the garage.

Evelyn pulled her mostly-dry raincoat off the peg Robin had hung it on earlier. "Is your raincoat totally waterproof, or do you want to borrow this again?"

"My coat is waterproof in Bend, but I'm not sure that's the same thing as waterproof when someone turned on the fire hose."

"Then take this." Evelyn handed her the coat, then opened a tall cupboard by the door and pulled out two pairs of waterproof pants. "You'll need one of these, too."

Eventually Robin found herself suited up in boots, pants, and coat, all of which were a little large and seemed designed for working on a fishing boat. Evelyn was in matching gear, but on her it looked natural. So did the sparkle in her eyes as she put a hand on the back garage door.

"Ready?"

Robin checked the tie on her hood one more time. "Ready."

She wasn't prepared for the noise when Evelyn opened the door. The immense roar of the wind through the trees tapped into some deep instinctual fear that said *Stay the hell inside*, but Evelyn was waiting, smiling at her. Swallowing hard, Robin stepped out and watched her shut the door of their shelter behind them.

"It's not so bad here," Evelyn called over the noise. "The house is still protecting us. A few steps out and it will get rough. Just stay right behind me, okay?"

"Okay."

She was right. Within five steps Robin found herself being pushed and pulled by the wind, and the amount of water hosing her down was beyond belief. She'd never seen rain like this before. It slammed into her from the side, paused as if it were taking a breath, and then slammed her again. Had she not been wearing the borrowed gear, she would have been drenched in two seconds.

She followed Evelyn down a well-worn path, and when they turned into a second path, she knew where they were headed.

"Are you insane?" she shouted over the storm. "We're going to the cliff?"

"Yes," Evelyn called back. "Just trust me."

She was asking a lot on a few hours of acquaintance and one kiss. Robin stopped to look back at the house, its windows shining like a beacon of safety. Most of the lights were on the first floor, with only one on the second: the desk lamp she'd left turned on so she wouldn't return to a dark room after dinner. As she stared up at her window, the curtain moved.

She jumped when a hand touched her shoulder.

"I promise you'll be fine," Evelyn said. Her earlier smile was gone, replaced by an expression of concern as water streamed off her hood.

Robin looked from her to the second-floor window, where a new shape was sitting on the sill.

Jackie, of course. Except she didn't remember leaving her door open.

A long-forgotten memory surfaced, probably brought on by helping Evelyn with the dishes. She'd been in the same position, washing dishes with her aunt, who had said, *Did you know that most people who live here never go to the beach?*

Robin had found that incomprehensible, because why live at the coast if you weren't going to take advantage of it? Then her aunt had said, *And I'm the only person I know who goes out in the storms. They think I'm cracked, but they don't know what they're missing. The only way to understand the power of the storms is to be in them.*

How had she forgotten that? All this time, she'd wanted to experience one of the storms her aunt had talked about, but somehow she'd lost the most important piece of all.

"Robin—I'm sorry. This wasn't a good idea. Come on, let's go back."

She tore her gaze away from the cat in the window. "No. We're going to the cliff."

"Are you sure?"

"I'm sure." Robin stepped past her and led the way, walking down a path she still knew by heart, though she hadn't trod it in twenty years.

The wind shoved at her, sometimes pushing her halfway off the trail before she could get her feet under herself again, but it didn't feel quite as threatening now. She was in the lead; this was her decision. Suddenly she couldn't wait to get to the cliff. She walked faster and then began to run, ignoring the call behind her. Another turn in the trail and a wall of wind hit her so hard that she stopped, shocked by the strength of it. She was at the cliff's edge, with nothing between her and the full fury of the storm.

An arm went around her waist. "This is as far as we go," Evelyn shouted. "But just feel it! Listen to it!"

Robin took one more careful step, just enough to see over the edge of the cliff. Far below, the waves were crashing onto the rocks with a ferocity she'd never seen before. She was mesmerized by the sight, by the feel of the wind pushing at her, by the sound of the rain spattering on her gear. She felt like a speck of insignificant life, a mere observer of a power far beyond the human ability to replicate or understand.

Evelyn leaned close, bringing her mouth near Robin's ear so she wouldn't have to shout. "Those weather reports, the ones that say what the top wind speeds are—they always get it wrong because the anemometer isn't here, at the very edge. The wind hits these cliffs and goes straight up, and right here is where you get the biggest gusts. By the time they hit the weather stations, even a few yards inland, the speed isn't the same. But here you're in the heart of it. And you can surf the wind."

She let go, took a step toward the cliff's edge, then spread her arms out and leaned forward. Her body canted to an impossible angle, supported by the sheer strength of the wind, and she stayed that way for several seconds before leaning a bit too far and putting a foot out to catch herself. Straightening, she shot Robin a grin. "Try it!"

At any other time Robin would have felt like a fool. But standing here, with her aunt's spirit practically buzzing inside her, nothing could seem more natural than to spread her own arms.

And it worked. She leaned more and more, testing the strength of the wind and marveling at its ability to hold her body weight. Then she leaned too far and had to catch herself, but a moment later she'd repositioned and was trying it again. She found the perfect equilibrium and laughed at the sheer wonder of it, of throwing herself into the storm and being caught and held.

Evelyn leaned beside her, and they looked at each other with matching grins.

"It's fantastic!" Robin shouted.

Evelyn's grin grew even wider as she nodded. "I know!"

They surfed again and again, competing to see who could lean the longest, and Robin could not remember when she'd felt this happy and free. Playing in the heart of the storm had woken something inside her, something that could never again be put back entirely. She never wanted to put it back. It made her feel more alive than she ever had before, and she understood her aunt's words. She hadn't known what she was missing.

"Thank you," she called. "For showing me."

Evelyn looked over, her eyes dancing and her face wreathed in a smile. "You're welcome. Thanks for saying yes. No one ever has before."

Only because you never got the chance to ask my aunt, Robin thought. She reached for Evelyn's hand and squeezed it.

With an answering squeeze, Evelyn turned back to face the cliff. Robin followed suit and they spread their arms, holding hands and surfing the wind.

Hours later, when they'd celebrated their heightened senses in a heated exploration of bodies, Robin left Evelyn sleeping on the living room couch and tiptoed upstairs. Despite the top-grade rain gear she'd worn outside, her clothes were slightly damp and she wasn't keen on putting them back on. A quick change into something warm and she'd go back to napping with Evelyn under the lights of the Christmas tree.

She walked down the hall, holding her clothes against her chest, and stopped dead in front of her door.

It was firmly shut.

But Jackie had been with them downstairs. Jackie had met them at the kitchen door when they'd come in, dripping and laughing.

So it couldn't have been Jackie in her window.

She turned the knob and opened the door, half expecting to see her aunt's ghost waiting for her. But the room was empty, looking just as she'd left it.

Moving quickly, she changed into dry clothes and stepped to the window. The storm was still fierce, lashing the glass with rain and howling through the trees. Beneath its roar she could make out the distant, deeper sound of the surf crashing against the cliff. She imagined her aunt standing at this same window, looking onto the same sights, and felt a peace that had eluded her for the past year. Aunt Jackie wasn't really gone.

This time when the ghostly touch brushed the back of her knee, she didn't jump. Instead she turned and scooped up the purring cat, holding her close and rubbing her cheek into soft fur.

"I know who you are. Thank you, Aunt Jackie. This was the best Christmas gift anyone could ever give me."

"What was?"

Evelyn stood in her doorway, wrapped in the afghan from her couch. Robin smiled at the vision she made.

"You. And this house, and the storm, and...Jackie."

Evelyn crossed the room and petted her cat. "Is she who I think she is?"

"Yes, but my guess is not always. You said she never did anything unusual except for appearing on your doorstep last Christmas Eve, and then appearing on my car this Christmas Eve." Robin pulled Evelyn into a one-armed hug, the cat contentedly snuggled between them. "Not that I'm an expert, but...I think she's just showing a little holiday spirit."

Mama Knows

CHERI CRYSTAL

It was as if my entire life had been leading up to this: sitting on a chartered tour overseas during the one Christmas that would change everything. That must have been how Mama saw it when she booked me an all-expenses-paid trip abroad for Christmas. Despite my protests that she should go instead, she insisted.

"I'm old. But you're young and fit. Go see the world before it's too late," she said.

Mama lit up like a kerosene lamp telling me about this great deal—five nights in London and five in Normandy—she got on the highly rated singles tour everyone was talking about. I was skeptical. Who was "everyone"? Certainly nobody from around these parts. And why should I listen to "them" anyhow?

Mama wasn't subtle about living vicariously through her only daughter, the only family she had left. I could no sooner disappoint her than cut off my own finger. She was really hot for me to check out the American graves at Omaha Beach and put flowers on Granddaddy's grave. She was too tired to make the journey herself. I figured she used age as an excuse to get me to understand the massive loss for the sake of freedom, so that I would think twice about wasting my own life. She harped on me about seeing it for myself that I finally agreed, just to shut her up.

Do you want to know why mamas are such pains in the ass? It's because they're always right.

Imagine a lonesome dyke on a straight singles' tour and you couldn't picture anything worse. It takes moving mountains to get a rise out of me, but I felt a rise of anticipation in seeing Europe and what all the fuss was about.

Mama hovered as I shoved all my stuff, including a hat I'd never wear, into a duffle bag.

"Geez, Mama, you do remember I'm thirty-five and old enough to figure this out on my own? Or are you getting soft?" I teased.

She clucked her tongue but let me be after that. Most folks thought I should have married and moved out ages ago, but I wasn't like most folks. Besides, if I left home, Mama would have to come with me. Easier to stay put.

It was time to leave. I made the huge mistake of calling my departure D-Day, and made other colorful remarks I regret. Mama had little tolerance for cussing, but avoiding bad habits for long periods was hard work and as a result, I received shitloads of Mama's slaps on the arm until I thought I'd welt. Once in our pick-up, Mama was unusually quiet on the drive to the bus depot.

We got out of the truck at the same time. All set with my brand-spanking-new passport in hand and foreign money in pocket, I gave Mama a hug and my best attempt at a cocky grin before I boarded the bus. There were tears in her eyes, which choked me up, but I'm certain no one could tell but her. If I'd said a word, I knew we'd both have started blubbering and that simply would not do. She could be a pain in the ass sometimes, but I counted my blessings for having her. I didn't exactly tell her this, but I suspected she knew.

It was a couple hours' drive to the nearest airport, where they had the kind of aircrafts that looked like the rubber band planes the Five and Dimes used to sell. The hairs on the back of my neck bristled when I discovered that I would be high in the sky in a tin box no bigger than the inside of an oil tank. Once we got moving, the rinky-dink flight turned out okay. Noisy, but the view was worth it. Hard to believe I'd never been on an airplane until then. Harder to believe was taking two airplanes counting the connecting flight from the USA to London Heathrow Airport.

Atlanta International Airport was a frickin' city in itself. Acres of concrete and tarmac took up more space from one end to another than the town and neighboring farms I grew up in, and the waves of people moving looked like a stampede. I hate to admit it, but I was a bit unnerved. Good thing I was tough or I'd have been shaking in my boots. I searched for the lady holding up the sign for our travel group. I'd sized up the crowd pretty accurately. They were from all over America, from California to New York and everywhere in between. There were proportionately more women than men and no doubt they were breeders on the hunt for suitable mates. Theirs was not my idea of the ultimate future, but I was going nowhere fast, so who was I to judge? Half past three decades, I knew it all, had seen plenty, and was fed up with hanging out in bars and job-hopping on the farms—farmers were having a raw deal most of the time, anyway.

Work, when I could get it, was all-consuming, long days spent doing hard physical labor, which never hurt anyone, but there was always time to hook up with a woman if she caught my eye. It was rare for someone like me, living in Small Town, USA, to meet many like-minded bedmates, but I got lucky more often than the cowboys I chugged beers and shot whiskeys with did. I didn't gloat about getting laid much, but the other farmhands were mighty envious. I never did take any shit from anyone, and I avoided a lot of fights because they usually backed off.

There was one other lesbian in town and she avoided me like the plague. That's how I knew she was gay. Girls like that made me laugh. They couldn't see that being different was only interesting if it was kept secret. Like a wrapped Christmas present, everyone wanted to know what was inside, even if it wasn't for them. But the minute the box was opened and the gift-wrap was torn to shreds, nobody gave it another thought.

But there was no doubt about me. Liking girls never was a secret I desired to keep. No sirree. I always dressed in boots, jeans, and T-shirts. I kept my fair hair short, and never minced words with the male farmhands. My body was strong and my hands rough. I was the token dyke and proud of it. I dared anyone to make a disparaging remark and developed quite the hard-ass reputation. Surely, I could take care of myself on a little trip across the Atlantic without any worries.

After risking life and limb aboard the "toy" plane from my hometown to Atlanta, I settled in the jumbo jet quite nicely. I shamelessly flirted with the hot flight attendant, who I could have had for breakfast, and had her phone number in my shirt pocket before the plane landed. Not that I was likely to use it, but it was nice to have just the same.

London was unbelievable. It didn't matter that the gals on my coach were chatty with each other when they weren't flirting with the guys, but they didn't have much to say to me. Everyone was nice enough, though, and I found myself immersed in history for the first time. What a trip! The world sure was vast and I wanted to know all about it. Mama was right. My horizons needed serious expanding.

I signed up for every excursion, except for shopping at Harrods. I ended up at the London Zoo instead. A wise move. We did the usual touristy things, like the Changing of the Guard at Buckingham Palace. The riverboat cruise down the Thames past Big Ben, the Tower of London, and London Bridge, among other notable sites, was good, too. Camden Market was quirky, all right. I was getting Mama's money's worth.

Lots of women in the city made my gaydar ping. I would have liked to get to know them, but there was so much to see, I didn't want to miss a thing. After visiting Covent Gardens for the street shows and Notting Hill for the outdoor market and to see where the movie of the same name was filmed, I was a bit let down about having to leave, but, as the schedule was rigid, I geared up for France.

Our coach was scheduled to board the Portsmouth Ferry to France on the 23rd of December. I got these fleeting pangs of loneliness—Christmas had that effect on Mama and me ever since Daddy died. Every year, Mama got that sad look in her eyes that I would just hate. I couldn't stand anything I couldn't fix. Sad turned to surly when she'd get angry at Daddy for leaving us. It was best that I left her alone to get over it, but I was worried sick that she was home alone.

We used to do Christmas right with all the trimmings, but that ended after Daddy took sick from the blood poisoning. He would have rather shot his own foot than admit to being ill. Had he allowed Mama to call Doc, he might still be alive. The year he died was the worse Christmas of my young life. At the tender age of ten, I became the "man of the house." Mama and I did all right once we got over the shock, but Christmas was permanently ruined. A shame she couldn't be here to see Europe for herself. She would have loved it. Everywhere I went, I took tons of photographs with my new instamatic camera with the built-in flashcube—that must have cost her a pretty penny—to show her when I got back.

When I heard, "All aboard, folks," all worries were forgotten, though. I hopped on the bus like a child going to Disney World before I realized my obvious exuberance just wasn't cool. I quickly posed disinterest despite being the complete opposite. That was me. Tough to the core, I liked to think.

The ferry was due to leave at 10:45 that night. The plan was for us to sleep aboard ship before docking in Caen around 7:30 the next morning. Our English tour guide bid us farewell after informing us we'd be equally pleased with our French tour guide, who would greet us there, and reminding us to book Christmas dinner ASAP. I scribbled my name on the roster on the way to choose a seat. There were a few empty rows, so I grabbed two seats to myself and spread out. I was not in a chatty mood and most of the people on the coach looked so straight, I wondered how they sat down.

I planned to sleep some after the bus took off, but with everyone in a festive mood, singing Christmas carols, serving Champagne in plastic cups and throwing popcorn at each other like a bunch of kids on a school trip, it was impossible to take a nap. I joined the rowdy group in one toast after another until the fizzy alcohol made my head spin. Beer and whiskey back home had never bothered me as badly. I wasn't used to fancy drinks. When I closed my eyes, I felt like Dorothy in Auntie Em and Uncle Henry's flying house on the way to Oz. But instead of thinking, "There's no place like home," I silently prayed, "Make it stop," until I had finally dozed off.

I was in a deep sleep when loud static and garbled words startled me to semi-consciousness. I caught the tail end of the bus driver's announcement over the loudspeaker, followed by a huge groan from the group. They were so selfish there wasn't a thing they didn't complain about. At times their behavior embarrassed me to be an American in England.

Pressing down on my temples with my thumbs to stop the figurative knife from making hamburger meat out of my brain, I squinted, hoping to block the light, and asked the nearest passenger for clarification of the message I missed. Apparently another coach had broken down and we had to pick up a few stranded travellers. We were en route to an out-of-the-way-stop to God-knows-where. I wouldn't have minded the detour except that long-distance highway driving, on the wrong side of the road, in an overheated bus was gruelling. The hot air of passengers who were so full of themselves and not shy about showing it added to my distress. And to top it off, after I'd imbibed a ton of Champagne on an empty stomach without ample water, I was close to hurling. Throwing up in public would not have been cool at all.

As if I couldn't feel worse, I had a wicked headache made more excruciating by the faintest light. God bless the lady who took pity on me when she handed over two prescription-strength-migraine-relief tablets, a large cup of water from her jug, and a few packages of Saltines. She claimed this "combo" had saved her many lost days due to severe suffering. After her profound act of kindness, I regretted placing my entire tour group into a thoughtless lump. Another sign that stereotypes weren't restricted to the het world.

Just knowing I was on the road to recovery, made my head and stomach feel slightly better, but not great. Waiting for the pain pills to completely work their magic, I shut my eyes again, which helped a lot. I slept for an hour or so when the driver made a wide turn, knocking my head against the wet windowpane as he drove into a bus depot. He promised it was the last stop before Portsmouth over the loudspeaker. I wished he'd turn down the volume.

Even through fogged-up windows and with a headache that miraculously had faded as the kind lady said it would, I couldn't miss the woman who narrowly escaped being flattened by our bus. I sat right up and quickly rubbed moisture off the window with the back of my sleeve to get a better look. After being smothered by breeders for much of the time, I detected a ray of hope. Having another lesbian aboard would spice things up. She could have been gay, but I was not totally sure. In a woollen skirt and thigh-high boots beneath a Shetland wool coat, she wore bright red lipstick and a colorful woollen cap with a pom-pom. I wouldn't be caught dead in pom-poms, and lipstick was a waste. It's not like I didn't know lipstick lesbians existed, but where I came from, there wasn't one. When the driver lifted the woman's suitcase, I noticed a bunch of stickers, including the rainbow flag, before he stowed the bag beneath the bus. A pride rainbow might be an obvious clue, but it wasn't foolproof. I learned that lesson the hard way, so I wouldn't be making that mistake again. She could just be a gay pride sympathizer, for all I knew.

She climbed aboard and sauntered down the aisle like it was a damn runway, making it no secret she was checking me out. Clue number two was the eye contact and slight smile. Determined not to share my seat I purposefully turned and looked away. If that didn't shout, "not interested," then nothing would. She was too high class for me. I might be a sucker for stereotypes, but the last thing I wanted was some snooty femme giving me an earful for the duration of the trip.

She took the hint and settled in the seat across from mine. With her snack, a bag of chips and can of Coke, tucked in the seat pocket, she fished in her expensive-looking and probably genuine-leather bag and pulled out a hardcover book and flashlight. She started reading, and I was amazed—I'd never seen anyone turn the pages that quickly. Maybe she was the brainy type.

It wasn't long before we were on the road again, the heater turned up high to blast us out. The femme woman made a big production out of removing her coat and folding it neatly in her lap before standing and stretching way up to place it on the rack above me, probably so I could smell her perfume. Her sweater hugged her curves, showing off nice, pert breasts, and from my vantage point, the underside of those perky numbers sure was fine. Maybe her scent was a bit sweet, but it was mixed with an earthy hint, and it kind of grew on me.

I stole a glance at her, and I thought I caught her wink at me. It was so fast, I couldn't be sure. I waited, silently daring her to do it again when she closed her book and gazed into my eyes. "See something you like?"

Taken by surprise, I said the first thing on my mind. "I was looking at your book."

She grinned with a sexy sideways glance, daring me to tell another lie. "Yeah, right."

She was frisky. I knew a good way to calm her down.

Next thing I knew, she jumped up and stowed her bag on the overhead rack with her coat. Then, keeping her finger in the book to hold her place, she slithered into the seat next to mine, forcing me to sit up straight and make room. She read quietly like a prim schoolgirl daring me to pull her hair or shoot spitballs at her. I was tempted. I grew curious to know the title of that book, but she concealed it on purpose.

While she was occupied, I summed her up. She was young, maybe twenty, and slim but with a little puppy fat. Her stark jet-black hair contradicted her dreamy soft brown eyes—kind of like serious business executive meets sweet seductress. She appeared just over five feet tall, falling short of me by six inches, I guessed. Not bad at all. Cute and compact on the outside, but I sensed there was a well-concealed commanding nature within. I could have some fun with her, but first she would have to learn her place.

Compared to the cold and blustery weather going on outdoors, the bus was getting warmer by the second with this chick sitting by my side. I had shucked my coat hours ago, but decided that I had to peel off another layer or sweat to death. I was glad I had thought to wear a T-shirt underneath or I'd have been stuck way overdressed.

"What are you reading?" I asked.

"*War and Peace*," she replied.

"You kidding me?"

"Yeah."

When she didn't elaborate, I took it to mean that she wasn't interested. Things cooled off fast as a result of that chilly introduction to Miss Snooty Pants.

The bus crept along. After what seemed like an interminable wait on a long line approaching the tollbooths, we were finally aboard the ferry. I'd never been on a ferry, much less an English channel-cross ferry that was more like a cruise ship. The brochure boasted spacious staterooms, comfortable lounge seats, money-exchange counter, boutique gift shops, bars, disco, dining room, snack bar cafe, a video arcade and a whole host of other amenities to make the trip pleasurable and seem luxurious. There were spectacular views from the many open decks for passengers strong enough to withstand the winter chill. I dared anyone to experience a Midwest winter before complaining about the cold.

I downed all three packages of Saltines at the same time, happy they were dry and salty because it settled my stomach. I was brushing the crumbs off my chest when the kind lady offered me a sandwich. She claimed that once the nausea was gone, I needed a full stomach to avoid feeling sick all over again. With immense gratitude I shook her hand so hard I nearly pulled her arm out of the socket. I often forgot my own strength. I returned her smile as I ate up. Ham, lettuce, cucumber, onion and tomato on brown bread with butter and English mustard tasted surprisingly good for someone who would never think to eat ham with butter and salad. Sampling foreign foods was making me quite the connoisseur—if you get my French. English food might be bland according to popular belief, but the amazing English pub that served up traditional recipes and the best beer I'd ever had gave new meaning to Rabbit Pie. One bite and I soon forgot I was eating a distant relative of Bugs Bunny. Thinking about the incredible brews I sampled and surprised at my renewed hunger, I was glad I had francs in my pocket for whatever my heart desired and my stomach could stand. I hoped French cuisine was as good as they claimed. Thinking about food meant I was feeling much better.

When it was time to board the ferry, we were reminded to take our overnight bags before we left the bus because suitcases would have to remain stowed below.

Miss Snooty Pants next to me was already standing and deliberately sticking her ass in my face. I caught a glimpse of the book title, some shit about Women's Lib. I figured she was a rioter, too. She was getting to me. I looked away and waited for her to go. Damn, who did she think she was, driving me nuts? She wouldn't share the title of a stupid book, but she had no qualms about wiggling her backside in front of my face or standing above me on tiptoes so her skirt brushed my jeans and I could asphyxiate on her perfume. If I had my way, she was in for a big surprise.

As it turned out, I didn't see Miss Snooty Pants while I was busy sharing a snack with the kind lady. She had told me, but

I never could remember her name, only her kindness. Thanks to her I was totally cured and unable to show my profound appreciation, I bought her a bottle of Côtes du Rhône in the gift shop, duty free too, and ordered the Plateau de Fromages des Regions de France from the a la carte menu—translation: wine and cheese. Amazingly I could read some French, but speaking the language was another story I didn't want to get into. After polishing off the plate of cheeses from the regions of France we then retired to the upper deck where the rowdy gang from our group was already assembled.

The nightclub festivities included music, but Christmas songs weren't conducive to dancing, unless you were drunk. It was the day before Christmas Eve, and I'd have thought they would have gotten the celebration started by then. Maybe the subdued atmosphere, even for a noisy bunch of characters, was because we had to be back on the bus before daylight. I was already noticing a few pairings amongst the natives. It was a singles tour after all, but I doubted I'd find anyone there.

With nothing much happening upstairs, I was on the way to find the reserved lounge seat area included in our ticket, when I realized I'd moseyed into the berthing area instead. The hallway was narrow. I stopped to read the signs and decided to head back out to the money exchange desk and start over. I turned, for a split second thinking I should hit the bathroom to brush my teeth, when someone ploughed into me from behind.

"Hey, watch it," I said, my fists clenched.

"You watch it. I know exactly where I'm going."

"It's you." I narrowed my eyes at her and stood tall.

"Are you going to move sometime this year?"

"The year ends in about a week, so I'd venture a guess at yes. Ask me nicely and I'll think about doing it sooner."

"Fine." I could tell she was trying to stay mad but failing miserably. The playfulness that she'd had in her eyes when we were on the bus returned until she sweetly added, "Excuse me, but would you kindly move your bodacious butt."

"Bodacious?" I repeated.

"You might be the most annoying woman I've met on this trip, but I can still notice a fine butt when I see one. Now, if you'll excuse me, my room is down that hall and I'd like to get there before we dock."

"You're not exactly painful to look at either."

"Is that your idea of a compliment?" Her lips clamped shut, but her eyes were opened wide. She had really pretty eyes.

She nodded down the hall. I clearly wasn't moving fast enough for her. As she tried to pass me, I backed against the wall to let her through. I held my hands up in surrender. Her tits grazed me, causing a chain reaction of events. She rolled her suitcase right over my boot. What a snotty bitch, but too cute to ignore. Before she could say another word, I pinned her ass to the wall with my hips pushed firmly against her belly, grabbed her face with my hands, and kissed her full on the lips, lipstick and all. This shut her right up. I was about to do it again too, but she slapped my face. I wasn't expecting that, but it didn't faze me. I guessed she had a change of heart, because she gathered the front of my t-shirt, twisting it in her fist, and pulled her suitcase and me along the lengthy narrow hallway.

We stopped in front of her room. She let go of her case, not my shirt, and opened the cabin door. Again, I grew dizzy from the smell of her sweet perfume. The warmth of her breath on my chin as she spoke enticed me further.

Her brown eyes, framed with lush lashes that could catch butterflies, softened. "I'm Billie."

It could have gone one of two ways. I chose the way that didn't dismiss her and promptly send her on her way. Our eyes held, it was nearly impossible to look anywhere else.

"Hello, Billie. I'm Roana, but folks call me Rue, because they rue the day they don't worship the ground I walk on." I laughed in response to her amused smirk. "I'm kidding. Not about the name, but feel free to worship me all you want." I was full of cocky grins before offering her my hand. All conflict aside, we shook hands on our new dubious friendship.

"What do you say we dump our bags and head to the bar for a quick drink?" I suggested.

"Sounds doable. What room are you?"

"I don't have a room." Our tour only included a reclining lounger. Mama's generosity was enough without paying extra for upgrades like staterooms just for a little shut-eye. I'd slept in barns with the livestock. I didn't need no fancy cabin. As it was, the assigned lounge seat was luxurious enough as there were plenty of benches aboard the ferry I could have used.

She interrupted my thoughts abruptly. "What do you mean you don't have a room? Where will you sleep?"

"I was looking for my lounge seat when we bumped into each other."

"We can leave your stuff in my room. This way." She had a mighty take-charge attitude going on there.

Dumping our bags was quick and efficient. I followed her out of her room, then through a maze of doors like a rabbit chasing a carrot. The nightclub deck was duly decorated. The tree was trimmed, garland was everywhere, and even mistletoe hung from the ceiling. But again I noted it was surprisingly empty for Christmas season.

"Must be a bunch of old farts on board," I commented at the lack of partiers. We ordered drinks, and she graciously accepted when I insisted on buying. She was such a girl. More girlie than ever after I learned she could talk the hind leg off of a donkey, without taking a breath.

"I'm spending one day in Normandy, and then I'm off," she said, popping a handful of salted peanuts into her mouth.

"How come?"

"I've always wanted to see Paris and hit the sights. I teach World History and plan to visit every part of the globe I can. Including the Champs-Elysées and Place de la Concorde, where King Louis XVI, Marie Antoinette, and many others were guillotined during the French revolution. Such a blood bath."

"That's awfully gory."

"It's history."

"Tragic history," I said.

"Didn't you visit the Tower of London while you were there?" she asked. It seemed like a challenge.

"Yes, and it was no skip in the park, either. There's no end to the forms of torture human beings are capable of inventing."

"That's a fact. Interest in torture and human suffering is hard to resist no matter what anyone says. It's why we can't help rubbernecking at crash scenes or watching the evening news on TV. Don't worry—I plan to partake in some tamer pursuits. Like visiting the Arc de Triomphe, and of course, I must see the city from the top of the Eiffel Tower."

I took a long swig of beer, Bass Draught for me and Stella Artois for her, sat back, relaxed, and listened. She was hip, coming from California and all, but her voice had a rhythm that led me to addiction. She was born in LA but moved to San Francisco, where she was the first girl at school to come out of the closet. She was brave and I admired her for that. It was getting late, but neither of us showed any signs of tiring. She barely took a breath, at least, none I could detect.

"...There's the Louvre, Notre Dame de Paris..." Her voice trailed off in a dreamy state.

All her plans meant I only had one night to get under her skirt. I'd never done it on a ferry before, but then I'd never been on a ferry with a fetching woman before.

She bought the last round. She sauntered back to our table, and plopped herself on the couch next to me, thighs up close so her free hand could roam up and down my leg. Every stroke made my desires harder to resist.

I had to make my move with this forward femme. Let her think it was her idea—that would be fine with me. By our last drop of beer, I reckoned I knew everything about her and despite first impressions, I was getting to like her. She was smart and funny.

"Unless we plan to sleep where we sit, I'd better walk you back to your room." I played it cool, spurred on when she didn't flinch at my suggestive tone.

"I'm ready, let's go." She stood and offered me both of her hands to help me up. I should have known this was just the beginning of her taking control.

I flashed a grin, which she returned with a wink. Light on my feet, and still holding her hands, I stood. She looked up at me when I said, "I suggest we get right to bed—together."

She had an adorable little nose that screwed up when she giggled. That's all the encouragement I needed. I offered my arm to escort her to her room. I even took the key from her to open the cabin door. Control was my middle name.

I barely got the door open when she pushed me inside, hurrying in after I did. She didn't have to wait for an invitation. Of course, the answer would be yes, but I had to put her straight on a couple of things. I looked around carefully. The ferry company boasted spacious staterooms, but in actuality, this room wasn't much bigger than a bull pen. I didn't care that it was cramped as long as it offered enough space for two. She completely relaxed in my arms; maybe this would be a good trip after all.

We faced each other and she started to move in close, but I held her at arm's length.

"Look, Billie, just so we're clear on this before it gets going, I'm not looking for a partner to cuddle. I like to fuck. If you think you can keep up, fine, if not, find someone else."

She looked put out at first and then grew defiant when she said, "I have no intention of marrying you either. Let's fuck or forget about it."

"I didn't mean to sound harsh, but I didn't want any misunderstandings later."

"Neither do I. Besides, we can be adult about this, enjoy what we have, and just move on. Shall we do this? It's almost Christmas. I know what I want. Do you?"

How could I keep the upper hand in this situation when she was full of sassy remarks? The bristles on my neck subsided one at a time, but that didn't mean I would be turned to mush by Billie or any woman. There was no sense in making this harder than it was. I reached for her shoulders to hold her still and kissed her, leaving no doubt about how it was going be or what I wanted for Christmas either. I forced my tongue into her mouth and then pushed her back against the bathroom door.

"You have too many clothes on. I see I'm going to have to peel you out of these, one layer at a time." I spun her around, lifted the bottom of her sweater, and pulled it over her head. For the time being, I left her creamy silk blouse on. I reached around and undid the top few buttons to ease the blouse down and expose the contours of her neck and shoulders. Taking tiny bites along the nape of her neck made her shiver, and she followed it with a delightful laugh. She opened the remaining buttons and let the blouse fall to the floor. It was such a tease to discover that she wore a camisole over her bra, concealing the treasures hidden beneath. I was ready to remove the cami, but she murmured, "Not yet." Waiting a few minutes wasn't a hardship. The feel of silk over pointy nips could make a woman howl like a hound dog in heat.

I ran my hands down her breasts and waist. I reached up under the hem of her skirt to grasp her thighs and pulled her ass into my crotch. I was packing, as usual, and wanted her to feel it, to judge her reaction. I rubbed my dick against her ass as I cupped her sex. Holding her in place with one hand, I let my other hand roam higher under her woollen skirt and searched for the waistband of her tights. I had to pull them down to bare her legs, but removing her boots was going to be a problem.

She must have read my mind because she swung around to face me and lifted her foot into my crotch. I grabbed hold of the heel and pulled so hard, I ended up flying backwards into a wall, but with boot-not-on-foot in hand. We laughed. She then hopped around as she tried to remove the other one all by herself. With tights pulled down below her ass and boots that fit like gloves, it would be New Year's Eve before she would be naked. We laughed harder, but spurred on by intense desire and her playful willingness, I longed to torture her pert little nipples, at the very least, and fuck her pussy from here to eternity, at the most. I pulled out the chair from beneath the desk and sat, legs spread wide, and waited.

"So, little girl, come sit on Santa's lap and tell me what you want for Christmas," I said. "Ho, ho, ho."

She swatted my arm, but feeling all naughty and nice, I play-fucked her ass with my crotch the moment she sat down on me. "Do you like that? I can stop now if you don't."

She murmured, "Don't you dare stop," in response. The crotch of her panties grew damp and fragrant. There was nothing sweeter than being responsible for the scent of a woman totally turned on and eager for me to have her. I moved the elastic of her pastel panties aside, slipped a finger between her slick folds, and supported her weight on one thigh. She threw her head back and rested on my shoulder, while I played with her from behind.

After a while, she got up and turned to face me. She pulled me up from the chair and kicked it aside, quite the feat in tight quarters, and ran her hand over my crotch. Her face lit up and her cheeks turned slightly pink. A great look, but not as perfect as when she screwed up her face. She drove me wild when she did that.

I whispered in her ear, "Tell me what you want, Billie."

Instead of answering, she lifted my T-shirt, and her mouth soon found my tits. My hips automatically lunged forward searching for contact. I didn't want to come too fast, but at this rate, I would if I wasn't careful. I hiked her skirt up and pulled her panties down. She kicked them off the rest of the way but left her skirt rolled up around her waist. Was leaving a few items of clothing on a security measure in case she planned a hasty getaway?

Not likely judging from her voracious appetite. She kissed me with such hunger that I backed her up against the door to regain some semblance of control. She unzipped my fly, getting my cock out before I could object.

"I want this for Christmas and I want it now!"

"Whoa there, take it easy." I took hold of her wrists, unlocked her fingers from around my dick, and started rubbing it around her opening, moistening both her and it copiously.

I needed to slow this down, but she was the most ravenous, insatiable woman I'd ever met. Her thrusting her hips into me with force was an aphrodisiac like no other. Her body searched for penetration, and I wanted nothing less than to give it to her good and hard. But I resisted. I reined myself in as best as I could, only to give in completely almost immediately. I slid into her slowly, but she pushed back hard. I started to withdraw my dick, but she sucked me right back in with the strength of twenty women, taking my cock all the way to heaven. I was losing control of her, and she was fucking with me in more ways than one.

I held her hips back against the door and attempted to do it my way, but she protested, "More, more, I want more. Give it to—"

I covered her lips with mine and fucked her mouth hard and fast with my tongue while keeping up the deliberate rhythm of my cock inside her pussy. Man, she was gorgeous, all squirming in my arms, submissive, rocking her hips, trying so hard to get more of my cock deeper inside, but letting me lead the next. She was putty in my hands.

Then I let down my guard. Bad move. Without warning, my cock was left stranded as she pulled my pants all the way down.

"One sec," she said, fetching something out of her bag. With glee, she held whatever it was behind her back.

"Whoa there, partner. What have we got there?" I asked, reaching for it.

She shook her head, but then whipped out the last thing I expected.

She probably hadn't bargained on me packing, but I hadn't expected her to have a vibrating dildo, either. Each time I had the upper hand, she evened the score. With my jeans around my ankles and her arm around my waist, she held me in place as if I was a fool. Not that I really wanted to be anywhere else. I slipped two fingers deep inside. Soon her pussy was squeezing the life out of my fingers until I was forced to surrender or die. I withdrew my fingers and kicked my pants away. She moaned for maybe a split second, but I had my cock back inside before she could draw breath. I was certainly up for fucking her with her own device after using my own. Maybe I would just tease her with both at the same time.

We were fucking machines. As I pumped her pussy, her hands were quicker than my eyes. She managed to put a rubber on the thick wand before placing it up against my cunt—from behind. No time to stop her. With the bulk sliding around in my juices, the next thing I knew, she had abandoned one hole for the other. She had the sheathed thing slicked and between my butt cheeks, pushing and twisting it into my ass faster than a bucking bronco throwing off a clueless rider. I'd have clamped shut, but this was not something I wanted to miss. Not many women were so bold. I had hit the jackpot with this one!

"Fuck, that feels good. So damn good. But…uh, you better stop."

She didn't listen to a word I said, but I couldn't shut up. "So fucking good. Stop or you'll…regret…it."

"Doubt that."

She was gonna make me come, and there wasn't a damn thing I could do about it. Or was there?

As I pulled my cock out of her, she pushed her plastic wonder harder into me, then pulled it away as I thrust into her again. We developed a rhythm that worked. I wasn't going to last long going at it like this, feeling intense pleasure from every orifice. We picked up speed. Without realising what was going down, I had given into her whim. I fucked her hard and fast and she was doing likewise. We were evenly matched, or so it seemed.

But my orgasm built up too fast.

"Damn it," I said. I couldn't stop myself. As I reached my crest, my dick playing my clit with each and every thrust into her pussy, she pushed her dildo into my ass. She was a frickin' magician, I tell you. Where she got the wherewithal to also suck my nipple, I haven't a clue, but she did that, too. When she bit down hard, I came like a fool with my head on her shoulder, shaking like a baby.

Fuck, fuck, fuckity fuck, I thought, shuddering like a pussy the whole damn time. What a letdown, I was used to calling all the shots, especially when it came to my own damn orgasm.

When my shaking subsided, she kissed me and slowly pulled the phallus out, which threatened to make me come again. I stifled the intense urge and blurted, "Fuck me. Sorry, I couldn't wait."

She pushed me back and we fell onto the lower bunk bed. She stripped off her skirt, straddled my hips, and pulled her camisole off. I unhooked her bra and set her breasts free. Completely naked, I couldn't take my eyes off of her and reached out for that first handful of silken flesh, but she stopped my hands.

"No touching. Hands by your sides. If you move, I'll stop." I surrendered. What the hell. Looking at her was prize enough.

Moving herself over my cock, she pulled herself open so I could see all her secrets. She proceeded to rub the end of my cock along her slit and around her swollen clit, then slowly taking me inside again. I lifted onto my elbows to watch my cock slide in and out until it got to be too much. I then flopped back onto the pillow and lifted my hips to meet her waiting pussy. I was getting closer to round two. She placed her hands against my chest to keep me down.

As she fucked me she played with her clit, getting herself harder and wetter. Feeling the start of another orgasm, I determined not to come before she did. I was supposed to be the one in charge here.

While rubbing her clit harder, she leaned closer. "Look into my eyes, Rue," she said. There she was, sliding up and down on my cock, and she wouldn't let me close my eyes or she'd stop.

"Watch me while I come. This one's for you."

With hardly a blink—well, maybe one or two—we came together. Again, I was reduced to mush. We came hard, and for me, this one lasted longer than the first.

Our shudders subsided after a time and she lay her head on my chest. Finally, with strength seemingly restored, she arose, her bottom still hot and moist on my belly, causing renewed stirrings down below. Leaning in to place tender kisses on my lips, cheeks, and nose, she lingered as she nursed my lips again.

"So, Rue, who did you say was in charge of this fuck?"

Was she kidding me? Did she really have to rub salt in my wounded pride? I didn't need to answer. She had made her point.

"Look, why don't you come with me to Paris? We could have a great time."

"It's a mighty tempting offer, but don't hold your breath. I have some shit to do." I didn't mention promising Mama I'd visit Granddaddy's grave. Gallivanting to Paris to fuck my brains out wasn't what Mama had in mind.

Billie looked crushed. Christ, why did I have such a big mouth?

She bolted, picked up my things in a messy bundle and handed them to me. Then she said, "Well, then, I enjoyed my Christmas present. Thanks for that. You can go now."

Fuck, fuck, and fuckity fuck. I dressed and left her cabin as fast as possible. What else could I do?

I must have fallen asleep, because the morning alarm call startled the crap out of me. My neck was sore. After all I'd said and the way I'd behaved, I didn't bother searching for Billie. I couldn't face her after she fucked me like I'm some kind of novice. At least she'd be gone soon. I planned to keep out of her way until the all clear. Trouble was, I had grown fond of her. I missed her sass and, okay, her ass.

I made it to the Normandy American Cemetery and Memorial in Colleville-sur-Mer, now a far cry from what it was like in 1944. I was in awe. Me, someone from shit-stomping country, who had never ventured farther than a stone's throw from home, was actually standing on the same soil as the men who fought in WWII. Unbelievable! I strolled around in an utter daze, holding directions to my granddaddy's grave in one hand and a bunch of flowers in the other. I'd never met him, but Mama shared her childhood memories often enough that it felt like I had.

The enormity of the history in that place was so grave and disturbing, I was glad Mama wasn't there to see it. Solemn sadness consumed me. I couldn't begin to imagine what went through my family's minds that day.

I was as proud as Mama was that her father had served his country, but the needless loss of human life put everything into perspective. Sure, there'd always be war, but on a more personal level, if I didn't plan for my future now, when would I? Mama worried about me being alone after she was gone. I made her hush up every time she mentioned her mortality. I didn't want to hear about it, and she knew that.

I was so deep in thought, I almost jumped out of my skin when I heard my name. I ignored it, but the voice grew insistent and closer. I saw her when I turned. She had gained on me, all out of breath from the run. I couldn't get away, but damn it to hell, there was no avoiding her now.

"Rue. Rue wait. We need to talk." She tried to take my hand, but I pulled away.

"You are such a horse's ass, trying to avoid me."

"I thought we were on the same page after I told you the score. Besides, you kicked me out, remember?" If I'd clenched my jaw any harder, my teeth would have broken. "Look, I have something I gotta do."

"Who are the flowers for?" She glanced at the rows and rows of white crosses. Her brown eyes softened enough to break my heart. We had one night. Yeah, it was a great night, but how could she have developed such compassion for me in such a short time? Caring too much, especially loving someone, meant loss was inevitable. Why risk it? I'd been doing fine on my own for thirty-five years. I didn't need Billie or anyone else to tie me down.

She tentatively placed her gloved hand on the sleeve of my jacket. I didn't withdraw this time. "You have someone here, don't you?" she asked.

"Granddaddy is around here somewhere." I looked off into the distance. The cemetery seemed to go on forever. There was a chill in the air and I couldn't imagine how the sun could shine or the plants could flourish on such a bleak place. But the sun did shine and the trees were winter-barren, but majestic and strong, some of the lofty pear trees having lived for 300 years, so maybe there was hope.

"Let me see the paper. We'll find him together."

I handed her the directions and gripped the flowers tighter. It was easier to let her lead the way.

I don't know how she did it, but she found him. Lt. Col. Inf. Division...my sight blurred. With her hand on my shoulder, I knelt down and placed the flowers on his grave.

"Are you okay?"

I gruffly replied that I was, but I wasn't really sure. I had no idea that seeing 10,000 graves would be this overwhelming and so profoundly sad. I stood there for some time just looking into the distance, fighting tears. There were white crosses and a few Stars of David, as far as I could see, and this was just the American portion. There were graves from other countries as well. I had never felt so humbled, so worthless with my arrogance, or so insignificant. After a while, I pulled myself together.

"Thanks for helping me find it."

"It was no biggie. I know what you said about last night, but I also know that it was more than just...you know. We were good together. Really good."

I had to agree with her.

"But if you'd rather waste your life, thinking you're better off alone, then suit yourself."

I had no answer. She was right, there was nothing I could say to fix the way it had always been with me. I swallowed hard, but just walked on past her up the road toward more graves, feeling sorry for myself. What was I doing? Standing in the middle of a massive graveyard. This scene could break even the strongest of hearts. I stopped dead in my tracks.

So many. I had no idea it would move me this way. It's not like I'd never been to cemeteries, for Chrissakes. I stood there for some time, just staring off into the distance at nothing in particular. Mama was right—we must never forget, and I needed something this Christmas to make me realize how precious life was and how wasteful it would be not to appreciate every moment of this ultimate gift.

The bus ride back to the hotel was very quiet. I guessed everyone felt the same as I did, silenced by so many young lives lost for the freedom we took for granted.

Billie kept her distance.

Later that day, we met up in the lobby while we waited for our ride to the Christmas dinner at a nearby restaurant. I thought Billie would be gone by then and I relaxed some.

But throughout dinner, I couldn't swallow away the sour taste in my mouth or ease the pain in my chest. Not even the French bread with creamery butter enticed me. Nor the wines I found downright delicious and the rich French food and pastries I'd been enjoying. I was busy chewing on regret when I glanced up from my seat to find her staring right at me. I couldn't look away. It was true, she was one fiery lady, too much for me to handle, but I knew I'd miss her.

She caught my eye and mouthed, "Come with me."

Maybe Billie and I would fizzle out, but if I didn't give us a chance, I'd never know that, would I?

I was tempted to turn away quickly, but I had no reason to go home alone, and I had ten thousand reasons to take a chance.

"I think I can fit in a trip with you to Paris. Care to join me for this lovely Christmas dinner in Bayeux first?" I asked. "If all goes well, we can do Paris after that."

Her eyes lit up with excitement, which made me feel like dancing around like a schoolgirl with her first crush, but I resisted. That's when I noticed she was dressed in her Christmas best, a velvet green dress with red trim made brighter with the biggest smile I'd ever seen. The kind woman seated to my left generously offered Billie her seat, and I thanked her profusely yet again. Maybe she was my guardian angel or something. I held the chair for Billie as she sat down, and I got the sweetest whiff of her perfume. I was ready to skip dinner and head right for dessert.

After I sat down, Billie leaned in close and slipped her arm through mine and whispered, "You won't regret this. We'll be good together. Merry Christmas, Rue."

"Merry Christmas, Billie."

And we've been really good together ever since.

Angels

JOAN ARLING

Being dead takes getting used to.

I can't begin to describe how it feels to be without a body or at least to feel as if I no longer have one. Jane was with me, though, and that was all that really mattered.

It had been an accident. A blown tyre caused our car to swerve from the road and careen down a ditch, obviously killing us. The last thing I remembered was the sound of our voices shouting each other's name, and then…then we were here.

We were not alone—far from it. For all they tell about the hereafter, the room—if you can call it a room—was full of people. Well, the souls of people. We might as well have been in the waiting area of a labour office. Time and again, a name was called, and someone walked through a door. The office or whatever was beyond that door must have had a second exit, because no one came out again.

Jane and I passed the time, or should I say eternity, reminiscing about the past and looking back upon our lives. Dwelling on the plans we'd had seemed futile, so we focused on how our demise would affect the people who hated us. Trying to think of someone dear to us seemed a waste of time, even with eternity to draw upon; ever since Jane and I had moved in together, our popularity had been at an abysmal low.

When the voice calling names became impatient, I looked up and realised it had been calling me for several minutes. Jane looked with wide eyes. No one had yet returned through that door, and the thought of getting separated was more than we could stand. I stood, grabbed her hand, and pulled her after me.

The office was like any other office—rows of filing cabinets, two desks back to back, one of them unoccupied. Only a clerk dressed entirely in white indicated that this office was not one in a million. He looked at us, and an expression of dismay settled on his face, which had not been cheerful to begin with.

"You are not supposed to enter in groups," he said. "Now which of you is Miss—"

"I am," I said. "This is my partner, Jane. Where I go, she goes and the other way around." I put my arm around her waist.

He gave us a sour look. "Have you any idea where we'd end up if every newcomer were allowed to continue as if still alive?" He waited for a reaction, but all he got was our tightened hold on each other. He shook his head. "No soul is compelled to stay here against her will. Considering the alternative, however..."

"Any time!" Jane's answer came like a bolt from the blue.

My heart leaped as she never as much as glanced at me for confirmation. God, did I love this woman. I nodded, momentarily at a loss for words.

He glared at me, then at Jane, before looking at the file before him. "Oh, I see, it's *you*...," he grumbled and pulled another file. "And *you*. Marked double-X at expected difficulty. Sit over there. I'll hand this upstairs." He pressed a button on an intercom and said, "Two cases of double-X in PR-4, form A-01 ... Triple even, from the look of them. ... Yes, I'll wait."

He cast a dark look in our direction. "Just a split eon."

The intercom came alive again, and he acknowledged, "Yes, I know where. They'll be there shortly."

He turned to us. "You'll be handled by the boss himself." When we gave him wide-eyed stares, he added, "The boss of *this* department, what did you think? Go through that door, then to the last office on the left. Now hurry."

The last we heard of him was a sigh as we entered the corridor.

Jane and I looked at each other, clasped our hands, and proceeded without a word. I could tell she was nervous, and she knew me too well to buy into my pretended coolness.

We headed to the last office on the left and were faced with a man so tall that we had to tilt our heads back to see his face. He was wearing, of all things, a *halo*!

"Hi, I'm Gabriel. You must be The Inseparable Two." He grinned. "Front office reported you to be a headache. But let's just see where we are with the two of you."

He indicated two chairs that were much more comfortable than the ones we sat in earlier. Oh well, boss's office, what would you expect?

He had two folders open before him, probably ours. He took another file from a stack and opened it.

"This one is labeled troublesome as well, but she'll probably be easier to handle." He looked at the two of us huddled together. "You know, this girl actually has something in common with you—she's gay too."

I gasped at hearing an arch angel comment on our sexual orientation.

His eyebrows twitched. "She is about to come out to her parents. Did you have trouble with that?"

Jane and I looked into each other's eyes. We'd struggled to keep off the street, with nothing and no one but each other.

"By the looks of it, she'll be kicked out. Now, her soul is not in a stable condition, and it's quite likely that, having nowhere to turn, she'll want to jump off a bridge."

Our hands tightened around each other. "Nowhere? No *one*?"

"Sadly, the girl she fell for wanted nothing to do with her." He paused. "The concept of deadly sin was not invented here, so she still has a fair chance of redemption. The thing is, our policy does not call for untimely arrivals." He looked at us and fell silent.

I empathised with the girl but was confused at the same time. Why was he telling us about her?

"If someone were to show her a reason not to hurry here..." Gabriel mused.

"Why do I get the feeling that you are leading up to something?" Jane said.

"Ah, clever girl!"

I glanced at her quickly, but for once, the patronising words did not cause her to flare up.

"Since I can't place the two of you together here and it's obvious you are prepared to spit ectoplasm if I don't and there is field work that needs to be attended to..." His voice trailed off.

"I think he's recruiting us as guardian angels," she said, not taking her gaze off Gabriel.

"In training," he said.

"We could be the first gay team of guardian angels." Jane broke into a smile.

"The first?" he muttered. "You have no idea."

And so we found ourselves on a road in the middle of the night, between a village and a railroad bridge, watching a freshly homeless girl trudging in our direction. She was so lost in her hurt that she didn't notice us standing in the shadows.

"What do we do now?"

"Well, we need some kind of distraction," Jane said. "Ready for action?"

Without waiting for my answer she ran toward the girl, pulling me behind her. Within seconds she stopped in front of the girl. "We can't leave her alone out here!"

"Come on! They're almost onto us!" I pulled on Jane's arm.

"No way. She's got to come." Jane grabbed the girl's hand and ran, pulling us both along.

We came to a crossroads and went in the woods, cowering and catching our breaths.

"What, what..." the girl stammered.

"Shhhh. Quiet, for heaven's sake," Jane said.

The girl looked from Jane to me, her eyes big in her lean face. "What the hell is going on here?" she asked in a whisper. "Who are you?"

I had used the time to come up with a story. "There's a bunch of...of hooligans out there, and they caught sight of us."

"And they started running after us, so we took to our heels," Jane said. "Quiet now. I think I can hear them!"

We listened carefully, but all I heard were the usual nighttime noises.

"I think we lost them." I stood and looked around.

"Do you see anyone?" Jane asked.

"No. I think we're in the clear."

They stood too.

"Jeez." Jane wiped imaginary sweat from her brow. "What are you thinking, walking alone out here after dark? What's your name, anyway?"

"Maggie. And who are you? And you're not walking around with a group of bodyguards, either."

"Oh, this is Angela, and I'm Jane. Our car broke down a few miles from here. We saw a sign that said we're close to a town. Could you show us the way?"

Wordlessly, Maggie pointed in the direction she had come from.

"Will you come with us? Or do you have a date or something?"

Maggie's eyes filled with tears.

Jane took her into her arms and let her sob against her shoulder. "There, there... Nothing is ever as bad as it seems at first sight."

Finally, when Maggie's tears dried, she led us back to a town called Nowheringham, which wasn't very far.

The rainbow neon sign of a bar was the only light in the dark town. Jane steered Maggie toward it.

I frowned and cleared my throat to get Jane's attention. When she glanced at me, I rubbed my thumb and forefinger together, indicating that we'd need money in there.

She smiled and patted her hip pocket, winking at me. "Look in your back pocket," she whispered.

Puzzled, I put my hand in my back pocket and pulled out a bundle of notes. I sucked in a breath. That was a lot of money, enough to carry us through a month had we been leading our former lives.

Maggie pulled away from Jane for the first time since crying in her arms. "Uh, I'd better get going now."

"Aw, come on. You showed us the way here. We'd be delighted to have you join us for a while."

"I've got no money." After a short hesitation, she said, "On me."

"Don't worry, we're on an expense account," Jane said.

I coughed to cover up a giggle.

Jane grinned, took the girl's hand, and pulled her into the bar.

I paused briefly and looked into the sky. "Thanks, Gabe." This job had unexpected perks.

"This has been the craziest night of my life." Maggie sighed as we settled into chairs around a table.

"What happened?" Jane asked.

Maggie fell silent. She finally whispered, "You saved my life, you know that?"

I grinned. "Hey, that's our j—"

"We couldn't have left you to the hooligans, could we?" Jane said.

"No, it's not that, even though that did frighten me."

"What is it, then?"

"I was going to..." She closed her eyes, but that did not stop the tears from running down her cheeks again.

"You were what?" Jane said, as though she was slow in comprehending, "That bridge? You were—don't tell me you were going to do something foolish. Why on earth would a girl like you—?"

"Because she wouldn't have me." Maggie wailed. "She was the world to me, but when her p-p-parents found out, she denied everything. She wouldn't even look at me." Maggie lowered her head onto her forearms.

"Oh God. What did your parents say?"

"They just threw me out." Her voice shook with the sobs that racked her body.

"Excuse me, may I ask what is going on here?"

I looked up.

A good-looking butch, maybe five years older than Maggie, stood next to our table.

Maggie raised her head.

"Mags? What are you doing here? And who are they? Did they hurt you?"

"Jenny? I had no... No, these two are friends. They've been..."

Jenny looked at Jane and me again, her face still hard. I had a feeling she'd thrash us if Maggie said the word. "You'd better come with me, Mags." She helped Maggie stand and then wrapped her muscular arm around the girl's shoulder. "No offence, ladies, but I don't know you."

With that she led Maggie outside, leaving us smiling at one another.

"Gimme five!"

"Yes!"

Gabriel looked up from reading our report. "Not at all bad. For first timers." He focused on me. "Do you usually call your boss by his first name? 'Gabe' indeed."

Before I could answer, Jane took my hand and squeezed it. "We got the job done, didn't we? Now what?"

His lips twitched. "You did okay. One week's vacation."

Doctor's Call

PATRICIA PENN

Fiona looked around carefully before slipping into the waiting room of the palliative care unit. Visiting hours were over and the room was abandoned; yesterday's newspaper lay discarded on a chair. For a moment she felt more like a character from a Jane Austen novel than a doctor on a busy shift. Her heart was beating loudly against her chest. She was fairly certain that a simple phone call should leave neither an accomplished physician nor a romantic heroine that anxious.

Even if it was a call she wasn't supposed to make.

It had been five months as of yesterday. Miriam's number was still saved in position one on her speed dial. Fiona told herself that she just hadn't gotten around to replacing it with somebody or something she might need to reach quickly, like her boss or Admission. She'd been working doubles ever since Thanksgiving, no time to play around with her phone. That was all.

Home, the display said as the phone made the connection, mocking her by stating as fact another piece of ancient history. Miriam's home wasn't her home anymore; intellectually she knew that. Yet her heart beat faster with every ring, and when the recording kicked in she exhaled with the violence of an addict getting a fix. The voice sounded painfully familiar, low and a little bit hoarse, sending a shudder of remembered intimacy down her spine.

"Hi, you've reached Miriam. I'm either not available right now, or I'm too lazy to pick up the phone. But don't worry, you can leave me a message. Happy Hanukkah and Merry Christmas!"

Fiona didn't leave a message. She closed her eyes, breathing in and out and allowing herself, for a second, to imagine that it was still five months ago. That she would open her mouth to say she'd be working late again because that patient had crashed, and that she was sorry, but she promised to bring Chinese, and "I love you, hon, talk to you later."

Instead, expectant silence settled in after the beep. Disconnecting the call, Fiona plopped onto one of the nondescript chairs. The back of her head hit the wall with a heavy, frustrated thud.

You're pathetic, she informed herself, but she'd known that already. She just couldn't bring herself to care.

An hour later she should have been on the way home, but with the looming prospect of her empty, half-furnished apartment, she never quite made it to the staff locker room. It was December twenty-third, and she had promised Dr. Kapstein from Oncology to take care of his patients through the Christmas holidays so that he could spend it at home with his wife and three children. So she dropped onto the couch of the doctors' lounge and immersed herself in the case files the old oncologist had practically thrown at her on the way out. Rounds wouldn't be necessary, he'd said. The resident would be at the ready to disrupt his skiing vacation at any point if she had any questions. He was so grateful for Fiona's offer, he'd assured her on his way to the elevator, leaving her with a stale sense that he'd forget her face and her favor by tomorrow.

The door opened. Bald, gangly Dr. Brian Eddleston sauntered in, as if he had any business crashing her floor instead of getting actual work done in the radiology labs where he belonged.

"No, I won't have time to go to the staff Christmas party tomorrow," she said rather unkindly, not bothering to look up. From the corner of her eye she saw Brian take one of the chairs and turn it around, straddling it to sit in front of her. He rubbed his head unabashedly.

"Not even with an astonishingly handsome and successful doctor such as myself?"

"I'm gay."

"That's not a problem for me."

"You're gay."

"Sexuality moves on a continuum," he said sagely, then shrugged and added in a normal voice, "Or so I keep reading in *Cosmo*."

She rolled her eyes, suppressing a chuckle. "Yeah, you're *so* gay." Looking up from the chart after all, she found herself facing her supposedly forty-year-old friend's self-satisfied smirk.

"In other news," she said, determined to change the topic and pointing at her charts, "did you know that Oncology is treating an eighteen-year-old for multiple myeloma? She's waiting for a bone marrow transplant now. It's wild: chemo, autologous transplant, none of that's an option anymore. And it's going to be a one-allele mismatch—unrelated registry donor—so she's running straight towards the light there. The whole hospital should be talking about this. I mean, she's eighteen. I bet Kapstein took her on just so he can publish about her."

"The hospital is too busy placing bets on whether or not that cute new nurse from the E.R. will turn out to be a lesbian when you woo her at the Christmas party."

"I'll be on-shift at the Christmas party."

"See, that's why they invented those little devices called pagers. Some might say they're old-fashioned, but they're really reliable in that they—"

"I'll look a little bit bad if Kapstein's crowning glory of a paper dies while I'm drinking fruit punch. He'll be at that party, you know."

Now it was Brian's turn to roll his eyes, and Fiona resisted the urge to tighten her shoulders defensively. It was as if her whole body wanted to curl up and present a wall. She'd been feeling like that rather a lot recently.

"I just...have a lot of work to do, okay?" She turned the page on her chart despite not absorbing anything it said since her friend had walked in.

"You've had a lot of work to do for five months," Brian pointed out softly.

His face had turned serious; she didn't even need to look at it to know. The change in tone hit her like a lightning bolt, the way a raised voice never could have. She immediately hated everything about it.

"Brian..." She put the chart on the pile in her lap, knowing that she sounded pained.

"Fiona," Brian said, in that firm voice of his that convinced patients to do a procedure, even though it would suck. "Listen to yourself. This isn't healthy anymore."

She shot him a furtive look. "Come on. It's just a stupid hospital function. Nobody ever really wants to go to those."

But Brian was shaking his head. "I'm not talking about the party. Forget the party for a moment. All this?" He made a gesture that encompassed much more than the charts in her lap. "It isn't good for you. You've barely moved into your apartment—"

"Yes, because I work all the time, all right?"

"Because you hide yourself away at work like you don't even want a private life anymore! Used to be that you and I would go out for drinks. You used to have friends. Now you're practically living at the hospital, and you pull all that crap where you do favors for people like you actually care about promotions, and the only people you ever talk to are old dying folks!"

Taken aback, Fiona leaned away from him, making sure he saw the way she raised her eyebrows to show how little he'd impressed her with that last one. She was a geriatrician who worked at palliative care, the unit for pain management. Most of her patients were in the last stage of their lives, yes. Many would never leave the hospital alive, but somebody had to take care of their special needs now that treatments had failed, and make things more bearable for them, and help them retain some dignity. Brian had never found anything wrong with that before. "Oh? Says the glorified brain photographer?"

Brian sighed as if she'd never made the quip, although she personally thought it had been a pretty good one. "I'm saying I'm worried about you." He hesitated. "It's been long enough, Fiona. Yeah, you didn't want a divorce, but there you have it anyway, and you've got to move on. Miriam—"

"Leave Miriam out of this," she snapped, her tone changing to something that sounded ugly even to her own ears. She couldn't help it, though. In truth, this whole conversation had been about Miriam from the start. Everything always was about Miriam these days.

No, Fiona didn't hang out with her friends anymore, because they had been *their* friends, and God knew which of them had known about the affair: the way Miriam had been cheating on her with some Parisian stewardess of all people, who probably had endless legs and a go-to plastic surgeon.

She still couldn't bear to think about it.

"Miriam was a bitch," Brian declared.

"Miriam was my *wife*."

"Yeah," Brian said. "And now she's not."

Frowning, he stood up, brushing imaginary dirt off his lab coat and placing the chair back in a corner. He would be working through Christmas as well, Fiona suddenly remembered in an angered, jealous way. It wouldn't be because he had no better place to go. His husband worshipped the ground he walked on, and was probably preparing the Christmas turkey already. Brian only had to work because he'd drawn the shortest straw in Radiology.

That thought left a bitter taste in her mouth. The sudden surge of anger ebbed off as fast as it had come when she noticed how petty she sounded even in her own head. Fiona slumped back, feeling tired and faintly miserable, like when she stabilized a patient after he or she had crashed and all was well, except not, because they would be dying anyway.

She really didn't want to go home. She didn't.

"I'm not hiding out," she muttered without looking Brian in the eye.

"Sure," he said. "That's why you're going to the Christmas party with me. I put a fifty down on you and that nurse."

Fiona groaned.

"We're called *Fragged*. Garage punk gone death metal. Band's touring through Ohio right now, but Doc Kapstein says if I'm lucky, I could catch up with them in New York in spring and play at least a song or two."

It was a lot of words to say at once for a hoarse eighteen-year-old who was undergoing chemo and high doses of radiation; they were systematically bringing down her immune system in preparation for a bone marrow transplant. Exhausted to the core, June Sekelsky was bald and a translucent kind of pale. Sunk into the pillows of her bed, tiny to begin with, she might as well have been a child. But there were tattoos of dragons snaking all over her arms, remains of clipped black nail polish still glued to her fingernails, and she seemed admirably determined to retain her sense of self.

Even more interesting to Fiona was the petite woman sitting at her bedside. Jessie McGee—June's fiancée, introducing herself with a politeness that spoke of a lifetime of strict nannies—stood in stark contrast to June: her careful prep school enunciation to June's Boston working class drawl, her health and radiant beauty to her fiancée's exhaustion. Jessie was African American, while June was white, though so discolored that the circles under her eyes looked like bruises.

Fiona admitted without shame that Kapstein's medical marvel had become two hundred percent more notable to her the moment she had turned out to be a lesbian.

Jessie took June's hand in her own gloved one, throwing her a sickeningly loving look, the rest of her face obscured by her facial mask. "My dad discovered them when they were playing at *T.T. The Bear's*," she said to Fiona. "He's a music producer. It's how we met."

June gave Fiona a weak smirk. "Don't forget to tell her that he's paying all my hospital bills, just 'cause I'll marry his daughter. He's awesome like that."

"That's what family does," her fiancée said in a soft and insistent voice, as if she had reminded June of that many times.

June grimaced, acquiescing unhappily.

The duty nurse finished checking the IVs. With a nod, she left Fiona to mark down June's status on the chart. As a palliative doctor, Fiona worked with a lot of cancer patients, and she'd be just fine in Oncology as long as nobody expected her to heroically do an emergency transplant. Having rounded on almost all of Kapstein's other patients before attending to June, she was already well on her way to settling into a routine. There wasn't a lot that could be done for the girl during transplant prep, apart from careful monitoring. She had kidney damage, but it was mild, and they could probably gently hydrate her through; if not, a nephrologist would be at the ready to start her on dialysis. The isolation room she was in minimized the risk of bacterial infections, as did the administration of broad-spectrum antibiotics, and the most worrisome new symptom she had reported this morning was a sore throat. Her hemoglobin was down but her platelet count remained stable, so all in all, things could be worse.

Apart from the partial match transplant she would be receiving next week, anyway. After that little deal with the devil, Fiona would likely be meeting June again while she died in the palliative care unit.

"It's good that you have somebody to stay with you." Fiona checked off the last couple of boxes. "This can't be how you imagined spending Christmas."

"Better than dying," June muttered, and Jessie looked like she was trying to be scandalized, except that she agreed.

"Me and the band are gonna all go bald for real the moment I get out of here," June informed Fiona, touching her head. "I think it looks rad."

"You're so full of shit," Jessie said fondly.

June shrugged. "Cancer sells, I bet," she said, and coughed.

Beneath her mask, Fiona forced a smile.

She might very well be seeing June in palliative care again, yes. But she shouldn't. The girl was young and obviously strong-willed, sick with a disease meant for Fiona's regular patients—sixty-five plus. A part of her felt like she should run from the room before the misery simmering beneath the brittle optimistic surface could make her choke. But at the same time—maybe because those two girls made for such an unbearably sweet couple—they infused her with an unfamiliar, unexpected, almost desperate sense that she should help. Eighteen-year-olds weren't supposed to die of MM. None of this was supposed to happen.

It was December twenty-fourth. It wasn't supposed to be a time of death, either. Fiona thought of med school, of when she'd still believed that medicine would be about improving people's lives.

That had been a very long time ago, though.

As Fiona had feared, the Christmas party wasn't the best idea Brian had ever had.

She forced a blank face. Standing with both hands wrapped around a glass of bad, non-alcoholic fruit punch, she had edged into a corner of the garishly decorated cafeteria, escaping from surgical fellows competing over who'd managed the most exciting flip on their snowboard during the last vacation, and bleary-eyed residents comparing the relative merits of ER night shifts during Christmas with those at Halloween. "When you've been puked on by Count Dracula, you've seen it all," she'd heard one of them say, and the other had smirked into his drink: "Only if he puked up blood."

Christmas meant working with an even shorter staff than usual, doing more shifts in a row than was technically allowed. Meanwhile, suicide attempts went up, as did turkey-induced salmonellosis, and the emergency room supplying the rest of the hospital with more and more work put a strain on everybody. Doctors and nurses alike dropped into bed like dead weight when it was finally over and slept until it was time to rinse and repeat all that at New Year's—with less salmonella, but more burn injuries.

All in all, physicians were about the last people on Earth who should be tortured with a Christmas party. Or so Fiona kept telling herself, despite the laughter all around. The lights and tinsel on the walls looked as fake as only professional interior designers could achieve, complete with a huge Christmas tree and a recording of trembling children's voices blaring "We Wish You a Merry Christmas" through the speakers on what was starting to feel like infinite repeat.

Through the crowd of chatting receptionists and security staff, Brian was making his way to her, a curvy blonde in nursing scrubs trailing in his wake.

Great.

It should have been her pager that saved her. It wasn't. Instead, her phone buzzed in the breast pocket of her lab coat, and Fiona pulled it out a second later. Waving it at Brian apologetically before discarding the punch and getting the hell out, she ignored the outraged face her friend made at her—another thing she rightfully didn't care about.

What she *did* care about was the caller ID, when she had a belated look at the display once the doors closed behind her, cutting off the noise in the dim hallway.

It was as if everything froze, after catapulting her back into the past.

Her hands shook when she raised the phone to her ear. "Miriam," she breathed.

You shouldn't have kept calling her. You knew you shouldn't have kept calling her. You knew she'd call you back eventually, and then what?

A part of her couldn't help clinging to the wild hope that Miriam would tell her all those things she'd imagined hearing when she was alone, lying on her bed with those sheets that didn't fit, because they were made for a double bed. Miriam had decreed that Fiona should have those, because she'd chosen them. But it had been Miriam's house and Miriam's bed, so Fiona had ended up with sheets she couldn't use.

Miriam's and *Fiona's* were categories that hadn't even existed in her head before the night she'd learned the truth.

Miriam's real voice sounded a lot more agitated than the cheerful recording from the day before, real emotion in place of multi-purpose holiday greetings.

"Hello Fiona," she said. It was a firm voice, learned in law school and well-practiced in court. "Listen, I don't know what you're playing at, but you have to stop calling me like this. It creeps me out."

Miriam would have looked at herself in the mirror before she called, straightening her shoulders and muttering those words to herself to check her tone.

Funny how that worked. Fiona knew that she would have done that, but it didn't take anything away from the effect. Miriam might as well have been talking to a stranger.

Closing her eyes, she took a deep breath to calm herself and not go into fucking cardiac arrest. She struggled for words.

"I'm sorry. God, Miriam, I'm sorry. I just…I've been trying to reach you. I didn't want to disrupt your holiday. Uh, it's just, there were some of your books in one of my boxes and I wanted to know if you would like me to—"

"Oh, cut the bullshit."

Fiona's mouth snapped shut. Miriam sounded weary and angry, like she was out of patience and tired of her ex. Fiona wondered if she was working through the holidays too, because she did that, especially when Fiona wasn't there to watch out for her. But Miriam's mind clearly wasn't on that. She continued with more determination.

"I don't know what this is about. But it's making me uncomfortable, all right? I know you're not trying to reach me at all! You call when you know I'll be at the gym, or at Kim's. You don't leave messages. You just call."

"Ah, I must have lost track of time. My schedules have been—"

"It's *over*, Fiona," Miriam said, an edge to her voice.

Fiona flinched. She couldn't help it. It *hurt*.

There was another pause.

Miriam sighed, as if she had been there to see.

"Listen, I'm sorry," she said, her tone implying that she was anything but. "I'm sorry I broke it off so abruptly, okay? I wasn't being fair to you when I did it that way. I realize that now. I thought that a clean break would be best for both of us."

Well-measured cadence. Sometimes, Fiona ended up telling patients lies exactly like this one. She didn't tell a dying man that his daughter hadn't cared enough to visit, or that the reason they couldn't reach his wife was because she had moved away to live in Spain.

"But it's been months," Miriam continued, "and you agreed to sign the divorce papers and all, and you keep calling my voicemail like some kind of stalker..."

"You left me!" Fiona exclaimed. The words spilled out, a wave of dry nausea accompanying them. She took a furtive look around, but the hallway was still empty. Still she lowered her voice to a hiss, retreating further into a corner. "What do you expect? You *left* me for some *stewardess*! Next thing, you say you never loved me anyway! Do you have any idea what that felt like? How do you expect me to just...to just..." Anger mixed with a helpless void, a lack of any available reactions. "How do you get over that? Explain that to me, please."

It was like she was trapped, like her life had knotted itself into this snare, tightening around her the more she moved, and she didn't even know why.

A moment of silence passed. Miriam seemed too far away, though her voice was too close, directly in Fiona's ear.

"That's not my problem anymore, all right? It's yours. Stop calling me. Goodbye."

There was a click when she hung up. Fiona resisted the urge to throw the phone against the wall, the way a character in that modern Jane Austen novel would who didn't have to care about propriety and what it would cost to replace a phone.

Sometimes Fiona thought this could only have been worse if Miriam had left her for a man.

None of it was ever real. That was the worst part, how Miriam had never loved her to begin with, despite stepping up to an altar with her. Relationships ended, even marriages, that was the way it went; Fiona knew that intellectually. But she'd never loved anyone else so much. This had been how she had wanted to spend the rest of her life, and for Miriam, it simply...hadn't been like that. She'd met another woman who worked better for her. A helpless part of Fiona kept insisting that Miriam should have warned her of that possibility up front, of how her marriage could be ripped away like a Band-Aid, disposable, applied only as long as required.

Laughter and "Jingle Bells" could be heard far away, muted by the walls of the cafeteria, and Fiona was sick of it, sick to her bones. She turned on her heel. She had two units full of patients to keep going until they perished.

June Sekelsky was the only patient on the Oncology floor who was awake. Remote control in hand, the young woman was following a Christmas special on TV with that mix of exhaustion and boredom exclusive to long-term patients. Jessie was nowhere to be seen, and it seemed like the stubborn glow that had fueled June's demeanor during Fiona's previous visits had left the room with her fiancée.

When Fiona entered, the young woman smirked without joy, not even bothering to raise her head from the pillow; yet it was surprisingly easy to picture her with defiant black eyeliner and a multi-colored Mohawk on a stage in a punk rock band, trashing somebody else's guitar and screaming "Fuck!" into a microphone.

"Anything interesting on?" Fiona asked, sitting down on the visitor chair. She would check June's chest sounds in a moment, to make sure that sore throat didn't grow into anything more worrisome.

June squinted at the screen, as if Fiona's appearance outside of rounds was quite ordinary, and she got courtesy visits by doctors all the time. Maybe she did; maybe her band was more famous than Fiona had thought, and there were fans amongst the staff.

"Dude called John visiting the family of dude called Sherlock. I'm not sure if they're gay or what; it's British. I think Sherlock poisoned his parents?"

"Okay. Please tell me you have actually heard of Sherlock Holmes before. Unless television has gone through some drastic changes recently, I'd say he's straight."

June snorted. "It's British," she repeated, as if that explained everything.

A moment of companionable silence passed as Fiona made an attempt to follow the story alongside June. Restlessness had befallen her, a need to move around and act, while at the same time, nothing that she could have done came to mind. She was trapped in the hospital, after all, and would be until Christmas was over.

"Your fiancée went home?"

"Christmas thing with the family." June's smirk grew. Although she'd started running a fever again and her mouth had to feel sore along with her throat, her voice remained strong. "Woulda dragged them all here if Nurse Leena'd let them in and all."

"Seems like a great girl."

"Oh yeah." June made a weak, wavy gesture, eyes still on the television. "They're all fab. Paying my bills and all, I mean, how great is that, right? Jessie thinks it's weird that I keep bringing that up, but it's, like, it's a *lot of money*, you know? Her dad's a real bigwig, though." She paused and closed her eyes to breathe before she continued, betraying how much the conversation exhausted her. "When we signed the contract with him, we totally thought we'd made it big. And then we kinda did, too."

Fiona looked at her hands for a moment, wrapped in rubber. Picking at the wristband of the glove, she thought of Miriam.

"I'm gay, too."

"Yeah. Figured," was all June had to say to that.

Fiona chuckled at her dismissive tone. Textbook generation gap; it made her feel old.

"Don't you have a place to be on Christmas or nothing?" June asked.

"Not how it works in a hospital. We can't close shop and go home."

"Coulda fooled me the way Doc Kapstein got the fuck out of here yesterday to eat turkey and shit."

Fiona laughed despite herself. "You're an orphan, I gather? There might have been a better bone marrow match in your family otherwise."

June averted her gaze. "Might as well be," she muttered, studying the remote control.

Fiona frowned.

Sometimes, her clinic patients over at the hospice prattled on about bone aches and shortness of breath for what seemed like hours until quite suddenly, they brought up the actual alarming issue, like the blood in their urine, hidden in some subordinate clause.

"June," she said firmly. "If you've got blood relatives out there—"

"Well I don't," June said, eyes still fixed on the remote.

Fiona tried picturing old, ever-distracted Kapstein questioning a stubborn young woman further after she gave him this answer but couldn't. So she may not have known which doctors June had seen before she came here, but she could bet that nobody at St. Anne's had pressed the issue.

"This is vital information, June," she said. "Listen to me. You're only going to receive a partial match transplant. Do you have any idea how huge the risk is with a MUD that your body will reject it? It's called donor-versus-host disease. I know they've told you about that. If there's any chance—any chance at all—that there could be a relative of yours out there, he or she could get tested and the odds that they'd match better are incredibly short—"

"You're not gonna find anybody from my family who'll donate anything for me!" If June had been on a heart monitor, it would probably have blipped in rapid elevation, sending nurses running her way. She tried sitting up, paling, the words followed by a coughing fit.

Muttering a swearword under her breath, Fiona reached out to steady her. But June had already caught herself, swatting her away weakly.

"I ran away from home back when. I haven't seen them in years; I have a new family now. The old one don't want anything to do with me!"

"Oh dammit, June..." Fiona hovered for a moment longer and then slumped back in her chair, eyeing the kid with a mix of shock and pity. After waiting to make sure that June had calmed down and that she had her full attention, she spoke firmly. "Tell me what happened."

June threw her an unkind look that showed how little she appreciated that question.

"I got out of there, all right?" she said defiantly after a moment. "I made it on my own. It wasn't hard. School is stupid anyway," she muttered to herself, taking an unsteady breath.

"I was playing at this club with some guys. Dude picks me up, says he needs someone to play guitar in a band. Next thing, we've got a contract with McGee, and I'm meeting Jessie and all."

Wow, Fiona thought. *Your regular lesbian* Oliver Twist. Except that June had cancer, and she wasn't speaking to her family that apparently *existed*. Fiona was fairly certain that nobody in *Oliver Twist* acted that stupidly, or readers would have rightfully complained.

She focused on the important part. "Why did you run away from home? Was it because you're gay?"

"Sure didn't help," June said cynically, still looking away.

The television was forgotten; in the corner of Fiona's eye, men were shooting at each other.

"I..." June closed her mouth, paused. Then she opened it again, angrily. "Shit happened, all right? They hate me. They want nothing to do with me. They said."

"And that was how long ago?"

"Three years."

"Geez, June. They've probably been too busy being *scared to death* for you to waste a thought on whatever it is you think you did so wrong."

But June was shaking her head already. "They threw me out. They said I'm a monster. So I ran. I don't need them anymore. I'd rather try the bad match than ever talk to them again."

Fiona couldn't believe this. "Even if it gets you killed?" This wasn't the time to sugarcoat the ramifications of that decision. She could have recited any number of ways that receiving the wrong transplant could do terrible, terminal damage.

June pressed her lips together. "Yeah."

"If they're really that awful," Fiona said, carefully handpicking each word, but getting more determined to get through to the girl. She felt more motivated to get to the bottom of this than she'd felt about anything in weeks, filled with a new, unexpected kind energy. "If they're really that bad, then what's wrong with using them for your health? You don't owe them anything. Call them up, tell them what they want to hear, laugh in their faces afterwards." She took a calming breath. "Do you have any siblings? You could ask them." A sibling was likely to match best anyway, a nine or even ten-out-of-ten match.

But June's face hardened even more—an angry, bald, sickly statue of pride. "Not anymore," she said, barely audible.

Everything that Fiona had just learned was such a *waste.* She couldn't believe it had taken a substitute from geriatrics to hit on this. June had been sick longer than she'd been a legal adult. This shouldn't be happening.

"They hate me," June said for the third time, like an incantation.

Why do people always throw the good things away? Fiona didn't understand. It was almost like they didn't need them. Like they didn't *care* that there were all these other, hollow people who'd never had the privilege of letting a chance like this one slip away. June was gay like her, and maybe that was a shallow reason to feel any kinship when there wasn't much else they had in common, but she couldn't possibly want to risk her life out of some teenage upset. She had cancer. It was a great and exciting case for everybody at St. Anne's except June.

Fiona wasn't sure if her thought process made any sense at all, or if it made all sense in the world. She wouldn't put up with it, in either case. She was tired of her life, tired of false Christmas cheer, when people could be doing actual good things instead. She was tired of managing pain but not improving patients' health, when this one here was young and strong and proud, and maybe didn't have to go down. June had a fiancée who loved her and a surprise career in music that sounded like it had been made for a movie. What was there to decide?

June was too young to know anything anyway, barely old enough to make the decision herself. When Fiona was her age, she hadn't even known she was gay, and her parents hadn't cared enough to give her either love or hate.

Much like Miriam, come to think of it.

If you don't like a thing, do something about it, she told herself and stood up.

Securing the phone number proved shockingly easy. The duty nurse accessed the complete patient file on the computer at the Admission desk, then turned the screen so Fiona could see without so much as pausing the game she was playing on her cell phone. The Oncology floor was always quiet, but now it seemed particularly so; the staff party had to be reaching its fabulous fruit punch peak about now.

June's complete history was located all the way down at the bottom, and there it said *Father: Joseph Sekelsky* and *Mother: Edith Sekelsky*. There were birth dates and job descriptions and an address. The last June had known, Mr. Sekelsky had been a factory worker.

Siblings: Tyler Sekelsky, deceased, it said, and a date from three years ago. Tyler had been two years younger than his sister.

Fiona didn't dwell on it.

Seeking refuge in an empty exam room, she had no problem finding the landline attached to the address, a poor neighborhood in East Boston.

"Yes," a harsh male voice answered when she called.

"Is this Joseph Sekelsky? My name is Dr. Porter. I'm calling from St. Anne's Hospital in Andover."

"Huh. What do you want?"

This was how people reacted to a call from a hospital when their circle of loved ones was both small and currently gathered in the living room in full.

Fiona took a deep breath. "I need you to come to the hospital, sir. I'm treating your daughter June. It's not looking good."

The sky outside the windows was pitch black by the time Mr. Sekelsky made it to St. Anne's. This late on Christmas Eve, the I-93 would be empty; a drive from East Boston shouldn't take over an hour.

Fiona identified Sekelsky immediately when he stepped into the mostly abandoned hospital lobby. His face was crunched into a frown and he was as short as his daughter, sharing her strong jaw, though where cancer treatments had left her skinny and haggard, he was badly hiding a beer belly underneath his ill-fitting, worn coat. He hadn't aged well, his skin an unhealthy shade of nicotine-yellow, and he looked like he had brought very little patience along.

"Mr. Sekelsky," Fiona said, stepping up and offering her hand. "I'm Dr. Porter. We spoke on the phone."

Mr. Sekelsky eyed her hand without taking it. "Where is she? She dead yet?"

Fiona attempted a smile, then waved him down the corridor towards Radiology. The receptionist was already glancing at them with too much interest. Radiology was close by. Nobody would be there but Brian, and he would either be asleep on the cot in the lab, or busy with an emergency patient.

Her smile transformed into a grimace when they had made it down the corridor. She turned towards June's father again.

"Thank you for coming here," she said. "I'm currently June's attending physician. She's being treated in our Oncology unit for multiple myeloma, which is a cancer that attacks her stem cells and her bone marrow. She's stable right now, but that's probably going to change. We're preparing her for a bone marrow transplant. It's the only way to prolong her life."

Mr. Sekelsky frowned. A number of emotions crossed his face, too many for Fiona to count, before it settled into something dark and defensive. Yes, she might have given him the impression that June had been brought in as a medical emergency, so that his immediate presence was required, but how else could she have made sure to get him into the hospital before Kapstein returned and took the case away from her?

A beat passed before Sekelsky asked, "Is this about money? She's eighteen by now. She doesn't need my insurance. Kid can get Obamacare now all she wants."

"I understand that the bills are taken care of, actually." Fiona collected herself, adopting her most serious and professional voice. "Mr. Sekelsky, your daughter is very sick. She needs that transplant to survive. However, the partial match found for her in the national donor registry has extremely shaky odds; it's probably not going to work. A donation by a family member will raise her chances of recovery considerably, if you or your wife are a match."

"She sent you after us to get a *transplant* from us?" Sekelsky exclaimed, and Fiona wondered if he was a little bit drunk, if this was a story of abuse by an alcoholic parent. *I got out of there*, June had said. But he didn't smell of alcohol.

"A bone marrow transplant, yes," she said evenly, despite her uneasy sense that something was off. "You can spare the bone marrow; it'll regenerate completely. We would only take about five percent, from your or your wife's hipbone. It's a very safe procedure. And no, she didn't send me. She didn't want me to contact you, in fact. But as her doctor, I have to do what's best for her health."

"Best for *all* of us if she dies!" Sekelsky growled, taking an angry step towards her that made Fiona retreat in surprise, although he was just moving in agitation. Sekelsky wasn't the type who'd dare hit a doctor; there was something intrinsically helpless in the man, a trait found typically in people who'd been poor all their lives. His kids, maybe he'd been hitting them, though suddenly Fiona wasn't sure about anything.

"Demon spawn is what she is! That kid made me and my wife's life hell, all those years! All that money that we spent to feed her!"

"Please, Mr. Sekelsky, hear me out," Fiona tried again. His voice was ringing loudly through the empty Radiology corridors. Her skin was crawling now, the situation so out of her control.

Sekelsky's Boston accent grew more and more pronounced the angrier he became. "You know what she did? Did she tell you what she did? Whore around before she was even twelve, that's what! Ran around with druggies and juvie court regulars. Dragged her little brother around with her to parties, the poor kid, when she was supposed to be watching him 'cause me and my wife had to work. She was *doing drugs* when she was supposed to be keeping an eye on him! Did she tell you any of *that*, huh? How them doctors called me up at work to tell me Tyler's dead because her and her friends were driving around high as kites? My little boy! Jesus Christ, he was only thirteen years old!"

Fiona wasn't a person who ran out of words easily, but today was proving a never-ending line of stutters, with nothing making sense. Yet again she'd been blindsided, unable to think of an appropriate reaction. "Mr. Sekelsky..."

"She did it!" Sekelsky sputtered, his eyes full of pain and his voice high and thin. "I don't care that she wasn't the one driving the car. She got her druggie friends to take Tyler on all their little joyrides. Let them drive her little brother around, stoned out of their minds on weed. Might as well have been her that smashed that car into that tree!"

Oh God. Fiona wanted to hide her face underneath her palm and whimper. This was...she didn't have a word for what this was. Not what she had planned, anyway.

"Running away was the only good decision that kid ever made!" Sekelsky seemed to be trembling; another person might have spat at Fiona's feet. "Now she's afraid of dying, huh? Well, she should've thought of that before she threw away her brother's life. Maybe it's God's will, wanting her to face up to what she did. If there's any justice in the world, that's what this is. That kid ain't my flesh and blood anymore!"

He turned, looking frantically around to orient himself and almost walking down the wrong corridor, but then he found the exit sign and stumbled away, the ruins of his life almost visibly trailing in his wake.

Well, that could have gone better, Fiona thought, although that was a massive understatement. She wanted to clutch her neck with both hands and hide from the world.

Seeing Brian down the hall, a stone's throw away, didn't help. Of course Brian would have heard—it was that kind of day.

Her friend was standing in the door to MRI 1, lab coat rumpled, cheek reddened where it had rested against a hard surface in his sleep. But he was looking wide awake at Sekelsky's retreating back, then turning to stare at Fiona with almost comically wide eyes.

They looked comical, anyway, to someone as close to hysterics as Fiona. Probably not so much to people who didn't feel like their life was suddenly breaking into little pieces in even more ways than before.

"The fuck, Fiona," Brian breathed, his usual wittiness falling off and making way for an expression that said that he didn't know how to process this, but it scared him. That was startling, too—Brian looking scared. "Tell me that wasn't what it sounded like, and you didn't actually go behind a patient's back to talk to her father! What in the world was that all about?"

"Just trying to make something right," she muttered, waving it off to show it didn't matter. She slumped against the wall.

Brian swore.

"Are you out of your *mind*?" he said in a lower voice, a concession to the fact that sound carried in these halls. Two big steps and he reached her, looking like he wanted to grab her, then reconsidered and rubbed his head instead. "That's a doctor-patient confidentiality breach, big time. Do you have any idea what the Dean will do if the patient complains about that? Remember last year, that whole mess with Jennings? People lose their license for that kind of crap."

But Fiona was so *tired* of doing nothing. She… God, she had no idea what she'd been thinking. It had seemed like such a good idea until Sekelsky showed up with a whole story that hadn't been what she'd expected, and the complex tragedy had poured down on her. She couldn't even make out who the bad guys and the good guys were in this one, too much information at once to immediately process. All she knew was that she'd had this great idea, until it hadn't been great anymore.

"Don't tell me you wouldn't do anything you could to save a patient's life," she ground out, although she couldn't look Brian in the eye. It shouldn't be a platitude; it should be a good reason, but it didn't sound like one the way she said it. "A couple of months and she's probably dead."

"You should *hope* that she'll be dead," Brian snapped. "Dead people can't sue." Staring at her for another moment, he shook his head. "What's wrong with you? This isn't a *House* episode. This is real life."

There was nothing she could say to that, and when she made a helpless gesture, he shot her a grimace.

"The fuck," he repeated. "You want to fall apart, you do it on your own time, where it won't destroy your career." Rubbing his neck for another moment, he seemed to reach a decision. "Go make sure your patient hasn't heard about this. And get her to understand if she did. I'll try and find out if that man complained to anybody on the way out. Didn't sound like a guy with a lawyer. You better hope this'll blow over," he muttered, already walking away.

Fiona resisted the urge to sink to the ground and curl up into a ball in the middle of the empty RAD corridor.

The magnitude of what she'd tried to do hit her, making her realize how much it had backfired. Why in the world had she ever tried to do anything like this? She didn't have a right to meddle in a patient's life. Nobody did. It wasn't her job, and it had been an arrogant thing to ever think differently.

It had been so much easier to try and fix June's life instead of her own, though. It had been easier than facing the fact that she couldn't handle her own problems.

She could admit that now.

At the Admission desk on the Oncology floor, Jessie McGee was waiting for Fiona, holding a phone in her hand. She wasn't wearing the hat and mask for the isolation room, and she looked astonishingly beautiful, with long waves of black hair and delicate features—if it weren't for that helpless look on her face distracting from the sight.

"He called me," she said without preamble. "He said we better stay away from his family forever, or else." Her face said he'd also spiced it up with some insults, probably aimed at her and June's sexual orientation, or how they were a mixed couple.

It took a moment for Fiona's brain to catch up. At first all she heard was that she was busted; it sent a cold shudder running down her spine fueled by a heavy dose of shame. Then she parsed the most important part: Mr. Sekelsky had Jessie's number saved on his cell.

He knew her.

"You've tried talking to him, too," she stated.

Jessie shrugged. "Yeah." She looked tired, a girl of eighteen or nineteen preparing to go off to a very good college, and madly in love with a dying girl. "June can't know," she whispered as if it were confession at the church.

I'd do anything too, her tone said.

Jessie pressed her lips together.

"It's not that bad," she continued, as if trying to convince herself as much as Fiona. She looked up, determined. "It's not that bad. June thinks she's going to make it. She's staying positive about it, and so should we. She'll get better with the unrelated donor transplant. She doesn't need her old family. She has us for family now."

How could so many wonderful and so many terrible things all happen to the same person?

Fiona wondered if she'd be willing to pay the price of a terminal disease if in return, she'd get an otherwise happy life, married to a Miriam in love with her. She wondered if she'd exchange Miriam for health, her marriage for a bone marrow match.

It would have been an easy question to answer before Christmas had come around, but it wasn't anymore now.

People stubbornly maintained the idea that all doctors should be infallible. Obviously, every med student learned the opposite the moment they saw their first real patient. Nevertheless, they too tried to keep up the illusion, partly because they clung to the hope that it would become reality one day and partly because it made their patients more compliant, their jobs easier to do. People sue human beings; they don't sue angels of mercy.

Fiona had always felt safe as a doctor. She'd felt competent, knowing she was already good at what she did or else she could read up on things and practice and improve. She might not be perfect, but she always knew what she was doing.

Now she felt lost and like everything was floating. The scare after her confrontation with Brian and Jessie had left her shaky. At the same time, she knew that state would pass, and everything would settle down in a better way than before, although she didn't yet know how. It was the strangest feeling.

June was lying curled up in her bed. For once she seemed too tired to keep up the proud façade, and she just looked faded and sick, the way every other patient in the cancer unit did.

"You know what creeps me out about the transplant shit?" she said without raising her head, sounding hoarse.

"What's that?" Fiona had taken a seat on the visitor chair again.

"That they kill off all my old bone marrow before they transplant the new stuff. With the radiation, right? Doesn't matter if a part of it is still healthy and stuff. They kill that dead, too."

"Medicine sometimes just works like that. Your own immune system is damaged, so it needs to be replaced by the donor's. But the old marrow has to be gone for that to work. You need to make space."

June shrugged, a small twitch of her shoulder. "Just seems weird that you've gotta destroy something healthy to grow something new, is all."

Fiona sighed, looking at the bald girl in the patient gown that the cancer had tried so hard to make anonymous. But it couldn't eliminate her attitude, any more than it could damage her tattoos.

It was late afternoon on Christmas Day. The sun was going down outside; soon the night shift would start trickling in. Kapstein had called, wishing her a Merry Christmas and assuring her that she didn't need to come in on her free day to round patients with him; handing them off to the night-shift resident would suffice. It was a strangely thoughtful gesture for the Chief Oncologist, who was known to never trust residents on principle and who she'd thought couldn't remember her face.

Fiona would return to St. Anne's to do doubles through New Year's, three long free days in between, and when she did, June would already have been relocated to the ICU after receiving her transplant. If Kapstein needed another substitute in that time, an intensivist would be the better choice.

She watched June for a while, resisting an urge to stroke her head; the gesture would undoubtedly have been met with dismay. June wasn't a child.

"Do you believe you deserve the long odds of the transplant because of what happened with your brother?" Fiona asked in a soft voice. She'd told June that she'd talked to Jessie about what had happened. Now that the first shock had passed, she had a hard time feeling guilty about the fact that she had tried to help, even if it had been for the wrong reasons.

Stress and treatments having worn her down, June's eyes started filling with tears. Angrily she brushed them away. "I'm eighteen. I can do what I want. I don't need them for anything now."

Then she muttered abruptly, "They left us alone all the fucking time."

"Your brother must have loved you a lot, trailing after you like that."

The tears were running down June's face now, silently melting onto the pillowcase.

"I didn't *want* him to go on a ride with those guys," she whispered. "But I couldn't leave him alone in the house."

Fiona remained quiet for a moment, hesitating. If she had learned one thing in these two days, it was that she shouldn't assume she knew enough to judge.

But now, she was clear on one thing: June was eighteen and allowed to make her own calls. She'd decided to go build her own life on her own terms, no matter the odds. No, it wasn't perfect, and the transplant probably wouldn't turn out well. But it was still her choice, not Fiona's. Fiona had different choices to make.

Suddenly it was impossible for Fiona to blink away the exhaustion of too many shifts in a row.

"You'll be all right," she told June quietly. It wasn't a promise, but a statement of fact. It had nothing to do with whether the transplant would take.

When Fiona made her way out of the hospital, the halls of St. Anne's seemed eerily empty, as they had throughout the Christmas shifts. She wondered if they ever really had been quiet, or if the strain of the last five months had made her see things that weren't really there.

An icy breeze and a heavy wave of snow hit her full in the face in the parking lot, which was entirely covered in ice. The snow poured onto her head as if a bucket had been dumped on her from the sky, and she surprised herself with a chuckle when she looked up, snowflakes tumbling into her eyes. She had always liked the way snow made her feel: free and slightly adrift.

Her car door was frozen to the frame, and it took two hefty jerks to get it open. When she slipped inside and turned the key, the radio came alive with a stutter, promptly spitting out another Christmas carol. It was "Jingle Bells" again.

Fiona wondered what she would do with herself in these upcoming days. Her empty apartment still felt daunting, the rooms too sterile and the walls too white. It didn't have any personality yet. Somehow, she'd always expected that would happen by itself. She'd open the door one day, and it would finally feel like home.

Now she thought maybe she should spend her free days painting the walls in a color she actually liked. Maybe she could invite one of the neighbors' kids to build a snowman in the yard, complete with a carrot for a nose; one of her neighbors was bound to have a kid.

One way to pass the time, she supposed.

Carefully navigating her car across the ice, Fiona turned onto the main road, rows upon rows of decorated houses left and right, lush Christmas lights and plastic Santa figurines on roofs. They might have looked silly, but a part of her still appreciated the trouble that people had gone to, the effort that they'd made to decorate the street for random passersby just because they could.

She thought about destroying things and making space for something new.

Flea

LOIS CLOAREC HART

It wasn't my fault. Honest! Who knew the kid would actually pull the fire alarm? Okay, so maybe I told him what it was, but I warned him in no uncertain terms not to pull it. Still, four-year-olds can be sort of unpredictable, so I probably should've known better. But really, I don't think it was entirely my fault.

I'm not sure the Boss will see it that way, though He's pretty good at overlooking the occasional mistake of His Guardians. Unlike Him, we're not perfect. He only expects us to do our best, and that is what I was trying to do.

I guess I should start at the beginning. My name is Flea, and I'm a Guardian. You people have a lot of different names for us: angels, faeries, sprites, pixies—the list is endless. But then, you also have a lot of different names for the Boss. He doesn't mind, so why should I?

My current assignment is the third floor of a large metropolitan children's hospital. It doesn't matter what city, because there are millions of us and my post isn't much different from that of many of my colleagues.

And look…about my name? For millennia I was perfectly content with my given name—Felicity. But we Guardians usually make our home in something unremarkable so that no one takes notice of us while we go about our duties. Once

I hitched a ride in Dr. Jess' briefcase to an out clinic, where their Guardian lived inside a pink ceramic pig. Each to their own, I guess.

As for me, I'd taken up residence in a small, stuffed toy elf that a child left behind many Christmases before. It was pretty cute, actually, with canary yellow woolen hair and robin's egg blue button eyes. The stitched-on smile is candy apple red, and its clothes were once a bright scarlet and forest green, though they've faded over the years. The white pompom on my hat and the bells on my curled-up slippers were lost long ago at the hands of an overexcited toddler; but other than that, I think I've held up well with age.

At least I thought so until the day about ten years ago when an arrogant young resident knocked me off the counter at the nurse's station where I normally sat. Instead of apologizing and picking me up, as any reasonable person would, he kicked me. I bounced off a file cabinet and fell back on the floor, one leg twisted behind my head.

He snarled at me as if I were Doctor Jess. She'd just chewed him out for his abysmal bedside manner, and he was hopping mad at the whole world.

"Where'd that flea-bitten thing come from anyway? It doesn't belong here."

I objected to that "it." I am a girl; make no mistake about it. Couldn't he see my delicate embroidered eyelashes and long, golden curls? Sheesh, what kind of doctor was he going to make? Luckily, all the nurses thought the young resident was a jerk, and they leapt to my defence. Polly picked me up and straightened out my limbs, while Judy and Alma scowled at him. Alma, the senior nurse on duty, spoke up on my behalf.

"She may not be the prettiest thing on the ward, but many's the child who found a little cuddle with that elf was just the thing to make a scary place a little friendlier. You leave our Flea alone."

Darn. That was it then; from that moment on, I was Flea. My fellow Guardians thought it was hilarious and ever after "forgot" to call me Felicity. Even Anemone calls me Flea, but at least when she does it, her eyes twinkle and her wings shimmer, which makes it easier to bear.

But back to the unfortunate fire alarm incident.

You have to understand what I do around this place. Contrary to popular belief, I'm not a miracle worker. Okay, I can do some minor stuff, but nothing like the Boss or those higher up the celestial hierarchy. Mostly, I pop up in the wee small hours of the morning when children wake up frightened, hurting, and wanting their mommies and daddies. They don't always see me, but I lie on their pillows and whisper in their ears, reassuring them that everything's going to be all right until they drift back to sleep. Or I sit on the shoulder of a scared parent as their child is in surgery. I try to give them hope.

Sometimes the Boss calls a child home, and then I cry with their devastated loved ones and wrap them in invisible hugs. It's those times especially that I wish I could work miracles at will, but that's reserved for far wiser beings who outrank me. I just do the best I can.

This particular day, Bobby was due to be released from the hospital. His left arm was in the cast that he needed after a tobogganing accident during the first snowfall of the season. His parents had been held up getting to the hospital to take him home, and he was bored with the cartoons the nurses thought he was watching. Bobby and boredom were a potentially potent mix, so I took it upon myself to entertain him.

To the average human eye, I was still sitting nestled next to one of the computers at the nurses' station, but actually I was perched beside Bobby, having an excellent conversation about his new radio-controlled fire engine. Adults rarely see me, but little kids often can, as long as adults aren't around. When his limited attention span waned, I suggested that we go down to the sunroom and put a puzzle together. He liked that idea and, in spite of his cumbersome cast, Bobby clambered over the metal railings of his bed like a monkey. As he dropped to the floor, he looked over at his roommate.

Teddy was engrossed in poking his green Jell-O and paid us no heed, so off we went, me riding on Bobby's shoulder. Since most of the children were having lunch, the sunroom was empty. Bobby's mommy had promised to stop at Mickey D's for lunch on the way home, so he had skipped the hospital's noontime culinary offerings. Smart kid.

Bobby dragged a chair over and took his favourite Harry Potter puzzle off the top shelf and tucked it under his cast. While he was up there, he noticed something on the wall beside the cupboard.

"What's that, Flea?"

"It's called a fire alarm. It makes a big noise, but it's for emergencies—only emergencies. You mustn't touch it."

Of course, he touched it. "What's an emergency?"

I got nervous at the way his curious little fingers were tracing the outline of the alarm box. "Why don't we go over to that table over by the window and put together your puzzle?"

"What's an emergency, Flea?"

So much for distracting him. I sighed. "An emergency is when something bad happens, like a fire starts and you need to let everyone know so that help can come."

He nodded and started to turn.

I breathed a sigh of relief, then my eyes widened. "No!"

Bobby pulled the alarm.

"Oh no, no, no!"

Bobby jumped when the siren clanged out through the quiet halls. He dropped the puzzle, hopped off the chair, and darted out of the room.

In his haste to leave the scene of the crime, I was knocked off his shoulder. I peeked around the door at the commotion in the hallways as nurses and orderlies scurried about in a rapid, but organized evacuation of the children.

"Oh, this is so not good." I huddled in the corner behind a large potted philodendron and waited for things to quiet down.

That's where Anemone found me, just as I knew she would. She's one of the supervisors of the hospital Guardians.

Inevitably, if I screw up, it's on her watch. This time she poked her head through the leafy fronds and laughed at the sight of my miserable face.

"I'm sorry, Nem. I didn't know he'd pull the stupid thing. I did tell him not to." I took some measure of comfort from the affectionate twinkle in her dark eyes.

"Flea, how long have you been working this assignment?"

I thought back quickly. I'd been here since they brought the first children into the old hospital. "Um, 'bout sixty or seventy years, I guess."

"And in that time, how often have children heeded a simple 'no'?"

I knew I'd already lost the argument, but I couldn't concede completely. "It could happen."

She smiled and pushed aside the big leaves so she could crawl through to my corner. Tucking her silky wings behind her, she sat beside me, took my hand, and patted it. "Don't worry. It happens to all of us, and there was no real harm done in this case. Bobby has already gone home, and all the other children are safely back in their rooms." Her smile faded. "But there is something else. I need you to help Nehemiah tonight."

"A bad one coming in?"

"A burn case." She sighed. "He's going to have his hands full, and I want you to be there to help."

Nehemiah was the Guardian for the kids in Intensive Care, and it wasn't unusual for me to be called in when he was overwhelmed with frightened, grieving relatives. At those times, Anemone would keep an eye on my kids as she went about her own duties. I'd be needed to offer comfort to a mother who couldn't believe that the child who had helped her make cookies hours before was now on the edge of death; or a father stunned by the abrupt way his safe, predictable world had been upended; and terrified grandparents who pleaded with the Boss to be taken in place of a child who had barely begun her life's journey.

I nodded. "I'll be there."

Nem gave me a light kiss, and a flutter rippled right down to my toes.

She stood, gracefully shook out her wings, and studied me for a long moment. “Call me if you need me. I’m always here for you.” With that, she launched into the air, swooped ’round the foliage, and vanished through the doorway.

I stared after her, my fingertips touching the cheek she’d kissed. I couldn’t help smiling, despite the grim duty that faced me that evening.

It was a tough shift. Nehemiah and I had our work cut out for us, but we kept the family sane and functioning while the doctors and nurses worked on their baby.

Anemone checked in once to assure me all was quiet on my floor, but I was too harried to stop and talk. I was frantically trying to convince the father not to leave the hospital with vengeance in his heart. He was determined to go after the babysitter. The girl had been texting with friends, and her inattention enabled the accident that left his two-year-old daughter badly burned and fighting for her life. The babysitter’s conscience would forever torment her, and no good for anyone could come of the father’s fury. I managed to calm him and redirect him to supporting his inconsolable wife.

It was well into the night before a tired doctor emerged from surgery to assure the family that their baby would live, albeit with a long road to recovery. The parents’ tears, which they had been battling fiercely all night long to hold back for each other’s sake, now flowed freely.

I was relieved to see that, and Nehemiah and I exchanged exhausted smiles.

“I can take it from here, Flea. They’ll be okay now. Thanks for all your help. Any time I can return the favour, just ask.”

I patted him on the back and left. I probably would never need to call on Nehemiah, but that was the way of the Guardians. We are there for our humans, and for each other, no matter what.

Weary, I went back to the nurses' station and slipped back into my elf body. I yawned and lazily eavesdropped on a conversation between two nurses who were updating charts between sips of strong coffee. Twelve hour nightshifts were no picnic, and I'd long ago learned the indispensability of the thick, black sludge they all seemed to subsist on.

"So, do you have any plans for the holidays, Jaideep?" Susan asked.

"I am taking my family back to India to visit my grandparents for two weeks. What about you?"

"Duncan wants us to go skiing and avoid all the seasonal fuss, but I have to work on Boxing Day, so I don't feel like going far. We're trying to reach a compromise." Susan shook her head and scowled. "This is the first Christmas I've had off since I started here, so I don't much feel like going away. He can't seem to understand that."

"My wife and I are lucky to both be off this year. Since we don't celebrate Christmas, I usually volunteer to work; but with the children out of school for two weeks, it was the perfect time to travel."

Susan reached for another file. "Yeah, luck of the draw, I guess. Mind you, Christmas was pretty quiet last year, so I didn't really mind working then."

She was right. In my experience, most parents tried to have their children home for the big day. With few elective surgeries scheduled, a lot of the patient rooms were empty during the December holiday, though there were always accidents and illnesses no matter what time of year it was. Last Christmas, Anemone was even able to spend the whole afternoon with me. I was hoping she could do that again this year.

Jaideep stood, stretching out his back with a grateful sigh as he did. "So, who got stuck on shift this year?"

Susan chuckled. "Well, you can figure Dr. Jess will be working, and if she's working—"

"Then Connie will be on too."

They grinned at each other.

I couldn't help a silent snicker. That was a slam dunk prediction. Despite her seniority, Dr. Jess always took the least desirable shifts, and inevitably Connie volunteered for the same duty schedule. Single for many years, Jess worked most holidays so that her fellow doctors could enjoy the special times with their families. Connie did it because she'd loved Jess with an unspoken intensity almost from the moment she'd first come to the hospital twelve years earlier.

Don't get me wrong, Connie was fiercely dedicated to her small patients, too, but it hadn't gone unnoticed amongst her colleagues that the usually highly competent nurse often got flustered and tongue-tied in Dr. Jess' oblivious presence.

I closed my eyes and idly contemplated the mystery of how humans managed to fumble such simple situations. I'd almost nodded off to the murmur of the nurses' chatter, when a warm presence materialized beside me.

Anemone put her arm around me and gave me a hug. "You did well tonight, Flea. I'm so proud of you."

She disappeared before I could respond, but it sure put a big smile on my face. As I drifted off into a well-deserved sleep, I wondered what Anemone would think if I gave Connie a little help in the Dr. Jess department. Technically, matchmaking wasn't numbered among my duties, but I decided that the Boss surely wouldn't object. Two lonely women needed a nudge towards recognizing what was right under their noses. Where was the harm?

I'd have to consider it further after a long nap.

It was Christmas Eve, and I still hadn't figured out how to get Dr. Jess and Connie together. I'd even sent a gossamer-mail asking advice from my old buddy, Naida, who specializes in romantic situations.

Unfortunately, she was tied up with a difficult case involving an international meeting of hearts. Apparently some cold-hearted government department was being irrationally inflexible about allowing the couple to be together—some nitpicking thing about crossing borders. As Naida pointed out with exasperation, trying to sway Homeland Security was like trying to sway the path of the moon: it could be done, but it would require persistence, time, and effort.

Naida's return g-mail told me I was on my own for now, though she said she'd be glad to help once she had gotten her pair of lovers together.

Being as this was my first foray into matchmaking, I'd watched Connie and Jess very closely for the previous couple of weeks. I was responsible for the well-being of the staff as well as the patients, but usually that entailed comforting them after losing tough cases. I'd never before played Cupid, but as soon as I started to pay attention, it was as plain as the painted nose on my face that Jess and Connie had deep—albeit unacknowledged—romantic feelings for one another.

The great thing about being inanimate—as far as the staff could see—was that I was free to observe them in their unguarded moments. Once I was on the lookout, the signs were obvious. I'd known in an abstract sense that Connie had been crazy about the good doctor for years, but now that I focused on Jess, it was evident that she wasn't quite as oblivious as everyone thought she was. She had a thing for Connie, too.

What I saw convinced me that each was meant for the other, but that if I didn't get involved, they were going to spend the rest of their lives exchanging shy smiles and not much else. Honestly, you humans do such a dance around each other. There'd be a lot less time wasted if you all just spoke up. But then, I suppose there'd be a lot fewer stories written, too, if everyone just blurted out their feelings willy-nilly.

I'd been taking notes since the night I overheard Jaideep and Susan, and there had been twenty-seven covertly longing looks, eighteen deep soulful sighs, and nine bright red blushes between the two of them in just two weeks. How could they *not* see what the other was feeling?

The night before, I started to giggle when I saw how Jess' gaze tracked Connie down the hall when she left the station to attend to one of her patients. Naturally, Anemone chose that moment to drop in on me and wanted to know what I was laughing about.

I put on my best innocent look. "Nothing, Nem. Just feeling good is all. Must be that time of year, I guess."

She gazed at me suspiciously. "Uh-huh. The last time I saw that look on your face, it was after an unexplained black-out that plunged the entire city into darkness for twenty-four hours."

Oh yeah. I'd forgotten about that. I'd been playing tag with a new Guardian when we had an unfortunate accident down by the city's central power station. But Anemone couldn't know what had happened…could she? I'd sworn the newbie to silence and thought I'd covered my tracks pretty well.

"Aw, Nem, that wasn't so bad, was it? Sure a few people were inconvenienced, but look at all the beautiful new babies that joined the world nine months later."

My beatific smile didn't have any effect. She knelt in front of me and stared into my eyes. Suddenly, all thoughts of Jess and Connie flew out of my head. All I could focus on was the feel of Nem's warm breath on my face and the delicate, enticing fragrance that filled my nostrils. I was seconds away from doing something that was going to be really hard to explain, when she pulled back.

I blinked. What the heck had just happened? Anemone and I had been friends for centuries, but I was acting like a star-struck pixie. Geez, I hoped she hadn't noticed.

"I know you've got something up your sleeve, but I won't press you for it now. Just try to stay out of trouble, all right?"

"Um, trouble, right. No, I mean, *no* trouble, no trouble at all. I promise."

Oh, that was brilliant. She's going to think I'd been nipping at the eggnog in the staff lounge again, and it had been at least thirty years since I made that mistake.

Anemone gave me one last suspicious look and flew off. I tried to stand up to go do my rounds, only to find my knees strangely and unaccountably wobbly.

Focus, Flea, focus. You're a Guardian, and you've got work to do.

Still unsteady, I tripped over a plate of shortbread cookies brought in for the staff by a grateful mother, did a somersault over a stapler, and landed feet first in a mostly-empty cup of cold coffee. With all the wounded dignity I could muster, I struggled out of the cup, ignoring the tinkling of familiar laughter that sounded in the distance. I brushed myself off and wrung out my slippers, very glad that human adults couldn't see me. My less than suave performance would not have reflected well on the reputation of the Guardian Corps.

It was a pretty uneventful night after that, and once my feet dried out, I was able to focus on the problem of how to get Dr. Jess and Connie together. I knew that if I could come up with a plan in twenty-four hours, I'd get some help from Christmas Eve itself. It's a special time, when the protective shields that humans wrap around their hearts loosen under the magic of the night.

With a little push and a little proximity, those two would finally open their eyes.

And now, here it was, Christmas Eve, and did I have a plan? Well, no, not exactly. Plotting and scheming apparently were not my forte. I'd just have to stay on my toes and seize any opportunity that presented itself.

It was almost midnight, and the floor was quiet. A couple of hours earlier, we'd had one little boy come in. He'd gotten so excited about seeing if Santa had arrived that he tumbled down a flight of stairs while trying to peer through the banister at the tree. Jess had seen to him in the ER and recommended that he stay overnight. The boy and his mother had taken up temporary residence in the last room on the right. They'd leave in the morning in plenty of time for him to open his presents.

I'd peeked in on them, but they seemed to be doing well, so I continued my rounds. A ten-year-old girl with Norwalk virus was doing much better. Jess hoped she could go home in a couple of days. Her parents had promised to delay the family Christmas until she could be back with her brothers and sister, so she was sleeping soundly with a smile on her face.

I was about to check on a toddler with mumps when the phone rang down at the nurses' station. I popped back there to see if it was anything I needed to be concerned with. Polly hung up the phone and closed her eyes for a long moment before she turned to Connie.

"Three-year-old female on her way from the ER. Looks like an abuse case—cracked ribs, cuts, and contusions. Geoff is bringing her up now."

Connie shook her head. These were the hardest cases for the staff. Accidents and illnesses were bad enough when the young and vulnerable were the victims. But when they dealt with the aftermath of deliberate cruelty, even the most experienced had difficulty steeling themselves to professional objectivity.

"I'll put her in 312. Did Geoff say if anyone would be with her?"

Polly shook her head. "He said not. Dunno where the parents are, but she came in with only the paramedics in attendance."

"Helluva Christmas." Connie walked down the hall to collect her tiny patient at the elevators.

I decided I'd better stick close, even though the toddler would undoubtedly be drugged and sleep through the night. This might be one of the occasions when my skills were needed more for the staff than the patient. I took their emotional welfare very seriously, and it looked as if I might be working overtime tonight.

The elevator doors opened. Geoff pushed the gurney, with all its attached paraphernalia, out into the hall. The child lay so still and small on the mattress. I couldn't help gasping at the sight of her tiny face, bruises half hidden under stark, white bandages, an oxygen tube running into her nose and an IV going into her foot.

Connie drew a sharp breath before she steadied herself.

"Yeah, sucks big time," Geoff said. "Makes you want to throw her lousy parents into a pit of lions to see how they like being scared, defenceless, and at the mercy of things that want to rip them apart."

I ignored them, landed at the foot of the gurney, and carefully made my way along the child's body until I knelt at her head. I stroked her matted hair as I asked the Boss to keep an eye on her. I felt His peace descend on the child and me, and was reminded that she was in His hands. That didn't necessarily mean she would survive, but whatever happened, she would be lovingly cared for.

Geoff rolled the gurney into Room 312 and lined it up beside the hospital bed that Polly had prepared for its new occupant. With infinite care, he and Connie transferred the child as I scuttled to keep out of the way. Geoff patted Connie's arm and pushed the gurney ahead of him out the door.

"Well, little one, you're safe now. We'll do our best to make you all better." Connie unwound her stethoscope from around her neck and warmed it in her hand. She laid the chestpiece against the child's chest and listened. Then she inserted a thermometer into one ear to check the toddler's temperature. Satisfied, she picked up the chart that had come up from the ER along with the gurney and made some notations. Reading over the notes, she frowned, until she came to the end, and then she smiled. "You're one lucky little girl. You've got Dr. Jess looking after you. Trust me, she's the best. She'll have you singing and dancing before you know it."

"Singing and dancing?" The low, amused voice came from behind Connie, and she almost dropped the chart as she whirled around and saw Jess standing in the doorway. I couldn't help giggling at the chagrined look on Connie's face.

"Well, it's a figure of speech, of course." Connie tucked a lock of hair behind one ear and turned back to her patient. "I don't really expect her to foxtrot her way out of here."

Jess chuckled as she moved to the opposite side of the bed. "So, then you're saying I couldn't really teach someone to foxtrot?"

I sat on the pillow, arms wrapped around my knees as I watched. This was the first time in my two weeks of observation that they had been alone—or almost alone—together. Connie's blush was so cute, and the look on Jess' face indicated she thought it was pretty attractive too.

"I'm sure you could teach anyone anything if you really wanted to."

"Thanks for the vote of confidence." Jess' words were quiet and sincere.

C'mon, Connie. Look at her. Her heart is right there in her eyes. Look at the way she's looking at you.

But my shy nurse wouldn't meet the doctor's gaze as she fussed with the blanket.

Dagnab it! What the heck is it going to take here?

Jess visibly withdrew and became strictly businesslike. I groaned. Another missed opportunity.

"So, how is Miss Tamara Dawn Fraser doing?"

Connie responded to Dr. Jess' brusque tone by rattling off the child's stats.

Jess nodded. "I made some calls after she came in downstairs. Seems young Tammy here has seen more than her fair share of the city's ERs in her short life, though this is the first time she's been admitted to our facility."

Her features clouded over with the shadow of her legendary temper. Her jaw was rigid and her gaze stern. Jess was famous for not tolerating fools or anything or anyone who endangered her kids. I'd seen a former head of the hospital kicked off the floor when he'd had the temerity to suggest a less expensive course of treatment for one of her patients. Nurses and parents loved her for the way she championed the children, but administrators and incompetent interns lived in fear of crossing her.

"If I have my way, this will also be the *last* time Tammy ends up in any hospital."

Her gaze glued on Dr. Jess, Connie nodded. I could see her utter faith that Jess would make things right.

I rolled my eyes. "C'mon, you two, look at what's right in front of you." It was to no avail.

Connie raised the rails on Tammy's bed, flashed Jess a bashful smile, then took the chart and left the room.

The look of loneliness and despondency that settled over Jess' face as she leaned on the bed rails almost broke my heart.

All right, I'd had it! There comes a time when you have to set subtlety aside and take the bull by the horns. Anemone claims I wouldn't know subtlety if it bit me on the nose anyway, so it was time to go with my strengths.

With a quick check to ensure the child was sleeping soundly, I left Jess gently stroking Tammy's hair and flew down the hall to find Connie. She wasn't at the station with the other nurses, and I located her in the staff locker room, sitting on a bench, hands dangling between her knees, looking every bit as morose and isolated as the doctor I'd just left.

"God, why am I so stupid? All I have to do is ask her if she'd like to join me for coffee or something. Then we could talk and get to know each other a bit... Yeah, right. Like I could manage to string two words together when I'm around her. I'm such an idiot."

I listened to Connie castigate herself and suddenly was struck by a brilliant idea. But I'd have to work fast.

Rushing back to Tammy's room, I ran into Jess coming out the door. I mean, I literally ran into her, though she didn't feel a thing.

I, however, ended up on the linoleum, my head spinning from the impact. Groggy, I picked myself up and weaved my way after the doctor. I caught up with her at the station. Perched somewhat unsteadily on her shoulder, I whispered fervently in her ear and planted a suggestion.

For a moment I didn't think she was going to heed me—the more strong-minded a person, the harder it can be to get through to them. Finally, she shook her head, set down the chart she'd been reviewing, and headed down the hall to the staff locker room.

I gleefully flew ahead to ensure that Connie hadn't left. She was leaning against the front of her locker, her head resting on crossed arms.

When Jess entered the room, Connie straightened and pretended to be opening her locker, but I knew Jess had noted the melancholy posture.

I slipped behind the doctor and quietly closed and secured the door. That thing wasn't opening again until I said so. With a grin, I flew to the top of the lockers and settled in to watch.

"Connie? Are you all right?"

Dr. Jess' tone was warm, compassionate.

Connie flushed but didn't turn around. "Um, yes. There's no problem. It's just…well, seeing Tamara and all—you know. Thanks for asking, though."

She still didn't turn around.

Never taking her gaze off Connie, Jess took a seat on the bench. She took a deep breath, and I sensed that at the very least, my suggestion that Connie really needed a friend right now had taken root.

"I know. The abuse cases are the worst. But I promise that she's going to be all right. Would you like to talk about it? I'm a pretty good listener."

That finally got Connie to turn around, but her gaze darted nervously from Jess to the door, and I knew that she'd try to bolt. Fortunately, though she didn't know it, I had circumvented that option. I smiled smugly.

Connie edged around Jess and shook her head. "Um, no, thanks anyway, but I'd better get back to work."

Jess watched her go, shoulders slumped. When Connie couldn't open the door, Jess rose to help her.

Jess, too, was unable to open the door. "What the…?"

I think I mentioned that I can't do big miracles, but little stuff like sealing a door shut is a piece of cake.

Connie hammered on the door, but the staff locker room was quite a distance from the nurses' station and none of the duty staff heard her.

Jess tried, with a similar lack of success. Finally both of them stepped back and looked at one another. Jess shrugged. "I think we're stuck in here until someone realizes that we're missing and comes looking."

Hmmm. That prospect didn't seem to upset the good doctor too much. Interesting…

Connie nodded and took a seat at one end of the long bench that bisected the rows of lockers. Jess settled at the other end and fiddled with her stethoscope. Each kept glancing at the other.

I blew out an exasperated sigh. Apparently, I was going to have to do something more drastic.

"Pretty weird about the door, isn't it? I never even knew it could lock."

Connie flashed a look at the door and frowned. "It doesn't have a lock."

"Mmmm?"

"It doesn't have a lock. Look at it."

Jess glanced over too. "Huh, you're right. Maybe the wood swelled up and made it stick."

"Could be." Connie was quiet for a long moment. "Why did you close the door when you came in?"

Startled, Jess studied the door. "But I didn't close it. I just wanted to see if you were okay."

Enough with the stupid door already. Get to the good stuff.

Exasperated, I leaned forward on the top of the lockers. I glared at them and vowed never to tread on Naida's turf again. It was a lot easier comforting distressed patients and their families than trying to work romantic miracles.

They lapsed into silence again, and I heaved a sigh. At this rate, my brilliant plan was going to come to naught. I blamed them entirely, because the plan itself was good…excellent actually, if I did say so myself. The magic of Christmas Eve, enforced togetherness and solitude, unspoken love burning hot and deep within their hearts… Honestly, what more could they ask for? They should be making out like love-starved teenagers by now.

Maybe I had to rethink my calculations.

I leaned back on my hands and stared at the ceiling. Where had I gone wrong? Would it be a little obvious if I conjured up some soft music and candlelight? Maybe a nice Cabernet Sauvignon… Not that I know a good wine from a sour glass of milk, but I once overheard an orderly recommend that when his buddy was planning a seduction. I guess providing a chaise lounge for them to recline on together might be going a bit overboard.

I sat up, prepared to work a little more magic, when Jess stood and went to her own locker. I couldn't see what she extracted, but she put something in her pocket and crossed to Connie's end of the bench. Straddling the bench and sitting about two feet away, she took out a candy cane and offered it to Connie.

"We could be in here for quite a while. I wouldn't want you to starve to death."

Connie accepted the candy and waggled it with a smile. "Your secret vice?"

Jess chuckled. "Well, I keep them for the kids, but I'll admit to having a sweet tooth myself."

"I know what you mean. Having a bakery in the basement hasn't helped my hips any." She peeled the cellophane off the peppermint stick.

Jess' gaze was glued to the way Connie's tongue slowly followed the curve of the candy cane.

Hah! This matchmaking gig wasn't so hard after all.

Jess swallowed hard and peeled her own candy. "I don't know, your hips look pretty darn fine to me."

All motion stopped as they just stared at one another.

I'm not sure who looked more startled: Jess, for having blurted out her observation; or Connie, for confirmation that the longtime object of her affections actually thought about such things. I hugged myself in delight.

"Um, I mean…I didn't mean…"

I'd never seen Jess so flustered. Oddly, it seemed to give Connie confidence, and she grinned.

"It's okay, Doc. It's not like I'm going to slap you with a sexual harassment suit."

Jess' face was fiery red. "That's a relief. I mean, I wouldn't ever want you to think... Not that I don't think you're... Oh shit..."

Connie and I laughed together.

"It's okay, Jess."

Connie sucked in a deep breath, and I knew this was the turning point...if she didn't back off first. I rocked back and forth, whispering encouragement. "Tell her, Connie. C'mon, this is what you've dreamed of. You know she feels the same way, but it's up to you to tell her. You can do it. I believe in you."

"I was wondering..."

Connie stopped, and so did my heart, just for a second.

Jess drew a bit closer. "You were wondering?"

Connie tilted her chin. "I was wondering if you might like to get some breakfast with me after our shift is over; that is, if you don't have any other plans."

Wow! I should've brought sunglasses with me. Jess' smile just about blinded me.

"I'd love to. I can't think of a better way to celebrate Christmas than to start it with you."

Okay, now it was a toss-up as to whose smile was brighter.

"There's probably not many places open on Christmas morning, but I make a mean Denver omelet and my apartment isn't too far from here."

Yes! I am *so* good at this matchmaking stuff. I must have a natural and heretofore undiscovered gift for it. Naida better watch out, or she's gonna lose her position to yours truly.

Thrilled, I watched Jess reach for Connie's hand. Oooh, looks like it was confession time 'round these parts.

"Your apartment sounds perfect." Jess delicately traced the palm of Connie's hand, while Connie stared, mesmerized. "I've been hoping... I mean, I've wanted to ask you out for a long time. Connie..."

Connie took a deep breath. "I think you're pretty special too. And I'm very glad that the stupid door got stuck."

Jess caressed Connie's face, as she closed her eyes and leaned into the touch. Two candy canes tumbled to the floor as the pair focused on something far sweeter.

I held my breath, and when Jess leaned in and softly touched her lips to Connie's, I hollered, "Yes!" and pumped my fist in the air.

"Flea, what have you done?"

I squawked and would've fallen off the top of the lockers, except that Anemone's arm caught me around the waist. I'd been so wrapped up in the love blooming in front of my eyes that I hadn't even noticed she had materialized behind me. Keeping her arm in place, she settled by my side, dangling her legs over the edge of the lockers, and looked at me.

"You haven't answered me. What exactly is going on here?"

I glanced down at the women who were now blissfully locked in a passionate embrace. Gee, it looked to me like it was pretty apparent what was going on, but judging from Anemone's stern expression, I suspected any smart-assery would not be well received.

"These two happened to get locked in here, and well, one thing led to another—"

"They 'happened' to get locked in here? That door has an enchantment on it that I could see from five floors up."

Nuts. I'd forgotten how sensitive Anemone is to the ethereal traces that magic always emits.

"Really? Huh. Wonder how that happened."

"Fleeeeeeaaaaa."

Well, as I learned long ago, when you're caught dead to rights, it's best just to 'fess up and take the consequences. I unsealed the door, and it swung open, startling the women who had been giddily lost in each other's arms.

They drew apart a little, and Jess slid her hands slowly down Connie's arms. Hands clasped, they sat for a long moment with wondering smiles, flushed faces, lips still parted, and eyes shining.

Without looking away, Connie murmured, "The door's open."

"Uh-huh." Jess' gaze was locked on Connie as if she might disappear.

"We should probably get back to work."

"Uh-huh."

I couldn't help it. I giggled. "Aren't they adorable?" Fearing that I'd sounded too unrepentant, I glanced out of the corner of my eye at my supervisor, but her stern expression had softened.

"I suppose they are."

I was grateful that she left anything else unsaid as we watched them finally rise to their feet. This was such a special moment. I had no idea if Jess and Connie would be a forever match, but the aura they were projecting right now was so powerful that it made me tingle from the top of my head right down to my toes.

Just before they reached the door, they paused. Jess drew Connie into her arms and buried her face in Connie's hair. "I can't seem to let you go."

Connie returned the hug just as fiercely, then pulled back enough to look at Jess' face. "Then don't."

Ah, there was that smile again. The joy between them was palpable, and I wriggled with delight. Whatever my interference might cost me, it would be worth it. As I watched them slowly release each other and walk out the door, hands touching and barely able to look away from each other, a happy tear trickled down my face...and was caught by a gentle finger.

Startled, I looked at Anemone.

She was gazing at me with an unusual intensity, her hand still touching my face.

I shivered, but it wasn't from fear of her disapproval.

"Nem?" My whisper was barely audible, but her wings seemed to quiver with the sound.

"What you did for them..." Her silvery voice was strangely hoarse. I stared, unable to say a word. "...it was beautiful.

They've been in love for so long, but just couldn't seem to take that first step. It was sad, really: so much happiness just one improbable kiss away...until you opened their eyes and hearts."

Somewhere in the back of my addled brain, I got the impression that there was a subtext to her words, but in the inexplicable desertion of my usual eloquence, I just gulped and nodded. "I didn't think the Boss would mind."

That squeak was me?

Anemone smiled, surely the most beautiful smile ever seen in this world or the next. "The Boss is always happy when His creations find love. You know it was His greatest gift to us all."

Oh, Boss! She was going to kiss me! Ooooooohhhh...

Then I fell, toppling off the top of the lockers at the first exquisite touch of her lips. Quicker than my eye could see, Anemone swooped down to catch me.

She cradled me in her arms mere inches from the floor, and I stared at her in awe.

She smiled. "I hope you're not going to do that every time I kiss you, because I plan on doing it often."

And she was as good as her word.

It's a good thing Guardians are really, really long-lived, 'cause we sure had a lot of lost time to make up for.

"Merry Christmas, my Flea." Anemone's delicate kisses covered my face.

I sighed happily, quite content to spend the rest of my life right where I was.

"Merry Christmas, Nem."

Meet the Lesbians

ASHLEY STEVENS

I SOUND LIKE I HAVE a slow air leak with all the sighing I've been doing in the past three minutes. I stare at the cell phone in my palm, one finger hovering above the key pad, and just when I think I have this under control, that I'm finally ready to dial her number, I jerk my finger away. Sitting on the uncomfortable sofa Kendall bought with the larger-than-life pillows, I press the first two keys and then hit the 'end' button. I hang my head. Between my feet is a gigantic dust bunny that looks like it's having an easier day than me. An agitated sigh from across the room pulls my head back up.

Kendall stands in front of me, arms folded over her chest. "I honestly have no idea what is so hard about calling your parents." She huffs. Her face is serious as a damn heart attack, and suddenly, I feel guilty. Girls are kinda good at doing stuff like that, aren't they?

"You don't know what she…what they're like."

"She's your mother for crying out loud. Call her already!"

I toss the phone onto the coffee table and rub at my eyes like a sleepy child. "Kendall, you really don't understand. My family is a little, well, different."

"Oh, whatever!" Kendall throws her hands in the air and walks into the kitchen. Twin staccato pops and low hissing drift to my ears, and then she's back, shoving a beer in my face, the cold aluminum of the Pabst can rubbing against my nose. "Drink this, your testes will drop, and you will call her."

"Fine." I sigh—again—and take a deep drink from the can. I dial her number quickly. I can't help scowling at Kendall. I would pout, but that just isn't appropriate at this point in time. I'm not going to get my way anyhow. The phone rings one, two, three times. On the fourth ring, I say, "I don't think she's there."

"Then leave a voicemail," Kendall snaps.

"I will, I will." The ringing stops. I suck in a deep breath to leave a message when there comes the familiar cadence of my momma's voice. Sometimes that cadence makes my eye twitch. This is one of those times.

"Deacon! To what do I owe this surprise?"

My slow air leak becomes a full-on pressure release. "Hi, Momma."

"I've been waiting for you to call me."

"The phone works both ways, Ma."

"Smart-ass. Anyway, we really need to talk about the holidays. Your aunt Dinah and I were thinking—"

"Actually, that's what I'm calling you about," I say. "I have an idea."

"Do share, then!"

How pathetic it is that I'm hesitating, that I'm searching for the courage to spit out the words I've actually spent time rehearsing. "I was thinking I'd come back home the week of Christmas and leave on New Year's Day."

The line goes silent, and I think maybe we've been disconnected, but then I hear my mother's infectious giggle. "You want to stay here for two weeks? That's awesome! Oh, we are gonna have so much fun!"

"Wait, I'm not finished. I'm not the only one coming home. I met someone."

"You what?" She gasps. "That's wonderful! What's her name? Where did you two meet? Tell me everything about her!"

Her enthusiasm makes me chuckle. She's always been easily excitable, kinda like a Chihuahua. A Chihuahua hyped up on crack. "Her name is Kendall. We met at Starbucks, and I promise I will tell you every last detail when we get there."

"Are you going to fly? Do we need to meet you at the Atlanta airport?"

"No. We're going to drive from Arkham to Atlanta, straight through. It'll take a day and a half, maybe two."

"Well, I guess I'd better start getting the guest room ready. Oh, and I need to break out your baby book and the photo albums! How soon can we expect you?"

"You really don't need to do that," I say. "Kendall and I have our last exam tomorrow. I was thinking we'd start the drive as soon as we're done."

I can hear her clapping her hands as she relays the information to Aunt Dinah. "I can't believe you're going to be here so soon! We really have missed you, Deacon. Your brother just got here this morning. He's going to be thrilled to see you."

"I can't wait to see him either. Tell Cullen I'll be there soon."

"I promise I will." The line goes silent for a moment and then she says, "You won't get here soon enough, sweetie. I'm so happy to have a full house for Christmas."

"It'll be a blast, Momma. Well, I need to study for my exam, so I'll let you go."

"Yes, you do that. Good luck. I love you so much, and please let me know when you two hit the road."

"I will. I love you too. Bye." With that, I realize the easiest part of this whole ordeal is over.

Kendall is grinning like a fool. "So I'll get to meet your mother and her sister and your little brother? Awesome! Didn't I tell you it wouldn't be so bad?"

I cut her a sideways glance. "Aunt Dinah's not exactly my aunt." How am I going to explain this one? Is seeing it in action easier than me trying to tell her about it? How can I tell her my momma and my aunt Dinah are lesbians?

"Oh? So you mean she isn't like a blood relative. I used to call my godmother my aunt. Anyway, we should start packing now. We need to get the GPS ready to go. Maybe we should bring some snacks along, too. What about presents?"

Things are going so smoothly right now. Honestly, I'm waiting for the bottom to fall out. "We'll figure all that out. Are you sure you're okay with this?"

"Of course I am." She's already up, heading for the bedroom. "It's only right that I meet your family."

I follow her into the bedroom, where she's lugging two large suitcases out from under the bed. I take the blue one and open it on the bed.

"I don't know why you say your family's so different." Kendall folds a pair of pajamas and lays it in her suitcase. "You and your mother seemed to have a perfectly normal phone conversation."

Here we go with the sighing again. "That's just it. They aren't normal. Nothing about them is. The conversation we had today was a total fluke and probably due to the fact that she was so surprised by it."

"I don't believe you."

"You should," I mumble.

Kendall rolls her eyes. "We all have our little quirks. They make us interesting."

"My family has more quirks than anyone knows what to do with. Just please take my word for it. They all march to the beat of a different drum, and it's usually one no one else can hear. I don't want you to be surprised or insulted by them."

Kendall walks to my side of the bed. She wraps her arms around my neck and kisses my cheek. She's so warm, so soft. "I will love them just as I love you. So what if it takes some time to get used to them? It's worth it because you're worth it."

As we cross the Georgia border, Kendall finally says it: "Tell me about your family. You really haven't told me very much about them, well, other than the fact that they're different. I'd at least like a brief introduction."

That's kind of hard to do. It's not that I'm ashamed of my family. On the contrary, I'm really quite proud of them. It's their individual characters, however, that make me leery. And then when you put them all together, yeah, it's funny as hell, but only if you get the joke.

"Well," I say, "there's my brother, Cullen. His nickname is Tank. He's a hulking, meaty creature who was a middle linebacker on the high school football team all four years. His neck looks like a pork roast, and he can crack all four knuckles on one hand just by making a fist."

Kendall wrinkles her nose. "I dunno, Deke. He sounds a little scary to me."

"Funny thing is, he's a total teddy bear. He cries when he watches *Steel Magnolias*, helps turtles cross the street, and picks up every stray dog. No lie, Kendall, we had six dogs once when I was a kid. Momma wanted to strangle him. Now he's a chemistry major at Georgia State."

"Aw! So he's just a big ol' softie. I think I'd pay money to see a man cry watching *Steel Magnolias.* Now tell me about your aunt Dinah. The one who really isn't your aunt."

"Dinah is a…a…a longtime family friend. She was there for my momma after her second divorce. She just kinda became a permanent fixture after that. Dinah's really cool and really funny. She's so laid-back, she may as well lie down, except during college football season."

"Why's that? I don't get it."

"She paces the living room, screams at the TV when her team plays, and once she's had a beer or six, it loosens her tongue." Insert nervous laugh here.

She looks pensive for half a second and then asks, "What about your mother?"

Just thinking about her makes me smile. I shake my head and snicker. "My momma is a hot mess."

"You keep saying that but then never elaborate. By the way, I find it incredibly cute you still call her 'Momma.'"

Heat creeps up my neck. "My momma is a free spirit in every sense of the word. She does as she pleases, says what she thinks, and doesn't give a rat's ass what anyone else thinks of her. She cusses like a sailor. One summer, Cullen and I bought an air horn and spent our entire vacation censoring her."

Kendall gives a belly laugh. "That's hilarious! What else?"

"My momma has always been one of my closest friends. There isn't a single thing under the sun I can't go to her with. Just beware: she's got one helluva temper, so don't cross her."

"Duly noted."

"She's also the reason why I love music so much, mostly heavy metal. I went to my first concert with her. Someone knocked me down and stepped on me while they were moshing, so she got in the damn pit and beat the snot outta everyone in there. Came out without a scratch on her."

Kendall grins big. "They sound awesome, Deke. You should be so proud of them."

I slip my hand off the wheel and over hers. "I'm proud of you." Yeah, I'm a smooth operator. "By the way, I've been meaning to ask you this, but I keep forgetting. Do you like pets?"

"Sure, I do. I have a dog back home."

"I mean, like, nontraditional pets."

"Like ferrets?"

"Uh, kinda, yeah."

"Of course! There's nothing in this world like a pet. Why do you ask? What kind of fur baby does your mother have?"

I flick on the turn signal to get off at the next exit. The car needs gas, and I need to stretch my legs. "I think it's best if you wait and see for yourself."

"Will you at least tell me its name?"

"Sappho." I have to stifle a chuckle, wondering whether she'll make the connection between the poet of Lesbos and my lesbian mothers once she gets there. "Let's tank up and get some snacks. We only have an hour and a half left until we're there."

Kendall cocks an eyebrow. "Whatever you say, chief."

Our journey from Massachusetts to Georgia is almost over. Then Christmas break with my big, gay family will ensue. What can possibly go wrong?

Past the hideous stucco house on the right, down to the third house on the left with the red front door and the tacky Christmas decorations, there is my childhood home. Not a thing has changed. Still the same lights, which never blink in unison, strewn on the house in no particular order. Still the same plastic nativity scene with Joseph's face half singed off from Cullen attempting to replace the lightbulb. Still the same inflatable Santa Claus driving his reindeer-drawn sleigh—even though it looks like he's boning one of his reindeer.

Kendall chortles and points at the house as we approach it. "Now that, my friend, is a hot mess!"

I press my lips together, praying to God, Allah, Cthulhu, Shiva, and anyone else who can possibly hear me that this trip won't turn out to be a mistake. "That's where we're going," I say as we pull into the driveway.

A couple of forms stand at the picture window in the living room.

I put the car in park and kill the engine.

"I didn't mean…"

I hold up one finger. "No, it's okay. It looks like Christmas shat all over the front yard. I know. The inside isn't any better." I want to give her a quick kiss, but it's too late.

The familiar groan of the heavy front door fills the still winter air, and Cullen is running for the car. It doesn't matter if I get out now or stay inside; either way I'm screwed, so I open my door slowly, quietly.

Cullen grabs me by my waist and throws me over his shoulder. I close my eyes as he runs around the yard, my head bouncing limp as a ragdoll. Everyone is cackling, even Kendall.

When he finally puts me down, he gives me a hard punch in the chest. "I freakin' missed ya, man!"

My momma and Aunt Dinah each plant a kiss on my cheeks and hug me tightly. My momma's long, gray hair smells like patchouli.

"Hey, guys."

"It's so good to have you home." Momma smooshes my cheeks together, making my lips stick out like a fish's. She kisses me again. "We have missed you so much! You have to tell us all about school."

"Please," adds Aunt Dinah. "We all want to know what it's like living in Massachusetts. We've also had to listen to Cullen nonstop for two days and could really use a change of pace."

"It's true." Cullen grins, and it's that grin that has always inspired me to sleep with one eye open.

We all share a laugh; then I realize Kendall is standing half behind me, holding my hand. I pull her to my side. "I would like you all to meet Ms. Kendall Mannheim."

Without waiting for an invitation, my momma hugs Kendall. "It's good to have you here, Kendall. We've all been looking forward to meeting you. Let's take this party inside. I've got some goodies fresh from the oven."

We all traipse inside, Kendall and I bringing up the rear. She whispers to me, "She's sweet, and so is your aunt. I dunno why you said they're weird. If anyone is weird, it's your brother."

"You'll see. They slowly suck you into the insanity. Don't be fooled."

Cullen turns around. "Did you tell her about the pig?"

I sigh and roll my eyes as I shove Cullen through the front door.

"Pig? What pig?" Kendall asks.

"I think what my brother meant to ask was did I tell you about what a pig he is?" I say loudly enough for both Cullen and Kendall to hear as I shut the door.

As we make our way to the living room from the foyer, my momma flutters out of the kitchen with a heaping plate of Christmas cookies.

I hang back and take hold of her elbow. "I haven't told her," I whisper in her ear.

"Haven't told her what?" she asks at normal volume.

I shush her. "I haven't told Kendall you and Aunt Dinah are lesbians."

"Oh." She nods and then says, "Okay, I gotcha. You're going to, right?"

"Of course."

We enter the living room, where Kendall has already been recruited to help decorate the Christmas tree. Cullen is running his mouth nonstop about God only knows what.

"...so then I told the guy not to mix it together, but he did anyway. It was like a damn flash bang went off in the lab! Man, was our professor pissed!"

Aunt Dinah groans. "If I put duct tape over his mouth, is it still considered child abuse? He is an adult now."

"But wait! It gets better!" Cullen is about to jump out of his skin if he doesn't get a chance to finish his story about combustibles, but as soon as he sees the cookies, we all enter into a blissful state of quiet. He snatches one off the plate before my momma can even put it down.

"Judas, Cullen! I know you aren't starving. That spare tire around your waist tells me they feed you good at Georgia State, or at least The Varsity does." She puts the plate down, frowning. "Where's Sappho? Did someone leave her outside?"

Cullen rises from his place on the couch and tiptoes as quietly as he can to the backdoor.

I think now is the best time to tell Kendall about our nontraditional pet, but the sound of hooves scrambling against the hardwood floor tells me I missed my opportunity. A black potbelly pig wearing a sweater is standing in the doorway, snorting and wagging its curly little tail. Sappho, Momma's anniversary present from Aunt Dinah six years ago, walks up to me, begging for her ears to be rubbed.

I turn to introduce Kendall to Sappho, but in less than two seconds, things are going to hell in a handbasket.

"Holy crap! It's a pig!" Kendall shouts and then stares, eyes wide.

Sappho is excited about this new human. In fact, I don't think *excited* is the appropriate word. This little piggy is all fired up. Sappho lets out the snort to end all others, kicks up her heels, and runs full force at Kendall. Sappho isn't huge, but she's big enough—sixty pounds of pure pork chop, bacon, and fat back. With the gracefulness and glee of a ballet dancer, she leaps into the air and knocks Kendall backward. The wind is knocked out of her as she lands; the ornament in her hand rolls away under the couch.

And now Sappho is snuffling and snorting and licking my girlfriend. Seriously? On what planet does this happen? Who has a pig for a pet? My parents aren't different enough by being gay so they had to adopt a pig, too?

My momma wrestles Sappho off Kendall while Aunt Dinah helps her off the floor and onto the couch. She pulls an ottoman from its hiding place and props Kendall's feet up. Then my jackass brother says, "Is it safe to laugh yet?"

I glare at him so hard that if looks could kill, Satan would have risen from the depths of Tartarus and made Cullen spontaneously combust. "Are you all right?" I ask Kendall.

"Yeah, I think so." She gingerly rubs her belly where Sappho's front hooves connected. "Is she like that with everyone?"

I watch as my momma continues in vain to restrain the pig. "No. Apparently, she's got a thing for you."

Cullen cackles. "Who'd have thought the pig's a lesbian, too?"

I throw the first thing I see, which happens to be a cookie, and then get scolded for all the crumbs.

But that pig is a smart one. She knows my momma is distracted. Sappho twists a few times and then is free from my momma's grasp. She comes barreling toward Kendall again but slows down once she gets to the couch. The next thing I know, Sappho is sitting on the couch, worming her way between Kendall and me, all while getting her fair share of piggy sugar.

"I have no idea what came over her," my momma says, shaking her head. "I was just waiting for her to start humping your leg."

Aunt Dinah has gone back to unpacking and hanging ornaments. It seems the excitement of the pig attack is dying down.

Carefully, I sweep cookie crumbs into my hand and let Sappho lick them off while Kendall scratches her ears.

Cullen ignores us all, shirking his decorating responsibilities so that he can stare vacantly at the television. He's watching *The Nightmare Before Christmas* for the millionth time with his mouth hanging wide open.

"Oh, would you look at this!" Aunt Dinah sighs wistfully to my momma. "It's our first Christmas ornament."

I don't even have to see it to know what she's talking about. It's in the shape of a heart. The front is like a mirror so that they will always see themselves reflected as the years pass. Etched on the front of the glass is one simple word: Always. As a boy, I liked to play with that ornament in particular.

My momma stands next to Aunt Dinah with a grin. "I still remember when you gave it to me, every single second. You had me stand underneath the mistletoe Cullen nailed on the door frame. You had me close my eyes. Then, when I opened them, you were holding it at your heart. Then we—"

"Who wants coffee?" I ask a little too loudly because what happened next was a total make-out fest and I don't want that to be disclosed. "Can't have cookies without coffee. Why don't y'all come help me? I don't know how to use your coffeepot."

My momma and Aunt Dinah look at me as if I've lost what few marbles I may have had to begin with.

I raise my eyebrows, hoping that they'll figure out I mean business. They're slow to follow, but eventually, we're all in the safety of the kitchen. My momma starts the pot of coffee while Aunt Dinah gets all the mugs. Me, I'm pacing.

Aunt Dinah hands me the sugar bowl. "Is there something wrong with you?"

"Apparently, Kendall doesn't know we're lesbians," my momma says.

"That seems like a key piece of information to leave out."

I rub my eyes until they hurt. "I know that. It's just I wanted to ease her into the idea. You guys know how hard it has been for me to have girlfriends stick around in the past. All I'm asking for is just a little bit of time to explain it to her. I figure, now that she's here, it's gonna be kind of hard for her to back out, you know?"

Cullen pops his head into the kitchen. "Can I help with the coffee?"

I know my brother far too well. "Let me guess. You just shoved three or four cookies in your mouth, and now it's dry as hell and you need something to drink. You aren't really back here to help."

"How'd you know that?" He straightens up as he walks into the kitchen.

"You have crumbs all over your face and down your shirt. Anyway, could you not make any more lesbian references? Please?"

He cocks an eyebrow. "Why?"

"Because I haven't told Kendall that Momma and Aunt Dinah are gay."

"Dude, not cool. You really should've told her that."

"Oh, shut the hell up!" I get Cullen in a headlock. I raise my knee to get him in the groin or stomach—whichever I can get before he beats my ass—but then the sting of the dreaded flyswatter licks my cheek. My momma has used it on us since we were kids. If we were naughty and she couldn't reach us, the flyswatter always could, perfect for getting at us in the backseat of the car.

"Both of you shut the hell up!" Momma roars.

Cullen and I are immediately quiet. So is Aunt Dinah for some reason.

"Quit picking on your brother, Cullen. And, Deke, just tell the girl the truth. Ease her into it if you feel necessary, but don't drag it out. Now we're all going to go back out to the living room; we're going to drink coffee and eat Christmas cookies and decorate the tree, and we're going to have a damn good time. So get your shit together!"

Back in the living room, Sappho is sound asleep on the couch, but Kendall is buzzing around the tree. She offers us a smile. "I got the rest of the ornaments up. There aren't any more in the box. I really like the Bettie Page one."

My cheeks are on fire. I roll up the sleeves of my sweater, trying not to notice Bettie's bullet bra from around the pine needles. Who has scantily clad female figurines for Christmas ornaments? That's a rhetorical question, by the way.

I sit down and prepare my coffee. Kendall eventually joins me on the couch, but Sappho doesn't even stir.

Cullen claps his hands together and rubs them hard. "I think we should plug this baby in and see what these lights can do."

I stop in mid-sip. "You mean you didn't plug the lights in first to see if they work? Like before you put them on the tree?"

"Nope." Cullen grins. "Sure didn't."

Aunt Dinah sighs and shakes her head. "He said he had a better idea. He brought his own lights and this thing." She motions to what appears to be a homemade control box or panel box.

"I rigged them to do some really cool patterns and stuff."

My momma nods. "He said he had it under control, so I let him do it," she says around a mouthful of cookie. "It was one less thing I had to worry about. Hey, anyone want some whiskey in their coffee? I just realized I still have my flask in my pocket."

Kendall leans in close to me and whispers, "Your mother has her own flask?"

"Don't ask questions," I whisper back. "Just keep it moving."

Cullen clears his throat, commanding our attention as he stands next to the tree with the box in his hands. "Ladies and gents, I present to you the best Christmas tree ever!" He flicks a switch, turns a knob, and...nothing. We sit there in an awkward sort of silence, staring at the tree as if we're all missing something. He flicks the switch twice and then turns the knob, keeps turning it until it can go no farther.

The tree comes to life with multicolored lights doing amazing things. Squares popping up here, all sorts of vertical and horizontal lines. It's impressive—until Kendall put her nose in the air.

"What's that smell?" She sniffs again. "It smells like burning hair and cooked meat."

Lightbulbs explode all over the tree, sending tiny fragments of glass to the floor. Deep within the tree, the first white-hot sparks of an electrical fire glimmer.

"Fire!" I shout. "Someone get some water!" I push Kendall behind me and run to the tree. What the hell am I going to do? Put it out with my bare hands? Not knowing what else to do, I stick my hand inside my shirtsleeve and start hitting the burning branch.

Something leaps from the tree and onto the floor.

Kendall and Aunt Dinah squeal.

The fire is starting to spread higher, catching the skirt of the angel tree topper. My momma and Cullen emerge from the kitchen with pitchers of water to douse the flame. They heave their pitchers at the tree. Water drenches the tree and everything around it, even the back of the wall. All we can do is stare dumbfounded at the tree.

"What the hell was that?" my momma shrieks. "And why does it smell like shit in here?"

Sappho is standing over something, nosing it around.

Cullen uses one foot to push her away and then bends down to get a better look. "Oh, sick!"

"What? What is it?" Momma asks.

"It's a squirrel that just rode the lightning." Cullen picks it up by the tail, holding it away from him.

Out of my own morbid curiosity, I go back to the tree, quickly unplug the strand of lights from the wall socket, and start pulling at the lights. There, securely attached to one strand, is yet another charred squirrel. Teeth marks cover the piece of plastic.

"Where did you get the tree at?" I ask. "Most places make sure their trees are free from critters."

My momma looks away. "Well, we didn't exactly buy it."

"What do you mean?"

"Trees are expensive, you know. So we just went for a ride one day, found this here tree, thought it looked nice, used the chainsaw, and brought it home."

I stand perfectly still, holding the strand of lights with the squirrel carcass dangling. "Where did you get it from? Please tell me you didn't steal it."

"Okay, we didn't steal it."

Aunt Dinah nods her head emphatically. "We're just borrowing it."

My eyeball is starting to twitch. Without another word, Cullen and I clean up the mess. We throw the squirrels into their mass grave (aka the garbage can) along with the blown lights and torched angel. No lights on the tree this year. Hell, we have only half a tree. I swear Murphy's Law is real.

My momma changes the channel to TBS. I overhear her telling Kendall how I tend to get my "panties in a wad very easily."

"We're in the same room. I can hear you fine." I take a deep breath, trying hard not to let my frustration show.

"I know you can, sweetie. I have no reason to say it behind your back." Her voice is sickeningly smug. She pats me on the back as she exits the room with Aunt Dinah on her heels.

With the stink of squirrel fritters still permeating the air, I excuse myself from the living room. Cullen and Kendall are completely engrossed in *A Christmas Story*. At this point, only one thing matters to me.

I've had to poop since we got here.

I take the stairs two at a time up to the guest bathroom, but I stop first to grab some reading material, *The Ape's Wife* by Caitlin R. Kiernan. Man, do I love that woman. With one Superman-style leap I'm in the bathroom, my pants are around my ankles, and I'm on the john. I've read six pages or so when someone starts banging on the door.

"Someone's in here," I call. "And will be for a while."

Kendall huffs on the other side of the door. "That's not good enough." She hisses like a big-ass, pissed-off anaconda. The doorknob jiggles and in she comes, her brow furrowed, lips pursed.

I, personally, am mortified. "Um, hi, Kendall. A little privacy, please?" Covering my lap with the book, I struggle to pull my pants up to my knees.

But she doesn't leave. Instead, she sits on the side of the bathtub and flushes the toilet. Her brow softens a little. "That was a courtesy flush."

I know I must be the color of a pickled beet. "Yeah, I figured. Can this wait just a few seconds?"

"I just saw something, and I'm not sure I understand it," she continues as if I hadn't spoken. "I'm hoping you can help me understand it, though."

"Can I please just finish pooping?"

"Why did I just find your mother and your aunt, who isn't really your aunt, making out in the pantry?"

She could have said she saw them kill Sappho and make pork ribs for dinner. She could have said she caught Cullen masturbating. Anything would have been better than that. I stammer; I stutter, and that only seems to piss her off more.

"Out with it, Deke! What the hell is going on?"

With a sigh, I give up on regaining my dignity. I let my pants fall back to my ankles. "Kendall, the reason my aunt Dinah isn't really my aunt is because she's my momma's partner. If they could get married in the state of Georgia, they would. I technically have two moms."

"So they're lesbians?"

"Yes."

Kendall's eyes narrow to tiny slits. I've seen that look before, and I know I'm screwed. "And you didn't think this was important enough to tell me? You thought it was okay to hide this? To keep a secret?"

"It's not what you think, Kendall. It's not like that at all."

But she's already heading out the door. She mumbles something as she stomps into our borrowed room and slams the door. She didn't bother to shut the bathroom door, though.

I scramble to finish my business and then fly downstairs. I find my momma and Aunt Dinah in the kitchen, talking softly.

"Have you two gone absolutely bat shit crazy?" Probably not the best way to start the conversation.

"Just calm down," Aunt Dinah says. "I know what this looks like."

"Yeah, it looks bad! Kendall won't even speak to me now. She's locked herself in our room."

"Honey, you have to understand. We spent so much of our lives in the closet before, we didn't think it would be a problem to go back in for a few minutes more."

My patience is wearing thin. What if this messes up any chance I'll ever have with Kendall? "Momma! You were playing tonsil hockey in a closet with food in it!"

"Well, at least we wouldn't starve," chimes Aunt Dinah from her place at the breakfast nook. She and my momma share a chuckle, but all I can do is roll my eyes.

"All I told you to do was to not act gay. Just to give me time to introduce the idea to Kendall and then I'd tell you when it was safe." As those words pass from my lips into the open air, I realize I have made a huge mistake. A hurtful mistake. An epic mistake. See, if Momma isn't happy, no one is happy. And I can tell by the look passing over her eyes that the excrement is about to hit the oscillating unit, if you catch my drift.

"Excuse me? Did you just say you want me and Dinah to not 'act gay'? You think this is an act? Like we can just turn it on and off as if it's something as inconsequential as a garden hose?" she asks me quietly. My momma is never quiet. This is very, very, very bad.

"Momma, that isn't how I meant it."

"Is that a fact, Deke? Because I get the feeling you might be just a little ashamed of us. Since we don't look like the cast of *It's a Wonderful Life*, you think you can't bring home a young lady who is important to you, who may even become part of our family. That's mighty shallow of you, boy. I thought we raised you better than that." Tears are welling up in her eyes. Her voice is beginning to crack and shake.

Aunt Dinah rushes to her side.

Now, I've seen my momma cry before, and I've even been the one to make her cry, but never over this. I can tell she's getting ready to let me have it again, but Aunt Dinah hushes her.

Hanging my head like a whipped puppy, I grab my coat and scuff out the backdoor. It's snowing now, pretty hard, too, by Georgia standards. Trudging out to the gazebo that will be surrounded by wisteria in the spring, I flop down in the big swing. I shove a hand in my jeans pocket. The little green box is still there, but I take it out and open it anyway. Nestled inside sits a brilliant pear-cut diamond for the woman I know I am meant to be with for the rest of my life. I brought her here to meet my family and so I could ask her to marry me in front of the three most important people in my life. Now everyone thinks I'm an asshole. I'm throwing myself a pity party now, and it's pretty damn pitiful.

"Whatcha got there?"

I jump at the sound of my momma's voice.

She's standing in front of me, wearing an old Slayer hoodie that was black once upon a time, and points to the box. "Is that what I think it is?"

"What do you think it is?" I ask as she sits next to me.

She leans in close and squeezes my knee. "Deacon, that is one beautiful ring. So, she's the one?"

"She's the one." I smile. "I never forgot what you told me about how you knew Aunt Dinah was the one. I kept that wedged in my brain. When Kendall came along, I just knew."

"And so it goes."

We sit quietly for several minutes, just watching the snow fall. I scoot closer to her after a while and wrap an arm around her shoulders. "Do you remember when I was a little kid and you gave me your 'super secret bestest piece of advice ever'? Do you remember what it was?"

"Always bring a towel?" she asks.

"No, but that was a good one."

"Hmmm. Was it always wear clean underwear just in case you wind up in the hospital and they have to cut your clothes off?"

I laugh out loud because she really did tell me that as a kid. "Not that one either. C'mon, Momma, think harder."

"Never mix food and sex. It's gross."

"No!" Now we're both laughing like fools. "You told me to never be afraid to apologize. So, I'm sorry for not telling Kendall the truth, and I'm sorry for expecting you and Aunt Dinah to be anyone but who you are."

"Oh, Deke," she whispers and kisses my cheek, "I'm sorry for snapping at you. I didn't understand the gravity of the situation. If you would have just told me what she meant to you and that you were bringing her here to..." She trails off, looking toward the backdoor.

Aunt Dinah, Cullen, and Kendall—all smiles—are heading straight for us.

My momma rises from her spot next to me. "Now's as good a time as any. Don't screw this up, Deke."

"Thanks, Momma." I chuckle. I stand, take Kendall's hand, and help her sit on the swing before sitting next to her.

Aunt Dinah has her arm around Momma's waist, and I realize she's wearing her ugly, bright orange University of Tennessee slippers, which makes me chuckle more. Cullen is holding Sappho, who is sporting a new sweater. A peace settles about me, and I know now is the time. But before I can speak, Aunt Dinah clears her throat.

"The house still smells really, really bad...and I think Miss Kendall would like to say something."

She actually looks like she's going to pop if she doesn't get it out. "Deke, I am so sorry. I overreacted." She takes my hand. "I don't care that you have two mothers—or a mother and an aunt who isn't really your aunt. That doesn't bother me one bit. I guess the part that upset me was that you felt the need to hide it. You know me better than that. You've been my best friend since the day you forgot your name when you introduced yourself to me."

"Dude, you really forgot your name?" Cullen asks.

My momma rolls her eyes. "You've got more game than that, Deke. Hell, Dinah has more game than that."

"It worked on you, didn't it?" Aunt Dinah retorts.

From the look in my momma's eyes, she's preparing her rebuttal, but, surprisingly, she keeps it to herself.

Kendall is about to continue, but she's said enough in my book. It's my turn, and I'm not going to screw this up. "I owe you and everyone here an apology. I wanted everything to be perfect. Dating has always sucked for me. Let's face it; I'm kinda awkward anyway. Then when it's time to bring someone home to meet the moms, well, you can imagine how well that has gone over before. But with you...it's...it's different."

"What do you mean?" Kendall asks, her head tilted to one side.

I give a quick glance at my momma, who looks back at me with a bright, approving smile.

"It's different because I can't imagine ever being without you. It's different because I want my family to love you the way I do and I want you to love them the way I do. I was so worried you'd think they were too weird or something." Without another word, I slide off the swing onto one knee. I open the ring box with shaky hands and let the words fall. "So, in front of the three most important people in my life and our family pig, Kendall Mannheim, will you marry me?"

Kendall's hands fly to her mouth, her eyes wide. Aunt Dinah and Cullen gasp. I can hear my blood roaring in my ears, my heart throwing itself all over my ribcage. Her silence is starting to worry me a little bit. Her eyes are growing glassy with tears. "Yes, Deacon! A thousand times, yes!"

I grin like a fool as I slip the ring on her finger. I look into her eyes, and my own tears streak down my cheeks.

She wraps her arms around my neck and cries into my shirt. When she pulls away, she plants a perfect, passionate kiss square on my lips.

"Lordy Jesus!" Cullen shouts, sounding like a southern belle drag queen. "We're gonna have ourselves a weddin'!"

"I think Sappho should be the ring bearer." Kendall sniffles and then laughs. "Just tie a little pillow to her back with the rings attached."

We all laugh and then decide to go inside when Cullen makes the observation that Sappho's ears are freezing cold. As we file inside, my momma and Kendall hang back for a moment, whispering on the porch. Eventually, they both come inside. My momma takes my face in her hands and kisses my forehead before disappearing into the warm glow of the living room. Kendall is right behind her, and she does the same thing.

"What were you two being all secretive about?" I ask.

"Your momma just wanted to make something perfectly clear to me."

I can't help my knee jerk reaction—the feeling of gut-wrenching doom. "What?"

Kendall wraps her arms around my waist and nuzzles my neck. "She said that she and Dinah are thrilled to have another child, especially a girl."

And even with the odors of fried woodland creature and Douglas fir hanging thickly in the air, even with the sounds of piggy snorts and Cullen's incessant yapping, even with my momma's flask, Aunt Dinah's ugly slippers, and their inability to keep their hands to themselves, I know this is my home and these loveable goons are my family.

Operation Jingle Bells

DEVIN SUMARNO

SUSAN SMILED AND HELD THE door open for her wife, who entered with her arms loaded with grocery bags. "Wow, that was quick."

Donna returned the smile. "I thought so myself. The store was actually quite empty for the day after Christmas."

"Morning, Mommy." Abby gave her mother a quick kiss on the cheek as she entered, carrying a small paper bag.

One hand on her pregnant belly, Susan ran the other over their daughter's blond hair. It was fairer than her own, and not as thick as Seth's. Today it was done up in a complicated French braid that was pinned up in a bun. Not a classical ballet bun, as Abby had explained to her once, but close enough.

"Lewis' work?" Susan asked. Neither Seth nor his partner, Julius, had mentioned that Lewis would be staying with them for the holidays, even though he was Seth's best friend, but it was obvious that it was the former dancer that had done Abby's hair.

Donna glanced up from the multiple packages of pasta she was unpacking. "Lewis slept over at the dads' house last night."

She subtly shook her head, and Susan took that as a signal to not ask any more questions. The crease between Susan's eyebrows remained, but she nodded a slight acknowledgement.

"And how's your head doing, love?" Susan asked softly, brushing her fingers over Abby's cheek.

"Better," Abby said. "Daddy stroked my head for a whole hour before bedtime last night. How's your head doing, Mommy?"

Susan shrugged. "Could be worse." She had been pain free when she woke up, but her neck was feeling a little stiff now. "What was Christmas dinner like at Grandma McKenzie's? Was she upset that you spent lunchtime with my parents?"

Abby climbed onto one of the stools beside the breakfast island. "Of course she was upset. And dinner was like always. Lots of talking about the company, about how Dad should persuade Uncle Alexander to join in, since it's a family business. Grandma went on and on about how brothers should be able to sort their problems out, and how she couldn't understand that they had fought over a guy like Daddy. She said that Dad could always go back to Lailani.

"That annoyed Dad so much, he even spoke up for Uncle Alexander. He asked Grandma what job she thought an architect could do in a toy company. And then there were more embarrassing stories about their childhood days together, and eventually they started yelling at each other again."

Abby took a bunch of grapes from a bowl on the counter and popped one into her mouth. "Dad told Grandma that I had a migraine and that we couldn't stay for long, but my guess is that he just didn't want to leave Daddy alone with Lewis for too long. We went home right after dinner, then Daddy and Lewis watched *Treasure Planet* with me."

Stowing eggs in the fridge, Donna urged, "Tell her what Grandma McKenzie got you for Christmas, Abby."

Abby grunted. "You don't wanna know."

One of Susan's neat eyebrows arched up. "Is it that bad?"

The girl made a face. "A riding hat and a trial lesson."

"Oh well. You know, she always wanted to have a little princess that she could pamper with dresses and doll houses and fancy hair styles and so on."

Donna said, "Hey, she's already got Alexander—"

"Donna!" Susan cautioned, smiling to soften the implied rebuke.

"Come on, Alexander uses more hair care products in one month than I buy in a year for all three of us."

Susan slapped her on the shoulder. "Let his hair be. He had a difficult upbringing."

Donna bit her lips. "Yeah. Prince Charming in the Tower of Brood."

Susan slapped her again, but had to grin herself. She turned to Abby. "Was Uncle Alexander there, too?"

Intent on the grape she was rolling around on the counter, Abby shook her head. "No. Dad said he had to work. That's why Lewis slept over at our place."

Susan caught another of Donna's glances and closed her mouth, biting her lip to keep from asking her next question. Her eyes widened as she watched Donna pull bottles of liqueur, wine, and spirits out of her bags and line them up on the counter. "Holy crap! Did you rob the liquor store? What's with all the alcohol?"

"Well, the fathers of our children, and all their friends, are coming here after two days of oh-so-happy holiday visits with their families." Donna gave her wife a pointed look. "I thought we might all need—"

"Can I go and search for the Twister mat?" Abby interrupted. "Lewis promised he would play with me."

"Sure, hon." Susan kissed the crown of her head and sent her off with a pat on the back. She waited until she heard the door of the attic close before turning to Donna. "So, what the heck is going on?"

Donna flinched as she turned a bottle of whiskey in her hands. "Nothing, really."

Susan sat on the stool that Abby had vacated. "You know something. Don't tell me otherwise."

Donna bit her lip and sighed. "Alexander called me."

"Again?"

"Yup."

"When?"

"Christmas Eve." Donna hesitated for a moment. "At my parents' house. When I was washing dishes."

"Oh." Susan knew full well they had gone for dinner with Donna's parents, but she didn't recall hearing anything about a phone call from Alexander. "Why didn't you tell me?"

"Because he asked me not to."

A frown appeared on Susan's face. That was something new. Donna and the rather restrained Alexander had taken a liking to each other, and during the last months they'd grown close. The number of calls between them had become more frequent over the last few weeks as Alexander's relationship with Lewis had become more complicated. But he'd never before asked Donna to be secretive about their talks. Susan didn't know whether to be worried or cross.

"Um, okay." She blew out a deep breath. "And...why did he call?"

"Actually, I don't know."

Susan raised an eyebrow. "You don't know?"

"He didn't want to talk about whatever was on his mind."

"Huh? He called you just to tell you that he didn't want to talk?"

"Uhm, yeah. Kinda. Sounds quite ridiculous when you say it out loud, but that was actually the gist of his call."

"You were in the kitchen for an hour and a half, on Christmas Eve."

"Yeah. There was a lot of sighing going on. Very *manly* sighing, of course. And I really did do the dishes, too." Donna sighed and wiped her face. "What I *did* find out is that there was some kind of an incident, and that Lewis isn't doing well. I think he was refusing to eat, at least Alexander said something about Lewis losing weight again. So Alexander brought him over to Seth's because he thinks himself incapable of helping him. At least that's what I think happened."

Susan studied Donna's face. "So," she closed her eyes, "we have no idea if Alexander and Lewis are coming tonight?"

"Uhm, correct."

"We don't even know if they're still a couple."

"Correct."

"We know that Alexander brought Lewis over to the dads' for the night."

"Correct."

"Again."

"Yeah."

"We know that Julius expected Alexander to be at their mom's last night for dinner, and Alexander didn't show up."

"Right."

"And we know that Alexander doesn't want to talk."

"Yup."

"Is he sure he doesn't want to talk about whatever the damn problem is?"

"I guess."

"Okay." Susan raised a hand. She had confirmed that she'd understood correctly, but none of it made any sense to her. "Just wanted to make sure I have it right. So, should we be planning to do something to help them sort things out? Get them an appointment for couples therapy, maybe? Or just lock Alexander up in the attic with Lewis and *make* them talk. In the event that they come, that is."

Donna sat down on a stool opposite Susan. "I wouldn't have a clue how to help them. I mean, Alexander wasn't even able to tell me what this is about, so… Hell, why do gay guys always have to be so complicated? And why do we only have gay friends?" She hid her face in her hands with a groan. "Maybe there would be less drama for us to sort out if they were all heterosexuals. Or women."

"Probably. But hey, Lailani is coming, too. She's a woman, and she's hetero. At least I hope so for Rupert's sake, since they're together. See, there aren't only gay guys on our list."

"Uhm, yeah. But she is Julius' ex-wife and Rupert is her husband. What I was actually referring to was us inviting other lesbians."

"We do have lesbian friends," Susan contradicted. "They're just part of happy families, so they're not likely to want to come to an anti-family Christmas party."

"I was talking about real friends, honey, not the strange couple we met on the ferry."

"Well, I guess the answer is because we're too busy with work to make friends of our own. When we moved here, it was just easier to adopt Seth's friends. That saved a lot of time. After all, I killed three birds with one stone—earning money while working with Seth in the pediatric ward, making friends with him, *and* finding a future father for our children."

Donna smiled at Susan. "Maybe we should put that on our list of resolutions for next year."

"Make new friends? Are you so unhappy with the ones we have?"

"You mean our bunch of gay perverts, who frequent a gay BDSM club and whip the skin off each other's backs every Thursday and Saturday? No, they're great. If they aren't yelling at each other, making big deals out of *not* talking about their problems, stressing the fact that they can't speak about their feelings, or otherwise behaving like infants, they're totally great."

"Are they really that bad? Is this only about Alexander, or is there something more bothering you?"

Donna sighed. "I guess the last couple of weeks have just been too much for me. The projects at work… Planning that damn charity ball alone took twice the time my boss had allowed. Then all the guys' private dramas." She shook her head. "I don't get why it's always me who has to deal with the little disasters."

She shrugged and fumbled the grocery list out of her pocket. "It started with Eric's move to Ridley. I understand, that Eric is asthmatic and allergic to everything that isn't made of plastic and food that has been genetically enhanced, but he and his boyfriend together can't even carry a stupid washing machine. Yeah, I understand that they are computer freaks and way too nerdy to eat on a regular basis, but hell, it was a washing machine, not an airbus. And why the hell is it me who always has to help out? Look at the McKenzies. Julius is what—six feet seven? And he constantly needs to rest with his broken heart syndrome. By the way—broken heart syndrome? Seriously? He can't even have a proper heart attack, like a real man. No, Julius McKenzie gets an old ladies' heart issue because his brother was angry with him. And yeah, there is Alexander, who is even taller, but can't help either, because of his back."

"He's soon turning fifty. It's not that easy for a man his age to haul heavy appliances up the stairs, you know."

"Amen to that! And who else? Seth is too fragile. And we won't even start talking about Lewis, who is fit, but in a non-muscular way."

"Or Phineas."

Donna threw up her hands. "Oh God. Yeah. Phileas. He's sweet, he really is, and I'm very happy that Bruce found someone, but hell, Phileas doesn't even reach my nipple line, not even when he's standing on his tippies."

"Phineas," Susan corrected, watching Donna's hands fiddle with the grocery list.

"Huh?"

"The boy's name is Phi*n*eas."

Donna looked up at her wife. "It is?"

"Yes."

"Since when?"

"Since *birth*, I'd guess," Susan said with a wry grin.

"Really?"

"Yes."

Donna smiled. "Well... How lucky I called instead of sending the invitations via e-mail. That would have been embarrassing."

"You mean just because you've seen him once a month for, what? Four years?"

"Well, to me he's just 'the boy.'"

"He's not a boy," Susan objected. "He's twenty-something."

"Yeah, that makes him twenty-something years younger than Bruce. Besides, you called Lewis 'the boy' for over eight years."

"Because Alexander calls Lewis that."

"You were the first one to call him that."

Susan shot her wife a puzzled look. She thought hard for a moment, then her mouth crinkled into a grin. "So I did. Let's get back to the subject at hand, should we?"

"I don't even remember what the subject was."

"Your rant about our family of friends not moving a washing machine."

"Oh yes, thanks." Donna took a deep breath. "Well, as I see it, Owen and Bruce are the only two guys in that bunch who wouldn't first gather the others for a counsel, and then get lost in drawing an info graphic on the three ultimate ways how to carry a washer upstairs. They both would just do it. But unfortunately Owen was posing half naked on a beach in Brazil at the time, and Bruce is in a wheelchair. So, if we should ever be planning to move, we really need some more lesbian friends—there'd be less talking, more working." She ran her hands through her hair. "Actually, I was talking about taking time to make friends. Or taking time to do *anything*, together."

Susan studied the look of uncertainty on Donna's face, and she knew what was about to come when Donna raised the paper in her hand.

"Well, can I…go through the list of the preparations for tonight with you?"

Susan rolled her eyes, but smiled as she took the list and pen from Donna's hand. "Would I ever say no to you? Ready when you are." She looked at her as if waiting for dictation.

Donna closed her eyes. "Okay. Picking up Abby and groceries are done. I called my boss, took my cousin's birthday gift to the post office, got Abby's pills from the pharmacy, and helped Bruce fix the sink. Huh… I've got the feeling that I have forgotten something important."

"Darling, you always have the feeling that you forgot something important." Susan crossed out each of the completed tasks on the paper. "It's a symptom of your control freakiness."

"You can't blame me, it's an occupational disease," Donna argued, and then went on going through the list in her head. "I'll have to check my e-mails to see if the dessert bowls I ordered for the New Year's dinner have arrived. Then I'll clean the bathrooms and mop the floors. You think just cleaning the kitchen and living room will be enough? They won't go upstairs, will they? Oh, and I need to iron the tablecloth."

Susan grimaced. "Honey, you know that this evening is supposed to be all about us not stressing ourselves out, remember? Besides, you just did the bathrooms last weekend. These are our friends. No one will mind if they can't see their reflection in the faucet."

"Do you think, I don't see what you're up to?" Donna grinned and lightly tapped the tip of Susan's nose. "You just want to have me sitting on the couch and watching *Sherlock* with you."

"You caught me." Susan smiled and shrugged. "It's just that over the last couple of weeks, you were everywhere but here, and next there will be the New Year's event at the music hall that you have to put the finishing touches on. It's just... I miss you. I'd like to spend a little alone time with you, before..." She patted her round belly.

"But I really need to wipe the—"

"Donna!"

Donna eyed her for a moment, then capitulated with a smile. She reached for Susan's hand and intertwined their fingers. She sighed dramatically. "Okay, no bathrooms. But... at least let me finish the list. Please?"

Susan rolled her eyes, but nodded. "That's fair."

Donna smiled as she took a deep breath to enumerate the last few points.

"Sooo. Owen will be here about four to make the dessert. Cream and eggs are here, the rest he'll bring himself. Lailani and Rupert will arrive at five, as will Bruce and Phineas. That reminds me, we need to get the ramp out." Switching gears, Donna gestured toward the pile of packages of pasta she'd bought. "You think that will be enough?"

"We could feed a whole football team and all their cheerleaders, and still have leftovers to pack doggy bags for everyone who is coming."

Donna winced at the reminder that she had probably bought enough food and drink for an army. "Yeah, I know. It's just that a pasta buffet seems a little lame to me. I mean, I set up events in five star hotels. Shouldn't I have come up with something fancier than pasta for Christmas?"

"Donna, take a deep breath. Christmas is over. We are just going to have a nice evening with our friends—no traditions, no pressure, no perfection. Just having some fun and relaxing with people who really care about each other. It was your idea. So, relax. Maybe it's 'just pasta' to you, but we all agreed on it, and we have two brilliant hobby cooks coming as well as a former professional confectioner. Everything will be all right. Okay?"

Donna's gaze shifted from Susan's face to the completed chores on the list between them, then back again. "Okay," she finally agreed. "But I'm positive I have forgotten something important."

"If it's really something important, it will come back to you soon enough. But now—you, me, sofa, and Sherlock!"

"God, Bruce, that smells delicious. What are you making?"

Donna was back in the kitchen after having helped Susan serve drinks to Lailani, Owen, and Seymour in the living room, and Rupert and Phineas at the dining table, playing Jenga with Abby.

Bruce smiled and shrugged. "My own creation, and Phineas' favorite pasta sauce. It's quite simple. Just white wine, cream, and pears. I'm guessing you'd like a bite?" He took a spoon from the silverware drawer and rolled his wheelchair back a bit so Donna could get closer to the stove.

She dipped her spoon into the sauce, blew on the bubbling concoction, and then took a small taste. She closed her eyes as she savored the treat, then she reached out blindly and squeezed his shoulder.

"This is *so* good. Thank you for making this."

"The least I could do." Bruce helped himself to a spoonful of Lailani's peanut butter sauce, which was in a pan on the other hotplate. He looked at the open kitchen door, then said quietly, "So, how's Susan? Don't take this the wrong way, but…she doesn't look too good."

Donna threw a glance at the door. She heard Lailani laughing and glasses clinking. "The…baby is fine. It's just that the last two days have been exhausting."

"Your parents?" Bruce studied her face.

Donna nodded. "Susan and I actually ended up having an argument about whose parents are worse."

"Oh? Sounds thrilling. Who won?"

"We couldn't decide. But I still think mine are the clear winners. Susan thinks her parents win because they kinda called me slut, in front of my daughter. And I couldn't defend myself, not at their table." She bit her lip. "I guess I didn't say anything because I think they're right. I mean…they did catch me flirting with a waitress at the charity ball. I had no clue they'd be there, but that's really no excuse. That makes me a slut, doesn't it? But Susan says that's something between her and me, that it's not her parents' business. And it's not like I've ever been welcome in their home. They just finally had a reason to express their dislike for me out loud."

"Sounds like an amazing evening." Bruce switched off the hotplate and then turned back to Donna. "So, what did your parents do to top being humiliated in front of one's child between entrée and dessert?"

Donna snorted. "Well, I can't really put my finger on it. It wasn't really anything they said. It was…subtle. My sister and her husband were there, too, with my nephews. Guess what my parents got them as present. A complete Playmobil knight's castle. And guess what they had for Abby. A pair of gloves and a book. Some story about a speaking dog." She flung her hands in the air, then dropped them in defeat. "It's not about the presents. We all know that Abby has everything she could ever want, and then some. It's not about the book, but they practically treated their granddaughter as bastard child. They didn't even bother to ask what Abby might like. Besides, real grandparents would know. Hell, Abbys is twelve, and even you know that she doesn't read animal stories anymore."

Bruce nodded and shared a sad smile with her. "I'm sorry to hear that. Hope Abby is okay."

"I'm not sure. I guess she was probably disappointed, but she didn't let it show." She sighed. "But what about you? I'm guessing your Christmas wasn't any better."

"Actually, it started out not too badly. I was drinking egg punch with Phineas' mother and watching *Some Like It Hot*. But when I was tipsy and encouraged enough to dare, I called my mother. Talked to her for not even two minutes. 'Everybody is fine. She is fine. Father is fine. Sister is fine. Nephew is fine. Thank you for your call. Hear you next year.' She didn't even ask how Phineas is doing."

"Shit." Donna frowned and bit her lip, then she took a deep breath, straightened her shoulders, and turned to the cupboard for some glasses. "Bruce, darling, you know what?" She grabbed the bottle of wine he had used in the pasta sauce, and poured them each a glass. "Christmas is over, and we survived another year. Tonight it's less family and more of *this*. Cheers!"

Someone knocked at the door at the same moment the phone rang. Donna set her wineglass down on the coffee table and leaned back to look out the window, trying to peek around the corner of the house. She didn't see a car.

"Wouldn't it be easier if you just went to the door?" Susan grinned. "I'll answer the phone."

Donna wrinkled her nose at her wife, but got up from the sofa and stepped over some extended legs on her way to the front door. As she neared the Jenga players at the dining table, she saw that Phineas' chair was blocking her way. When he didn't notice her, she cleared her throat.

"Oh, sorry. Am I...? Yeah, um...sorry." He flushed and shifted his chair aside, bumping against the table. "Oh shit!"

Phineas flung his hands forward to catch the tower of wooden Jenga bricks that was swaying dangerously, but he grabbed thin air. The tower toppled, some bricks flying over the edge of the table, and one of them tipping Rupert's glass. The white wine splashed onto the table cloth, then missed Rupert's leg by an inch as it formed into a puddle on the floorboards.

"Oh God. Shit! I'm sorry." Phineas jumped up and leaned over the table, trying to catch the rolling glass, but the sudden jolt moved it even closer to the edge. Before it could fall to the ground Rupert caught it with his left hand. "Shit! Oh, I didn't mean to curse." He flushed bright pink, then hid his face behind his hand. "Sorry."

"Phineas?" Bruce's voice from the kitchen held a hint of alarm. "You okay?"

"We're all right. Everything's under control," Rupert called back, reaching for a paper napkin from the holder on the table.

Donna squeezed Phineas' shoulder reassuringly and gently pushed him back onto his seat. "Don't worry. Abby's heard worse language." She chuckled. "I'll fetch you a cloth. Just let me open the front door first."

Still grinning, Donna opened the front door and found Alexander, a bag filled with presents in each hand.

"Hey, merry after-Christmas!" Bags and all, he held his arms open for a hug.

Donna accepted the embrace, patting his back. "Good to see you. Come in."

Alexander followed her in, placed his bags on the sideboard, and shrugged out of his cashmere coat.

"Would you mind hanging that up yourself? I need to get Phineas a cloth."

Alexander threw a glance through the open living room door. When he saw Phineas kneeling with a paper napkin in hand, a broad grin settled on his face. "That's funny. No matter what kind of party I attend—Phineas is always on his knees."

"We're lucky, this time it's not raspberry juice on a white carpet," Donna whispered.

"Well…I wasn't exactly talking about his penchant for spilling drinks, but rather for his talent for certain other… activities." He hung his coat on the rack. "But hey, the evening is far from over, hmm?" He winked at her.

Donna rolled her eyes, but winked back as she took the cloth Owen handed her from the kitchen doorway, a pastry tube in his other hand. She handed the cloth to Phineas as she passed through the dining room, and then proceeded into the living room.

Alexander picked up his bags of gifts and followed her. "Good evening, everybody." He waved at the group in general and carefully stepped around Bruce's boyfriend, a lascivious grin still on his face. "Merry Christmas, Abby." He crouched down to give her a proper hug. "How's your head doing?"

Donna smiled at seeing Alexander's tenderness with his niece. She helped herself to one of Owen's petit-fours from the tray on the coffee table. "Honey, who's on the phone," she hissed softly.

"Our stepson," Susan said as she put the phone down. "Eric wanted to let us know that he'll be late. He and Ridley are still at the office, fixing some bugs in the level design. Apparently their boss just told them that the new level has to go online next week."

"The game with the little chocolate bars trying to survive the school yard? Cool." Donna licked molten chocolate from her fingers. "Did they say how late they'll be?"

"He said we shouldn't wait dinner, but he'll be furious if they arrive and we've already exchanged presents."

Donna shrugged, emptied her glass, and took another chocolate. "Shouldn't be a problem. We saved our holiday gift exchanging for this evening. An hour more or less doesn't make a difference."

"Is Eric your stepson, too?" Seymour asked softly, from the arm chair in the corner of the living room.

Susan smiled at his confusion. "I guess so. He's Julius' son, and we're the mothers of Julius' other children. Well, Abby is, of course, but soon to be plural." She patted her belly.

"Seymour might have a point," Donna mused. "Since neither of us is, or has been married to Julius."

Alexander chuckled. "So by your reckoning, Seth is Julius' partner, so he is Eric's stepmother?"

"Um..." Lailani cleared her throat. "I still insist on being Julius' only wife, so how about calling Seth Eric's stepfather?"

"But isn't Rupert his stepfather, since he *is* married to Lailani?" Susan protested.

Rupert chimed in from the dining table, "I don't mind sharing. It's fine with me if Eric has two stepfathers."

"But we're the mothers of his half-sister. Doesn't that make us his stepmothers?" Susan leaned back on the sofa and took a sip of her tea.

Alexander stood close to the coffee table. "Logically, that should make you his half-mothers. But we could simply decide that Eric is too old for having stepparents. I mean... he's just two years younger than Seth, so..."

Donna raised an eyebrow at Alexander. "Do I hear a note of..." She decided that she shouldn't suggest "jealousy" as she had intended, so she substituted, "...a note of disapproval in your voice?"

"Out of my mouth? Concerning my brother? Never!" He hefted his bags of presents. "Um, shall I put these under the tree?" He nodded at the empty space under the fir and gestured towards the bags of gifts that already sat next to the tree.

"Oh, right. Geez, I even forgot to bring down the presents. I don't know whether I'm coming or going these days." Donna sighed. "Yes, why don't you start? Maybe we should sort them into piles by name?"

Alexander looked around at the eight people who were already present. "Sounds reasonable."

"Abby, wanna help me?" Donna stood and held a hand out to her daughter.

"Shall I lend you a hand, too?" Phineas rose from his knees and hung the cloth over the back of his chair.

Alarm bells jangled in Donna's head, but she didn't let her anxiety show. "Sure. Can't do any harm."

Followed by Abby and Phineas, she went to the upstairs wardrobe and took out the presents that she and Susan had wrapped in blue and silver striped paper. She handed Abby the watch for Julius, the perfume for Seth, and the audio books for Lewis. She took the headphones for Eric, the old school Game Boy for Ridley, Owen's book, and the spoon lures for Rupert. That left concert tickets, massage gift cards, and dive vouchers, as well as the leather bag for Alexander for Phineas to carry.

Donna knew that giving the unbreakable to Phineas was a good idea when he missed the last step and stumbled forward, almost dropping his parcels. He recovered his balance just in time.

"Got 'em!" he called out. "Everything's fine."

Donna bit her lip to repress a comment, but she saw Bruce's half curious, half worried glance into the hall.

In the living room, she knelt down next to Alexander and ordered her packages around the tree, then took the others from Phineas and Abby. She rechecked to see that everything was in place, then she helped Alexander with ordering his gifts as well.

Taking the last box out of his bag, he looked at Donna, his brow wrinkled. "Uhm..." He glanced pointedly at Susan, who was chatting and laughing with Lailani and Seymour on the sofa. "We seem to be a present short."

Donna stared at him, glanced at Susan and then back at Alexander. She felt herself go pale.

"Is...something amiss?" Alexander asked softly.

She got up and fled into the kitchen.

Alexander was after her in no time, carefully closing the door behind him. Bruce and Owen turned from the stove in alarm.

"Donna? What's wrong?"

"I forgot." She exhaled. "I forgot to order it."

Bruce threw Alexander a questioning look, but he just shrugged.

"Donna?"

She didn't seem to hear. She rested her elbows onto the counter and hid her face in her hands. "I did it at the office. I remember typing down the email address. I wanted the package delivered to the office, but then A…a customer called, and I forgot to send the order."

"What are we talking about?" Owen asked.

"Susan's Christmas gift," Alexander supplied.

Donna mumbled into her hands.

Bruce looked over at her. "Oh shit. What was it?"

"A calendar," Donna groaned out between her fingers.

There was silence for a moment before Owen said, "Couldn't we get a different calendar? If we hurry, we could make it to a store before closing."

Shaking her head, Donna still didn't look up. "It was a limited edition. Handcrafted. The photos are of untouched landscapes around the world. The sheets come in single printings, in an art folder made of laid paper. You won't get something like that downtown."

The doorbell rang, but not even that made Donna react.

Abby called from the hallway, "I'll get it." A moment later there was the sound of the door opening, followed by Julius' voice.

The quartet in the kitchen fell silent. They didn't want to draw attention to the kitchen.

When they heard the sound of footsteps going towards the living room, Bruce sighed in relief. "So, we need a last minute gift," he summed up. "Is there something we can buy online? A music download? Netflix subscription?"

"How about a gift card?" Owen suggested.

Donna snorted and shook her head. "Susan says only strangers resort to gift cards as presents."

"How about a trip for the two of you?" Bruce offered.

"And when could that happen? When Abby leaves for college?"

"Maybe just a weekend?" Owen mused. "Before Susan…" He didn't finish.

Donna shrugged, her face resigned. "I guess I'm just gonna have to tell her that she will get her gift next week. If it's still in stock." Her shoulders sagged.

Bruce put a comforting hand on her arm. "Maybe you could say that the delivery took longer than anticipated. After all, it was holidays."

She looked at him with a sad smile. "No. I know you mean well, but I shouldn't lie to her. I just have to admit that I fucked up. Again."

After another long silence, Alexander approached her, phone in hand. "Donna?" His voice was soft. "It's this one, isn't it?"

Donna turned to him, and he held his smart phone in front of her.

"This was the link you sent me a couple of weeks ago, asking my opinion? I'm sorry I never answered."

She nodded.

"It's handcrafted, you say?"

Donna nodded again, and he nodded as well.

"Huh."

She tried to read his suddenly furrowed brow. "Huh what?"

Alexander handed the phone to Bruce. "What do you think?"

He raised an eyebrow. "Um…what do you mean, what do I think. What do I think about what?"

"Actually, it's simple. I mean…it's made by hand. So…"

Bruce's eyes suddenly widened in realization. "Are we talking about…? Huh. I'm not sure if we can manage that in what…two hours?"

Donna looked from Alexander to Bruce to Owen and then back. "Excuse me, but what are you talking about?"

Alexander smiled at her. "Saving your ass, the way you save ours all the time." He turned back to Bruce with a shrug. "It's worth a try, isn't it?"

Bruce studied his face for a moment, then turned back to the smart phone. "But we don't have the photos. If you copy them from the preview, they would be too small to print in poster size. Not to mention that it would be illegal."

"When something is handcrafted, a company will usually offer options for personalizing the product. Donna could say that they had a B-version or that she called and requested something special, or something like that."

"So, you're thinking of using your own pictures? That could work. But you can't just copy some pics from photo stocks, either. Chances are that Susan would stumble over them at some point."

"Exclusive shots." Owen fell into their musings. "In other words—private material." He peered over Bruce's shoulder at the display and reached out to browse through the preview of the calendar that Donna had meant to order. "That shouldn't be a problem. I know more photographers than I have friends, and these are just trees and deserts and rocks. Instagram could do the rest to get that artsy look."

Alexander nodded—seemingly more to himself than to anyone else—and drew pad and pen out of his inside pocket. "Okay, let's get started. We should assign the tasks. Owen will get us the content. Eric and Ridley can do the design." He scribbled down some notes.

"If I can get my assistant on the phone, I'll ask her if she can get us an art display folder like this," Bruce said, tapping the picture on the phone. "She's in contact with several galleries. Maybe she can organize something. But I'll need to know the size of the printings. And we would need someone to drive to the museum and pick up the folder."

Alexander nodded. "Do you happen to have a printing press at the museum that can print high quality photos in such formats?"

Bruce shook his head. "Not really. We commission a printer for everything that's larger than a simple eight by ten info advert. And I'm sure they're closed for the night anyway."

"Okay. We need to think of something. And we need a delivery boy, too." Alexander sighed. "Donna, is there much of that paper left that you used to wrap your other presents?"

"Um…I'm not sure. And we keep the wrapping paper in the cabinet in the living room, so I can't check on how much we have without making Susan suspicious."

"That should be the least of our problems." Alexander brushed his hand through his hair as he thought. "Okay, priorities. I'll call Eric, and you…" he looked at Owen, "…get us the photos. Eric will need high resolution files. Bruce, you call Linda. Maybe she can put together samples of art display folders in different sizes, and we choose later. I'd like her to start right away, if she can. If we wait until we have the final sizes of the photos, it could be too late."

As Bruce and Owen nodded in agreement, Donna blinked and swallowed hard. "And what am I to do?"

"You just relax," Owen ordered as he hit the call button.

"But I'm the professional event manager. I should totally be doing all that myself," she objected.

"Relax! We mean it!" Bruce took a bottle of cream liquor from the counter and set a shot glass in front of her.

Donna caught herself staring blankly for the second time that evening. Her mouth open, she watched the three men take to their phones. Lacking anything else to keep herself occupied, she took a seat on one of the kitchen stools and poured herself a full double shot of Bailey's, as she had been ordered.

Alexander was the first to get someone to answer his phone. "Eric, it's me, Alexander. Where are you right now? … Oh, shit." He stepped to the window and looked out. "Drive on. Really, drive by and don't stop. I need you to turn around and get back to the office."

Donna thought she heard tires screeching.

"Jesus!" Alexander chuckled. "No. No zombie apocalypse but another kind of an emergency. Let me explain it to you…"

"Linda, I need your help," Bruce said, covering his other ear.

"Hi, Mitch. It's Owen Hall." Owen was in a corner of the kitchen, speaking into his phone. "Remember Cambodia last June? … Listen, this might seem a strange question, but do you happen to have shot any unpublished photos of the abandoned rice terraces?"

Sitting amidst the muted cacophony of the worst last minute plan she'd ever heard in her entire career, Donna downed the double shot and poured herself another. Just in case all this didn't work, she could always escape the "no gift" fallout by passing out. Now and then her mind registered snatches of the hasty calls surrounding her.

"Send them via express messenger. They can send the invoice to my private address."

"I'll take them all—every photo that has no people in it and screams out 'natural.'"

"Does your college happen to have a printing press? … No? Thank you anyway."

When the kitchen door suddenly swung open, there was instant silence as the men awkwardly hid their phones. Donna shook her head, actually surprised that nobody started whistling in feigned innocence.

It was Phineas, and Bruce was the first to exhale.

"The mob is growing hungry. I'm supposed to ask when we can start the buffet." He took a close look at the four occupants and frowned. "Um… What's going on in here?"

Alexander laid his hand on Phineas' shoulder and drew him closer. "Phineas, good that you're here." With a knowing smile, he looked down at the young man whose head didn't even reach to the middle of his chest. "Go, tell them, that the buffet will begin in a few minutes. Then fetch my brother and Seth—inconspicuously!—and come back here. We need your type."

"A blond?" Phineas asked, a curious look on his face.

"A bumbler."

Phineas brow was still furrowed as he was gently shoved out of the kitchen, but he didn't comment or ask questions.

"Julius, too?" Donna asked, her eyes wide.

A grim expression on his face, Alexander nodded. "Unfortunately, we need his type as well."

Bruce chuckled as he looked up at Alexander. "A well-built guy?"

Alexander shrugged. "An alpha."

"Okay, is everybody clear on what they're supposed to do?"

Donna studied the faces of the six conspirators gathered around her kitchen island like generals around the map of a combat area, all staring with more or less comprehension at Alexander's scribbled notes.

After a moment, Julius shook his head and crossed his arms over his broad chest. "No, I'm not clear. Not really."

His brother suppressed a sigh. "How come I knew that you would say that?"

Julius shrugged. "Maybe because your little plan isn't as 'Danny Ocean worthy' as you think."

Alexander straightened to his full height, towering over his brother. "Got a better idea?"

"Boys!" Donna interjected. "Could you save your pissing match over Seth for another holiday? You have work to do for me!"

"She's right," Bruce hurriedly agreed. "We all know and all agree. You, Alexander, lost, but you're absolutely entitled to be mad at your brother. You, Julius, didn't play fair and should still feel ashamed. But not tonight. And after all, Seth's virginity was lost years before either one of you knew him, so why still bother with claiming rights?"

"Excuse me!" Seth blurted, but his expression was more amused than indignant.

Bruce raised his hands in surrender. "No offense, just saying! We have important things to do, and we can't waste time talking through *that* same old issue between you two."

"They're right," Julius admitted.

Donna thought his tone was a bit grudging, as though he was reluctant not to press his "claim" on Seth, but she wisely stayed silent.

"Yes, they are," Alexander commented through gritted teeth. After another moment of staring Julius down, he took a deep breath. "So, would you like to ask a question, or make a suggestion?"

Instead of making another snarky comment, Julius took a deep breath and blew it out slowly. "Let me see if I have this clear. I drive to the printing office with the paper Donna will give me. There I will hopefully meet my son. It will look the least suspicious to Susan if I am the one to take care of that because I'm the one who's always on the go, and also because I have the connection to the printer. We will print the photos on the specialty paper in the poster-sized calendar design that Eric will bring along on a USB stick. Then I drive to the museum, where Linda is waiting for us in Bruce's office. We'll carefully tuck the calendar pages into one of the art display folders, ask Linda nicely if she can wrap it up for us in a feminine, artistic way, then drive back here. Before I come in, I call so you can create a rear diversion while we smuggle the gift under the tree. All this, totally unnoticed by the en—um…Susan. Does that about cover it?"

"Wasn't that difficult to understand after all, was it?" Alexander praised. "We'll start the buffet now, and all move over to the living room and have a bite. After twenty minutes or so, Bruce and I will retreat back here to base camp to work on the frame design." He looked at Phineas. "You and Seth make sure that Susan doesn't come into the kitchen while we're working. But first, you'll help Donna get that roll of paper. Gentlemen, boys, Donna," he tried to keep a serious look on his face, but couldn't suppress a grin, "Operation Jingle Bells has begun. Good luck!"

Donna took one last deep breath, then went into the dining room with a bowl of meat sauce. Seth followed her with another full of pasta, while Julius carried the plates.

"Dinner is ready!" Donna announced with a bright smile to the guests still in the living room, and then she rushed back into the kitchen to get another pot of sauce. When she returned, she watched from the corner of her eye as Julius went to Susan on the sofa, reached for her hand, and gently pulled her to her feet.

"Susan, dear, the security agency called," Julius said. "An alarm has gone off in the factory. I'm afraid I need to go down there and make sure everything's okay."

"Now?" Susan's mouth twitched, but she didn't look surprised.

"It shouldn't take too long. We had a false alarm only last week. Turned out to be a raccoon."

Susan sighed. "Well, okay. But drive carefully, will you?"

"Aye, captain." Julius nodded. "Oh, by the way, we forgot to bring Seth's migraine pills, and his head is killing him. Do you think you could give him one of yours?" Having set the stage for Seth's diversion, he went back to the kitchen.

Susan turned and studied Seth, who was about to sit down at the end of the dining table. "So, the stress of Christmas has gotten to you, too?" she said with a worried smile.

Seth shrugged. "Kinda. But no need to tell *you* about that, huh?"

Susan shook her head. "Do you need just regular painkillers, or the heavy duty stuff?"

For a moment, Seth hesitated, and Donna could see how he struggled not to turn to her for a clue. "Um…the heavy duty, please."

Donna cursed inwardly, knowing Susan kept her migraine pills in several spots all over the house, so that she didn't have to go upstairs in a case like this. She might not even have to leave the room, and there went the plan.

Rupert joined them at the table, and now looked at Seth with a sympathetic smile. "Migraine?"

Seth nodded, making an agonized face.

"We didn't know we both suffer from migraine attacks until Abby had her first one." Susan sighed and stroked her belly. "That's why we decided that Julius would be the biological dad in this round."

She went to the cabinet, opened a drawer, and pulled out a blister pack that she handed to Seth.

"Just stay. I'll get you some water." Susan smiled at him and then went towards the kitchen.

Seth turned to Donna, who could only stare back in alarm. Seth's head shot back around to Susan. When Phineas appeared in the kitchen doorway, balancing the last bowl of sauce in his hands, Seth nodded at him and tilted his head toward Susan, mouthing, "Stop her!"

Donna saw Phineas' expression turn from "How?" to "Oh, no!" in less than half a second as Susan reached the door.

Phineas closed his eyes, the mental sigh clearly visible on his face. With a turn of his hip, he stepped aside to let Susan pass, bumped his elbow on the door frame, jerked in sudden pain, and tumbled half a step forward—directly into Susan.

"I'm sorry," Phineas exhaled, a millisecond too early.

"Whoosh" went the cheese sauce as it flew from the now half-empty bowl.

"Huuuh," Susan heaved, as the warm, creamy mass splattered on her blouse.

Seth was the first to move. He was at her side in no time. "Whoa, Susan, you okay?" He grabbed a napkin from the table to mop at the dripping, then he took her hand. "Come, I'll help you wash that out." He gently drew her out of the room, towards the staircase.

The last thing Donna saw of them was Seth's hand waving behind Susan's back, gesturing for her to hurry up and retrieve the paper.

Rupert took a handful of napkins to help Phineas clean up the floor for the second time that evening; Lailani tried hard not to dissolve in laughter. Seymour looked up from the CD case he had been studying, and glanced from one to the other. He obviously had no idea what had been going on.

Donna pulled herself together and hurried to the cabinet. "Here, I have more napkins," she said, snatching them out of the cabinet along with the roll of silver and blue paper, and handing them to Rupert in passing. With the gift wrap pressed close against her, she rushed into the kitchen.

"Got it," she breathed as she handed the roll to Julius. "Your turn. By the way, Bruce, your boyfriend is a genius!"

Bruce wore a mix of pride and worry in the expression on his face. "Nobody's seriously hurt, right?"

Donna grinned and shook her head, while Julius slipped into his jacket and Alexander whipped out his phone with a smirk.

"Eric? Rudolph is ready for take-off. Talk to you soon."

Donna checked her watch. So far, the plan had worked well, with Bruce and Eric exchanging their data in a constant flow, and Alexander coordinating the moves of his chessmen throughout the city. But with every minute passing, she grew more nervous. When Alexander's phone rang, she jumped.

It was a brief call.

"The Three Kings of the East have arrived." He touched her shoulder. "It's time for the final strike. Ready when you are, Donna."

She took a deep breath. She wasn't sure what she felt more nervous about—that they had to smuggle a poster-sized calendar past Susan, or that Alexander had said he would improvise the diversionary maneuver. She went into the living room and stood close to her wife.

"Susan?" She smiled apologetically at Bruce, who had been engaging Susan in conversation to provide a distraction. "Sorry to interrupt, but could you come with me for a second?" She feigned a look of concern. "It's about Alexander."

"Oh God, what is it this time?" Susan said, alarmed, but she got up from the couch.

"I don't know. He said he wants to talk to you." Donna's lips twitched as she suppressed a tell-tale grin. "But he's making his sad face."

"The brood of doom?"

"No. It's more the 'my man pain has heartache' sort of face."

Susan couldn't make a remark about that, as they were at the kitchen door. Alexander sat hunched over the island, his shoulders sagging, his fingers playing absently with an empty glass.

Susan's annoyance instantly turned to worry. "Hey, what's going on here?"

Alexander made a show of lifting his head ever so slowly, but even Donna was taken aback when he looked up at them with reddened eyes. She wondered how he had accomplished that.

"Hey," he said softly. "There you are."

"Have you been crying?!" Susan moved close to him and laid her small hand on his. "What's wrong, huh?"

Donna moved to his other side, which put her next to the window. She could see Julius, Eric, and Ridley waiting by their cars. With a triumphant smile, Eric held up a large package. Donna nodded, which was the signal for Alexander.

"I'm..." Alexander's voice cracked.

"Is it about..." Susan nodded towards the living room, where Lewis had been talking to everybody except Alexander all evening.

"No." He shook his head, and tears spilled from his eyes. "Not at all. It's just, I'm..."

"Hey, we're back." Julius' voice came from the hall, as they had planned.

Before Susan could react, Alexander plunged forward and pulled Susan into a tight hug. "I'm just so happy for the four of you!" he burst out, crying shamelessly into Susan's hair. "I mean…I always wanted a family myself, and now I'll be the uncle of three. And this time I'll have the chance to be there right from the start. It's all so…overwhelming!"

Over his shoulder, Susan threw Donna her "What the heck!" look, but Donna just shrugged, gesturing Susan to hug Alexander back.

Susan closed her arms around him in a comforting embrace. "That's…nice," Susan soothed, her eyes shut tightly, patting his back while Alexander sobbed.

Per the plan, when Eric knocked on the kitchen door, Alexander released Susan.

"Hey there, we finally ma—" Eric looked at Susan's tear-stained blouse and Alexander's reddened eyes. "Oh, sorry, didn't mean to disturb." He raised a hand in apology.

Alexander straightened up. "Oh God, I'm sorry," he murmured. He cleared his throat and picked up the empty shot glass that was actually Donna's. "Cream liquor always makes me sentimental. I hope you don't mind too much." He took a deep breath and wiped his tears. "So, now that our company is finally complete, how about opening presents?"

Donna should have felt relieved when she entered the living room, but she was suddenly more nervous than she'd been the entire evening. Her heart raced when Susan positioned herself in front of the tree and cleared her throat loudly.

"Um, could I have everyone's attention for a moment?" Susan waited for the room to grow silent. "Before we start unwrapping gifts, Donna and I would like to make an announcement." She shifted from one foot to the other. Unsure of who she should look at, she turned to her wife.

Donna took Susan's hand and nodded encouragement.

She smiled gratefully and turned to their guests. "We know it's an anti-Christmas party, but since our little family is all here now and we all love surprise gifts, we thought there wouldn't be any better time to tell you." Susan sighed heavily, squeezed Donna's hand and laid her other hand on her stomach. "Julius, Seth, we're having twins."

Donna waded through the mountain of discarded wrapping paper, sparing a thought for the environment, then deciding that it was not an evening to feel guilty about not being green. After the first brief look of panic had faded from Julius' face, and the congratulations and cheers were finished, Phineas and Abby handed out the presents. Operation Jingle Bells had been a complete success. Susan was delighted by the custom-made calendar and had Julius hang it up the instant she had finished flipping through the pictures.

Now everybody was sitting around the dining room table—drinking, enjoying dessert, and talking. The ambience was as relaxed and warm and joyful as Donna had wished it would be. She sighed as she enjoyed the scene for a moment before she continued stuffing the wrapping paper into a plastic bag.

When two long legs appeared before her, she looked up at Alexander, who smiled as he crouched down beside her.

"Congrats, Donna." He nudged her arm with his elbow. He reached out and picked up a ball of crumpled paper. "Just between the two of us, it wasn't a customer's call that distracted you from ordering that calendar, was it?"

Donna froze, then took a deep breath. "No, it wasn't," she finally admitted.

Alexander nodded slowly, his gaze wandering over to Lewis, who was playing Twister with Abby, as he had promised. "I'm sorry I've caused you such stress," he said. "I really am."

"It's okay. I mean, it's not that you did it on purpose. It's just..." She shrugged.

"...too much," Alexander finished for her.

"Yes."

He nodded again, looked over his shoulder at the gathering around the table, and then reached into his pocket and drew out a square object. "This is for you." He handed her a small booklet with a blank cover. "The others helped me with it."

Donna studied his face for a moment before she took it from his hand and flipped it open. It was a pocket calendar with handwritten notations. Browsing through the pages, she found twelve more gifts.

January: Eric—fixing broken laptop.
February: Owen—spa weekend.
March: Lailani—shopping for children's room.

Alexander grinned. "We decided not to do a rushed photo shoot in the garage. You really need more lesbian friends. Especially given your news, I guess this will be more helpful. I'm Mr. April, by the way. I'll build that garden shed you asked me to help you with last spring."

Deeply touched, Donna looked at him with watery eyes. "This is so sweet of you." She sniffed back the tears. "Thanks. Really. Also for what you did today. That was award worthy."

"It was, wasn't it?"

"It was absolutely brilliant. Still...somehow, I still have a feeling that something is...missing. Huh. Well, never mind. Thank you. Again."

"No problem. It covers my 'making amends' resolution for next year. So, one thing sorted, I'll move on to the next. Excuse me?" He touched her arm, got to his feet, and slowly went over to the corner of the room, where Abby and Lewis were playing Twister.

"And?" Susan crawled onto the bed and let herself carefully drop on her side next to Donna. She sighed as she stretched. "Have you remembered whatever it was you thought you forgot?"

Donna bit her lip, then smiled and reached for Susan's hand. "Um…kinda."

"So, what was it?"

"Ummm… Telling you that you're the most fabulous wife of all."

"Oh. You haven't said that in a while. Regular adulation of my awesomeness should be put on your next list." Susan snickered. "But besides the fact that it's true, what makes you say that?"

"Many reasons." Donna grinned. "One is you convincing me a couple of years ago that it would be a good idea to adopt Seth's friends."

"Ha. Sounds like you think that the guys aren't that bad after all." An amused expression on her own face, Susan studied Donna's features. "So we strike 'making friends' from our to-do list for next year?"

Donna nodded. "Yeah, I guess. There won't be much time for that. We'll be too busy coordinating our twelve volunteer babysitters."

Susan smirked and cast a glance at the tiny calendar on the nightstand. "Oh yes, we'll make good use of them. After all, there will be enough babies for all of them. I mean… actually it's perfect that we're having twins. That way, each McKenzie can have his own baby."

Donna laughed. Sighing, she curled up against Susan. There was a long moment of silence before Susan broke it with a lengthy clearing of her throat.

"Um…Donna?" Susan squeezed her wife's hand. "Now that we're alone, I wanted to tell you something. I'm sure you've probably wondered about it already. Your present…

There...was a delay in the delivery. After all, it was the holidays. So...your present is still on its way. I hope you're not mad."

Donna stared into the dark for a long moment before she burst into laughter as the last tensions of the evening eased away. "Oh well." She giggled. "You know, there can only be one Operation Jingle Bells per Christmas."

Donna laughed as she imagined the confusion on Susan's face. She felt Susan shifting next to her, trying to see her expression so she could catch a clue.

"Um... Operation what? Is that the Bailey's talking? Did you even hear what I just said? I don't have your gift."

Donna took a deep breath to stifle her amusement and reached for Susan. She pulled her closer and placed a kiss on Susan's temple. "Never mind, honey. When my gift arrives, I'll tell you the whole story."

One Hot Tamale

CATHERINE LANE

THE NARROW, SMALL SERRANO CHILE is almost pure heat. Chefs and other people in the know place this chile at the top of the Scoville scale. Near the bottom, on the other hand, is the Anaheim chile. Often called simply the plain green chile, it is also long and thin, but this chile brings very little heat to a dish. The green chile is used primarily to impart the subtle and traditional flavors from south of the border. But when mixed, watch out, because just the right balance of these two chiles can lead to...One Hot Tamale

Colorful fruits and vegetables in overflowing containers lined the sidewalk. Vendors in singsong voices offered free samples. The warm Southern Californian sunlight shone through the organic honey display on the first table, casting a magical, golden glow on the whole scene. The farmers' market sprang up in the hospital parking lot every Thursday like a dance scene from *Brigadoon*, and this particular Thursday, everyone who entered smiled a little deeper and stepped a little lighter—everyone except the woman who stood at the entrance under the hospital's banner: *Healthy Eating—Good Food, Good Choices.*

Marisol closed her honey-brown eyes and sighed deeply. She ran a hand through silky dark hair and willed her foot to take a step into the line of stalls. Ordinarily, a trip to the farmers' market in the middle of December was a time of joy. Buying all the ingredients for the Christmas tamales rang in the holiday with both bells and whistles. But this year was different. Horribly different. She would go home with all the fresh ingredients spilling out of the basket on her arm to an empty house and putter about her kitchen, soaking the corn husks and stirring the chicken broth into the masa harina all by herself.

Never before had she made the tamales alone. In years long past, her grandmother had steadied her hand as she, a little girl in long braids, added the masa flour slowly and carefully to the base mixture. Then her mother had ushered in a whole new modern era with the Tex-Mex spicy avocado cream addition. Legend had it that her mother had dreamed up the concoction as she stared at the avocado soap dispenser while she washed the Thanksgiving dishes. By December 25, almost like a Christmas miracle, the delectable spicy and creamy sauce made its successful debut.

This year should have seen Marisol and her girls building the tamales in their own kitchen, as the women of her family had for years. But her ex, Carrie, had ruined the tamale tradition, among other things, when, the day before Valentine's Day, she admitted to Marisol that she had slept with another teacher—who was married, no less—at her school.

"I think I'm in love," she had opened the conversation as they strolled around their funky Topanga neighborhood. For a brief moment, Marisol had thought it was the start of a fun new game to usher in the holiday, but her smile had fallen as soon as she saw the hard look on Carrie's face. The full conversation that followed had frozen her heart, and now, nine months later, a tamale party for one was not going to thaw it.

"Hey, beautiful." The fishmonger who set up his coolers right by the honey stand winked at Marisol. She had bought a salmon fillet from him once, and since then he had always greeted her the same way. She smiled wanly. There was no real sentiment in the compliment. She had heard him greet every woman from six to sixty that way, and the creepy breathiness of the way he drew out the "ful" at the end of the word finally drove her into the market.

The chile and pepper kiosk, her destination, lay smack in the middle of the market, a terrible spot between the artisan-roasted nuts and the perfumed soaps. Even so, it was always packed. Today in the crowd, a man with the light blue scrubs of a surgical nurse stood over the poblanos, inspecting each one carefully.

"Hey, Carlos," Marisol said.

Carlos raised a hand to wave happily at Marisol as she approached. His scrubs, a size too small, stretched over his chest, revealing rippling muscles underneath. He claimed that he just took whatever the laundry gave him, but Marisol had many times seen him riffle through the piles of clean scrubs to find the size he wanted. The other male nurses made fun of him, but Carlos had immediately taken her side in the break-up. He could go around in a jockstrap if he wanted to, as far as Marisol was concerned.

"Oh hi, Mari! What are you doing here? I thought this was your day off." He leaned in for a hug, smelling deliciously of Obsession for Men.

"It is, but I'm making tamales this weekend for the girls. So I came for the ingredients."

"A tamale party? That's wonderful. Are they coming over?"

"No, it's just me. Things are crazy. The girls have finals and a softball tournament, and my schedule here at the hospital is all over the place. But there's one night somewhere in all of that mess where the girls and I can have dinner before they leave for Hawaii. I thought I would do one Christmassy thing, and we'd eat tamales."

Marisol shrugged. For the most part she was writing Christmas off this year. She had already signed up to work on Christmas Day, telling everyone that the overtime was great. Frankly, with the girls on their beach vacation with Carrie and Mrs. Homewrecker, who conveniently owned a condo on the Big Island, there was no real point to celebrate. Her cousin who lived in the Bay area had invited her up, Carlos and Mark too, but she didn't want to throw gloom over the holiday for anyone. The hospital would be the best place for her.

"What are you getting?" She forced herself to focus on Carlos and not the empty days ahead.

He held up a dark green pointy poblano. "Mark said he wanted chile rellenos this weekend, all Bobby Flay style, with the cornmeal crust and the goat cheese."

Marisol raised an eyebrow.

"I know. What can I say? I love him." He dropped two perfect chiles into a plastic bag with an exaggerated wave of his hand. "Don't tell my mother."

His gaze drifted over her head, and then his eyes went wide, very wide. "Oh my God." He silently mouthed the words. Pushing Marisol aside, he stepped into the path of a tall woman with pretty almond-shaped eyes and black hair styled in a spiked pixie cut.

"You're ... you're that woman on the cooking show contest." Carlos bounced up and down on his toes. "You won the whole thing with the cod and coconut broth dish, right?"

"Yes," the woman said. "It's a curse to be known for your food rather than your name. Jenny Kwon."

"I'm Carlos. Mari, did you see that episode? Oh my goodness, the colors in that bowl. It was like a piece of art."

Marisol nodded. She had seen every episode, in fact, of that season. The woman standing beside her looked better than she had on the show. On TV she raced around a hot kitchen and even hotter personalities. It had been barely controlled chaos. Here she stepped with purpose; her motions were quick and energetic, her face radiated calm. Not classically attractive, but everything about her screamed confidence. That was better than pretty, in Marisol's book. She met the woman's gaze for a moment, and then let her eyes drop. Jenny's scrutiny, too open and too inviting, bored into her, probing places that had been very cold for a long time.

Carlos looked from one woman to the other. He tipped his head for a moment and ran a darting tongue over his lips. Then a sparkle lit his dark eyes. "Jenny, this is Marisol. Marisol, this is Jenny."

"Nice to meet you." She fixed Marisol with another lingering look and waved her hand in the direction of the chile and pepper stand. "What do you know about these?"

Marisol couldn't immediately find an answer. People these days only looked at her as a nurse or a mother. Jenny peered at her like she was an attractive woman. She didn't quite know how to answer.

"Oh my God. Marisol is a wonderful cook. Ask her anything."

"Stop it. Jenny's a professional."

"Don't let a win by one vote fool you. I actually know very little about Mexican cuisine." Marisol again said nothing. "I came over to see if there were any Thai chiles. It's not the season, but you never know. Of course, now I don't see any, so I guess I'll just stand here like an idiot."

Carlos reached out his foot and kicked Marisol into a response.

"The Thai chile is spicy, right?"

"Yeah."

"Then the serrano could be close." Marisol pointed to the narrow red chiles in the basket closest to them. "It's spicy and hot, but it also has real pepper flavor, not just heat."

"Then it's made for me." Jenny reached up for one of the thin plastic bags that hung on the crossbars of the kiosk roof. She wrapped it around her hand like a glove, and then took another. She grabbed a couple of the serrano chiles and stuffed them inside the second bag. "What are you getting?"

Carlos struck through the opening like a viper. "Mari's getting green chiles. She's making green chile and cheese tamales for Christmas. It's a Mexican tradition. You haven't lived until you've had her tamales."

This time Marisol kicked Carlos—harder and on the shin. "Ouch. Seriously. She's embarrassed, but it's true."

"I'd love to taste them," Jenny said simply. Again she cast that open and inviting look at Marisol, who had no idea how to interpret this statement. Was she serious? Was she just aggressively dedicated to bettering her craft as a chef? Or was flirting with anyone she met on the street just her way? How was anyone supposed to navigate these waters? She had been out of this game way too long.

"You can." Again Carlos jumped right in. "She's making them this weekend."

"Carlos!"

"Thursday is her day off." He rushed the words out before anyone could stop him. "We'll meet back here next Thursday at, let's say, the same time. Noon?"

"Carlos, I'm sure she's too busy to come back next week." She marveled that she wasn't blushing, but the coldness, Carrie's parting gift, still circled in her chest.

"No, it's okay. My uncle has a standing appointment here. I brought him today. I could come next week too. Believe me, I could use some brownie points with my mother." She handed the bag of chiles to the vendor, who finished a text on his phone before he weighed them.

"Two bucks," he said with a yawn.

Jenny dug the money out of her pants pocket, while Carlos and Marisol watched as if she were creating performance art. She tucked the bag up under her arm, and then whipped up her hand to shake Marisol's with a firm, poised motion. "It's a date."

"Okay." She raised her arm slowly to meet Jenny's outstretched one.

"Nice meeting you too, Carlos."

"Till next week, then." She strode away with quick, light steps.

Marisol spun to Carlos, eyes flashing with a chilling stare. "What the hell?"

Carlos shrugged. "She's hot. Really hot."

"I'm not—"

"No. No. No. I am sick and tired of you moping around. And now with Christmas right around the corner and the girls leaving, you really need something or someone else to think about. Consider it my Christmas present to you."

"We don't even know if she's single."

"We know she broke up with her girlfriend while she was on the show. Thank goodness, that she-devil was one scary bitch. I know it's all about editing, but seriously, have you heard more bleeps in a row on network TV?" Carlos produced the money for his poblanos. "And she called it a date. She's single."

"I just wanted to come in to get some chiles in quiet."

"Mark my words. She's the ingredient you came to get."

Marisol punched him in the shoulder.

The next Thursday, loud pounding on her front door woke Marisol up out of a deep sleep. The clock read ten a.m., but she had had a late shift at the hospital the night before, assisting on two complex surgeries, and for her it was still the middle of the night. She stumbled through the house, finally stubbing her toe on the heavy wooden cabinet by the front door that her grandmother had brought with her from Mexico.

"Son of a bitch," she said as a ragged painful jolt ran up her entire body. "Who is it?"

"Your fairy godfather. Open the door, Marisol." She heard Carlos's practiced lisp outside the door.

"For Christ's sake. I just got home a few hours ago." She twisted the first deadbolt open on the door, and then the second one she had gotten just a week after Carrie had moved out.

The door opened to reveal Carlos grinning from ear to ear. Dressed in a bright orange T-shirt just a smidge too tight, he thrust one of two large coffee cups into her hand. "I know. That's why I came bearing gifts."

"And why exactly are you here?" She tried to keep the annoyance out of her voice. Carlos was probably her best friend now, and he had gone to the trouble of stopping at her favorite coffeehouse, which required an illegal U-turn on the way up the hill. A long pull at the coffee, and the burst of caffeine running down her throat definitely put her in a better mood.

"To get you ready, girlfriend. You can't show up in sweats and a Sparks jersey like you did last week."

Marisol thrust her free hand onto Carlos's chest to prevent him from entering. "I'm not going. Jenny's not going to show up. We both know she only agreed because you ramrodded her into it."

"She's coming. I saw the way she looked at you." He grabbed her hand at his chest and gave it a gentle squeeze.

"Carlos, you always read way too much into things."

"So you say. Did you make the tamales?" Carlos bounced through the dining room into the kitchen. He went straight to the fridge and opened the freezer. Over two dozen neat little tamales, all tucked away in their corn husks, sat modestly on one side. Carlos whistled through his teeth. "Mari, they look beautiful."

"They turned out pretty good." Actually, the whole day had gone better than she had expected. The quiet of the kitchen was not what she was used to—the tamale parties at Christmas existed in part to bring the women of the family together—but she had found something else that day among the pots and pans: herself. Smoothing the masa into the corn husks, spreading the cheese and chile filling, and folding and tucking the husks around the tamales acted like a therapy session for her. Carrie didn't take the best part of her away when she left. Even if the other woman was ten years younger and ten pounds thinner, Marisol had the strength of several generations of hardy, resilient women running through her veins.

Like her great—grandmother, Lucia: the first woman in her neighborhood to start her own business, a tiny food cart that sold these same tamales from huge aluminum vats on the outskirts of Mexico City. Or her grandmother, Maria: a woman who had picked up her entire family and shamelessly manipulated the coyotes to get them to California when her husband died. And her mother, Rosa: a woman who had battled cancer with strength and dignity. Marisol conjured each one up as she built the tamales, and they had all stood beside her that day as she pulled the last tamale out of the steamer. The whole experience grounded her in a way she desperately needed. For the first time in ages, she could feel a slight thaw in her chest.

Carlos tapped his finger on three of the tamales. "Raul from the cafeteria is going to help us. He'll steam them up, and then when they are ready, we can meet Jenny."

"Okay, that's a great plan and all. But don't you think appearing with beautifully plated tamales is a little weird or desperate or something?"

"Marisol, stop." He took a seat at the kitchen table and patted the chair next to him. She sat down, and after taking the coffee from her, he grabbed both of her hands in his. "You know I love you. And so I say this out of the kindness of my heart."

"That's never a good start." She tried to slip her hands out of this sudden intervention, but his muscles rippled underneath his shirt as his grip tightened.

"When we first started working together, you were hot and spicy and full of life. Maybe not a serrano but a jalapeno, which is better. Heat with flavor. Now, honey, I know Carrie hurt you. But I'm not even sure you are a chile any more. I look at you now, and sadly, I only see a plain ol' pepper. A sweet pepper, for sure. But I miss all that fire, and I think deep inside of yourself, you do too.

Marisol rolled her eyes. "How long did it take you to think up that metaphor?"

"The whole ride up the hill, but that's not the point. You need to remind yourself of who you are." He gave her hand a gentle squeeze. "And it's not a bell pepper."

She raised her head to meet his gaze. Carlos pinned her with an earnest look. He was right. She almost heard the ghosts of Lucia, Maria, and Rosa saying "*sí, sí*" in unison from the shadows of the kitchen. She blew out a deep breath with a loud rush. "Fine. What am I wearing?"

She regretted that question ten minutes later as she stood in the middle of her bedroom. Carlos had tossed half her wardrobe onto her bed and the other half on the floor in search of just the right outfit. Nothing measured up to his casual yet sexy vision. Finally, he pulled out a thin cashmere sweater that would cling to her in all the right places.

"I haven't worn that in ages."

"Good. Then it will feel like a brand-new outfit. Go hop in the shower. And make it a hot one."

Raul had been better than his word. The Dutch oven and steamer were ready for them the second they showed up. And now noon struck from an old clock tower given to the hospital by a long-forgotten donor. Carlos and Marisol—who had cleaned up well, thanks to Carlos—stood by the chile kiosk. The clock gonged its last bell.

"See, I told you. She's not coming."

"And I told you she is. Look."

Jenny, long and lean in slacks and a blouse, walked briskly toward them. She held her shoulders back in a way that somehow opened up both her body and her day to the possibilities that life might throw at her. She waved as soon as she saw them standing by the kiosk.

"I'm glad you're here. You know, I stupidly left without getting your cell numbers, and people are flakey." She nodded to Carlos, and then let her gaze linger on Marisol. "Hi."

"Hi." A thin wave of heat curled in her stomach. Marisol, not actually believing deep down that Jenny was going to show up, had no plan on how to proceed.

"We're set up over here." Carlos led the way to a table surrounded by folding chairs, which the farmers' market had put up to encourage more buying. Marisol lagged behind, mostly to watch Jenny walk, but also to try to figure out exactly what was happening in her stomach.

Three plates, each with its own tamale still steaming from the hospital kitchen, adorned the table. In the middle sat a plastic container full of a bright green tomatillo salsa. Next to that, diced red peppers completed the Christmas color theme.

"*Provecho.*" Carlos pulled out the plastic chair for Jenny.

"It means to make the most of it," Marisol said as she sat down as well. "Kind of like bon appétit."

"I will. It looks great." Jenny picked up the plastic fork. "Very Christmassy. I like the red and green."

The unwrapping of the tamales gave them all something to do, so the quiet wasn't as unsettling as it could have been. Marisol watched and waited as Jenny dug into the soft, plump package of masa and brought a forkful to her mouth.

"Wow. This is good. Much lighter than other tamales I've had." She cocked her head and chewed thoughtfully. "Do you tell your secrets?" The tone was unassuming, but the glance that came with the question suggested that she might be asking about more than a simple recipe.

"She does." Carlos nudged Marisol with his elbow.

"I add pureed kernels of corn to cut the heaviness of the masa."

"Smart."

"You'll have to get her alone for the all the other secrets." Carlos laughed to soften his inference.

Marisol shot him a warning look. It didn't say all she wanted it to—mostly that if he wanted to flirt with Jenny, then he would have to go out with her. But it was already too late.

"Sounds great." Jenny picked up Carlos's lead and ran with it. "In fact, you guys should come over as a thank-you for all this. I'll cook something this time. Carlos, do you have anyone special?"

"Mark." Carlos went all doe-eyed. "He's a doctor here. My mother's very proud."

"I'll cook for everyone, then. I'm free next Thursday. That's your day off, right?"

Marisol nodded, although she was not at all sure how she felt about all of this. Too soon, too fast. Wrapped in her overwhelming self-confidence, Jenny came off like one of those German high-end knives made from one hunk of steel, the kind whose edge is so honed it could hack away anything. She was certainly cutting to the core of something here, but was Jenny trimming off all the cold, hurt, and bruised parts that Marisol still had, or chopping her up into bite-size pieces to devour?

"What's your info? I'll text you." Jenny handed Carlos her phone so he could input his contact information right into it. His fingers flew over the keyboard with a practiced dexterity.

"You'll come, right?" She looked at Marisol almost hungrily. There was no mistaking it now. This really was a date, and Jenny had just opened up the night to all other date-like activities. The coolness returned.

"Carlos, does Mark have that night off?" Marisol attempted to close the door a bit.

"He's taking a whole week off," he said without looking up. "I'm putting your info in too."

"Yes, I'll come—if we're all there." She nodded twice to make her point clear.

"Gotcha. Table for four." Sudden beeps came from the runner's watch on her wrist. "I gotta go. My uncle's ready. It was delicious, Marisol. I hope my meal turns out half as well."

Jenny picked up her plate and the others to clear the table and melted into the crowd of the market like the Ghost of Christmas Present. The whole encounter couldn't have lasted more than twenty minutes.

"That was quick."

"But fruitful."

"And embarrassing. Thank you very much."

"You gotta get over all that. You, honey, have your first date in nine months. Congratulations."

"It's not a date. You and Mark will be there. Right?"

"Right."

A week later, Marisol found herself holding a very expensive bottle of wine and carefully picking her way up a steep stairway in the Hollywood Hills—alone. The plan had been to meet Carlos and Mark in the Von's parking lot near where they all lived and make the drive over together, but Mark had wanted to check out a new gym on the Westside first. Carlos texted earlier that day with the simple message "Meet you there."

Marisol wasn't born yesterday, and she had certainly watched Carlos manipulate her and Jenny like a medieval matchmaker from practically the first moment in the marketplace. She had texted back "Need proof." So Carlos had taken pictures out the car window as they drove from the gym to Jenny's house and sent them to her in ten-minute intervals. Marisol had waited in another Von's parking lot, this time in Hollywood, until Carlos had texted a picture of Jenny's house festive with white Christmas icicles with the message "We're here." Now that Marisol was climbing the stairs, she noted that the icicles looked better in person.

Knowing that her friends were already inside comforted her. She had showered, dressed for the evening, and even put on makeup as if she were just going through the motions. If this were a date, shouldn't she be nervous? At one point she even imagined Jenny, long and lean, moving around her kitchen in that efficient way of hers. It was a nice image, and she even started to imagine Jenny doing other things. Wisps of heat began spinning ever so slowly in her chest, but then the cricket noise her cell phone made took her right out of her fantasy. The girls' happy voices came through loud and clear all the way across the sea.

"Mom, we swam with dolphins!" Their delight doused the heat immediately, since she had not been there to see such a feat. Apparently it wasn't enough to own a condo on the beach. Mrs. Sluttypants also knew someone at a dolphin preserve.

Marisol stepped onto the front landing and gave the door a quiet knock. It opened immediately. The crisp, piney scent of a fresh Douglas fir greeted her, and then Jenny smiled a warm hello. She stood in the hallway, hand on the door, with the lit and decorated tree right behind her in the living room. The scene could've been the model for a Norman Rockwell holiday lithograph, but Jenny's white blouse painted a different story. Buttoned only three-quarters of the way up her chest, the top barely hid the promise of small, full breasts inside. Marisol took a quick step back; she could practically feel the heat coming off Jenny. She had to admit, Carlos was right. Jenny was hot.

"Hi." Marisol barely tore her gaze away from the shirt to glance around the house. "Where are the boys?"

"They didn't text you?"

"No. Why?" The bottom of Marisol's stomach dropped out.

"Carlos called hours ago. Mark twisted his ankle pretty badly at some fancy new gym this afternoon. Carlos said he was trying to look all studly for the hot young men there. And something else about a doctor being the worst patient imaginable. He took Mark home to get ice on it as soon as possible."

Marisol wanted to punch something. She could totally hear Carlos telling the story with an earnestness that would have made it seem true over the phone, especially to someone who didn't know him that well. But she, who did know him, had been royally played. They must have driven over just to take the picture of the house and would be halfway home to the Valley by now. There had never been any gym at all.

"No. They didn't text me."

"I hope he's okay."

"Oh, he'll be fine." Although Marisol had visions of twisting more than their ankles next time she saw them.

"So the night's ours, I guess."

Jenny invited her into the kitchen. Marisol expected the set from the cooking show—a pristine chef's kitchen with sparkling granite counters, matching backsplash, and stainless steel appliances. Something much more homey and grounded greeted her. The kitchen felt lived-in, as if some really good meals and some really bad ones had all found their beginnings here. White walls and cabinets flowed into the butcher-block counters, and pops of vibrant colors in the form of handles, bowls, and containers brightened the look. The warm, rich smell of tomatoes ripe from the vine and fresh herbs like rosemary, thyme, and sage rushed to her as soon as she entered. A recently used pasta maker sat on the counter with a dusting of flour like Christmas snow all around it. This was who Jenny really was. Take away those pretty eyes and the tight body, and at her core Jenny was a warm hearth on a cold night.

Marisol relaxed the second she stepped over the threshold. Her breathing slowed, her shoulders dropped. Her anger at Carlos and her anxiety about what was going on at a beach and bedroom twenty-five hundred miles from there began to melt away—a Christmas miracle or the testimony to the power of really good food?

"Pasta?" she asked.

"Surprising, huh? Most people see me and think all I cook is Asian. And I do. It's my specialty, after all, but my mother's mother was Italian. Christmas for me and us has always been about pasta and fish." She gave the meat sauce on the stove a quick stir with a wooden spoon "We called this the Christmas pasta. I don't even know its real name."

"It smells absolutely delicious." Her stomach leapt up to meet the aromas wafting about the kitchen. Suddenly, she was starving.

"It's the first thing I learned how to cook. Nonna was the real chef in the family. See, you are not the only one with kitchen secrets." She scooped up a taste in the wooden spoon and brought it to Marisol. "Taste?"

Marisol nodded and reached for the spoon. But Jenny held it back and said, "Open."

Marisol did as she was told, and Jenny slid it in, dropping it neatly on her tongue. Sexy as hell. Marisol rolled the taste around in her mouth. She identified short ribs, pancetta, and Italian sausage, both hot and sweet. "Oh my God," she sighed. "It's delicious."

Jenny stepped back and smiled. "Is that for tonight?" She pointed to the forgotten wine bottle in Marisol's hand.

"Yeah. Sorry." She handed a bottle of Cabernet Sauvignon over to Jenny. She had let the salesman at her local wine store talk her into buying the bottle earlier that day. She had asked for a good first impression, and he had practically guaranteed her one with this particular Cab. It had certainly put an impression on her wallet. "But if something else works better for tonight, just put it up for later."

Jenny read the label and chuckled. "No. This is perfect. Look." She grabbed a bottle of wine from the counter and handed it to Marisol. It was the exact same wine down to the year. "It's a sign."

"Well, only if you want to date the salesman at the Wine Cellar. It was his choice."

Jenny stepped up to her and raised a hand to her cheek, cupping it for the briefest of moments. Her palm was hot, and Marisol's cheek burned where the touch had been. "For the record, I only want to date you. I knew it the moment I saw you at the farmers' market." Still standing close to Marisol, she pinned her with a frank look that demanded an answer.

The heat from her cheek wound its way down her throat and settled in her chest, sending tendrils deep into her heart. Jenny's touch was strong enough to melt the edges of the frost that had lived there since Carrie's confession. Suddenly, she wanted to play this game to see where it would go. She even remembered being good at it once.

"You might want to reconsider. The salesman does have great taste in wine."

"Yes, but can he make a tamale?"

"Probably not as good as me."

"I bet he doesn't do a lot of things as well as you do."

Jenny searched Marisol's face with her eyes and took a small step closer. Jenny was so close now that she could feel warmth coming off her body in waves. Marisol closed her eyes and imagined that warmth enveloping her. It felt very good to be back in the heat after so long.

"My tamales are good. Really good. But sometimes lately, I think the cornmeal may be a little bland. I think I may be ready to kick it up a notch."

"You mean add more spice?"

Marisol nodded. She could feel Jenny's breath coming out in ragged bursts.

"A dash or two right now?"

"Yes." She met Jenny's gaze, still so open and full of invitation. This time she didn't shy away. This time she willed Jenny to take that final step to her. They were inches apart now, their mouths close but not touching. For being so quick and efficient at everything else, Jenny painfully drew this part out. It was all Marisol could do not to slam her lips into Jenny's. To stand there so close, letting the heat and promise of the coming kiss surround her was maddening. Butterflies that hadn't flown in ages opened their wings and started to flutter deep in Marisol in response to the sunshine that Jenny brought. When Jenny finally did drop her lips onto Marisol's, the kiss was everything she desired—warm, soft, tender. She tasted of all the wonderful things bubbling away on the stove and the potential of much more exotic meals down the road.

Goose bumps shimmered across her arms as Jenny ran both hands up them and finally tangled her fingers in Marisol's long hair. She pulled Marisol even closer. The kiss sizzled and deepened. Jenny's tongue dipped into Marisol's mouth and stroked hers. Marisol shuddered with desire. She stroked back and wrapped her arms around Jenny's lithe frame. The heat of the kiss wound its way to the center of Marisol's heart, and with a glorious burst, the last of the frost and hurt melted away completely.

All it took was one scorching kiss. Just like that, Marisol found her inner jalapeno and got her chile back—all in time for Christmas.

Elfin Magic

R.G. EMANUELLE

THE TRANQUILITY IN THE CHRISTMASTOWN maze was broken only by the sound of moving parts and mechanisms at work. I strolled through it, taking the opportunity to center myself in those last moments before Christmastown opened to the public and things went nuts. There was something magical about the decorated trees, twinkling lights, and mechanical figures beckoning to shoppers. The little worlds that Stanton's Department Store created with stuffed animals, trains, toys, and lights made people feel young and hopeful. Like anything at all was possible.

At the end of the maze, I bypassed the rooms where multiple Santa Clauses would, within minutes, have hundreds of children (and some adults) sitting on their laps, and headed toward where I was working for the holiday season: Santa's Shoppe. Once the kids had their photos taken with Santa, the adults came to me to have them printed and pay for them.

I entered the register area, clocked in on the computer, and waited for the madness to begin. I quelled my roiling stomach with some tea and contemplated how I'd ended up here, upselling photo packages in an elf costume, playing to parents' sentiments to squeeze as much money out of them as possible. The first customers came, and the nonstop parade began.

Four hours later, I was aching to go on my break. My feet throbbed and I was about to pass out from hunger. I was keying in my employee identification number to clock out on my register when I looked at the next customer in line. A woman holding a little girl's hand. The woman had long, dark hair pulled back from her forehead with a headband, exposing delicate features with softly rounded cheeks and a small perky nose. Her black coat was unbuttoned and I glimpsed a tight, purple sweater.

I cancelled the clock-out sequence. "Next customer in line," I said. "Right here." I made eye contact with the woman and waved her over. She smiled as she approached my register and handed me her ticket.

"Hi, Merry Christmas," I said with all the enthusiasm I could muster, which was much, considering how unnerved I'd suddenly become by the woman's dark brown eyes boring into mine.

"Hey, I thought you were going on break," my co-worker said.

"Yeah. After this customer." I turned back to the woman and smiled as I scanned her ticket. Photos of her child on Santa's lap came up on the computer screen. She pointed at the customer screen. "Look, sweetie," she said to the little girl.

While the woman looked at the screen and spoke to the child, I watched her and when she smiled, a warmth filled my chest.

I became aware of my elf costume. Painfully aware. My green, one-size-fits-all smock with the ugliest flower pattern ever splashed across the chest and shoulders, my baggy red pants tucked into my fake boot coverings, and best of all, my hat with points and pompoms all around it. To completely humiliate us, they tagged us with special identification bracelets—fuzzy "white snow" stuff with our elf names glued on with sparkles. Mind said "Jingles." Sexy.

"Are you magic?" the little girl asked me.

"Of course I am. I make all kinds of things happen."

I thought I saw a gleam in the woman's eyes. A mischievous, wicked gleam. I put on my best elf face and asked, "What kind of photo package do you want?" There was a little more quaking in my voice than I would have liked.

"What kind of package?" She raked her eyes over my chest and I almost choked on my saliva. "Oh, I think we'll go for the Special Santa Package," she said. "What do you think, Lindsay?" The child nodded her head. "Two of each picture, please. And the CD."

"Okay." I fumbled with my mouse to print out the pictures and set up the CD files to process her order. When the photos came out of the printer, I busied myself putting them in the cheap cardboard frames that customers got for free. I felt her eyes on me but I didn't dare look up. Not only because I'd probably do something stupid, but I needed to keep moving so I could go on my break and not get punished by my manager, who I liked to call the Elf Overseer.

The little girl shrieked with laughter. "I can't wait to show Daddy."

Damn! There's a baby daddy.

When I had everything in a bag, I looked up to hand it to the woman and my heart almost stopped. She was staring. Boldly, unabashedly staring, with a particular look in her eyes that made me feel naked and for once, I was glad for my elf suit. My face was burning. The elfin world around me stopped for a year or two, until she reached for her bag.

"Th-thank you," I sputtered. "Merry Christmas."

"Merry Christmas," she said, her soft, penetrating eyes locking on mine.

She took little Lindsay by the hand and left. When she was out of sight, the world started moving again. The throngs of people rippled into motion, the sound of the choir elves singing "Here Comes Santa Claus" rose up, and the smell of my own sweat told me it was time to take my break.

The days of the Christmas season went by rather fast as hundreds of people wanted color memories of their children while they were still innocent and naive, before they became cynical and mistrustful. I had been doing this for the last couple of seasons but I had lost that wonder, that exuberant child-like expectancy and enchantment that comes from Christmas. My enthusiasm had been diminishing over the years, but this job had just about killed it. And I hated my stupid elf name. It belonged to someone who still felt that magic.

But there must have been magic in the air two days later, when she came back to the Shoppe.

Like a drone, I was processing people's orders with a happy elf expression pasted on my face. "Next in line," I called out. She stepped up to my register and I recognized her right away. The woman who had warmed my insides.

"Oh. Uh, hi. Weren't you here last week?" *Yeah, that was smooth.*

"Yes, I was. You remember." She beamed, as if she'd been given the thumbs-up signal for some secret plan. I locked my knees for fear they'd give in.

"Yes. I do." I dropped my gaze low to look for her little girl but didn't see her. "Where's your daughter?"

She frowned before answering. "My what? Oh, the little girl I was with? That was my niece."

Her niece! A ripple of glee went from my chest to my groin.

I thought I saw a twinkle of amusement in her eyes. I don't know how I tore my gaze away, but I spotted the Elf Overseer eyeing me. I turned back to the woman and pretended I was showing her photos. Pointing to the screen, I smiled and said, "So, what are you doing here?" A furtive glance told me that the Elf Overseer was still watching me.

"Aren't you due for a break now?" the woman asked. "You were the other day, right around this time."

She'd remembered the time of my break? With my finger frozen on the face of some random child on the screen, I turned to her. "Uh, yeah. Soon." I pretended to key in some numbers on the keyboard and tried to think of something witty to say. The woman stood there watching me and I tried to control my quickening breath.

Another elf appeared behind me. "Go on break," she said. My stomach did a somersault and I couldn't tell if it was pleasure or fear to be able talk to the woman for real. I clocked out and as I approached the half-door that enclosed the register area, I became aware of my elf costume again and worried that any chance I might have with this woman would be gone as soon as I stepped out and showed myself in all my elf glory.

She walked over to meet me. A big, pearly grin graced her features. Was she amused? She leaned in and whispered, just loud enough for me to hear over the din, "That is the cutest outfit I've ever seen."

The warmth I'd felt that other day returned and covered me from head to toe.

"Listen, it's getting really hot in here," she said. "Do you want to go somewhere quiet? I'd love to talk."

"Uh, yeah." My brain raced as I tried to think of where we could go and have privacy. Then it came to me. Despite my better judgment, I said, "I know where."

"I'm Leisha, by the way."

Shit, I didn't even think to ask her name. A gorgeous woman with an exotic name. I wondered what the hell she wanted with me.

When my brain kicked back into gear, I responded, "I'm Maddy,"

"Nice to meet you, Maddy." She held out her hand and I took it. She squeezed ever so slightly and accompanied the handshake with a searing look that would have taken down Mother Teresa.

My tongue was dry, so I gestured for her to follow me.

Through a maze of makeshift corridors constructed from particleboard and Sheetrock, I led her to a display of stuffed bears. There had been some mechanical difficulties with it, so it was blocked off from the rest of Christmastown. All that stood between the crowds and the construction site was a black curtain.

"What's this?" Leisha asked.

"You'll see. We can have some privacy here."

The bears were mounted on a four-foot hut-shaped structure to create a cave, and the center was filled with additional bears. The display was supposed to be like a scenic Easter egg—you looked into the cave and there would be some scene enacted. A stupid idea from the get-go.

One by one, I began removing bears from the center of the pile and tossing them aside. When I had dug out enough of the stuffed critters, I took Leisha by the hand and pulled her in. It was a tight squeeze but cozy. We lay down on a mattress of police officer bears.

"Should we be in here?" she asked with wicked glee.

"No," I said.

From somewhere inside the cave, I heard a little jingle. All that fur created great acoustics but it also dulled sound, and I couldn't tell where the sound had come from.

"I have a confession," she said, lying down across the bears. "I was here before I came with my niece and I saw you. I told my sister I'd take Lindsay to see Santa, just so I could see you again."

"You did?" I could be suave when I wanted to, but Leisha was sweeping me off my feet and I felt tongue-tied like never before.

"Yes. I was shopping and I saw you on your break. Well, I assumed it was your break. You were sitting outside the entrance with a bottle of water." She looked away shyly. In the light filtering in from the gaps between the bears, I saw her blush, and it was so cute. "I was hoping to see you again."

I was a little lightheaded and my heart pounded. I swallowed as best as I could and cleared my throat. "After seeing me in this outfit? Hardly this season's style."

Leisha had an expression that I could only describe as seductive. "I think you look adorable," she said. And I knew she meant it.

"Please don't take this the wrong way," she continued, "but I'd really love to make love to you."

Don't take it the wrong way? How does someone take that the wrong way?

Despite my occasional lack of finesse, I'd never had a problem getting dates—women seemed to like a five-foot-eight, short-haired runner type, even if she made a freakish-looking elf—but I'd never had someone flat-out tell me something like that.

Something happened when she looked into my eyes. I don't know if she cast a spell on me like a Christmas witch or sent some kind of fishing line into my soul, but I wanted to give her everything. It became important to me to please her. As creepy as it may sound, I couldn't help but picture us as a couple and having a life together.

But right now, at this moment, this beautiful woman wanted to make love to me and I was more than willing.

I stretched out on top of her and slid my arms around her waist. Under the canopy of fur and miniature costumes, I could see her face clearly—smooth, sculpted cheeks and delicate lips—and I wanted to get to know every centimeter of her. The skin on her neck was warm and slightly damp as I kissed it, slowly. With her hand on my shoulder, she stopped me with a look of panic.

"Suppose someone catches us?"

"They won't," I said. What I really wanted to say was, "Who cares?" The thought of someone catching us actually gave me a little thrill. I straddled her leg and began grinding against her thigh as I continued kissing her. Our lips fit perfectly and glided together easily. I practically devoured her.

Furry bears create a lot of heat, and sweat coated both of our faces. My breath was hot in my lungs and she began to pant. We stopped to catch our breath.

"Ouch," Leisha said. "Something just stabbed me." I reached beneath her to see what had poked her. A little plastic badge was sticking up in a most awkward position. She laughed. "I've never made out in a pile of bears before."

"So, there are things you *have* done in a pile of bears?" I asked, waggling an eyebrow.

She gasped and I could see by the mischief in her eyes and the slight upturn of her mouth that the thought titillated her. I wanted nothing more at that moment than to bring her to the pinnacle of ecstasy, in a plush world of softness and comfort, any way she wanted it.

A sound caught my ear. There it was again—a jingling. Leisha didn't seem to hear it, apparently because she was too busy dispensing with her shoes and pants. I tried to make more room for us by shoving her things against one wall of bears, but I pushed a little too hard because the walls began wobbling. I froze, waiting for the wall to either stop wobbling or collapse altogether, revealing the sins of the flesh as committed by two lesbians to the sounds of the faithful visiting Christmastown.

Thankfully, the walls stopped wobbling. I exhaled and began unbuttoning her shirt. At the same time she began to pull at my clothes so I sat up to take them off. My clothes were a little more complicated than hers, however. I'd already dispensed with the hat and it sat absurdly in a little pointed heap by the cave entrance. My costume pants, now damp, clung to my jeans like plastic wrap. I sat up, pulled off the fake boot covers, and rolled the pants down until I was able to remove them. By the time both pairs of pants were off, I was so hot that my elbows and knees were sweating. I knew my face was beet red. I pulled the stupid smock over my head and tossed it aside. The bemused look on Leisha's face would normally have unnerved me but I was a woman on a mission.

When I finally got her blouse open, I was stunned by the sight of a red satin bra with white feathery trim. A sexy Mrs. Claus. Right between her breasts was a single bell.

"So, that's where that jingling was coming from," I said, completely enchanted. "I thought I was losing my mind."

She just smiled.

My mouth dampened with the sweat between her breasts and the feathers tickled my cheeks. I glided down her middle, my lips hovering just above her skin, making her shiver. When I reached the top of her panties, I stopped. They matched the bra, and had a little white bow and a little bell in a very strategic place.

"Do you wear Christmas underwear all season long?"

She looked at me, with a flash of wickedness and shook her head. "Uh-uh."

Holy crap.

The satin was smooth beneath my fingers, and I brought my index finger down to tinkle the bell. She squirmed and my already blazing desire was turned up even more. I lifted the bra over her breasts, which fit perfectly in my hands when I cupped them, and she moaned. I reached down to her hips to pull off her panties, but stopped. She'd gone to the trouble of putting on this sexy underwear, I felt bad taking them off. Then, as I explored, I realized that I didn't have to because they were crotchless. Well, they had a crotch, but it was open in the center for easy access. I felt her wetness and dipped into it with my finger. She lifted her hips, inviting me in, but I wanted to feel her from the outside a while longer.

The sounds of Christmas cheer got louder outside the bear cave as the afternoon throngs descended on Christmastown, and the heat of frenzied humans reached our huggable hideaway. I licked Leisha's moist skin, from her throat to her shoulders, and she sucked in her breath. I pushed my thigh into her crotch, bumping it gently but firmly.

Above the Christmas din came another sound. The jingling sound. It was faint at first, but the harder we rocked, the louder it became. It reminded me of a classic Christmas story: *It started in low, then it started to grow.*

I looked down at Leisha's bra, bunched up above her breasts, and knew that it wasn't that, and it couldn't be the underwear, as my thigh was still pressed into her. I stopped, remained still, and listened. But the jingling had stopped, too, so I continued kissing her.

Again, the little jingle.

I looked up sharply, intent on discovering the source of the sound. Holy shit, it was the bears. The bells on their little coats and hats were tinkling away. It sounded like we were riding in a sleigh that just happened to be pulled by a team of Care Bears. I knew no one would hear us—the real problem was the integrity of the structure.

Leisha took my hand and pushed it downward, sending a clear message of "fuck me." So I brought my hand back down to her crotch and continued stroking her.

The walls began to wobble again, and I was gripped with fear that the whole thing would come crashing down.

Jingling and swaying. And hot as hell.

We were going to get caught for sure. In the midst of the Christmas jolly that was being had all around us, we were going to get caught butt-ass naked.

I was trying to decide what to do when voices came from outside the structure. It was not the voices of visitors going through Christmastown on the other side of the curtain. These were clearer. Closer.

Panic seized me and Leisha's face now sported a wide-eyed look of alarm.

"The damn gears got stuck," a man said. "So they had to take the damn thing apart."

"So it's just sitting here like this?" another man said.

Oh, great. Just what we wanted—to put on an X-rated show for a couple of idiot guys. *Muff Divers in Christmastown.*

"Yeah, there've been so many other problems this year they didn't want to spend any more time on this. They may never get to it."

Afraid to move, I held my breath. Leisha stared up at me. I wanted to put her mind at ease, so I gave her a quick nod to let her know that it would be okay.

"So what do you want to do with it?" the second man asked.

My heart almost stopped. Through a protective instinct, I almost shifted so that my entire body would cover Leisha's. So what if they saw my bare ass? I just didn't want Leisha to be humiliated. But something told me to just stay still.

With my hand still in her crotch, I bent my head down onto her shoulder to mask my breathing, now labored because of the heat and my nerves.

I stopped breathing altogether when the structure began to rock. There was jingling all over and a bear fell from the ceiling onto my head with a thud. I didn't know if Leisha heard the thud or if the sound was just in my own head, but for a soft, furry toy, it sure as hell hurt.

"How sturdy is this thing anyway?" I heard the second man ask.

Leisha's nails dug into my shoulders and she bit her lip. Was she laughing?

And just like that, our plight went from tense and embarrassing to comical and inconsequential.

The bears stopped rocking. Outside, the other man responded, "I don't know and I don't care." He was apparently ignoring the sturdiness question. "If it ain't their priority, it ain't mine."

"Okay, let's go."

The sound of their footsteps fading was like a cap being removed from a bottle of soda—everything just released. My breath, Leisha's laughter, and both our muscles seemed to unclench.

"Wow, that was close," I said, trying to catch up with my missed intakes of breath. Sweat was dripping from my face and a drop landed on Leisha's chest. I tried to pull my hand from between her legs but couldn't. The snow shit on my stupid ID bracelet had gotten caught on the little bell. Yanking it caused a ripping sound, so I stopped.

"What's the matter?" she asked.

"I'm stuck," I whispered. This began a new wave of laughter, and I joined in. The whole thing was so absurd. She laughed so hard that tears rolled down her cheeks.

She sat up as best as she could, her laughter diminishing into chuckles, and reached down to help me. With all four of our hands in her crotch, we pulled the bracelet free.

She leaned back on her hands and took a few deep breaths. Sweat coated her forehead and upper lips, and she looked really hot. In both ways.

"Listen, why don't we take this somewhere else?" she said.

"I have to finish my shift."

"I know. I meant after."

A little thrill ricocheted through me. "I'd love to."

It was a tight squeeze with both of us trying to dress, and we kept falling over ourselves, which led to more giddiness and chuckles. The bell on her panties tinkled as she slid her pants back on, and the sound made me smile.

I poked my head out and looked around. "All clear. Let's go." We crawled out and together we adjusted the bears, putting them back into place. I almost didn't see Snowflake, a helper elf, standing there looking at us. She had a mop and bucket in her hands, so she was probably on her way to clean up some kid's mess.

Dread prickled my spine, until I realized that I didn't care. I grinned and, pointing to Leisha, said, "Replacement elf. I'm showing her around." Leaving Snowflake with a puzzled look on her face, I led Leisha toward the staff elevator, out of the way of the public. "I'm really sorry about that," I said.

"Are you kidding? That was hilarious. Although, I must say, I'm a little disappointed. I've never had sex in a bunch of bears before."

"No, can't say I have either. Too bad we didn't actually do it."

"Are you going to get into trouble?" she asked.

"Nah. And even if I do..." I shrugged. "I'm sick of Stanton's Fascist Christmas Regime anyway."

At the elevator, I pressed her against the wall and kissed her. I couldn't help pouting for a moment. "You must be disappointed."

"Why?"

"I didn't perform any magic acts."

Leisha looked at me. "On the contrary," she said, the tip of her forefinger on the top button of my elf smock. "I've had more fun this Christmas than I've had in a long time. I think you've performed some magic here."

Her soft eyes were so inviting and gentle that for the first time since I was a kid, I believed in Santa Claus. Without my asking, he had sent me the Christmas present I most needed.

"So, Jingles, it looks like we have some unfinished business. Can I take you to dinner first?"

"I'd love that."

"Okay, I'll pick you up. Five, right?"

"I'll need a few minutes to change."

"Oh, you're changing?" she said in a wounded voice. "Too bad. That outfit's kinda cute. Besides, wouldn't I be the envy, walking into a restaurant with a Christmas elf?"

My cheeks grew hot. "Umm, no, not really."

Her laughter filled my ears and I fell in love with it. It was more melodic than any bell, and her smile was superior to any Christmas present. Her sense of humor beat all. My stomach knotted at the thought that I might fall for even more of her.

She stepped into the elevator and turned. "I'll meet you downstairs at the main entrance." I nodded and watched the doors slide shut.

When I was back at my register, the Elf Overseer gave me a stern look from across the room. I was a few minutes late returning from my lunch.

"Nice of you to join us, Jingles," said the elf whose lunch break was delayed.

"I'm sorry," I replied, stifling myself. "I got tied up."

At that moment, I decided that I loved my elf name. It was appropriate after all. I chuckled.

"Oh, you think this is funny? This is cutting into my time," the elf said. With an irritated look, she stomped away. I began taking customers again and with each woman who approached with an excited or crying child, I wondered if she'd ever had sex in a pile of stuffed animals.

Then my thoughts turned to Leisha lying almost naked among the bears, squirming under me. And I craved more. More of Leisha and more of the things she had made me feel. Her laughter and deep brown eyes made me believe in magic again. I wondered what other plush worlds I could have her in, and I hoped that she wanted to see me long enough to try them all out.

First Christmas

JEAN COPELAND

I peeked at Lily from the kitchen, studying her dark chocolate eyes behind her rhinestone-encrusted glasses. Perched on the corner of Martha's sofa, she looked pensive after our discussion about the book club choice that week, *The Great Gatsby*.

"Lily, you haven't said a word since we finished," Carol said. "Something you'd like to share with us?"

Lily, soft-spoken and ripe with ageless beauty, offered a slight smile. "Even though I've recovered from the cliché of a cheating husband, I'd be lying if I said all the infidelity in *Gatsby* didn't remind me of Frank."

"Me too," I chimed in as I helped Martha gather the dessert plates and coffee cups. "Cheating wife, I mean."

Carol shot me a playful look. "Yeah, Erin, you're recovered, all right. That's why you still commune with this old lonely hearts club every Friday night."

"I beg your pardon," I said. "It's a book club, and I come for the stimulating literary discussion and Martha's strudel."

Lily looked at me with a grin.

Carol glanced out the window into the rainy night and turned to Lily. "I hope it won't be flooded or icy under that bridge when I take you home."

"I'll take her home," I said. "She's on my way."

She really wasn't, but for that sweet face, I would have chauffeured her to Canada.

A glass of chardonnay was my compensation for the ride home. Lily built a small fire in her family room and lit a Douglas fir candle. The recessed lighting low, the stage was set for seduction—if only she had been so inclined.

Halfway through her first glass, Lily curled her feet under her on the sofa and brought up *Gatsby* again. "I'm really enjoying the novel," she said. "I could never have appreciated it in high school the way I can now—the whole idea of being haunted for years by a lost love. Oh, it gives me the chills."

I nodded. "Unlike in tenth grade, I'm actually reading it all the way through without Cliff's Notes. Even for a cynic like me, totally down on relationships, I couldn't help getting swept away by the tragedy of it—how we're all just 'boats against the current, borne back ceaselessly to the past.'"

"Oh, I love that quote," she said. "The one thing I don't like is how Fitzgerald doesn't show us a thing that went on between Jay and Daisy when Nick left the room. What did they say? What were they feeling? That was the most exciting moment in the novel. Why would he skip over it?"

I shrugged. "I think leaving it to the readers' imaginations heightens the sense of possibility. Haven't you ever wanted someone so bad that it made you..."

She shook her head.

"Well, no doubt you will. It gets everyone, eventually." I felt sad for her. How could someone have been married for twenty years and not know that feeling?

"Hey, can I make an odd confession?" she said. "I never thought of gay relationships as being the same as straight ones."

I shrugged, not surprised. "What did you think happened in them?"

She shrunk into the plush sofa and hesitated. "I used to think they were just about sex. In my defense, I grew up in the white bread capital of the Midwest."

I grinned. If it were anyone else, I would've been savagely offended, but her candor was adorably innocent. "I should be so lucky. Obviously, you've never heard of lesbian bed-death syndrome."

She shook her head and recoiled as though it were a contagious disease.

"Sparing you the unpleasant details, I can assure you gay relationships are as real and wonderful, and awful as yours."

"Oh, I know that now. You must think I'm so ignorant, but honestly, I've never had a problem with gays, and I'm all for marriage equality."

I teased her with a handshake. "I guess now we can be Facebook friends."

She giggled and slapped my hand away. "I can't believe how comfortable I am around you. I feel like I can talk about anything."

"I feel the same way. You seem surprised."

"It is a little surprising if you think about it. I'm straight and a mom, soon to be a grandmother. We're just very different people."

I twirled the stem of my empty glass. "With one major thing in common. We're both rebuilding our lives. I may not have had kids with Vanessa, but I spent almost fourteen years of my life with her. I thought we would be together forever, and then at forty-one, I found myself starting over."

As she nodded, Lily's olive skin shone in the glow of her white Christmas tree lights. "When you told me about Vanessa, it felt like you were describing Frank and me, especially when you said it wasn't just Vanessa you lost; it was your whole way of life. Another person rips it out of from under you, and you're left to piece it back together on your own."

I agreed, wishing I could touch her. "I couldn't piece together a life I'd built with someone else. I had to learn how to live without being half of something."

"I'm finally figuring out how," she said, straightening her posture. "My sister keeps trying to fix me up with guys she knows, but I keep saying no."

"It's only been eight months." The prick of jealousy surprised me. I enjoyed seeing Lily every week at Martha's, and we had started texting or talking on the phone a few times a week. A new guy in her life would pose a serious block to that situation.

"At first, all I thought about was finding someone else," she said. "Frank wasn't alone. I didn't want to be either—more like I was afraid to be. But now I actually like it."

"I've been single for almost two years," I said. "I love the freedom. I'm getting to know who I really am, which is something I couldn't do with my identity tangled up in Vanessa and me as a couple."

"Do you know what's really going to suck?" she asked.

"Never meeting anyone ever again and dying alone?"

She giggled. "No. Christmas. Christmas is going to suck."

I nodded. "Your first Christmas alone."

She nodded, too. "Thanksgiving wasn't so bad because my daughter and her husband came to my sister's, and we all had a nice time eating and drinking—lots of drinking." She offered a devilish grin.

"Why can't you do that on Christmas, too?"

"They're driving down to my son-in-law's parents in New Jersey. I can't complain. He's spent the last three up here with us. Besides, it may sound weird, but Christmas has always been such a romantic holiday to me."

"Did you and your husband have some special tradition?"

She gave a vague shrug. "There's something so romantic about cuddling on the couch with all the lights out, nothing but the fireplace and Christmas tree, a mug of hot chocolate or a glass of good wine. And then maybe it leads to love making. I've always had the fantasy, but reality never quite lived up to it. I'm afraid I'm such a hopeless romantic that it sets me up for disappointment every time."

Silence hung between us as I fantasized about acting out every part of Lily's reverie with her. "Wow," I finally said. "I don't think I'll ever look at Christmas the same way again. Thanks for making me dread the next five weeks." I winked at her.

"Well, maybe we can have a special holiday book club meeting with the girls closer to Christmas. I'm sure Martha would appreciate the company, too."

"And if Martha's strudel won't ease the ache of a spouseless Christmas, nothing will."

She grinned as she poured us refills and raised her glass to mine. "Here's to Martha's strudel."

I chinked my glass against hers. "And to great friendships that keep us sane," I said and hid a sappy smile behind a long sip of wine.

She licked her lips after the toast and drew her eyeglasses back into her hair. Suddenly, everything sexy about her came alive. The way my body tingled, there was no doubt that if I pursued this friendship, I'd ring in the New Year in a support group instead of a book club.

Over the next week, I sent Lily a few texts that danced precariously between sincere compliments and shameless flirtation, the latter of which I diffused with smiley faces and an over-abundance of "lols." When my toes did shuffle over to the flirty side, she seemed almost ambivalent.

"I'm in my late forties, about to be a grandmother in two months," she said as she picked through pink layette sets during our first Christmas shopping venture. "I'm not sexy at all."

"Lily, don't you know what a cougar is? It's a sexy, *older* woman."

"I know what it is. I just can't believe you think I'm one."

As she bent down to examine teddy bear feety pajamas, her delicious décolleté peeked out from her V-neck sweater.

"Trust me," I said. "You meet all the criteria."

We were at a critical juncture in conversations like this. As I became more and more brazen with my remarks, her tolerance level bent to accommodate each one.

"You're a very attractive woman, Erin. I don't get why you're still single."

"I have discerning taste. I'm very happy to wait for Ms. Right." I was proud of myself for sounding so smooth, until the stack of boxed baby booties I was leaning against toppled to the floor.

She snorted with laughter as I scrambled to gather up and restack the boxes. "I get a kick out of you," she said.

I shifted my coat and bags of gifts from one hand to the other, following Lily as she drifted around racks of baby clothes. As "Baby, It's Cold Outside" filled the stuffy department store, something, maybe a lack of adequate oxygen supply, dared me to lean toward her and whisper, "If you were a lesbian, would you go out with me?"

"Oh, it would definitely be you."

I'm not certain if it was the response itself or the speed and conviction with which it was said that shocked us more. She stopped browsing, and we exchanged glances like we were back in high school and the teacher caught us passing notes.

"Uh, I'm going over to men's fragrances," I stammered. "I've gotta try to upgrade my dad from Old Spice this year."

"Okay, uh, I'll pay for these things and meet you over there," she said, avoiding my eyes.

In the car heading home, we were suddenly Fitzgerald scholars, examining *Gatsby's* enduring social relevance and deconstructing Myrtle as a metaphor for the common woman oppressed by the white, well-heeled patriarchy—anything to steer us out of the Valley of Awkward. As we neared her street,

I caught her looking at me. My better judgment vanished like the moon behind snow clouds, and my mind schemed for an invitation in for a nightcap.

"I'm so glad it's Friday," I said "I can sleep in tomorrow. You feel like stopping somewhere for a quick drink?"

"I have wine at my house—unless you want something else."

My heart and I shared a secret smile. "No, wine is fine."

As we nestled on opposite ends of Lily's sofa, I found myself less able to curb my desire for her after each sip of Malbec. I studied her lips forming each word, imagining my fingertips touching her skin, my mouth falling on hers.

"Do you feel okay?" she asked. "You look a little flushed."

"Oh, yeah, I'm fine." I pressed my fingers to my hot cheek and steered her attention back to the intriguing conversation we'd started after *Gatsby* on the way home from the mall. "So other than traveling, what else is on your post-Frank bucket list?"

She giggled. "Post-Frank—I like that. Let's see, I don't know. I'd like to think I'm open to adventure of any kind. What do I have to lose, right?"

"That's what I always say."

"What have you come up with?" she said.

"Um, I think I'd like to try snowboarding and visit Greece to see the ruins and, well, I think I should just leave it at that."

"Why? What else is on that list?" She narrowed her eyes and grinned.

I played along. "I better not."

She kicked my foot from her end of the sofa. "Just tell me."

"Nah, you'll get mad."

"Why would I get mad at what's on *your* bucket list?"

"It involves you."

"Now you better tell me, you jerk."

What a turn-on when she got feisty like that, and I was feeling reckless from the wine. I hesitated, just long enough to stir up some drama. "To kiss you."

Lily's jaw seemed to come unhinged.

"See? I told you I should've kept that one to myself."

She laughed nervously. "No, I'm glad you didn't. We said we could tell each other anything."

"That's what we said."

She grinned, shaking her head.

"Ever think of adding 'kissing a girl' to your list?" I said.

"No, I never had—until recently." She stretched her legs on the coffee table and sipped her wine.

"Would I be the girl you'd want to kiss if you wanted to kiss a girl?"

She laughed out loud. "That sounded like lyrics from a Julie Andrews musical."

"Oh my God, it totally did."

After I sang the line in my best Julie Andrews falsetto, we collapsed into laughter.

Once we calmed down, I said, "So you've thought about it?"

She nodded, staring into the fire.

"Would you slap me across the face if I kissed you now?"

"Slap you? What's a kiss between friends?" She shrugged coolly as her fingers dug into the fringe throw pillow clutched to her chest.

I blushed as I whispered, "If we're going to get anywhere, you have to come closer."

"Duh," she said with a smile. She set her wine glass on the end table and scooted over.

I leaned over and kissed her gently, savoring the hint of Malbec on her lips, expecting her to back away. Instead, she took my hand and pressed it on her cheek as we kissed. When I flicked my tongue against hers, she responded with a soft moan. I eased her down against the decorative pillows, and she grabbed my face with both hands and kissed me harder.

"I love how your lips feel," she whispered. "You're so soft." She caressed my back and then squeezed me to her.

"All girls are," I said in her ear.

"But you're the only one I've ever made out with." She slipped her hands up my shirt, digging her fingers into my skin.

When I bit her earlobe, she squeezed me tighter.

"We should stop," she said.

I made a half-hearted attempt to sit up, but she wouldn't release her grip on me. She searched my eyes as though in them she could solve a million mysteries

She kissed me again, and for a while, we helped each other forget all about a lonely Christmas.

After she shifted to her side, I draped my arm over her like a blanket, waiting for her afterglow to fade and to be ushered out the door, baby, no matter how cold it was outside.

I woke with a chill to the dying embers and checked my watch.

"Lily, I have to get going," I said, lifting her arm off me. "It's almost four."

"That late?" She slurred her words, still half asleep. "Why don't you stay?"

Anticipating the particular awkwardness of a morning-after breakfast, I declined her offer.

I drove home to the hum of tires hugging asphalt and icy wind through my cracked window, pondering the numerous reasons our night together would likely end our friendship. I hoped it wouldn't, but what if she woke up and in an attack of guilt resented me for seducing her?

I spent all Saturday starting and cancelling text messages to her. Finally, about nine that night, I picked up the phone and called her.

"I'm not sure whether to tell you how much I enjoyed last night or apologize," I said.

"Don't apologize. It was wonderful."

"Then you don't hate me?"

She chuckled softly. "Not at all, but I haven't been able to think straight all day."

"Nice pun."

"What? Oh, ha ha. Speaking of that, does this mean I'm not straight anymore?"

I had my suspicions of what it meant, but I felt compelled to reassure her. "Oh, I don't think so, Lily. One experience doesn't decide whether you are or aren't anything."

"But I enjoyed it—I mean I really enjoyed it, more than I ever did with my husband."

I felt so petty grinning into the phone, but how could I not at a revelation like that? "I don't know. Maybe he just wasn't the greatest lover."

"I was with a couple of other men before I married Frank. I don't ever remember feeling like that, and I don't just mean physically. The whole experience was so different, so emotionally gratifying."

I loved what she was saying but hated the distress I heard in her voice. I sighed. "I don't think I have the answer to what you're asking me, Lily. Like I said, one experience is nothing to get nervous about. Lots of straight people have tried it."

"But I bet not so many straight people felt like this the day after."

"Like what? Guilty? Violated? Degraded?" I said it half-joking, only half.

She chuckled. "No, you fool. Quite the opposite."

I wanted to ask for clarification, but I didn't. I liked the sense of possibility in leaving it to my imagination.

She exhaled deeply. "I should probably stop thinking so hard about it."

"Right, and, hey, now you have something you can cross off your list, too."

"Hmm, I wish it was that simple. Last night was much more than just a bucket list adventure, Erin. That I know."

"For me, too." After a brief silence, I said, "Well, I guess I'll see you Friday if you still want to go to Martha's."

"Of course I want to go. Erin, I hope this isn't going to ruin our friendship."

"It won't for me." I sounded confident, but I couldn't imagine how I could be near her and resist reaching for her hand or her irresistible lips. After making love to her, I realized I had been in love with Lily before we'd even kissed.

"It won't for me either," she said. Yet the week came and went without as much as a text from her.

By Friday afternoon, the text I'd been driving myself crazy waiting for all week finally arrived. She asked if I could pick her up earlier than usual so we could talk over dinner.

As I waited for her to broach the subject, Lily pushed around more of her Caesar salad than she ate. I was convinced I was the cause of the glass of pinot she ordered instead of diet Coke. She remained quiet. All I could do was prepare for the inevitable.

"Erin," she said.

Here it comes, I thought. "Hmm?"

Her mouth opened, but nothing came out. And then, "How is your wrap?"

"Spicy. Want some fries?" Suddenly, I wasn't hungry for any of it.

She shook her head. "Erin, I can't stop thinking about you." She looked into her plate and jabbed her fork into a grilled chicken strip. "And I can't believe some of the things I'm thinking."

"I've been thinking about you, too."

She dropped her fork in her dish and scratched her chin. "I mean I've tried to stop, to focus on other things. God, I really want to kiss you again, but I know I shouldn't."

"It's okay. Look, I never expected to be more than your friend anyway."

"How can I have a relationship with you? I'm not a lesbian." She pushed her plate away and dabbed her mouth with a napkin. "But I keep thinking about being with you again, making love with you. I want to make love *to* you." Her eyes grew dark and dreamy. "This feels like one of those movie romances where the woman gets all breathless and swept away. I always thought those stories were just in some writer's imagination, but that's how you make me feel." She let out a deep sigh. "That probably makes me a lesbian, huh?"

I smiled and pointed a long French fry at her. "Probably."

Her eyes widened.

"I'm teasing, Lily. Look, you'll figure this out eventually, whatever there is to figure out."

"I don't know. I just know I love being with you and talking with you and kissing you. But I don't know what it means. I don't even know what I want it to mean."

"Maybe we shouldn't see each other for a while, you know, so you can process all of this."

She sat up straight in the booth and sighed. "I think that's a good idea."

Wait a minute. I just said that to be polite. She wasn't supposed to take me up on it.

"I hope you understand," she added.

What could I say? Yes, I understood, but I was also crushed. The inventor of the bucket list never stipulated that all wishes were subject to cruel and swift cosmic irony.

"I understand," I said. "Maybe we should skip Martha's tonight, too," I added, indicating the snowflakes in the streetlight. "It would be really inconvenient if I had to crash on your couch because of the roads."

"You wouldn't be on my couch. That's the problem."

I glanced out the window again. "No, the real problem is that only one of us sees that as a problem."

"I'm sorry, Erin. I just don't know what to make of all these crazy feelings. This is the last thing I expected to happen to me."

"Do you think I expected it?"

"No, but at least you're used to this kind of thing with a woman," she said. "I feel like I've been totally broadsided."

"I can imagine. But who can really anticipate what's going to happen next in life?"

She lifted an eyebrow. "I haven't cared much for surprises since the last one was Frank walking out on me."

"Would it have hurt any less if you knew it was going to happen?"

She shrugged and looked out at the snowflakes piling quietly on the windowsill. "I could've braced for the fall."

The following week, Lily declined my invitation to pick her up for book club. In fact, she wasn't going at all. "I'm helping my daughter wrap Christmas presents," was her reason.

"Who wraps anymore? Isn't this the age of the gift bag?" I replied in jest, but there was no giggle on the other end.

I knew it was an excuse. I knew I had to give her space, as much as she needed, forever if she needed that. As the holiday drew closer, I went to the drug store and leafed through the remaining Christmas cards—'for my wife,' 'a new love,' 'seems like we've always been in love.' When was Hallmark going to cater to the sorely underrepresented market of those who fell in love with someone they never should have slept with? It was impossible to find a generic card that expressed my feelings. I settled on a 'thinking of you' card with a classy silvery bulb on it, wrote by hand what burned in my heart, and left the rest to serendipity and the US Postal Service.

Christmas night we sat on barstools around Lily's kitchen island, sipping amaretto-laced eggnog. After a noisy afternoon with my large family in my brother's small house, the soothing hum of a Sinatra Christmas CD smoothed out the edges the amaretto missed.

Lily took a sip of her drink and licked the hint of foam off her lip. "So was Santa good to you today or did you get coal?"

"Santa brought me the best gift ever last night—your text."

"Your card was beautiful," she said. "And since three weeks away from you have done nothing to help me forget you or move on, it was something I needed to do for myself."

"I've missed you, Lily. I don't know if I should say that, but it's true."

"You should say what you want to say."

I offered a cautious grin. "I will if you will."

She exhaled deeply. "I'm happy when I'm with you, Erin. I've felt that way even before we slept together."

"Me too." I put my hand on hers, and she grabbed hold of my fingers.

"Remember when I told you I used to think being gay was just about sex?"

I nodded as my skin tingled with the recollection of our passion.

"Now I realize I wish it was that simple." She paused as her lip quivered. "My heart has never missed anyone more, my body's never craved anyone, and my thoughts have never been so involved with anyone until you. I'm in love with you."

I took her by the waist and kissed her like I was about to wake up from the best dream ever.

We walked into the family room where the fire blazed. She stopped me by the tree and kissed me in the glow of its white lights. "Thanks for making me love Christmas again."

We sat on the couch, and she pulled me into her arms. "By the way, I think I now have a pretty good idea of what went on between Jay and Daisy that afternoon."

"That Fitzgerald," I said, shaking my head with a smile.

Season's Meetings

ANDI MARQUETTE

Rae glanced at the departures board yet again. Cancellations were piling up like the snow on the tarmac, so she figured it was just a matter of time…yep. As she watched, the status of her flight went from "delayed" to "cancelled." She sighed, not surprised, but still bummed. At least this was her home airport. She took her phone out of her pocket and speed-dialed Jeri, who picked up on the first ring.

"Where are you?" she demanded.

"Hey, sis. No deal. Flight's cancelled."

"Shit. Did you even get out of DC?"

"Well, sort of. Reagan Airport is in Virginia, you know."

"Smart ass. You know what I mean."

"Sorry. Technically, no, I didn't. I guess that's good. I won't have to sleep in an airport, at least. The snow's coming down here pretty hard."

"Can you go see if they can get you out tomorrow? I know that's Christmas Eve, but at least you'd be here for Christmas Day. The boys would love to see you."

Rae smiled. "That's because I'm their fave lesbian aunt."

Jeri tsk'ed. "You're their fave and only aunt, period. And it's because you happen to draw really cool graphic novels."

"Oh, I get it. They only like what I do. Not who I am," Rae teased.

"That definitely helps. Especially when you draw them both as superheroes and make their own private comic book panels. Their friends are so jealous." Jeri laughed. "Will you check the flights?"

"All right." She adjusted her backpack on her left shoulder, her duffle bag on her right, and moved closer to the wall, out of the flow of harried passengers. "Don't get your hopes up, though. The Weather Channel says this is sticking around tomorrow, too."

Pause. Sigh. "I don't like the thought of you spending Christmas alone—" she stopped, and Rae silently finished her statement: Even though you've always hated this holiday and would prefer to ignore it completely.

"Hey, it's all good," Rae said. "James told me to call him, even on short notice. He and Alex always have a Christmas dinner gathering and I have a standing invite. I won't be alone." She fibbed that last part, since she wasn't sure she felt much like spending time with anyone on Christmas. No, she'd never been one for Christmas. Most likely, she'd work.

"Are you sure?" Jeri sounded worried. It reminded Rae of their mom when Rae couldn't make it home for the holidays when she was in art school. Rae tried to find any excuse not to come home and have to deal with their father's drinking and yelling. And their mom would end up in the kitchen crying. It became a habit for her, avoiding Christmas. This year, she'd tried to do something different and break the negative connotations. She looked up at the board again. Didn't look like that was going to happen. But at least it'd be a quiet holiday, snowed in like this. Not necessarily negative. But it still carried some weight from the past.

"Positive," Rae said. "There's nothing to be done about it. I'll call you once I know more. If I have to, I'll reschedule for the boys' birthday in March. There's got to be some kind of sporting event going on that a couple of eleven-year-olds will want to check out."

"And that's why I'm so lucky to have a lesbian as a sister. She can take care of all the male role model stuff for my sons."

Rae grinned, in spite of herself. "Okay, let me go take care of this. I'll let you know what I find out."

"Okay. Bye," Jeri relented. She'd stopped pushing Rae about the holidays years ago, especially after Rae came out, and it was something Rae appreciated about her sister. She was glad she'd sent the boys' Christmas presents at the beginning of the month. At least she could feel like she was involved that way.

She hung up and made her way to the United counter at the gate through which she had, at one time, been scheduled to depart. Her phone beeped with a text message and she checked it. James, telling her they'd set an extra plate for dinner on Christmas Eve, from the looks of the weather. Rae texted back: "So right. Checking with airline anyway." A couple minutes later, her phone beeped again. "Girl, u know u ain't goin anywhere. Come to dinner. Nvr know who u'll meet." Rae texted him back that she'd call him later and she put her phone back in her coat pocket. He was always trying to set her up with someone. Although maybe she'd take him up on it. She hadn't done so well picking the last girlfriend, who'd ditched her a week before last Christmas. Shit. She really needed to break the Christmas curse. Maybe next year.

The line was just a few people deep. Resigned to her fate, Rae took the last position. She set her duffle bag on the floor and kept her backpack on her shoulder. No sense standing here with extra weight. She watched the front of the line. Most people were like her, just resigned to rescheduling, and didn't hassle the counter agent, but Rae noted that no one was happy about the situation.

She also wasn't last anymore. That position belonged to a woman who had moved into the line right behind her. Rae dubbed her "Art Gallery" because she looked like the kind of woman who represented artists and sponsored openings at swanky lofts somewhere. Smooth, classy, and maybe a little aloof. She was standing with her back to Rae, texting on her phone. Rae continued to check her out. Long black hair, but she had it pinned up. Expensive black cashmere coat. Rae's gaze went lower. What's this? Black jeans? Black motorcycle boots? Now that was an interesting look for a chi-chi art gallery chick. Rae started making up a storyline for Art Gallery's character, and decided that rather than the Moneypenny to James Bond's 007, she just might *be* 007.

Art Gallery hung up and put her phone into her chocolate-colored leather shoulder bag. She then dug around for something else, and her cell phone fell out onto the floor. Rae picked it up and held it out for its owner.

"Thanks," Art Gallery said, grateful, as she took it. "Kinda disorganized at the moment." She flashed a smile.

Rae guessed her accent as New England. Boston? "Join the club." Rae smiled back. "Were you going to San Francisco, too?"

"Yes. Not tonight, though, obviously." She shrugged and smiled back. "Shit, as they say, happens."

Rae nodded, strangely charmed at the statement, and at the hints of mischief in Art Gallery's dark eyes, and moved, in a weird way, by the sight of a woman in a cashmere coat and motorcycle boots.

"Bummer," Rae said, trying to continue a little bit of conversation. Art Gallery had a nice voice.

"Oh, well. Probably doesn't help that I'm not a fan of holiday travel," she said. "Seems it never really works out the way it should."

The line moved and Rae pushed her duffle along with her foot while Art Gallery pulled her rolling carry-on.

"That's the truth."

"Maybe I'm just a grinch," Art Gallery added. "I'd rather just stay home with a cup of coffee and a book on Christmas."

"That's not grinch-y. That's practical. Maybe if we all did that, there'd be less stress this time of year." And fewer expectations, fewer fights, fewer freak-outs.

"And fewer crowded airports."

"Which would make spending Christmas in one less of a hassle."

Art Gallery laughed, then, a rich, velvety caress. Uh-oh, Rae thought. Lust virus warning.

"And maybe even enjoyable," Art Gallery said.

"You never know."

Art Gallery nodded, and for a few moments, she kept her gaze locked on Rae's. "No," she agreed. "You don't, do you?"

Rae wanted to respond, but her throat had gone dry. Fortunately, it was her turn at the counter, and another agent had opened another line at the same counter, so Art Gallery was able to get her flight squared away, too. She flashed another smile at Rae before she turned to the counter.

"I'll be right with you," the agent said to Rae.

"Okay." She waited, pretending to just be waiting for the agent when in reality, she was working up a story line. Art Gallery would make the perfect superhero for one of Rae's graphic novels. And a really excellent date. Hell, she was the perfect adventure. Kind of enigmatic but approachable. Incongruous quirks, like a long cashmere coat and big, clunky boots. She'd have a big, black bike, and really sexy shades and black leather riding gloves. And she'd have a vulnerability beneath the bravado that could melt stone.

Yeah, Rae thought. A perfect mix of means well and mysterious. The kind of woman Rae was drawn to, much to her never-ending chagrin. She wasn't doing so well in the dating arena these days. But she'd settle for a couple of nights with Art Gallery, here. Who needed dates when a rendezvous with a pseudo-superhero would do?

"Ma'am? Can I help you?"

Rae focused on the agent, trying to ignore the fact that Art Gallery was a few feet to her right. Weird little sparks zinged around in her stomach. "Sorry. So lay it on me. Any chance of getting out tomorrow?"

The United employee looked at her like she'd just grown an extra head.

"I'll take that as a no," Rae said, adding a rueful smile to her statement.

The agent relaxed and smiled back. "It'll take a lot of tomorrow to dig out," she explained. "I'm sorry. This is a really bad storm. We probably couldn't get you out until the morning of the twenty-fifth, but if you're desperate, I'll put you on standby, but we're trying to juggle all kinds of people."

"No guarantee I'll get out tomorrow?"

"No, unfortunately. I can't say it won't happen, but I can't say that it definitely will."

Rae debated for a moment. Well, what the hell? No sense trying to get her ass to California when she might not have but a day or two there. "Yeah, that's what I thought. So can you reschedule me for March, maybe? Same destination?"

The counter agent relaxed even more. "Let me see what I can get worked out. When?"

"First weekend. That Thursday. Returning Sunday evening."

She typed away at her keyboard. "Done." She waited for the new documents to print out and she slid them into a holder. "I'm really, really sorry about this. It's such a bad day for a storm."

"Sh—I mean, it happens. Merry Christmas," she said, trying to sound genuine. She glanced over at Art Gallery, who was pointing something out on a paper she held to the agent helping her. She was engrossed in the conversation.

"Same to you," the agent said. "Thanks for your patience."

Rae gestured at the line that had grown behind her. "Thanks for yours." She picked her duffle bag up and moved away from the counter, trying to act nonchalant while she stole glances at Art Gallery, who was just finishing up. She stepped away from the counter and slipped her arm through the strap of her shoulder bag and looked at Rae. She approached. "Hope you got your flight worked out," she said.

"Yeah. Hope yours is worked out, too."

"As best it could be. Thanks for chatting. Take care."

"Same to you."

Art Gallery hesitated, like she wanted to say more, but instead she gripped the handle of her rolling carry-on suitcase, and left the gate area. Rae willed herself not to watch her leave, willed herself to look through her new flight information, but she lost the argument and stared after her. And was *so* busted. Art Gallery had stopped to put her new documents into her shoulder bag and she looked right at Rae and held her gaze for a long moment, another smile on her lips. Then she was off, into the crowd.

Rae cleared her throat. Weird, how she wanted to chase after her and ask her—ask her what? To dinner? To grab a cup of coffee at an airport? She didn't even know if Art Gallery was single. Or into women. Rae forced herself to go near the window that overlooked the tarmac, where ground crews worked in the twilight to plow paths that were covered within minutes. The snow was at least eight inches deep and it was still coming down hard. Estimates were anywhere from twelve to eighteen inches, more snow than they'd seen in this area in years. The great Christmas blizzard, newscasters were probably calling it by now.

She set her bags on the floor and opened the document holder so she could text Jeri the new info. In addition to the new itinerary and receipt, the ticket agent had included a one hundred dollar voucher for a future flight. That was a nice holiday present, though she would've preferred the visit with her sister and nephews. Whatever. She'd spent holidays alone in the past. Not like she could change the weather, after all. She thought about Art Gallery, and what her plans for the holidays were. Like it mattered now. She was long gone, which was sort of sad, somehow.

Rae put the papers into the front pocket of her backpack and hoisted it to her shoulder before she picked up her duffle bag, dreading the drive home, but knowing it needed to be done. At least she was at Reagan Airport and not Dulles. Ten miles versus thirty.

She headed back to the main terminal, thinking that she'd call James when she got home, though she still wasn't sure she wanted to go to a dinner party. She'd probably end up staying home tomorrow, given the weather. Which was fine. She had to do some more work on the latest project. Rae thought again about Art Gallery, and her long black coat and motorcycle boots. Definitely more pleasant than thinking about a holiday dinner party. She got to the lower level and set her bags down while she zipped her coat up. Thus prepared, she slipped her arms through her backpack straps, got it settled, and hefted her duffle bag to her shoulder.

Ready, she exited through the sliding doors, prepared when the winter air slapped her bare face. It made her think of broken ice across a pond. Here, protected by the airport's overhang, the streets were wet and slushy, but the few cars that crawled by were coated with snow and ice. A sloppy, nasty night. She'd worn her combat boots because she'd just weather-treated them. Hopefully that would help with the worst of this.

She waited for a cab to pass before she crossed the street toward the parking garage where she'd managed to find a spot. She glanced to her right, wondering who else might be braving the weather and standing outside. The cab passed, leaving Rae a clear shot but she didn't take it. Art Gallery stood about fifty yards away near the curb, talking on her phone. Was she waiting for a cab? No, she didn't grab the one that had just gone by. She stood near a shuttle sign. A hotel, Rae thought. She's going to a hotel.

Rae started to head over to her but stopped. What was she doing? What would she say? "Hi. Want a ride?" Crazy. She hunched against the cold and resolutely crossed the street instead, without saying anything. Art Gallery had clearly made arrangements. She was waiting for a shuttle, chatting on the phone with a friend/girlfriend—hell, maybe even a husband. Had she been wearing a wedding band? Rae thought back, but couldn't recall. There. End of story. Right? Right.

Ten minutes later she had loaded her bags into the back of her trusty Subaru all-wheel drive and she buckled up and prepared to brave the elements. It'd be at least forty-five minutes home in this, if not longer. At least. And only ten or so minutes back to the terminal. She made her decision. Why not? It was practically Christmas, after all.

She steered out of the parking garage to the terminal rather than the airport exit. Fortunately, a layer of snow covered whatever ice might be underneath and it wasn't too bad, as long as she was careful. As she approached the terminal overhang, she slowed down a little bit more and got into the shuttle lane. Art Gallery was still waiting, but she wasn't on the phone anymore. A couple of other people stood near her, apparently waiting for the same shuttle. Rae pulled up right in front of her and rolled the passenger side window down.

"Excuse me," she said, loud enough for her to hear.

Art Gallery bent a little to see who was addressing her. She smiled. She had a great smile. The kind that made Rae think about slow dances and warm nights. "Hey," Art Gallery said, sounding a little surprised.

"Not to disrupt your plans, but I live in DC and I don't mind giving you a ride to wherever you need to go."

She came closer to the car. "That's awfully nice of you, but I don't want to put you out."

"You're not. I'm offering."

Art Gallery regarded her for a few seconds, and those weird little sparks Rae had felt at the gate resurfaced in her gut. "Dupont Circle?" Art Gallery finally said.

"That's my neighborhood." And Rae was already unbuckling and practically out of the car before Art Gallery could say anything else. "Here," Rae said. "I'll put your suitcase in the back. Get in. It's warmed up."

Art Gallery didn't protest and did as she suggested. Rae slammed the back of the car shut and returned to the driver's seat. Her passenger was already buckled up and ready to go. She'd rolled the window up. "You're right. It is warmed up. Thanks."

"You're welcome." Rae belted herself in and pulled back into the traffic lanes, which were mostly empty. "I'm Rae, by the way."

"With an 'e'?"

"Yeah."

"Nice. I'm Erika."

Not quite a superhero name, Rae thought. But it was smooth and classy, like its owner. "Good to formally meet you. Where to?"

"The Madera. Do you know it?"

"On New Hampshire? Nice place. Artsy." And about fifteen minutes' walking time from her apartment. Convenient.

"Yes. And now I won't bother you too much so you can concentrate on driving."

Rae laughed. "It's okay. Just don't ask me to read anything."

"Good, since I'm not normally one for awkward silences."

The sparks had increased, and Rae was warm in spite of the night.

"So what's in San Francisco, Rae?" The way she'd added her name to the end was kind of sexy, like punctuation with a wink.

Rae exited slowly onto the main thoroughfare that would take them back into the city. "Family."

"You were going to visit them for the holidays?"

"'Were' being the operative term here, yes." Rae lightened the statement with a smile as she settled in for a slow drive following the ruts left by a few other intrepid drivers before her. The plows had been through, but already another layer of snow had fallen on the churned-up slush. Fortunately, most people seemed to have decided to go home early, and traffic was light.

"Sorry about that," Erika said, in a tone that seemed to convey genuine concern.

"On the plus side, I do live here, so it's not that big a deal to go home from the airport. Still, there's no chance I'd get out of here until Christmas Day, so I had to postpone a visit." She shrugged. "Someone said earlier today that shit happens." Rae glanced over at her and caught her smiling. She refocused on the road.

"So she did. That was kind of tacky. Probably shouldn't swear at a first meeting."

Rae grinned, but kept her eyes on the road this time. "I rather enjoyed it."

"Then I won't apologize. At least not for that." She left a little hint of possibility at the end of that statement, like she was leaving clues about some of her inner workings that Rae had to unravel. Sexy.

"So what about you? Are you from San Fran?" Rae asked in a salvo to regain her equilibrium.

"No. I'm based in New York, actually. I was visiting a work colleague here, and then flying to San Francisco to visit friends for Christmas."

"So your holiday plans—"

"Out the window," Erika said with a laugh. "Good thing I had a feeling this might happen. I made another reservation at the hotel right before I left for the airport. If I had actually boarded the plane, I would have canceled. Looks like I'll be taking the train back home."

"Smart move, on both counts." Rae envisioned Erika notifying the hotel via a miniscule headset like in *The Matrix*. "So you're just passing through for business, then?" Maybe she was a government agent. Rae could see that, too. Rae steered for the exit, across a ridge of snow.

Erika waited to say anything until they were safely on the ramp. Rae eased the car to an almost-stop at the bottom of the ramp, but since there wasn't any traffic, she turned without a full stop. The streets were slick enough here that she didn't want to spin out on the ice. Once again, Erika waited a few moments before continuing the conversation.

"Mostly. I figured I'd get that last meeting in before Christmas shuts everything down for a bit. I was able to visit an old friend who lives here, too."

Rae made a noise of agreement as she worked her way around a semi. "So what kind of business are we talking about?" That was much less personal than asking about the old friend. She tried to sound just interested, like anyone might be when talking to a stranger at, say, an airport while waiting for a flight.

"I'm a literary agent."

Secretly, Rae gave herself a high five. She'd pegged Erika as involved somehow in the arts. She hadn't quite nailed the field, but she was in the ballpark. "Cool. What areas?"

"Science fiction, fantasy, and mystery, mostly. But I also have some paranormal authors I work with."

"That is *seriously* cool." Rae geared down for a right-hand turn.

"I'm glad you think so. Most people's eyes glaze over when I reveal my secret identity."

"No, that's really excellent. Tell me some authors you've placed."

Erika named a few and Rae threw another glance at her. "Excellent. The power behind the throne, huh?"

She laughed and a really nice warmth flowed up Rae's legs into her chest. Uh-oh. She was definitely coming down with what seemed to be a lust virus. Damn.

"I take it you read those genres," Erika was saying.

"Yeah. Kind of neat to know that I met the agent of a few of the authors I'm familiar with. And you know, you could always just tell people you're an agent, to prevent the eye-glaze thing."

"And how would that work?" she asked, with that little punctuation wink that made Rae breathe a little faster.

"Easy. Somebody asks you what you do, and you just say 'Oh, I'm an agent. Just got back from DC, and now I'm on a new assignment.' It's not completely wrong, after all."

Erika laughed again, but this time it was a sultry little chuckle and the warmth coursing up and down Rae's legs turned into a burn, bordering on an ache. Definitely the lust virus. Double damn.

"True," Erika said. "So what about follow-up questions?"

"You tell people you're looking for a few good spies. Or vampires, maybe, since you acquire paranormal. Then, when they think you're totally nuts, that's when you drop the 'literary' part in."

"I see. It's how I'm packaging my field that might be the issue."

"Exactly. It's in the branding."

"Do you work in advertising?"

"No. I'm a graphic artist, actually." She slowed as the car in front of her was trying to turn right.

"*That* is seriously cool. What venues?"

"Graphic novels, mostly." Rae turned left onto Twenty-third Street. They were almost at Erika's hotel and that definitely calmed the lust virus down. A little.

"So give me one of your biggest titles."

"*Wolf Moon* series."

"No way. You're *that* Rae Trent?" The surprise in her voice made Rae tingle a little more.

Rae shrugged, shy. "Yes, that's me, but there are a few others who work on the series, of course. We're waiting on text for the next volume, actually."

"I cannot believe I'm sitting in the car of a woman who draws for *Wolf Moon*. That's a great series."

Rae maneuvered the car around a traffic circle and exited onto New Hampshire. "Glad you like it. The next one's supposed to be out in June, but you didn't hear that from me."

"I heard nothing," she said in a fake mysterious voice.

Rae pulled up in front of the Madera Hotel, getting as close as she could to the curb. It resembled a 50s or 60s-era upscale apartment building. A maroon awning extended from the front entrance to the curb and fortunately, the hotel staff had done a good job shoveling and clearing. "All right. Here you go," Rae said, hoping she didn't sound as wistful as she felt now that the ride was over. She unbuckled and got out before she did something even crazier than offer a ride to a stranger. Something that involved lips, tongues, and a whole lot more. "You okay getting out over there?" she asked as she took Erika's bag out of the back and held onto it, so as not to set it down in the snow.

"Got it, thanks." She got out and shut the door then stood on the curb just in front of the awning, waiting.

A hotel employee approached, bundled in a long winter coat and hat and gloves. "Good evening and welcome to the Madera. Can I take that?"

Rae let him take Erika's bag and he, too, didn't set it on the ground and hence, the snow. He started to walk back toward the hotel's entrance, but Erika didn't follow him.

"Thank you so much for the ride and the conversation. It made what might have been a shitty night definitely not that way." She dug into her shoulder bag and pulled out a business card. "Email me, will you? I'm going to try to get out of here tomorrow evening, but I'm not holding my breath. Probably Christmas Day, more likely. But I will be checking email. I would really like to chat more."

Rae took the card like it was made of glass. "Will do," she said, trying to sound casual.

"Good. Thanks again."

Rae nodded, thinking that the way the snow fell on Erika's hair and long, black cashmere coat made it a sort of magical tableau and even if she wasn't really a superhero, she definitely had some kind of magic. "You're welcome," Rae managed. "Thanks for the company."

She smiled and turned away but she stopped halfway to the entrance and looked back at Rae. "Email me."

Rae raised the card at her. "Yep." And she watched her go inside, her coat almost swirling around her black jeans like a cape. She stood in the snow for a bit longer, not sure why, until a car pulled up behind hers. She got back into her car then and placed Erika's card on the passenger seat, like it was a placeholder for her. Rae put the car in gear and pulled away from the curb. Another fifteen minutes and she'd be home, and she'd resolutely vow not to email Erika that night. Too weird. And it might come across as desperation. But for what, Rae wasn't sure. Erika had her thinking all kinds of things, and a lot of them didn't involve clothing. Damn lust viruses had a habit of doing that to her.

Tomorrow. She'd email Erika tomorrow, when she was a little more sane.

Rae woke up the next morning and looked out the window. No way in hell was she going in to the office today, she thought, as her phone rang. She checked the ID. Speak of the devil. Leon.

"Hey, Mr. Supervisor Guy. What's up?"

"Merry Christmas Eve. Did you get out of DC last night? Because I will be amazingly surprised if that's the case."

"And I'd be really pissed, because it would be four in the damn morning if I did."

"Oh, shit. That's right. I'm sorry. Is it?"

"No," she said with a laugh. "I'm still in DC."

"Then I'm sorry again because you didn't get to see your sister for Christmas."

"Shit happens, as they say." Rae thought again of Erika, and cleared her throat while she pulled sweatpants, sweatshirt, and thick socks on. She moved her phone from shoulder to hand when she finished. "So what's the word?"

"Do not—I repeat—do *not* attempt to go to the office. The city's pretty much shut down. Just stay home and draw pretty pictures. And call if you need to."

"Where are you?"

"Home. See you day after tomorrow, if we haven't all died in the snowpocalypse—oh, are you good for Christmas Day? Lynette and I can set a place for you. You'll love her mom," he finished, with just a hint of sarcasm.

"I'm good, but I really appreciate the offer. Thanks, bro."

"It's there if you need it, even last minute. All right, stay warm. I've got to call the rest of the crew. Later."

"Yeah. Later." She hung up, relieved. Leon's energy level was always high, and though she appreciated it most of the time, early in the morning was not one of those. She went to the kitchen and placed the phone on her counter while she ground coffee and got her coffee pot ready. Did Erika drink coffee, she wondered, and if so, how? She pegged her as woman who would appreciate a strong cup of dark coffee, maybe a little splash of cream, but no sugar.

While the coffee brewed, she went into the guest room, which also doubled as a studio, and turned her Mac on before she opened the curtains and let the day's light in. Wow. At least a foot of snow. No, more than that, she guessed as she looked down on the street and the white lumps that at one time were cars. Leon was right. The city was shut down. An SUV braved the street, but other than that, the world was snowed in. White Christmas for sure, and definitely excellent coffee weather.

Her radiators creaked and hissed cheerfully, and she was glad to be on the second floor because she got the heat from the downstairs apartment, too. Great light, nice space, and reasonably priced, for DC. Rae filled her coffee cup and went back to her computer so she could check her email before she started working. And then maybe she'd think about sending a message to Erika. Speaking of—Rae put her cup down and went to the closet by the front door.

She had put Erika's card in her coat pocket last night. Her fingers closed on its smooth surface. Again, handling it like it might break, she took it back to her studio and set it on her light table. If she was going to email her, all she had to do was reach for the card. She stared at it for a moment. She hadn't even really read it, so she didn't even know what Erika's last name was.

Maybe she was afraid she'd jinx something. Jinx what? A chance meeting in an airport? Stupid, Rae remonstrated herself. She settled into her chair, took a sip of coffee, and opened her inbox. An hour later, she went back to the kitchen and fixed a peanut butter and jelly sandwich, which she ate standing at the counter. Another cup of coffee, and she was ready to start drawing. Back in her studio, she turned her speakers on, selected one of U2's early albums on her iPod, and settled in at her drawing table. Every now and then, a little tone emanated from her computer, letting her know when an email came in, but she ignored it and worked until noon, stopping only to make more coffee and go to the bathroom.

While the second pot of coffee brewed, she started sketching another panel but stopped when she realized that she'd just drawn Erika, in black jeans, black boots, and a long black coat, standing next to a big black motorcycle, eyes hidden by sunglasses. "Wrong comic," she muttered, though she was pleased about the new character. She set that drawing aside, though she kept coming back to it, adding details to the version of Erika she'd started. Maybe she'd scan it and send it to her later on.

Or maybe not. Erika might think she was stalking her or something. Some people got a kick out of being in a comic book. Others, not so much. Her phone rang.

"Hey," she answered.

"You are totally coming to dinner," James said, the Southern in his accent emerging.

"I am?"

"Yes, you big ol' grinch, you. I know how you are this time of year, but deal with it. Just think of it as a regular party."

"With red and green and a big tree with ornaments—"

"Fine. Ignore all that. You didn't get to see your sis and nephews, so Alex and I will be your surrogate family. And Devya's coming with a friend, so you won't have to sit and talk to us the whole time."

"Thank God for small miracles."

"Girl!"

She laughed. "All right. What time?"

"Five. Start putting on your winter gear so you look like that kid in *A Christmas Story*. Which Alex is playing non-stop here, just so you know."

"Actually, I like that movie. All right. Should I bring anything?"

"Nope. We've got it covered. See you soon." He hung up and she went to get another cup of coffee. It would be fun to hang out with the boys. And they always had really good food.

She brought her fresh cup of coffee back to her studio, opened her email inbox and scanned through the messages. The most recent caught her attention because she didn't recognize the sender. Maybe a fan. Rae opened it, and had to read it twice before it registered that it was from Erika.

Hey. I'm pretty sure this is the email address of Rae Trent, who I met last night at the airport and who gave me a ride to the Madera. Forget the email and please give me a call. My number's on my card.—E

Possessed by some force she couldn't control, Rae's arm shot out and she grabbed the card off the light table. Where'd she put her phone? Kitchen. She took the card with her, sparks zipping around her stomach again, and dialed the number before she opted not to. And by the second ring, it was too late to change her mind.

"Erika Myles."

"Hi. It's Rae." The words felt weird in her mouth, like she'd been eating cotton balls. Her heart was pounding way harder than it should have been.

"Hi, stranger," she said, and the unexpected warmth in her voice only sent another cascade of sparks through Rae's veins.

"Hey. I guess you decided to stick around today, huh?"

"I did. I got busy trying to find an email address for you. Which wasn't as hard as I thought it would be. And you have a great website, by the way. I really like your work."

"Thanks." The sparks were now fireworks. "Oh, sorry I didn't get a chance to email. I got kind of busy on this project I'm working on." That sounded rude. Rae winced.

"Don't worry about it. What I'm wondering is one, if you can actually get out of your house and two, if you're busy tomorrow. I know that's Christmas Day, but a girl can always hope."

She didn't even need to think about it. "Yes and no."

Erika laughed, and the sound made Rae ache in a way that she hadn't in a long time. "So which is it?"

Rae grinned. "Yes to the first, no to the second."

"Well, then. Since I'm here in DC at least through tomorrow, do you feel like killing some time with a visitor? I'd like to buy you a drink."

"Definitely," she said before she ran Erika's request through deeper analysis. "What time?"

"You know what? I'd like a little more time to chat than just an evening drink. How about lunch tomorrow instead? I'm sure we can find some alcohol somewhere."

"Probably. Lunch it is." And maybe dinner? A girl could definitely dream.

"I'm going to have to impose on you and ask that you come here, though. For obvious reasons."

"Sounds great." Rae leaned back in her chair. Date? Not a date? I suck at this, Rae thought, desperate for something witty or at least not idiotic to say.

"The restaurant here is pretty good," Erika continued "And yes, they are open tomorrow. The show must go on through Christmas, they said. Especially since this place has a bunch of people stranded. If I recall correctly, there's a bar."

"That sounds fine. Noon?" Did she at least sound cordial, and not like she was completely freaking out?

"Excellent."

"Are you okay for tonight?" Rae was prepared to invite her to Christmas dinner with James and Alex, and since they always took in strays, it would've been fine. The question was whether Rae could make it through without coming across as dorky as she felt.

"I am. My old friend invited me to dinner. Thank you for asking."

"Oh, okay. Good. Guess I'll see you tomorrow, then."

"Looking forward to it. Bye." She hung up and Rae stared at her phone. Oh, God. What would she wear?

"Darling," James said in his silky baritone when he opened the door for Rae. "Don't you look edible." He made "nom nom" noises as he leaned in and pecked her on the cheek.

"I feel like I should represent for the lesbian nation when I come over here. Lose the flannel and Birks, you know." She handed him the bag wrapped around the wine bottle then took her scarf and hat off and shoved them into the pockets of her old Army coat that hung mid-thigh on her. James wore jeans and a nicely tailored rose-colored shirt that contrasted nicely with his dark skin.

"Girl, stop." He took her coat with his free hand and hung it on a peg near the door. "I told you not to worry about bringing anything." He pulled the bottle out of the bag and made an appreciative noise. "But in this case, I'll make an exception."

She laughed. "I'm trying to overcome my issues with Christmas. Let me buy you some booze." She unlaced her combat boots and as she placed them on the mat beneath the coats, she paused, staring hard at the pair of black motorcycle boots that stood beneath a long black cashmere coat.

"Who—" she started to ask James when a petite dynamo of a woman flung herself into Rae's arms, laughing.

"So glad you're here," Devya said as Rae managed to set her down and extricate herself. Even dressed in faded jeans, baggy maroon sweater, and thick gray socks, Devya always looked like she should be in a Bollywood film as the gorgeous leading actress.

James laughed. "Girl, you could lay out a linebacker with a tackle like that." To Rae, he said, "C'mon and get some Christmas cheer." He turned and Rae started after him, glad she'd worn her thickest socks though she knew James or Alex would have loaned her a pair.

"Cheer's in the kitchen," Devya said. She brushed past Rae as they entered the big open space of the modified loft James shared with Alex, furnished with tasteful Ikea and select antiques. Lots of exposed brick, which gave the space a warmth Rae enjoyed. Their table could normally seat eight—three on each long side and one on each end—but tonight it was set for five. A Christmas tree stood near the picture window, and it was like something out of a magazine. Its lights glowed blue and white, throwing reflections off some of the ornaments and Rae thought about seeing Erika tomorrow, and Christmas suddenly seemed okay.

"Honey, look what blew in," James called.

Alex poked his head out of the kitchen. "Rae's in the house," Alex teased as he did a hip bump with her. "Get this party started." He had on an apron to protect his shirt, a light sage. He also wore jeans, but unlike James, who was in his stocking feet, he had house slippers on. Rae was glad she went with jeans herself, though she'd picked a gray button-down shirt, her thumb-of-the-nose to Christmas.

Devya gestured past him at the interior of the kitchen. "Come and meet a really old friend of mine."

Rae was sure her jaw dropped when she saw Erika leaning against the kitchen island, a glass of wine in her hand. She almost felt around with one of her feet to see where her jaw had landed so she could put it back before anybody noticed. And oh, lord, Erika was wearing a different pair of jeans that looked like a favorite pair, from the way they hugged her hips and thighs. She had a white tee on underneath her button-down shirt, a blue a few shades darker than her jeans. But the quirkiest part was her thick red socks. She wondered if Erika wore them and her boots at her New York office.

"I'm not as old as Dev claims," Erika said, a really nice smile on her lips that lit up her eyes, too. "And actually—" she glanced at Devya before she looked at Rae again. "We've met."

"Seriously?" James brushed past all three of them, carrying another bottle of wine. "Where?"

"At the airport." Erika gave Rae a little wink. Or maybe Rae imagined it.

"Yeah. Yesterday, actually," Rae managed, heat racing from her head to her feet and back again.

"I want to hear this story," Alex said. "But first, munchies on the table. Honey?"

"Be right there." James finished opening the bottle of wine Rae presumed Devya and Erika had brought and poured another glass, which he handed to Rae before he took a cheese platter out of the fridge.

"But Devya didn't actually mention your name," Erika said, and she shot Devya an accusing look.

"Forgot," Devya said with a shrug.

"I—" Rae started but Devya grabbed Erika's free hand.

"I have to show her the view," she said. "I'll bring her right back," she said sweetly to Rae as she pulled her out of the room, an apologetic expression on Erika's face.

"Back in a few," Erika said. "Don't go anywhere." She smiled and Rae managed to nod, hoping she didn't look as nervous as she felt.

She turned toward Alex and pecked him on the cheek, to distract herself. "Something smells super good." Alex was a whole lot shorter and slighter than James, who had played college football and still maintained a physique along those lines. James, on the other hand, was more bookish, though he liked some sports. He played a mean game of racquetball.

He grinned. "James wanted a Southern dinner."

"Oh, no. You did *not* make fried chicken for Christmas." Rae brushed past him to the stove, a stainless steel match to the refrigerator and dishwasher. Even the kitchen looked like fabulous gay men from Ikea had designed it. "You did." She turned with a huge grin. "I will totally marry both of you."

"Collards on the back burner," Alex said, smiling back. "And cornbread."

"Squash casserole," James added from the doorway. "Baked macaroni and cheese."

"That's it. I'm marrying into this family," Rae said as she took another deep breath, savoring the smells, and remembering how her favorite aunt in Mississippi would cook a meal like this when she and Jeri went to visit as kids.

"Along with my mama's sweet potato pie." James finished.

"Seriously. Let's elope. Right now," she said.

James laughed. "Let's crack this wine instead." He handed the bottle Rae had brought to Alex, who used one of his myriad kitchen gadgets to open it.

"This is going to be really good with the chicken," Alex said as he smelled it. "But then, wine is pretty much good with everything." He set the bottle aside so the wine could breathe. "So. Erika?" He gave her a pointed look and she knew she was blushing. "Uh-huh," he said. "She's a good-looking woman."

"Seems nice," James added. "Classy but down-to-Earth." He stirred the pot of greens. "And single." He raised his eyebrows at her. "And of the right persuasion. So Devya says."

Rae shrugged, trying to appear nonchalant, and sipped her wine. He laughed and went back into the other room, much to her relief. She watched as Alex took the pieces of chicken he was frying out of the pan and set them on a plate to drain. "You have no idea how great it is to have this for Christmas," she said.

"It's a nice break." He looked over at her. "Helps with some of the holiday aversion this time of year. Good food, good wine, good company. Do things a little different, make some different memories."

She took another sip. "It's great. Thanks for inviting me."

"If you said no, James was going to go and physically carry you out of your apartment."

She laughed.

"Whether Erika was here or not," he added, sly. "All right, dinner in about twenty minutes," Alex announced. "Go on out there and socialize." He shooed her out of the kitchen, and her stomach clenched in both anticipation and anxiety at the thought of interacting with Erika face-to-face again. Devya was pointing things out to Erika through the picture window on the other side of the room and James was busy with the sound system. Rae joined the two at the window.

"It's a gorgeous view," Erika was saying. She smiled at Rae.

Devya nodded as she ate a small piece of cheese. "The boys have such a great place. I'm glad you're here to enjoy it."

Same here, Rae thought.

"And you could have been more specific about your ride to the hotel yesterday," Devya said, giving Erika an affectionate glare.

Erika shrugged, sheepish. "I thought 'super interesting graphic designer' *was* pretty specific," she said.

"A name might've been nice. Though you're right. Rae is hot."

At that, Erika coughed and even in this light, Rae could see her blush.

Devya laughed and shot Rae a smile. "You were actually the super interesting *hot* graphic designer," she elaborated.

"Thanks," Rae said, knowing a flush had spilled out over the collar of her own shirt, and glad that by the window, the light was dim. She thought about the drawings she'd done of Erika as a superhero, and the flush spread. She studied the wine in her glass.

"Oh, I love this song," Devya said as a slick bass groove emanated from the speakers hung tastefully around the room. "Be right back. I'll check on Alex." She went back into the kitchen and Erika cleared her throat.

"Sorry. I didn't want to embarrass you," she said.

Rae shrugged. "I'm flattered." She took a swallow of wine for bravery and added, "It's mutual. Except you're the super interesting hot literary agent."

Erika regarded her over the rim of her glass, a different kind of smile on her lips. Rae flushed again, but this kind of flush was not the kind that showed.

"So how do you know Devya?" Rae asked, trying to lower her pulse rate with distraction.

"Boarding school in Massachusetts. I was a perpetual Christmas orphan and she was always bringing me to her family gatherings this time of year. Guess that hasn't changed all that much," she finished, looking around the loft.

"Sometimes those are the best Christmases." Rae looked out the window, all too aware of Erika's proximity. She picked up a trace of her cologne, sort of crisp and spicy, and looked over at her.

"True." She held Rae's gaze, and even in the softer light on this side of the loft, the expression in her eyes indicated that she was not at all sorry she was a Christmas orphan this year.

"Y'all dig in," Alex announced as he emerged from the kitchen carrying a huge platter of fried chicken.

"I think I want to marry into this family," Erika said as she followed Rae to the table.

"Take a number," Devya said as she put the casserole dish of macaroni and cheese next to the chicken.

She and Alex loaded the table up, James refilled all the wine glasses, and as Devya directed Rae to sit next to Erika, Rae thought that maybe Christmas didn't have to suck after all. Erika's voice and her laugh and the way her dark hair fell around her shoulders made that clear, as did the few instances when her hand brushed Rae's as if by accident, though the little spark of mischief in her eyes said otherwise. And by the end of the meal, Rae had practically forgotten why she traditionally hated this time of year, and after they'd helped clean up, she was actually disappointed that Christmas Eve was nearly over.

"Ladies," James said as Rae, Devya, and Erika suited up for the cold. "Let's do this again sometime. Maybe I can talk Alex into making it a holiday thing."

"That would be totally cool. Devya? How about Indian next year?" Rae adjusted her scarf before she zipped her coat.

"If we get snowed in again, definitely. If not, we could do it on the day before Christmas Eve." She pulled her gloves on.

"I'm in," Erika said as she finished buttoning her own coat up. "At some point, we can do a New England seafood Christmas."

"That would be excellent." Alex hugged each of them, and James did the same. "Be careful out there and call if you get stuck. We'll come and save you."

Rae glanced at Erika in her long black coat and big black boots, and knew who she'd much rather have pull her out of a snowdrift. "Bye, guys. Merry Christmas," she said, and meant it.

"Do you want a ride?" Devya asked as Rae opened the front door. "It's on the way to Erika's hotel. Not a big deal."

"Okay."

"Oh, give me a minute. I forgot to check something with Alex."

"All right. We'll meet you outside," Erika said. "We're dressed for it, after all."

"It'll just be a few minutes." And Devya left the foyer. She hadn't put her winter shoes back on yet.

Outside on the sidewalk, Rae breathed in the icy night air, liking how it was almost like an aperitif. Erika adjusted her scarf and the two of them stood near the main entrance to the lofts, where the glow from the lights inside added a soft yellow to the red of the Christmas lights strung on the awning. Rae was painfully aware of being alone with Erika, and she combed her brain to think of something amusing to say, to hide how nervous she was.

"I had a thought," Erika said, relieving Rae of the responsibility to talk first. She stood about a foot away, a little smile playing on her lips. "And maybe I'm being presumptuous, since neither of us is that into Christmas."

"Hey, I'm willing to change my mind."

"Me, too." Erika looked up and Rae followed her gaze, to the big bunch of mistletoe that hung above the main entrance. She hadn't even noticed it going in.

Erika dropped her gaze back to Rae's, and what Rae saw knocked anything she might have said out of her mouth.

"So let me help change your mind," Erika said softly and then she leaned in and before Rae had time to register anything, Erika's lips were against hers, soft and warm and oh, so delicious and fireworks blasted down Rae's spine all the way to her feet. She was sure the snow beneath her boots was melting.

"That totally worked," Rae said as Erika pulled away. Her heart pounded so hard she was sure even her heavy coat couldn't muffle it. "Christmas might be my new favorite holiday."

Erika smiled. "Mine, too." And she kissed Rae again, this time for a little longer, and the tip of her tongue traced a bit of Rae's lower lip and Erika's gloved hand gripped Rae's. Erika pulled away again much too soon but out of the corner of her eye, Rae saw Devya through the glass doors, getting off the elevator.

"Can I get more of that tomorrow?" Rae asked.

Erika smiled. "Definitely. It'll be Christmas Day, after all."

Rae was pretty sure that wouldn't be enough, but Devya was at the door.

"Okay," Devya said as she emerged from the building. "I'm parked right over there. You two ready?"

Rae caught Erika's gaze. "Totally," she said. "Totally ready."

"Same here," Erika said.

Devya gave them both a puzzled look but moved toward her car. Rae didn't even notice how cold it was anymore and after Devya dropped her off and she was back in her apartment, leaning against her door, her boots dripping on the mat and a huge grin on her face, she knew she had changed her mind.

Christmas definitely didn't suck.

Kitmas on Peacock Alley

LEE LYNCH

IN MEMORY OF SWEET PEA LYNCH

It is Kitmas Eve on Peacock Alley. Hollyday lights twinkle through a fog just soupy enough to mask the frantic activities of a dozen cats preparing our anyule fancy feast. In one and one half hours Santy Cat arrives and street kitties from all over the Mission District and Noe Valley come to Peacock Alley for their edible gift. This is the time we celebrate the union of Santy Cat and her partner Kit Kringle, the sacred matrons of all felinity.

I am Sue Slate, Private Eyes, and my office, with a sweeping view of the Alley, is my base of operations.

My brother Dumpster takes a delivery. "Bring the bay scallops in here toot sweet!" he howls around the catnip stogie that lives in the corner of his mouth and is always setting his whiskers alight.

"Hold your mousies!" growls Bad Tuna Gat, transformed for this day from schoolyard nip-dealer to Robin Hoodwinks. His cohort Roarie dumps the cartload into an orange crate.

Dumpster checks the load on his clawboard and escorts the strong-paw duo out. Roarie does wheelies with his cart, screeching all the way down Fourteenth Street.

"All right, you guys," I say. Instilling discipline into the ruffians of Peacock Alley is not in my job description, but somebody's got to do it.

"Let us hustle before the Alice Blue Gowns get a whiff of our contraband and confiscate it."

"Yo, Slate!" calls Yellow Ethel. She is a punk street kitty who needs to exchange the chip on her shoulder for a clean and sober chip on her collar. "Is that the last shipment?"

"If Leonora's chicken liver sauce is here."

Leonora, in apron and bedraggled furs, stirs a hot pot. "Creamed liver sauce! Come taste!" She is a changed woman since she gave up the Feline Potential Movement to join AlaCat after the breakup with Yellow Ethel. I suspect they are flicking tails at each other again.

Old Miss Kitty herds volunteers into cleaning scallops. She talks a blue streak about her days as a street stripper and meter pole dancer, whiskers all but twirling with gayety.

"Humphrey!" I shout at a shaggy white elder.

"Humph, humph, humph," he says, pretending that he is not eating every seventh scallop as he works. I request Woogie, the pianola player, in tuxedo already, to assist him.

We are hard at work when into Peacock Alley stumbles the scrawniest pre-teen tidbit of stripey long-tailed fur I ever have seen. She proceeds to teeter to my paws and fall over, bleating and looking sweetly up into my eyes as if I am Coddess-On-High.

"Hey," says my compassionate brother. "Street kittens aren't allowed in here till midnight. Is she drunk?"

The bag-o-bones turns her sweet gaze on Dumpster as if to share her love with him. Dumpster's head tilts up, his snarly mouth goes soft, and he says, "Aww, ain't you cute?"

"You're all heart, Dumpster," says Yellow Ethel. She asks the young one, "I seen you around the Mission, haven't I? Your name is Sweet Pea." She turns to me. "Her late mom has the distemper. It makes the kittens like this. Fallover problems. No meower."

"How do you know her name is Sweet Pea?" I ask.

"I just know," Ethel replies with an annoyed swat of her tail.

"Distemper, did you say?" asks Miss Kitty, paw to her ear, whiskers trembly. "Does the ragamuffin have the virus?"

Yellow Ethel says, "Do not be alarmed, Miss Kitty. The kittens who survive as long as Sweet Pea are not sick anymore. They are only wobbly."

Without warning, the kitten flings herself across the Alley and lands on her back. Her paws kick the air like an upended bug.

"And have awesome fits," explains Ethel. She hurries to the kitten and gives her loving licks to clean her eyes.

Sweet Pea reassembles herself onto all fours and with much cheer staggers back to us, beaming up at Ethel.

"What's the matter with her?" Dumpster asks. "Cat got her tongue?"

Sweet Pea opens her little mouth wide, showing a pointy pink tongue and tiny white teeth. However, no sounds come out.

"Like, wow," says Ethel, snapping her halibut gum. "Kit Kringle must be looking out for this one."

The door to the storage cellar opens with a flair and who should appear but torch singer Tallulah Mimosa. I admit to the simultaneous arrival of a chorus of angels between my ears at this sight. Tallulah wears my favorite fur pant suit for the occasion: svelte black, gold, and cream. Her black half-mask shrieks allure across the room.

"We're finally finished with the gifts," she announces, smoothing the lapel of my stripey three-piece suit with a white-gloved paw. She rubs noses with me, then looks down. "Who's this? Tiny Tim?"

Sweet Pea sways, obviously as much in my Tallulah's thrall as I am.

"Aren't you enough to win over even Bad Tuna Gat."

We explain that Sweet Pea lives on the streets and just walks in.

"You look just like one of Santy Cat's elves, Sweet Pea," says Tallulah.

"Never mind all this pawlaver," says ancient Miss Kitty, doddering toward us with a bowl of chow. "Dig in, kit."

And Sweet Pea does. Chomping and falling, righting herself and packing it in, flipping onto her side, getting up and chowing down. Olley comes out of her bar with a jigger of water and the kitten polishes that off too.

"Holy mistletoe," I exclaim in consternation. We are all looking at one another like, "The streets are mean to the most fit of us. How can this little Sweet Pea survive?"

"Ho, ho, ho," rumbles Dumpster, shimmying his belly which drag's about a fur's width above the ground. "This reminds me. Santy Cat's tummy pouch is filled with nothing but space just about now. I am not at all certain it can fill out my red uniform. Give me early eats."

Turtle Dove bats his eyes. He is just returned from having his claws done. "My man Dumpster needs his strength," he says.

Dumpster's paw darts toward a carefully made shrimp cocktail. I leap to the rescue.

As per usual at this juncture, Turtle Dove screams. I land on my brother's back, claws spread, and as per usual he flails at the air in front of him. Sweet Pea falls back and watches with wide eyes. Miss Kitty and Yellow Ethel comfort her.

Unfortunately, this altercation rouses a sleeping monster. A new People, Emily Values, had moved into OUR neighborhood in summer and immediately was promoted to feline enemy number one. I say if she does not like living in Peacock Alley where Tallulah Mimosa sings nightly and draws deservedly great crowds, then she can move into that church across the street, outside of which she spends many hours introducing herself as Misses Emily Values, Emily Values, Emily Values until the words ring in my ears.

"Scat," she screeches." We ignore her. She grabs a broom. "Scat,you vermin-infested,rabies-carrying,oversized rodents!"

I hold Dumpster back from attacking her ankles.

"It stinks to the high heavens out here!" the People Emily yells.

We slink into my office and line up to block the door. Sweet Pea thrusts herself through just before the broom lowers.

Misses Values explodes. "Lord save me from you noisy, smelly pests! A decent Christian woman can't live in a clean place in this day and age with these godless homosexuals and their pet-worship. I'll have you all carted off to the pound!"

Everyone in our lineup yowls as she makes her way back upstairs. Most times we can flee the various do-gooders and bad-doers who want to remove us from our domicile. But not tonight! We must serve up the feast with love and good cheer!

All pledge to work quietly. I go about my business only to find that Sweet Pea decides to be my sidekick. I tell her to catch some Z's, but how can I ignore those sweet, beseeching eyes.

"Okay, pal, stick with me. I am about to do some detecting to find a way to save our Kitmas celebration. But you must be very, very quiet. It is levendy-fifteen P.M. and we must hasten."

We enter a crawl space I know, making our way through the dark. I hope the kitten does not have a noisy fit.

From a hole the size of a small cat, gnawed by a varmint with no respect for the privates of others, we spy Emily Values in her kitchen. She sits at the table, a telephone before her. She is sighing.

"If only my son would call," she laments to herself. "If only I had a friend to ask over for a turkey dinner." Her head sinks into her hands. "At least there is a service tomorrow. Maybe some sinner will need me."

I whisper, "Holly Kitmas Cactus. She is only lonely and unhappy, Sweet Pea. This makes People crabby. When they are crabby, they take it out on littler beings."

Sweet Pea looks at me, looks at Emily Values, back at me, eyes big as milk saucers.

I say, "So the conclusion to this dilemma is quite simple. Can you solve it?"

Sweet Pea does not yet grow into her ears which loom like twitchy pink satellites on her little head. Her eyes grow brighter. She licks my muzzle.

"Right!" I say. "We must make this People, Emily Values happy! But how? It is now levendy twenty-five!"

I do not know if the stress precipitates her fit, but just then the kitten launches herself. She flips up, lands on her side and proceeds to kick the stuffing out of the Emily's wall.

"Holly garlands!" I cry.

All this is not lost on Misses Values. "No!' she shrieks. "Now they're in the walls! Cats! Mice! Rats! Bats! Homosexuals! Snakes! Scorpions! I'm calling the building manager!"

There is silence. "Not the manger!" Roarie roars.

We scrubble out of there the best we can, but it is too late! Our feast is doomed!

Sweet Pea hangs her head as if she blames herself. I gather the others together and we discuss solves. Move?

"Impossible!" meows Leonora. "There are too many tasties!"

Woogie laments, "Think of the pianola!"

"Humph, humph, humph," Humphrey declares.

"Be sensible, darlings," Turtle Dove says. "Kitnap the miserable woman."

"With the manger on his way?" Bad Tuna Gat snarls.

"He's right for once, Sue Slate," says Tallulah Mimosa. "The manger will see us leap over every fence, rush through every alley, and tear across the streets." She patted her eyes dry with those beautiful fur mitts of hers. "He will call in the National Guard Dogs!"

Roarie roared, "Not the National Guard Dogs!"

Bad Tuna Gat clips him one, but no claws. "Shut your flap, you wimpy house cat."

"Whatever shall we do?" keens Miss Kitty and faints like a silent star.

Humphrey lumbers over to where Miss Kitty lies and harrumphs her awake.

"Oh, Humphrey!" purrs Miss Kitty. "You do care about little old me."

I roll my eyes at Tallulah. She all at once appears alarmed.

"Sweet Pea! Sweet Pea! Where is our Sweet Pea?"

"Holly jinglebells!" I say. "Where is that Sweet Pea?"

"We must find our little spirit of Kitmas!" Yellow Ethel proclaims.

"Why?" asks Dumpster, showing off his red Santy suit. "We got me, the one and onliest Santy Cat."

Turtle Dove shrieks, "Your Santy costume! It has a spot on the front! Let me lick it clean!"

"Hold onto your fake eyelashes, Turtle Dove," says Big Tuna Gat. "Not in front of the kittens."

"Stop the bickering!" I say.

We spread out and search every nook and cranny for Sweet Pea.

Outside the Alley we hear the growling excitement. The street cats are lining up.

This is when we hear the screech of tires and the sound of heavy boots at the front door of the building.

"I hate this part," hisses Dumpster. "Skip to the end."

"Oh no! The manger!" Says Miss Kitty. She faints again.

We see shadows of man People on the curtains of Emily Values. It is hopeless. We stand, frozen with panic. We cannot hear what they say.

If only I can find a way to lead Misses Values out of her lonely state. After all, is not Kitmas about miracles?

In a flash, all over the city, mission bells chime. It is Kitmas Day. The street kitties line up for blocks, their fur unkempt, their ears ragged, eyes tearing, but tough as pails and ready to PARTY! The ushers look to me. Are we leading them into a trap?

The All-Edison Band strikes up its first notes and Tallulah Mimosa jumps onto the tin stage over the Peoples' yard. She grabs her Mike, who holds a tinsel-trimmed megaphone for her. Before she sings, she announces the disappearance of Sweet Pea. The crowd promises to search the party for her.

Servers ladle out the delicacies. Olley paws out milky. "MIL-KEE! MILK-EE!" she bawls. Santy Cat Dumpster swaggers along the line dispensing catknit mousies while the rest of us hold our baited breaths. The ushers tell the kittens to behave themselves when they run this way and that way, nabbing each other's mousies.

And then the miracle does come. There in her doorway is Misses Emily Values. And in her arms, satellite dish-eared, smiley-eyed, is Sweet Pea. The kitten turns her little head and nuzzles Misses Values cheek. Emily cries crocodile tears.

That little mite of a kitten is all love and spunk. To save Kitmas, she flails her way back to the lion's den and beams that looks of love into Emily's eyes.

The fog lifts. The band stops. Tallulah announces the discovery of Sweet Pea and how she saves Kitmas. After the cheers are ceased, she sings, a cappella, the holly Kitmas song: "When the Moon's on the Rise, Santy Cat Flies."

Not an eye in Peacock Alley is dry.

"Oh, my sweet little pea," says the People.

Yellow Ethel winks at me. "I told you that's her name."

Sweet Pea leads Misses Values out among us. We rub her legs and lick her hands. Kittens jump at her apron strings and fall back squealing with giggles.

"I never knew," says Emily. "I never knew there was so much love in the world." She gets on her knees between Santy Cat and glittery Turtle Dove. She prays: "Thank you for showing me where my love is truly needed. I will protect all your creatures and never judge one of them again."

In the arms of Emily Values, the spirit of Kitmas purrs.

A Champagne Christmas

CLARE LYDON

GEORGIA'S FACE CREASED WITH CONCERN. "Are you sure this is a good idea?" She'd been in the bath longer than she should, and her fingers were beginning to prune—not a good look for a lesbian. Behind her, steam trickled down the pale blue tiles.

"Yes, I'm positive." Milly ran a hand through her long, dark hair, flashing her girlfriend her hundred-watt smile. "I've told you a million times."

Despite her misgivings, Georgia grinned back. She filled a plastic jug with warm water from the tap and tilted it over her head, closing her eyes as the water sluiced down her face and body. She swiped a hand across her eyes to get rid of the excess before opening them. Georgia could see Milly was picking at the skin around her thumb again.

"It'll be fine." Milly sat on the closed toilet lid. "My mother's going to love you."

The water rushed one way as if in a panic as Georgia's body slid down into the bathtub and she submerged herself fully, before coming up for air seconds later. She took a moment to regain her senses.

"Your mother has never met me." Georgia pinched the end of her nose and opened her eyes wide. "And, have you told her yet?"

Milly cocked her head. "Told her?"

Georgia rolled her eyes, smiling. "You know."

Milly waved a dismissive hand. "Yeah, I told her...sort of," she said. "Okay, no *actual* details but... Anyway, it's going to be fine." She paused for effect. "She's fine, *we're* fine. Christmas will be *fine*."

Georgia stood up, water cascading off her tanned skin, taut stomach, rouge nipples. She placed a hand on the shower screen. Milly licked her lips and offered her the cream towel she'd been holding on her lap. Georgia took it and vigorously dried her thick, grey hair, then straightened up and leant forward for a kiss. A familiar tingle fizzed down her body as their lips connected.

"Darling one." Georgia's face was inches from Milly's. "In my experience, which I think we can agree is considerably more extensive than yours, a situation attached to that many 'fines' is usually anything but. So, is it fine if I just stay here, eat chocolate, and watch Christmas films by myself?" A grin played around the corner of Georgia's mouth as Milly shook her head.

"That is definitely not fine. In fact, it is totally unfine." She kissed Georgia's lips and grazed the top of her naked thigh with nimble fingers. "We're spending Christmas together," Milly insisted.

"Even though your mother will likely think I'm the cradle-snatcher from hell?"

Milly laughed and stood up, her height matching Georgia's. "She's much better with everything these days, I told you. She's dealing with everything in a far more...relaxed way since Dad..."

Milly looked down at the floor, but within seconds she flicked her head back up and kissed Georgia full on the lips. "And anyway, once she sees how fantastic you are, she'll see why I love you. Plus, you're the same age. You might even become friends."

That drew a low chuckle from Georgia, who propped her left foot on the bath and began to dry her leg. "That's what I love about you," she replied. "Your youth, and therefore your eternal optimism."

Jane took a deep breath as she strode to the front door, wiping her hands on the blue-and-white chequered tea towel. She'd been cooking all morning and the house screamed festive—strings of cards hanging from the staircase, tinsel around door frames, and a riot of red and gold on the dining table. Nobody could accuse her of not embracing the Christmas spirit, but she would have to admit to a touch of Christmas fatigue. Both her daughters were bringing their new partners home, and Jane was going to have to wear her "Best Supportive Mum" face for the next forty-eight hours.

Through the glass front door, Jane could see her daughter Milly and the outline of her new partner, Georgia, beside her. Georgia. How ironic that Milly had chosen a Georgia too. Jane hoped she was better for Milly than her Georgia had been for her. But had she ever truly been *her* Georgia?

This Georgia appeared to be wearing a shocking purple coat. An artist, Milly had said. Jane supposed statement colours came with the artistic territory. She clicked the latch, swung the door open and shook hands, smile frozen at half-beam.

"Happy Christmas, Mum." A bag with bottles of wine clinked in one hand, while Milly pulled her mother into an embrace with the other and brushed her chilled lips against Jane's warm cheek.

Milly was wearing a new red scarf, Jane noticed. Had Georgia bought it for her?

Jane accepted a bottle of posh-looking red from her daughter's new love. She tried not to stare at Georgia's greying hair, the laughter lines creasing her face, or the instant recognition in her eyes that was reflected in Jane's own. It couldn't be, could it? But Jane was pretty sure it was. Her blood froze in her veins.

"So lovely to meet you," Jane said, tasting fear on her tongue.

Georgia's handshake was firm, her hands soft, moisturised. Just as Jane remembered them.

"You, too," Georgia said.

The last fragment of doubt Jane had was wiped away. She'd have known that voice anywhere. She could see the clouds of disbelief forming in Georgia's eyes.

Avoiding Milly's stare, Jane took their coats and ushered them into the lounge. Georgia had changed her perfume since they'd last seen each other, but *she* smelt the same. Her scent held promise and excitement, just like always. Jane was suddenly very aware that she was wearing an apron with an image of Rudolph on it, his giant fluffy red nose protruding from her stomach.

"What can I get you? I've got fizz, white, red? Or a beer, if you'd prefer."

Jane heard her voice going through the social niceties, but they sounded like someone else's words, in someone else's lounge completely. She felt her cheeks flush scarlet as the pair sat on her brown leather couch as if it was an everyday occurrence, Milly immediately reaching for her girlfriend's hand.

Georgia was her daughter's girlfriend. Jane suddenly found the thought of getting through the next forty-eight hours overwhelming. She concentrated on controlling her facial expression and bit her lip. Georgia's legs were still longer than the M1.

"Let me help you," Georgia said.

Her voice was gravelly; it hovered in the air long after Georgia had closed her mouth. She sprang up from the sofa with an uneasy smile etched on her face.

Jane couldn't stop staring at the shock of grey hair. Why didn't Georgia just dye it like most women their age? It was cut sharply, though, and Georgia still had a chiselled jawline direct from Greek mythology. She also still possessed piercing emerald green eyes that made people weak, her daughter included, apparently. A loved-up smile on her face, Milly was staring as if Georgia *was* a Greek goddess.

"Some fizz to get the day started?" Georgia directed at Milly, who nodded.

Still assertive, Jane noted. She opened her mouth, closed it, opened it again. "Right. Won't be a tick," she said, gathering herself.

Georgia made an "after you" gesture, and Jane walked ahead into the kitchen with as much poise as she could muster. She heard Georgia suck in a breath as she walked past her. No change there, even thirty years on.

The succulent smell of roast turkey and all the trimmings hit Jane's nose as she entered the kitchen. It was the perfect Christmas scene. Until the door closed.

"Is this some kind of fucking joke?" Jane hissed. "Is there a hidden camera I'm not aware of?"

The colour drained from Georgia's face. She moved to the other side of the kitchen and opened one cupboard, then another.

"What are you doing?" Jane asked.

Georgia swung around to face her. "At this point, I think we could all do with a drink, don't you? Where do you keep your glasses?"

"Above the microwave." Jane pointed.

Georgia opened the white cupboard door and took down three champagne flutes, then prised a bottle of Tattinger from the fridge. "I see you still have expensive tastes," she commented, determinedly focused on the champagne.

Jane exhaled. "Are you seriously dating my daughter?"

The scar on Georgia's arm stood out against her skin as she removed foil from around the cork. Jane remembered the night Georgia had sustained it in Henry's Bar. She also remembered only too clearly what had happened later that night.

The room started to spin, and Jane tried to hold onto the kitchen bench for balance. When she regained her equilibrium, Georgia was staring at her with concern. Her red dress clung in all the right places. How dare she come into her house over thirty years later looking this sexy? But then, this was Georgia.

"You okay?" Georgia reached out and touched her arm.

Jane shook it off with a frown. "Don't," she snapped. "Just don't."

"And the answer to your question is yes." Georgia popped the cork, tilted a glass, and began pouring champagne. She chewed at her lip. "And before you say anything, I didn't know she was your daughter. How could I possibly know? I met her in a bar a month ago."

Jane pressed her palm against her forehead and shook her head in disbelief.

"But now that I know, it makes sense," Georgia added. "She looks like you. And she's beautiful inside and out, just like you." Georgia handed Jane her glass of fizz and held up her own. "Happy Christmas, Janey, even if it is thirty years late." She emptied the glass of champagne. "Your daughter." She shook her head. "It explains a lot, though."

Jane drained her glass too, then slammed it down on the countertop. Given how delicate the flutes were, it was amazing that it didn't smash.

"You have to leave. You have to leave *now*. This is...this is crazy. I bought you a *gift*."

"Did you really?" Georgia raised an eyebrow. "That's more than you ever did before."

"We weren't really on gift-giving terms that Christmas, were we?"

"Everything alright in there?" Milly called from the lounge.

"Yes!" they both chorused back quickly and loudly, before locking eyes. Gazing. Staring. For too long.

Georgia exhaled a long breath. "I... This is...too bloody strange."

"She's twenty-three, you know. You're fifty-four, or had that bit slipped your notice?" Jane's poise had all but evaporated, the remnants exploding silently around the kitchen.

Georgia sighed. "I'm aware of the age difference almost every day. I didn't just wake up one morning thinking, 'I know, I'll go snag myself a twenty-three-year-old.' It just happened."

Jane snorted with disbelief, making a face as she cracked her ankle against a cupboard door. "You know you're too old to use that line, don't you?" To take her mind off the pain in her ankle, she poured herself another glass of champagne and drank it swiftly.

They stared at each other, the silence between them broken only by the sound of the turkey spitting and the potatoes roasting. Jane swore she could even hear the bubbles fizzing in her glass.

"Oh my god," Georgia said, her hand flying to her mouth. "Does this mean that Paul's…" Her eyes widened.

Jane nodded. "She told you?"

"About her dad, yeah, but I never put two and two together." Georgia poured another glass of champagne, downed it, and then drew herself up to her full height, sighing loudly. "I'm so sorry. He was a great guy. I always thought that, despite everything…"

Jane bit her lip and nodded. Before she knew it, Georgia's arms were around her, enveloping her, soothing her. It felt safe and comforting to be held, despite the fact she knew Rudolph's fluffy nose was burrowing into Georgia. Jane could feel Georgia's heart thumping.

The doorbell broke their connection. Jane pulled away, went to the sink and ran the cold tap. She needed a glass of water; the champagne had muddled her thinking. As the water hit the stainless steel sink, the timer on the oven sounded.

"Fuck," Jane muttered. Everything was happening at once, too quickly. She cleared her throat. "I can't…" She turned to look at Georgia as she rallied. "Can you baste the turkey? That'll be Joanna, and I need to go and sort myself out."

She opened the kitchen door. "Milly, can you get the door!" Jane called, before disappearing into the downstairs bathroom.

Georgia grabbed the oven gloves and carefully lifted the turkey out, the heat of the oven licking her face. The bird was massive. Just how many people did Jane have coming for dinner? A slew of old college lovers perhaps, just to add a bit more zest to the festivities? Her heart was still racing at breakneck speed, her face flushed as she followed Jane's instructions, basting the turkey and accompanying veg. It was good to have something to concentrate on. She was just lifting the turkey back into the oven when Milly appeared.

"There you are, and why are you doing that? You're a guest, for god's sake."

A sexy smile played on her lips, and Georgia recognised it as Jane's smile.

"Where's Mum?" Milly asked, leaning in for a kiss, her breath warm on Georgia's face.

Georgia quickly shut the oven door and took a step backwards before their lips could connect, suddenly aware the kitchen was an extremely small space. She'd run her tongue up those thighs that very morning, tasted Milly, had her fully. She felt slightly sick. Milly, her current love, daughter of Jane, her former love. Darling Jane, who had broken her heart.

"She just nipped to the loo," Georgia replied.

Georgia pushed her hair off her face and smiled at Milly. She was desperate to leave, but Milly grabbed her hand to draw her out of the kitchen. She hastily deposited the oven glove on the counter before she left.

"Come into the lounge and meet Joanna and Josh," Milly said. "He seems lovely," she whispered over her shoulder, "if a bit scared."

Georgia shook her head. Josh didn't even realise that whatever his faults, this was a "battle of the partners" he was about to win hands down.

"Jo, Josh, this is Georgia," Milly said, pulling her close, putting a protective arm around her waist.

Georgia smiled and shook hands, absently looking around the room for an escape route. There were no exit doors or inflatable slides, so she'd have to be inventive. Sickness. A headache. A migraine. Yes, a migraine was perfect.

Where Milly took after Jane with her dark hair, brown eyes, and skin as pale as a porcelain doll, Georgia could see

Paul leaping out of Joanna at every turn—his nose, his smile, his easy-going manner. Everything she didn't want to be reminded of about good old Paul. Poor old Paul. What was it was like for Jane, seeing him reflected back at her every day of her life?

"Lovely to meet you at last," Joanna said, flashing a smile so wide Georgia thought it might fall off her face. Josh, as befitted many young men in London these days, wore narrow jeans, a beard, and a worried smile. He shifted from foot to foot, holding a bag of gifts in his left hand. Behind her, Georgia sensed Jane returning to the room. That was confirmed by Joanna's smile notching up a level, in tandem with Josh's worried glance.

"We were wondering where you were, Mummy!" Joanna pulled Jane into a hug.

As introductions were made, Georgia stepped aside and took stock of the situation. She still couldn't quite believe this was happening to her, but apparently this *was* her Christmas 2013 and she *was* in this room in Muswell Hill.

Joanna held Jane at arm's length and studied her. "You okay? You look like you've been crying."

Putting a tissue to her nose, Jane batted her comment away. "Allergies. And too much champagne. Talking of which, let me get you a drink and go check on the dinner." She hurried out without a single look towards Georgia, Joanna hurrying after her.

"I can get us our drinks, Mum, you sit down," Joanna said, but Jane was long gone.

"She's acting very strange," Milly said, sticking out her bottom lip. "Was she okay when you were getting the champagne?"

Georgia sighed as she felt Milly's hand on the small of her back. Perhaps running screaming out the front door was the best option. She kissed Milly's cheek and then gently pushed her away.

"I'll just go and get the things from the car," she said. "You keep Josh company."

Milly, in full-on happy family mode, was happy to oblige.

Georgia grabbed her handbag, strode out of the lounge and down the magnolia hallway. She would have expected better from Jane than magnolia. Then again, Jane had been offered colour in her life and she'd rejected it for a life of conformity, a life of beige. Perhaps this hallway suited her perfectly. This, and the overhanging pelmets on her curtains. She never, ever thought she'd have a friend with pelmets.

Outside without a coat, the wind took Georgia's breath away and lifted her hair away from her face. It whipped around her legs, sliced at her ankles, nipped at her neck. She reached her blue Mercedes, flashed the key fob, and sank gratefully into the driver's seat. She considered her next move. Which was what, exactly?

The obvious option would be to start the engine and drive away, remove herself from the situation and leave Jane to have a family Christmas with her two daughters. But what about Milly? All her things were in the suitcase, all the presents in the boot. She couldn't very well just drive off with all of them, could she? Besides, how on earth would she explain it? Milly knew where she lived, where she worked, where to find her. It wasn't like she could just disappear.

Georgia sighed as she pulled down the sun visor and flipped the mirror open. She might feel freaked, but at least she was looking normal—mascara intact, hair still passable. She scrabbled in her handbag and found her favourite lipstick. She reapplied, then reached down and took off one of her black heels, kneaded the ball of her foot with her thumb. She wished she'd taken up her brother's invitation and gone to his house for Christmas. At least that would have been dull and predictable. But then, that's why she hadn't said yes in the first place. But this…

Okay, she could do this. She took a deep breath and put her hand on the door lever just as she heard some knuckles rapping on her window. A furious Jane was peering down at her. Georgia hit the button and lowered window.

"Is this your default setting?" Jane asked.

If the window had been closed, the harshness of her words might have shattered the glass. Panic stuck in Georgia's throat as she stared up at Jane's crazed eyes.

"Don't give me that look. You left me all those years ago, now you're going to do the same to my daughter? On Christmas day?"

Was Jane going to reach in and punch her? Georgia edged away from the door, just in case. "I wasn't going…"

"Plus, you've had too much bloody champagne to drive," Jane added. Her eyes were drilling a hole into Georgia's skull.

Georgia saw the net curtains in the living room twitch, and knew Milly had clocked the scene.

"I just came out to catch my breath and get the suitcase and presents," Georgia said. "I bought you a present too. Trying to make a good impression." She got out of the car and walked round to the boot, Jane's heated gaze following her the whole way.

"What is it? A dagger? Some poison?" Jane asked. She crossed her arms over her chest defensively.

Georgia's mouth curled into a snarl. "How terribly Shakespearian." She pulled the grey Samsonite case out of the boot, along with the bag of gifts. She glanced at Jane, whose body was heaving so visibly that it looked like Rudolph was having a very bad day. "I brought Bollinger, actually. Safe choice, I thought. Perfect choice, it turns out."

The corners of Jane's mouth flickered upwards slightly and her bravado deflated in front of Georgia's eyes.

"I…you… You can't come back in," Jane said.

Jane now looked freaked, and Georgia knew this wasn't the course of action she'd talked herself into in the bathroom mirror. Georgia set the case on the pavement. The bag of gifts clinked when she put it down, and she looked at Jane with an eyebrow arched in question.

"Which is it? You don't want me to drive off, or you don't want me to come back in. You can't have it both ways." She sighed. "That's what you've always wanted, but life doesn't work like that."

Jane's lips drew into a tight line, and Georgia could see her internal struggle. She might not have ridden to Jane's rescue all those years ago, but she found that she wanted to do that now. She exhaled sharply.

"I'm going to make this easy for you," Georgia began. The hairs on her arms were standing on end, and she wasn't surprised. It was icy cold in more ways than one. "I'll come back in, drop off the presents, have a drink, and develop a sudden migraine. Then I'll leave."

Jane was staring at her, watching her mouth move, licking her lips. If Georgia hadn't known better...

"And Milly?" Jane said, snapping out of her thrall. "She doesn't deserve this. And that's on top of the fact that she's too young for you."

Georgia closed her eyes and rubbed the bridge of her nose. When she re-opened her eyes, Jane was still there, but now Milly was standing beside her with a puzzled look on her face.

"What am I too young for?" she asked, eyeing her mother with suspicion. "I told you on the phone she was older than me. What are you doing, throwing her out?" Milly's voice was on the edge of hysteria.

Georgia stepped forward and touched her arm. "It's okay, darling."

"No, it's not okay!" Jane and Milly yelled.

Georgia looked over at the door, where Joanna and Josh were standing shoeless on the threshold, mouths open, hanging onto the doorframe. Perfect.

Shaking her head, Milly burst into tears and stared at her mother. "I can't fucking believe you'd do this. I thought after everything...*everything*, you'd support my choice of partner. I love her, Mum." Milly took a deep breath. "I love her!"

Georgia winced; Jane let out a hollow laugh.

"You don't love her. You don't even know her. You've known her five minutes." Jane fixed Georgia with a stare that kept her rooted to the spot. "You don't know her at all."

"And you do?" Milly asked, wiping away tears and sniffing continuously.

"Yes, I bloody do," Jane said.

"Just because she's thirty years—"

"She's thirty-one years older than you, not thirty. Thirty-one!" Jane's voice boomed off the pavement, slapping bare skin, denting car bonnets. "I know her. I went to university with her. She nearly broke me and your dad up with her games, her lies—" Jane abruptly clamped her hand over her mouth.

"My games? *Really?*" Georgia said, disbelief coating every word. "You're the one who played games, you're the one who declared your love but wouldn't commit. So don't fucking talk to me about games."

They stood on the pavement glaring at one another, legs apart, torsos pitched forward as if they were about to engage in actual combat. Georgia and Jane—street fighters both.

Georgia could see Milly trying to make sense of it all, struggling to put together the pieces of the puzzle. She knew when she eventually got the entire picture, the ending would not be the happy one she'd hoped for.

Seeing the confusion in Milly's eyes, followed closely by incredulity, Georgia clocked the scene from the street—neat lines of trees, box hedges, frosted windows, flashing tree lights. And on the pavement in front of number forty-nine, a Shakespearian plot played out: the dead father, the jealous lover, the jealous mother, and Georgia squarely in the middle. She'd have laughed if it hadn't been so farcical.

Just at that moment, it began to snow.

"Am I..." Milly's gaze shifted from Georgia to Jane, then back to Georgia. Her index finger pointed from one to the other. Two snowflakes settled on its tip, before melting into nothing. "Am I getting this right—you two?" Her nostrils twitched. "You two?" she repeated numbly.

Jane stared at the pavement. Georgia looked up at the sky, as if for Divine intervention, then reached out for Milly, who immediately shrugged her arm away.

"It's not what you think," Georgia began. "Well, not exactly what you think. Yes, your mum and I knew each other in college, but it was complicated—"

"By Dad?" Milly said.

The snow was falling in earnest now, and when Georgia looked over at Milly's crumpled face, she was wearing a hat of snowflakes. She looked absurdly seasonal.

Milly threw her hands in the air. "I don't understand. Am I sleeping with someone my mother has already slept with?" She instantly clapped her hands over her ears, as if that would somehow keep her from knowing the answer.

Georgia heard footsteps coming down the pathway, and she turned to see Joanna. She had her hood up over her head, and all Georgia could see were two wide, frightened eyes staring out of the pale face.

"What's going on?" Joanna whispered. "Mum? Milly?" Even though she had addressed her mother and sister, she was looking at Georgia.

Georgia brushed snow off of her face and smiled softly. "What's going on is, it seems I've outstayed my welcome." Georgia's eyes flicked to Milly. "I'm sorry." She shrugged. "I honestly didn't know."

Jane took her hands away from her face and stared at Georgia.

Georgia set the bag of gifts down in front of Joanna, along with Milly's suitcase. Her heels clicked against the pavement as she moved back to the car. It was snowing harder now, but her body was impervious to the cold, her shoulders rigid like girders. She cast a final fleeting look at the trio standing in a row in the snow, raised a hand in defeat, and opened the car door.

Jane took a step towards her. "Georgie…"

Georgie. Jane was the only person who'd ever called her that in her life. Usually behind closed doors, when Paul was out, when she was sure nobody would hear. Georgie. Georgia glanced at Jane and caught the longing in her eyes. Somehow she knew it wasn't the last time in her life she'd ever hear Jane say it.

"Happy Christmas," Georgia said to the three stricken women standing on the pavement.

As her body settled in the driver's seat, she felt relieved to be in her own safe space, a metal cocoon. She was comforted by the thud of the heavy car door as it shut her in.

They were all still watching her.

"Drink the good champagne first," Georgia called out the open window, then pressed the button to close it. Her window sealed out the rest of the world. The engine roared to life. Without a backwards look, Georgia drove forwards, into the rest of her Christmas Day.

First Christmas

A Sigil Fire Story

ERZABET BISHOP

Sonia stared at the scene in the kitchen with disbelief. Its normally pristine surface was in complete disarray. Flour covered the counter, the smell of something delicious baking was in the air, and Fae, her blood-witch vampire girlfriend, was singing Christmas carols like she was Patsy Cline incarnate. Dressed in low-rider skinny jeans and a vibrant, red tank top, Fae shimmied around the kitchen with a snap in her step. Her long, black hair was loose and flowing, and Sonia had to fight the urge to pin her lover to the counter and run her fingers through it while ravaging her lips.

She loved to watch Fae in the kitchen. The normally badass, "don't mess with me or I'll shove a sword up your nose" woman was pure magic when she wielded a spatula. Or any other kitchen equipment, for that matter. Sonia grinned, a low simmer of heat spreading between her thighs as her eyes followed Fae's every move.

Jellybean rested next to the kitchen door, her small, black, hellhound face fixed on Sonia. It seemed even Jellybean didn't know what to make of Fae's behavior.

As Sonia rounded the corner into the kitchen, she caught sight of a stack of cardboard boxes and a half-decorated tree started in the front window of the living room. She'd left for work, and everything had been normal, and now, she'd come home to Chaos Comes to Christmas Town. "What are you doing?"

"Getting ready for the Yule party, what else?" Fae came around the kitchen island and placed a light kiss on Sonia's lips.

"Party?" Sonia leaned next to the island and let the scent of baking goodies settle over her. Still dressed in her fetish costume from the day's shoot, she felt like a pornographic elf.

"I like the corset," Fae crooned, her eyes sliding up and down the length of Sonia's body.

"Thanks. Monty said I could wear it home this time. It feels great." Sonia did a pirouette and took a bow, letting her full breasts come dangerously close to falling out of the corset. It had been a long afternoon at the photo shoot, but Monty was happy with her work, so it had been worth it.

"Mmmm. Someone is going to get a spanking for that one. Definitely on Santa's naughty list." Fae tisked and waggled her finger, reaching for a spatula.

"What?" Sonia bit her lip and giggled, scurrying around the island. Something dinged, and she jumped. "What did I do?" Her voice rose in a panic, her eyes darting around the room to find the source of the sound.

"You've never baked cookies before?" Fae padded over to the oven and snapped up the hot pads camping on the counter. She opened the door to the oven, schlepped the pans out, and laid them on the stove. The spicy scent of freshly baked cookies filled the kitchen.

"No." Sonia turned away, more than a little awkward. "I've never really had Christmas or Yule before. It was always...I don't know...something for other people. And about takeout."

Fae set the hot pads on the counter and came around the island. "I had no idea."

Sonia shrugged. "It wasn't something I ever thought about. I modeled a sexy Santa suit here and there, but that's been about it." She walked over to the cookies, the spicy scent tempting her nostrils. "That smells amazing."

"Thanks." Fae leaned back against the counter, lifting her eyebrows. "So in all your years, you've never been to a Christmas party or a Yule celebration?"

Sonia's lips twitched, and she met her lover's eyes. "You have to understand: I was an angel before I was changed into this." She held out her arms and sighed. "I didn't remember anything from before, and, like I said, the only time the holidays meant much was when Jeannie popped over for a drink or when I had to model for a magazine standing next to someone else's Christmas tree."

"We always had Yule at my house." Fae gazed off into space. "My mother was the neighborhood Yule goddess of light." An amused smile tilted up her lips. "She had me baking cookies and making presents by hand at the age of ten."

"You're kidding."

"Nope." Fae grinned. "I keep forgetting you've only been here a couple of months. It feels like you've been a part of my life forever." She walked over to Sonia and tugged her toward the living room.

"Where are we going?"

"You'll see."

Fae dragged her to the spare bedroom and pulled open the top of a chest of drawers. "Open your hand."

"Okay." Sonia lifted her palm and cocked her head.

"Here."

Sonia looked down and found a small, round shape made from yarn with beads sewn into it. The dark evergreen yarn was over-dyed, the colors natural and earthy. The beads sewn into the fiber were red and resembled shiny ornaments made in miniature. It was topped off with a red bow. The shape reminded her of something.

"What is it?"

"It's a wreath, silly." Fae chortled. "I made it last year. It gets slow at the shop, so sometimes I pick up my mother's old crochet hook and make some quick presents for people. It's fun."

"You made this?" Tears prickled behind Sonia's eyes. "I can keep it?"

"Of course." Fae looked at her curiously. "Are you crying?"

Sonia turned and shook her head. "No." She stared at the tiny wreath and at the wonderful woman who surprised her every day and smiled. *My first Christmas present.* "I'm happy."

"I'm telling you, Monty, you won't believe it." Fae hugged the phone to her ear. "I want everyone over here right now. She's gone to grab a bite of someone at the bar, and I need all you guys *tout de suite.*"

"She's been to a Christmas party before." Monty growled through the phone. "At least, I thought so. We had one at the studio a few years back." Fae could positively hear him counting back the years in his head.

"I don't think so." Fae shook her head, even though she realized the demon couldn't see it. "She's completely clueless about Christmas. They must have scrambled her brains pretty good when they changed her into a succubus. I mean, what kind of former angel hasn't gotten the down low about gingerbread cookies and little crocheted wreaths? It's unnatural."

"No it isn't. Our girl's been through a lot." Monty paused, his rich, chocolate voice revealing his surprise. "Come to think of it, she wasn't there. Always ducked out before the festivities started. Every time."

"I thought so." Fae mused. "Every year, we have the party over here at Forbidden Ink. It helps me keep relations with the customers, and with Cirque Nocturne hanging around longer than normal, I kind of want to have an extra fun one. I want them to stay in town. Will you help me give her a good Christmas? I want her to understand she's got a family that loves her."

"She does." Monty agreed. "The girl is special. But the guys can't come right now, actually. There's been some trouble at one of the clubs downtown. A zombie was sighted in one of the back alleys. Not a good situation."

"Crap."

"I know. Got to get a lid on it quick or it'll start to spread. But anyway...I digress. What time do you want this shindig to start?"

"No, you hold it like this." Fae grabbed Sonia's hands and tried to position them around the crochet hook.

Sonia squirmed in frustration. "I'm hopeless." She moaned, holding out the knotted-up piece of yarn and the ugly swatch of stitches. "This is hideous."

"No, you're not hopeless," Fae said. "But you are pretty frustrating."

"Hey!" Sonia's lips slid into a frustrated pout.

"Come on. Put that down for a minute. I want you to come into the kitchen. We have to make some crescent cakes for the party and stir the soup."

The whole second floor was decorated stem to stern with holly, Christmas trees, and garlands. Holiday music filled the air, and even Jellybean seemed to realize there was something going on. She roamed from table to table, sniffing out possible tidbits in need of rescue. Platters of chicken and vegetables were laid out along the sideboards, and an assortment of cakes and pies lined another table to the other side of the dining room. The tree sparkled in the front window, laden with white lights and crystal snowflakes. It was a dream.

One of the girls she'd seen down in the shop nodded at Fae as she headed out the door.

"Thanks, Wanda."

"You're welcome! See you in a couple of hours."

"Did you drop by the bookstore and the bakery?"

"Yes. Now stop worrying." Wanda grinned. "It's going to be amazing."

Sonia gave Fae a dubious glance. "I'm not sure why you're trying to make me into a domestic goddess, Fae. I'm not." She frowned.

"I realize that. But a few people from the shop are coming, and I wanted some time alone with you before they show up." Fae winked. "Monty's even coming this time."

Sonia perked up, laying down the offending crochet hook.

"Whoop! Really?"

"Yes. Perry and what's-her-name are supposed to come too."

Sonia rolled her eyes. "Her name is Charley."

"Yeah, yeah." Fae whistled as she finished a batch of cookies and slid them into the oven. "Whatever. She's still a pain in the ass."

"Who else?" Sonia eyed her suspiciously. Her lover was hiding something.

Fae looked down, pretending to be busy putting dishes in the dishwasher. "Oh, you know…a few people."

Sonia bit her lip and tried not to panic. "I'm not sure how to have Christmas, Fae."

"It's easy, babe." Fae tucked a strand of red hair behind her ear and smiled. "You just come to the party and gawk at the pretty lights, eat a few snacks, and if you're especially good, you might get a present."

The timer dinged, and Fae reached down to take out the tray.

"But you already gave me a present." Sonia pointed to the small crocheted wreath pinned to her blue T-shirt.

Fae blinked. "You haven't taken it off."

"No. You gave it to me. It was my first Christmas present. Why would I ever take it off?"

"How about I help you?" Fae pressed her lips to Sonia's and wound her fingers in her hair. Her hands cupped Sonia's breasts and Sonia moaned. "Come here." The shimmering lights of the tree flickered in the darkness of the room. Fae urged her forward with beckoning fingers.

Sonia sat down on the carpet in front of the tree.

Fae followed close behind and sank down beside her onto the floor. Their lips met, and Fae groaned. “They’ll be here in an hour.”

“Good. I want to see what you look like underneath my first Christmas tree.” Sonia breathed, desire moving under her skin like molten fire. “No clothes. Just you.”

“Your eyes are so beautiful in this light.” Fae tugged Sonia down to meet her hungry lips. One of Fae’s fangs drew blood.

“Ow!” Sonia drew back, quirking her lips into a grin. “So, you’re going to be feisty tonight. Oh, good.” Her life had changed so much since she had met Fae. The sex between them did something for Sonia on a primal level that went way beyond the norm. They fed off each other—Sonia giving blood, Fae giving her the life force she needed without having to feed as often. It was sexy and hot, and Sonia had never been as happy as she was right now. Her needs as a succubus were met. But there was so much more than that between them.

“You have no idea.” Fae grinned, the feral being in her coming out to play. “Look under the tree there. The package with the red paper. Open it up.”

“But I can’t open it yet. Christmas is still a few days away.” Sonia wiped a loose strand of hair out of her eyes.

“Oh well, I guess I’d better get back to my party preparations. Wouldn’t want to forget to…I don’t know… maybe rearrange my sock drawer before they show up.”

“Ugh. You’re incorrigible.” Sonia got on her hands and knees and shuffled under the tree to find the package in question. Moments later, she held the shiny, red-paper-covered box in her hand and brought it back with her.

“Now, open it.” Fae sat back up, folding her legs beneath her.

Sonia grumbled and did as she was asked. The paper was slick under her fingers. She let her hands roam along the seams and tried to peel back the tape without ripping it.

"Oh my Goddess, give me that." Fae scowled. "You just rip it. Like this." She grabbed hold of one end of the paper and tore, leaving the wrapping hanging off in tattered pieces.

"Hey!" Sonia pouted. "I was getting there."

"So is Christmas, and, at that rate, it's going to be here before you even get past the first piece of tape."

"Mean..." Sonia rolled her eyes and stared down at the ravaged package in her hands. She tugged the torn wrapping off and considered the box sitting there.

"Open it."

"Okay, okay." Sonia lifted the flap on the cardboard box, revealing two smaller boxes within. She reached inside and picked up the larger one.

"You can open them both, but what do you want first? Naughty or nice?"

Sonia blinked, indecision eating at her. "Naughty."

Fae grinned. "Good. Open that one."

Sonia lifted up the lid on the glossy black box. Buried within a layer of tissue paper was a wooden paddle, her name painted on the wood of the business end.

"Oh, my God." Sonia stared at the paddle with wonderment. She and Fae had been exploring impact play, but to have a paddle of her own...Tears prickled behind her eyelids, and she gave Fae a wobbly smile.

"Do you like it?" Fae moved forward and took the instrument from Sonia's hand.

"I love it." She wiped a tear, reaching over to place a kiss on her lover's lips.

"Well, I figured we could try out that nifty song about Rudolph the Red Nosed Reindeer and see whose was brighter—his glow-in-the-dark nose or your ass after I swing in a little holiday cheer." Fae swung the paddle.

Sonia giggled. "You're terrible."

"Yes. But you love me."

"I do. I really, really do."

"Good." Fae's eyes sparkled in the dim light. "Now, open your other present."

Sonia reached into the bag and scooped out the smaller black velvet box. "What is it?"

"Open it, silly."

"You…" The little black velvet box sat there patiently waiting. Small, it loomed large in Sonia's mind. It had to be jewelry. Nothing else looked like that. In the past, men had tried to offer her trinkets in exchange for her love, but none of those offers had been true. Not really. Just bribes for a physical bout of succubus-induced bliss.

This was. It was real, and for a moment Sonia's hands shook as she moved to pull apart the hinged box. The sparkling lights of the tree illuminated the diamond engagement ring as it winked against the black velvet. The trembling in Sonia's hands increased, and the tears she had been holding back let loose with a torrent of want and need. "Fae…" she choked out. "I…"

"You don't like it." Fae had moved away and was standing by the window, looking out at the street. "I can pick out something else if you'd rather."

"No! Yes. I mean, I love it. Come over here, please." Sonia wiped her eyes and opened the box again, just to make sure she hadn't imagined it. She picked up the white gold and diamond ring and slipped it on her finger, dropping the box to the floor. The fit was perfect. "Why do you do that? Don't run away from me." Sonia sniffled and swallowed, her voice wobbly and full of emotion.

Fae stared at her with large eyes. "I couldn't stand it if you said no."

"So ask me, then."

"Will you marry me?" Fae knelt next to her, a careful expression on her face when she saw the closed box on the floor next to Sonia's feet. "We've only known each other a short time, but I can't imagine a day going by without you here in my life. A night without you in my bed. A family without you in it."

Sonia held up her left hand, the diamond glittering as bright as any star. "Yes. Oh yes."

"There's nothing you could give me that could top this." Sonia wriggled the fingers of her left hand and rubbed her backside, wincing at the heat that still rolled beneath her skin.

"Hmmm. I don't know. That Santa is full of surprises." Fae winked and laid out the last of the party favors on the table next to the door.

"Yeah. Shiny red things." Sonia shuddered and rubbed her sore ass.

Fae laughed. "I hope you're ready."

The doorbell rang, and a steady stream of demons and humans Sonia had seen around town paraded into their home. It was the holidays, and she knew Fae would be pleased, but Sonia was more used to social situations happening outside of her home and not in the middle of the living room. It was something she was working on. She loved Fae, and sharing the holidays with her friends was important to her.

Sonia backed up against the wall and tried to pretend she was part of the scenery. Always, she had been on the outside looking in. She'd always felt awkward in large groups, especially during the holidays, like some part of her realized she was severed from the light and couldn't figure out how to find it again.

"There you are!" Monty came through the door and lifted Sonia into a bear hug. The demon was smiling, his eyes shimmering red. A large Nordic blond man in a reindeer sweater joined him on the left.

"Howard, how do you put up with this guy?" Sonia gasped as Monty let go and her feet touched the floor once more.

"Easy. He makes a killer eggplant parmesan." Howard winked, and his lips curved into a smile, revealing a hint of fang.

Monty grinned. His eyes narrowed as he picked up on the sparkling rock hanging from Sonia's finger. "Something I should know, kitten?"

Sonia giggled. "Yep. She popped the question."

"Oh, honey." Monty pulled her into another hug. "I'm so happy for you both."

"Thanks." Sonia's reply came out muffled as she pulled away from the demon's chest.

"Have fun, kitten. I need to show Howard the tree. He wants one and can't decide on colored lights or white."

Sonia chuckled and turned her gaze onto the room. The party was in full swing. Laughter and holiday music filled the air with joyous frivolity. She fingered the ring and sighed. It was perfect. Jellybean romped from guest to guest, begging tidbits of food, and Fae was in her element. Dressed in her leather pants and a red sparkling tank top, her lover was radiant. She flourished as more and more people showed up.

Sonia drifted toward the hallway, ambling toward the stairs to the roof. It was irrational, but she needed to be by herself for a bit. She'd always been this way, alone in a crowd. It wasn't that she was unhappy. But she was restless.

She pushed the door open and stepped outside onto Fae's cultivated rooftop garden. It was a space that Sonia came to whenever she felt like a fish out of water.

The weather had been mild for December, but a storm was brewing in the distance. The scent of snow bit into her skin, and suddenly, the blue sleeveless dress she wore wasn't enough to keep the chill at bay.

The sigil on her arm sizzled to life, and the door to the roof opened. Magic was in the air, a winter's kiss on the horizon.

"There you are." Fae made her way across the garden and smiled. "Too much holiday cheer?"

"No. I just needed a minute. It's been a pretty intense day." Sonia sat down on the stone bench and winced. Her bottom was still sore, but it was a pleasant burn.

"Do you want me to sit with you?"

"I don't want to take you away from your guests." Sonia smiled. "I just want to watch the stars."

Fae nodded and bent down to place a kiss on Sonia's lips. "We're about to start the white elephant gift exchange. Come down when you're ready."

"I will."

The door closed, and Sonia was once again alone with the elements. A flake of snow drifted down, singular in its majesty. She captured it in her hand, the icy radiance melting upon contact with her skin.

"That's how I feel." She whispered her words to the heavens. "Like I'll burn with the heat and never, ever cool down enough to just be."

One after another, flakes of snow began to fall. Clouds covered the moon, and the snow began to fall in earnest. Sonia sat, letting the flakes pelt against her body. One after the other they melted. She lifted her hands once again to the gray and tempestuous sky, and one last perfectly crafted flake drifted into her hand.

The sound of sleigh bells echoed through the night, and the merry sound of a deep belly laugh resounded through the sky. Out of the corner of her eye, Sonia thought she saw…no. It couldn't be. Santa was a myth. Wasn't he?

Sonia looked down at the flake in her hand. Instead of melting, it began to change. Cold blue fire burst from the crystal of icy radiance and began to twist and shape it into something else. Something…other.

"Goddess." Sonia laid the throbbing ball of blue fire on the bench and backed away, uncertain what to do. Her sigil flamed on, power itching across her skin.

The ball of fire grew, and suddenly, the light went out, leaving a white furry object still and silent in its wake.

"Oh…" Sonia padded carefully toward the bench and knelt down, gingerly touching the creature and turning it over. A small furry canine face, eyes bright with winter fire, looked back at her. The little dog whined and cuddled against her hand, a tiny mop of white fur that half glittered in the white glare of the security lights.

"Well, I'll be." She cradled the little pup against her breast and crooned. Her vision clouded with happy tears as the puppy snuggled into her warmth.

She lifted the tiny snow beast into her arms and brought her inside. Fae was waiting in the hall, watching her come back down the stairs.

"Who's that?" Her brow arched upward.

"It seems the heavens thought I needed someone else to care for." Sonia grinned.

Fae laughed. "I thought I heard Santa's sleigh up there."

"What are you up to?" Sonia growled, suddenly suspicious.

"Of all the things in heaven and earth, never ask. Just accept the gift of family." Fae kissed her, drawing an irritated yipe from the puppy in Sonia's arms.

"It seems like Snowball there doesn't like getting squished between us," Fae quipped.

"Snowball…I like it." Sonia eyed her lover. "You didn't have anything to do with her, did you?"

"Now, why would you ask that?" A dimple crept into Fae's mischievous smile.

Sonia shrugged. "I don't know. You're always full of the darndest surprises."

"Merry Christmas, baby." Fae drew Sonia's hand to her lips and pressed a kiss against it. "Now, let's get back to the party. Jellybean will be waiting to meet her baby sister."

Sonia pressed a kiss to Snowball's tiny furry head and smiled.

"Oh yeah, Perry's here," Fae snarked as she headed back into the fray. "He's in the front room playing Twister with what's-her-name, and she's kicking his vampire ass."

"Charley! Her name is Charley." But, nevertheless, a grin settled across her face. The night was somehow fuller, as the furry creature in her arms shifted and got more comfortable, her little puppy mouth opening up in a yawn, only to close again quickly.

"I love you, little one." Sonia stood in the doorway and watched her friends play in front of the sparkling Christmas tree. "We're home."

Home for Christmas

T.M. CROKE

Carter's heart thudded to a stop as the stream of red cascaded down the right hand side of the Departures screen.

This can't be happening.

A snowstorm had struck with fury, and now every plane east of Ontario was grounded. That included Toronto, where she and her partner Amelia had recently arrived after a five hour flight to make their connections. Amelia was going to see her folks in Halifax, and Carter was on her way to St. John's. Apparently they were going nowhere tonight. They would be lucky to get another flight by Christmas Day, or even Boxing Day.

Risking a glance to the side, Carter held her breath as she waited for a reaction from Amelia, who was rhythmically tapping on her iPhone, her mouth twisted in concentration. Amelia swiped dark bangs away from her equally dark blue eyes, eyes that Carter found herself lost in on a daily basis.

"Damn."

Amelia's exclamation startled Carter from her reverie.

"This website is useless. Guess we should go find out how bad this is."

Carter gripped the handle of the luggage cart, ready to follow Amelia to the ticket counter. "At least it happened here and not in Halifax."

Amelia turned to face Carter. "At least if we were in Halifax, we wouldn't be stuck in the airport."

"*You* wouldn't be stuck in the airport," Carter retorted.

Amelia was very close to her family, but they had never accepted that she was a lesbian, never acknowledged or accepted her relationship with Carter. At Christmas, that translated into separate holiday celebrations for each of the six years of their relationship.

Amelia's eyes narrowed as she slapped Carter's arm. "They wouldn't leave you stuck in the airport alone."

"Good to know," Carter said with an incredulous grin. Amelia might have believed that of her parents, but Carter wasn't so sure.

Carter had wanted them to stay at home in Vancouver and celebrate Christmas together, but Amelia's need to please her parents made it unlikely that would ever happen. It was a tired and familiar discussion, but she was glad they had gotten past the argument about the holidays and were able to tease each other about it.

Amelia rolled her eyes as she linked her fingers with Carter's. "Come on, let's find out what's going on."

Air Canada's service counter was bombarded with stranded travelers desperate to reschedule their travel plans.

"It's going to be okay." Carter rubbed Amelia's arm. "Hopefully the storm will pass quickly, and we can catch a late evening flight."

Forty minutes later, they reached the front of the line at the ticket counter, where a harried woman attempted a smile. Carter thought that her expression said she had been yelled at one too many times that day. People lost all their Christmas spirit when it came to travel delays.

"Good afternoon. How can I help you today?"

"Our flights to Halifax and St. John's have been cancelled." Amelia handed their boarding passes to the agent. "We need to rebook."

The agent tapped her computer keys. Her mouth formed a tight, thin line as she reluctantly relayed the results of her search. "It looks like the next available flight to Halifax is tomorrow morning at 10:15, with the connection to St. John's departing at two."

"We'll take it." Carter turned to Amelia. "One night. We'll survive, right?"

"Right. When we finish up here, I'll try some hotels to find a room."

Her voice cracking with fatigue, the airline agent interjected, "We've already contacted a number of hotels in the area, and unfortunately everything in the vicinity is booked through the next few days." She smiled sympathetically. "We're offering blankets and small pillows, as well as meal vouchers."

Carter closed her eyes and counted to ten. She and Amelia only had this one night together for the entire holiday; could they possibly spend it in the airport? She shrugged. People had done it before and apparently survived no worse for the wear.

With their new travel documents in hand, Carter and Amelia tucked their blankets and pillows atop the luggage on their cart and moved out into the crowded airport until they found a spot they could stop and discuss their options.

"Bet you're wishing we were stuck in Halifax now," Amelia whispered with a smile.

Carter leaned in, her lips brushing Amelia's ear, causing her to shudder. "I'll take my chances with the airport." She stepped back with a chuckle.

Amelia smiled back. "Say that to me again in the morning, when you're stiff from lying on a chair all night."

Carter pulled her phone from her jacket pocket and tapped out a text to her younger brother, notifying him of her change of plans. "Done. I texted David and told him we were delayed. He'll tell Mom and Dad."

"If only I could get away with a text." Amelia blew out a deep breath.

Carter kissed her forehead. "You call your parents. I'm going to scout out the airport."

Carter returned to find Amelia leaning against a wall, engaged in an animated phone conversation, their luggage cart propped against her leg. Her body slumped forward as she ended the call, which Carter assumed had been with her mother. She looked tired, Carter thought, and it was only the beginning of a long night.

Carter grasped Amelia's hands in hers and tugged her forward. "Come on." She pulled Amelia against her in a warm embrace. "Grab the cart and follow me."

"Where?" Amelia grabbed her jacket, which she had thrown across the cart. "Most of the chairs are taken."

"Come on. I've found us a prime spot, and I don't want to lose it," Carter blurted out in delight.

"You found us a room in a four star hotel?"

Carter rolled her eyes. "Oh, come on."

She led Amelia down a hallway to an almost secluded alcove, where she took the handle of their luggage cart and tucked it against the wall.

"Here?" Amelia questioned indignantly. "You want me to sleep on the floor?"

Carter stared back at her. "It will be more comfortable here than trying to sleep on chairs. I'll spread the blanket so we can stretch out, and it doesn't seem to be that busy down here, so we'll have some degree of privacy. We can pretend we're camping." She grinned.

Carter knew that Amelia hated camping, but she shook out one of the blankets and laid it on the floor in invitation.

Amelia took a moment to size up the small space, then gave in with a loud sigh. "I guess it's better than nothing."

Carter was surprised by how easily Amelia had given in. "That's my girl," she said in a low voice, rubbing Amelia's arm in a comforting gesture.

Giving Carter a half-hearted scowl, Amelia grumbled, "You better have cards or something in your bag to entertain me." She dropped down on the blanket.

"I have my iPad. We can watch a movie later." Carter knelt down on the blanket in front of Amelia and cradled her face in her palms. "It'll be Christmas morning before you know it."

Their eyes locked, and twin smiles appeared on their faces. In the rush of the day, it was only now that Carter realized this would be the first Christmas they would actually be spending together in their six year relationship. For so many years they had made separate plans with their families, but now they would be together on Christmas Day. It didn't matter that they were spending it on a dirty floor in a crowded airport, just that they would be together when they woke on Christmas morning.

Amelia laughed. "Who thought the first time we would get to spend Christmas holidays together would be in an airport."

Euphoria poured from those few words, and Carter's eyes lit up as she kissed Amelia soundly. "You okay here if I go get us something to eat before everything closes?"

Amelia nodded. "Okay, but don't be long."

Carter quickly kissed her again. "Back in a flash." She stood and strode toward the concourse, Amelia's soft laughter trailing behind her.

The shops were crowded with people picking anything and everything off the shelves. Carter snagged a few packets of almonds and a couple of bottles of water. Snacks in hand, Carter hurried through the airport in search of a sandwich shop to use the food vouchers.

In a way, it was like any other day at the airport and not at all like Christmas Eve. Of course, it was an international airport, and not everyone celebrated the holiday, but then, as she turned a corner, the glow of a beautifully decorated Christmas tree appeared before her.

She stood and stared. A tingle danced down her spine, and Carter's smile widened. She was determined to make this Christmas an amazing experience for Amelia, starting with the small gift she had slipped into Amelia's suitcase earlier that morning for her to find when she got to Halifax. Carter would have to distract Amelia when she returned, or wait until she was asleep before taking it out. Seeing Amelia's face light up when she opened it would be a thousand times better in person than over a choppy ten inch screen on her iPad.

She turned away from the tree towards a small deli, searching her mind for ways to make this a Christmas to remember.

After a few shopping stops, Carter made her way back to their airport home with food in hand. Stopping about thirty feet away from their campsite, she stood and stared at Amelia, who sat propped against the wall, her legs stretched out in front of her, crossed at the ankles. Long dark hair tumbled about her shoulders, framing her delicate face. Her cheeks were flushed and her lips slightly parted. Carter's heart skipped a beat. She was definitely the luckiest woman in the world.

As if Amelia sensed her presence, blue eyes turned in her direction. A slow smile crossed Amelia's face, and Carter's knees shook. Despite the many years they had been together, one look from Amelia still made her heart flutter.

Carter bridged the gap between them, and Amelia grabbed for the plastic bags in her hand.

"What did you get?"

"Hey!" Carter held the bags away. "It's a surprise," she teased, knowing full well that Amelia hated surprises.

Amelia rolled her eyes. "I am starving. I hope you brought me something good to eat, or your hunter-gatherer status might be called into question."

Carter laughed as she pulled out a sandwich and handed it over. "Turkey, mustard, no mayo," she said, listing off the ingredients she knew so well.

"Yum." Amelia smiled as she accepted the sandwich.

"I did splurge and pick up a pack of chips for us to share."

Carter had barely held them up when Amelia snatched them from her. Chuckling, Carter took out her own sandwich, casually setting the other bags down behind her carry-on, away from Amelia's prying eyes.

"So...many people around?" Amelia asked between bites. "It's so quiet here, it's as if we're the only ones around."

"There's still a lot of people milling about, killing time. When it gets later, more people will be hunkering down, I suspect. There are all sorts of makeshift sleeping areas popping up." Carter finished the last of her sandwich. "After dinner, you should take a walk around the airport to stretch your legs and have a look."

"And find some coffee."

Carter smiled. "Yes, find some coffee. I forgot. After you finish your dinner, you should see if you can find a Starbucks.

Crumpling her sandwich wrapper, Amelia said, "That hit the spot. Your hunter-gatherer status is still in good standing, but I still need coffee."

Amelia got to her feet, grabbed her knapsack, pecked Carter on the cheek, and departed. She was gone so long, Carter wondered if she had caught a plane to Colombia to get the beans first hand, but when she returned with small white cup, Carter's eyebrows raised.

"Starbucks was closed, but I managed to find a vending machine." Amelia frowned as she pointed at the cup. "They say its coffee, but I think they skimped on the beans."

"That good, huh?" Carter kidded, enjoying the smile that the warm elixir put on Amelia's face. Coffee was her one true addiction.

"It's caffeine. You know how I hate to go without." She plopped down next to Carter. "Everything is closed now, and people seem to be settling down for the night."

Carter put an arm around her and sighed. Content. It was the first word that came to her mind. Amelia filled her with such contentment. Their first Christmas together, Carter thought, but would it be their last? Would their tradition of spending separate holidays ever change? Would Amelia's parents always have the priority hold over her? Carter wanted to think that at some point, she would come first. It was silly, really. For the last six years, they had gotten through the holidays just fine by celebrating on another date, but now that Fate had given them this day, she couldn't help wanting more.

They sat in comfortable silence, people-watching and playing chess on Carter's iPad. Carter lost every game, distracted by her opponent. As the hours crept by, they took turns stretching their legs by wandering about the airport, bumping into other wayward travellers, returning to share the stories with one another.

The night was winding down as they sat snuggled together reading. Amelia yawned and rested her head against Carter's shoulder.

Carter kissed the top of her head. "Stretch out, get comfortable." She smiled at Amelia's sleepy eyes. "It's going to be a long night."

Amelia quickly acquiesced. She threw off her shoes, lay down, and wiggled her toes against Carter's hip. "Why don't you curl up with me," she asked through a deep yawn.

"I want to finish this chapter," Carter lied. She knew Amelia would be asleep before long. It had been a long day and they were both exhausted, but Carter's excitement was keeping her awake.

"Well, read fast, and then come cuddle."

Warmth enveloped Carter as Amelia wiggled her toes on Carter's thighs.

"Oh yeah?" Carter wanted nothing more than to curl up with Amelia and wrap her arms around her, to kiss and touch her, but they weren't alone. That didn't satisfy her active libido. After six years together, time had not diminished the desire Amelia stirred in her. She peered out into the airport where a few people were still trying to find a place to settle for the night, and then she looked back at Amelia and waggled her eyebrows.

"Get your mind out of the gutter. I just want you to keep me warm." Amelia chuckled and curled onto her side.

When she was asleep, Carter eased away and watched her for a while. She could have continued doing so for a long time, but it was getting late and she had many things to do before she would get the chance to close her own eyes.

Carter quietly eased to her feet and stretched. No matter how often she moved, the hard floor still made her stiff. She gingerly bent to retrieve her now mostly empty knapsack, and then she set off on a quick trip around the airport to get what she needed.

Her first order of business took her down one concourse and through another, stepping over people resting in bunches on the floor. In the centre of the aisle between two departure gates was the Christmas display she'd spied earlier. Again she stared at the tree, mesmerized by the twinkling of its gold and glitter decorations.

As she fingered the bows, she took a quick look around to make sure that no one was looking or wandering nearby. If not for the fear of getting caught, Carter would have lifted the whole tree and carried it back to their airport home. Borrowing four or five balls and a small amount of ribbon would have to do. She would return them tomorrow; she just wanted to make Christmas morning special for Amelia.

Childhood memories washed over her, memories of enchantment and wonder. This was the way she hoped Amelia would feel when she woke in the morning.

A large red teardrop bulb with gold glitter stood out, and Carter delicately lifted its hook from the supporting branch and placed it into her knapsack. With a racing heart and trembling fingers, she liberated a few more ornaments from the limbs of the artificial tree.

"And what do you think you're doing?" a stern voice questioned from behind.

Carter jumped, covering her mouth to suppress a scream, then she reluctantly turned around. "Um…I… This doesn't look good, does it?"

The security guard folded her arms across her ample chest and shook her head. "No, it doesn't."

Carter released a nervous breath. "I was just trying to *borrow…*" she emphasized that she was not stealing the ornament. "…a few things to decorate for my girlfriend so she would have a nice Christmas morning. It's our first Christmas together."

The confession came out in a quick jumble. Carter hoped her honesty would persuade the husky security guard that she wasn't doing anything wrong.

Eyebrow raised, the security guard studied Carter hard.

Carter swallowed. *What kind of trouble am I in? Is it a felony to borrow Christmas ornaments in an airport?*

The security guard stared at Carter, her stoic expression unchanging.

Surely she wasn't the only hopeless romantic caught doing something stupid at Christmas. What was supposed to be a quick trip to pick up a few things was now going to bite her in the ass.

"Come with me."

It was a command, not a suggestion.

Shit. Carter followed behind the security guard. Weren't they supposed to read her her rights or something?

She knew the airport was large, but as she was dragged through concourses and white walled back corridors, she doubted she would find her way back if she was ever free to go. *I hope Amelia doesn't wake up and worry about me. I should have left a note.*

They stopped in front of a plain door painted the same colour as the walls. Except for the black scuff marks on the bottom panel, there was nothing on it to tell Carter what lay behind. The long corridor behind them was empty, dead quiet, a whole other world going on behind the scenes beyond the view of clueless travelers. Carter wiped a bead of sweat from the back of her neck. Any possible trouble she might get into for borrowing the Christmas decorations became a secondary concern as she realized she had just followed a stranger into the bowels of the airport at two in the morning.

Carter closed her eyes, and Amelia's face filled her mind. Was she wondering where she was? All Carter could think about was getting back to her.

The sound of jangling keys dragged her from her despair. The door was now open, and the guard motioned her inside.

Carter obediently walked into the small room. There was a round table in the middle and a loveseat against either wall. A small kitchenette in one of the corners was equipped with a Keurig, a sink, and a tea kettle. It looked like a snack room or staff hangout. Unsure of what she should do, she froze as the security guard moved past her.

The guard grabbed something off the counter, turned, and started to laugh.

Carter stood rigid in the centre of the room, afraid to move as fear knotted her stomach.

The guard pushed the object toward Carter, who blinked.

"Don't just stand there, take it," the guard said, her laughter changing into a smile.

Carter stared down at the guard's hands. She held a small Christmas tree, complete with decorations. Carter blinked again and awkwardly extended her hands to accept the tiny Charlie Brown Christmas tree. "Thanks," she murmured, totally confused.

"I know what that first Christmas feels like." The guard beamed at her. "I've worked so many Christmases here, I can't even remember how many. At least I get to go home to my wife tomorrow morning. You can borrow my Christmas tree. Just drop it off at Security before you leave tomorrow."

Feeling like a kid at Christmas, Carter cradled the tree. "Thank you! You have no idea what this means. I will make sure it gets back to Security tomorrow, I promise."

"Just make it special." She smiled and put two candy canes in Carter's shirt pocket. "And all you need for that…is you."

As the guard guided her back to the main concourse, Carter learned that her name was Kris, and she couldn't help but think she had found her own Kris Kringle. Kris and her wife had been together for just over ten years. Both from the Toronto area, they officially tied the knot two years before. They chatted about their significant others, Carter's face alight as she told Kris about Amelia.

Within sight of Carter's temporary home, Kris bade her adieu and "Merry Christmas" before heading in the opposite direction.

Holding the Christmas tree securely, Carter rushed back to their corner to lie down beside Amelia. Carter found her curled on her side, her knees tucked up and her hand resting under her cheek, her other arm draped across her abdomen. Her wayward dark hair fell over her eyes, and Carter thought she detected a smile on Amelia's face.

Trying not to wake Amelia, she quietly placed the tree and all the trimmings down next to their sleeping area. It was close to three, and Carter was fading fast. Her earlier adrenaline high was rapidly fading. She gently drew back the zipper on Amelia's suitcase and fished through its contents until her hand cupped the gift she had strategically placed inside earlier that morning. She tucked it under their tree, then knelt for a moment to admire Amelia's features before stretching out behind her.

Amelia shifted into Carter's embrace and mumbled in her sleep. Carter feared she might wake, but she settled, her breath a steady cadence to the beat of her heart beneath Carter's hand. Its beat lulled her.

Content that their Christmas Day would be as special as she could make it, Carter drifted off to sleep, her most precious gift wrapped tightly in her arms.

Daybreak came quickly, and despite only a few hours of sleep, Carter was already awake.

The airport had come to life at an ungodly hour. People milled about, shuffling their luggage toward the rousing airline counters in hopes that the delays of the previous day would not be repeated. Choruses of "Happy Holidays" and "Merry Christmas" echoed against the walls.

Amelia stirred beside Carter, her blue eyes fluttering open, focusing on her surroundings.

"Merry Christmas, sweetheart," Carter whispered, kissing her temple.

Amelia closed her eyes again, apparently debating waking.

Carter's lips tickled Amelia's cheek until she squirmed, a bright grin gracing her face. "Mm," she mumbled. Blue eyes opened and stared up at Carter.

"Sleep okay?" Carter asked. She herself remembered nothing after falling asleep with Amelia in her arms. They could have been sleeping on a bed of rocks, she wouldn't have known.

"Yes. Did you?" Amelia brushed the loose strands of hair from Carter's face. "Merry Christmas, baby." She kissed Carter's lips. "Our first one where we're actually together. I guess you got your Christmas wish."

"Not the way I envisioned it, but I'll take it," Carter admitted with a smile.

Amelia stretched in her arms, her curves gliding under Carter's hand. Carter's body responded, and she shook her head. She wasn't supposed to be having lascivious thoughts whilst lying on the floor in the middle of an airport, but with Amelia's body directly beneath her fingertips, she couldn't help it.

She sat up behind Amelia and forced herself to focus on her plan to pamper her this Christmas morning. "Come on, sleepyhead. We should get up." Carter twined her fingers with Amelia's and pulled slightly to coax her.

Sitting up, Amelia stretched and yawned. "Why does it have to be so damn—" Her eyes went wide as she turned slowly toward Carter, tears welling in her eyes. "You did this?" She gestured toward the festive display.

Carter shook her head, "Me? No. I think Santa had a layover while he was waiting out the storm."

Arranged before them was the borrowed Christmas tree, neatly decorated with miniature ornaments. Taped to the wall were the larger ornaments and bows Carter had borrowed from the bigger tree. Next to the tree was the pair of spare socks Carter kept in her carry-on in case of lost luggage, only now they were filled with the traditional treasures of her childhood stocking—an orange, an apple, a banana, and a small toy she had gotten from a bubble gum machine. It was impossible to find the loose shelled nuts her mother used to fill the spaces in her and her brother's stockings, so a bag of roasted almonds served as a suitable substitute under the circumstances. Topping off the goodies in the stockings were the two candy canes Kris has bestowed upon her.

Beneath the tree lay a small, square box wrapped in glossy silver foil paper.

Amelia was silent for a long while as her fingertips skimmed over the festive display, and Carter's palms started to sweat. Did she like it?

"How?" Her blue eyes turned to Carter. "Never mind, tell me later." She laughed, brushing pieces of gold glitter from Carter's cheek. "I love you."

Three simple words that meant everything to Carter.

Amelia leaned in. Her lips barely brushed Carter's, but the tingle resonated through her entire body.

"I love you too," Carter declared, resting her forehead against Amelia's.

"I can't believe you did all this." She shook her head, and her hair tickled Carter's face.

Carter blushed. "Well, you know me, always the romantic."

"This is the nicest thing anyone has ever done for me," Amelia confessed. "That you would go to all this trouble to make Christmas special for me when we're stuck...here." Her eyes glistened with tears.

"I don't care where I am, as long as I am with you." It was true.

Taking a moment to peer down the hall through the large window overlooking the tarmac, Carter saw that the snow had subsided and the cleanup crew was hard at work with shovels and plows. The calm after the storm meant they would be going their separate ways today. A tinge of melancholy gripped her and she wished they were home, tucked in their bed, celebrating Christmas morning together. They'd open their presents, and then Carter would make breakfast while Amelia prepared the turkey and popped it into the oven. Carter chuckled. She knew they'd end up back in bed once the turkey was roasting, and it would be a wonderful day with just the two of them.

Looking at Amelia, she knew it didn't matter. They would make the best of this, their first Christmas morning.

Amelia leaned in and kissed her, and this time it wasn't just a brush of her lips, it was an out and out "make your toes curl" kiss.

Carter didn't want to let the moment go, but thoughts of the crowded airport pulled her reluctantly away.

Amelia's eyes lit up. "So, do I get to open my present now?"

Carter removed the present from under the tree, fingering the glossy paper before handing it to Amelia. She bit her lip in anticipation as Amelia slowly, carefully unwrapped the tiny present.

"Open it."

Carter's excitement was palpable. She wanted to see Amelia's face when she looked inside the box. She had wanted something different this year, something to show Amelia that she loved her and that her love was infinite.

Amelia gazed down into the box, gasped, and then looked up at Carter with tear-filled eyes.

Carter swallowed audibly and reached for the contents of the box. She took a deep breath. "I saw it and immediately thought of you." She held up the white gold chain with a delicate infinity symbol dangling from it. The words "love forever" were engraved on the inside of one of the loops. She draped the chain around Amelia's neck and managed to close the clasp despite her shaking hands.

Carter sat back, then cradled Amelia's face in her hands. "I love you now, I'll love you always. You're my heart, my home, my family." And she kissed Amelia with every ounce of love she could convey.

"Oh, sweetheart, this is the best Christmas ever!" Amelia stroked the pendant, then looked up at Carter. "I have something for you, too."

"You do, do you?" Carter teased, feeling she had the best Christmas present ever.

Amelia rummaged through her knapsack, pulled out their plane tickets, and handed them over.

Why was Amelia giving her their plane tickets? They still had a few hours before their scheduled departure.

Amelia nodded at the tickets in Carter's hand. "Open them."

She slowly lifted the flap. Tickets. She looked up in confusion.

"Well?"

"Well, what?"

Amelia rolled her eyes. "Read one."

Carter's eyes went wide. Amelia had changed their tickets. They were not scheduled to fly out to two separate destinations; they were flying home, together.

"Really?" Carter breathed.

Amelia nodded. "Really. Merry Christmas, beautiful." She wiped a wayward tear from Carter's face. "You're my family, and it's time we start our own family traditions. I want to put up a tree," she laughed as she gestured at Carter's socks, "hang real stockings, and burn the turkey. But mostly, I just want to spend the holiday with you."

"Christmas with you is all I've ever wanted. At home or someplace else, it doesn't matter."

Carter captured Amelia's lips in a soft kiss, and the sights and sounds of the airport fell away.

"I love you," Carter whispered against her lips.

"I love you, too," Amelia said, her eyes twinkling. "Let's go home."

The Spirit of Christmas Past,

Christmas Future

S. M. HARDING

"You said yes?" I asked. My eyebrows must've hit my hairline. "You barely know her."

Brit held out her left hand and let the firelight explode the facets in the diamond. "Isn't it gorgeous?"

"You met her at the Halloween party and Thanksgiving's only a few days away. Marry her?"

"This is what I've been waiting for all my life. The woman I've been seeking since I can remember."

"Your whole life? All twenty years of it?" I tried to lower my volume. "What happens to college, kiddo?"

"We plan to travel a year or so, then I'll go back and finish up," Brit said, still captured by the flashy diamond on her hand. "Share the joy with me, Auntie Dee. Don't be so suspicious."

"It's my job."

"Was. You're retired."

"Right. There's no such animal as a retired PI." I got up and put another log on the fire. My dear niece had been raised in the rarified atmosphere of the Gold Coast. She'd been indulged by her father and ignored by her mother to the point of hearing "no" so rarely she'd lost its meaning. How she remained a basically good kid amazed me. "So you're going to do the whole June bride bit?"

Brit expelled a long breath. "That's so straight. We're getting married in upstate New York at a lodge." She dug through her backpack. "Airline tickets for you and Robbi and we made reservations at the lodge. Transport to the lodge, too."

She handed me a packet with a smile that didn't leave room for much else on her face.

"When?"

"Christmas Eve, but we made the reservations for the whole week."

I just stared at her. "*This* Christmas?"

Brit grinned at me, kissed my forehead and ran out the door with the wave of a bon vivant.

"You have as much sense as your father," I yelled at the closing door. "This is so wrong."

Robbi poked her head around the doorframe that led to the kitchen. "So we're going to New York for Christmas?"

"Shit, I don't know. She's way too young for a step like this. Married? She's rich and probably easy pickings for some low-roller."

"She's well off, but not loaded like one of those robber baron families," Robbi said as she took the chair Brit had vacated. "And DJ, she's a Riordan. Headstrong, stubborn as you are. The perfect way to push her into something is to tell her not to do it."

I opened the packet and examined the tickets. Brit had included a brochure from the picture-perfect lodge. "I wonder how many of the family she's invited."

Robbi leaned her head back. "She looks so much like you, she could be your twin."

"You need your glasses, lady. Or you're remembering back a lot of years," I said.

"Do you? Remember when we were young? Remember the night we met?"

"If I ever forget that, shoot me."

Robbi pursed her lips and threw me one of those looks.

"At No Exit." I hadn't thought about that night for years, maybe because our life together had gotten better every year, except for a hiccup here and there.

"You walked in so cocky, big grin on your face. On top of the world."

"I'd just wrapped up the Cotswold case. Cashed the check and it didn't bounce. It meant I had enough money in the bank to keep the agency afloat for another year."

"Your first year, wasn't it? A rough year?"

"Nobody wanted a female PI anymore than City Hall wanted female cops. Closing that case changed my luck, all the way around. Saw you sitting up at a chess table totally engrossed in the game."

"Not totally. I saw you come in covered in snow and watched you shake it off. Take off that old ratty watch cap. You still run your hand through your hair the same way."

I remembered what a bitter cold gale had swept off the lake that November. How ice had formed early on Lake Michigan and began to hump the beach across the street from my apartment. How the windows of No Exit had been steamed up from the espresso machine that took up the whole back wall. How the ever-present coffee aroma warmed my soul. And how the classic blonde on the little raised dais stirred my interest. And more. "My lucky night."

"And how long did it take you to bed me, DJ?"

"Bed you? Shit, it may have been years ago, but it wasn't an historical novel." I lifted the footrest on my section. "We didn't sleep together for a whole month, if that's what you mean. Nor did we get married a month after that."

Robbi cleared her throat. "We're still not married."

I had no answer for that. Marriage to me had always meant the trap straight women fell into, and got screwed getting out of.

"To quote the song, 'put a ring on it,' DJ." Robbi wiggled her ring finger.

"Really?"

"We're getting older," Robbi said. "In case you hadn't noticed."

"Our lawyer drew up all the papers, POA and all that stuff."

"How well did that work for Nancy and Tracy?" She rose. "Times are changing and I think we've waited long enough to file a joint tax return."

"So that was the purpose of our trip down memory lane?"

"No. Just remember what I said." She took my hand and turned to me. "I want you to remember how we felt when we were so new to each other. That's how Brit feels now." She kissed my hand and rose

"Check out her bride-to-be if you have to, but don't destroy her happiness with your own cynicism."

I watched her go into the bedroom and pull down the comforter. Robbi was the only comforter I needed. I'd been so sure of it when we first got together, if it'd been possible, I would've put a ring on it that night.

The next morning, as I walked into a nondescript building at 809 Clark Street, I was swept by a tide of nostalgia. My first office had been a cubbyhole at the back of a finance office storefront on Glenwood, a few doors down from No Exit. I paid my rent by running record checks on their loan applicants. Lotta shoe leather back then. Now my agency had twelve employees and offices on one whole floor of this building. Another niece, Kate, had taken over the day-to-day operations and I only poked my head in when I got bored—or stumbled onto something.

I waived to the receptionist and tapped on Kate's open door. "You have a minute?"

"Of course, DJ," Kate said, motioning me to a conversational grouping by the window.

"This is a matter of some…delicacy," I said as I sank into the leather chair.

She sat opposite me and waited for me to start talking.

I smiled and nodded. "You can't go blabbing to the family. Did you know Brit's getting married? At Christmas?"

"She's what? Oh, shit." She sat back in her chair, shook her head. "That kid has absolutely no sense."

"So you didn't know. How about the rest of the family?"

"Haven't heard a peep and you know it'd be all over even if it was a rumor. Who's the lucky gal? Or guy? She isn't marrying some guy. Please tell me she hasn't lost all her Mother wit."

"Gal. Georgina Salazar."

"The one she met at my Halloween party? You've got to be kidding."

I handed Kate a paper with all of Salazar's basic data. "Do a deep background check. Brit is really head over heels. I don't want to spoil it for her but that woman could be a con for all we know."

Kate scanned the sheet, then laid it down. "I gather Robbi's taking her side?"

"Always the romantic. She reminded me of when we met." I smiled. "That did make me think about the situation. But if anything turns up hinky about Salazar, well, that's a different story. I know I can't prevent Brit from getting hurt, but I don't want to see her financially screwed."

"I'll get on this right away." She rose. "I won't say anything to the family because they'd kidnap her and put her in a nunnery."

As I rode the L back to the north side, I flashed back on that first night at No Exit when I'd met Robbi. When her game was finished, I'd sat across from her and opened with some lame line like, "What's a girl like you doing in a place like this?"

She'd taken my measure with an assured gaze from brown eyes so dark they almost appeared black. "Playing chess and getting ready to hear some poetry. Are you a chess player? Or a poet?"

I'd grinned. "Both, and world-class." Oh, the lies had tripped away so easily those days. I never worried about the consequences.

She'd raised an eyebrow. "Really."

I studied her hands, long-fingered and slim and paint-stained. "You're a painter?"

"Not hard to tell that, is it?"

She'd had me with the raised eyebrow. It took years of practice in front of the mirror before I could raise my right one and I never did get the left one to cooperate. I bought her a double shot, settled next to her for the poetry reading and offered to walk her home. It turned out she lived down Eastlake Terrace about two blocks from where I lived. When we stepped into the tiny lobby of her building, her face was rosy from the cold and her eyes sparkled. I wanted to kiss her, but I had no idea how she'd react.

"You ever go to Women and Children First, you know that bookstore on—"

"If you're asking if I'm gay, the answer is yes. And yes, I'd like to see you again." She handed me a slip of paper. "Call me, DJ." Then she gave me a kiss on my cheek and went through the inner door before I could pull myself together. Nobody ever declared their perversion to a stranger. To anybody, unless it was in a gay bar.

I'd been hooked and all she had to do was reel me in. I didn't want to deprive Brit of a love like Robbi's, my lifelong rock and soul, but I didn't want to see her crushed either. As I switched trains at Howard Street, I tried to weigh the benefits of watching her make her own mistake or poking around in her sweetie's life. No question about it. Robbi had had to run the gauntlet of my dad and my brothers. All cops, all used to grilling a suspect until they gave it up. Robbi had charmed them as much as she had me. I rode the rest of the way to my Evanston stop smiling like a fool.

When data began to come in from Kate the next day, I called Brit and asked her to join me for lunch.

"I wondered how long it'd take you to call. I'll be in the loop tomorrow. How about Billy Goat?"

"New or old?"

"Let's try the new one on Lake Street. Okay?"

She was, of course, late. I'd about finished by the time she took her seat across from me. "Doesn't have the same atmosphere, does it?" she asked as she looked around.

"No smoke-stained walls, no smell of grease and the furniture's still in one piece. Very different."

"You're going to be difficult about this, aren't you?"

One of my eyebrows went up in the controlled lift. "About what?"

She glared at me. "I suppose you've done your background check on Georgi."

"Not a deep one, just skimmed the surface. Why don't you tell me about her?"

She took a bite of her burger and chewed a long time. "She makes me laugh, Auntie Dee."

"Why don't you cut the cute stuff? You haven't called me 'Auntie Dee' since you were eight. Level with me, are you just in lust—or do you love her?"

She leveled a stare at me. "How would you have described what you felt for Robbi two months after you met?"

I shook my head. "We're talking about you. Period. I want a real answer, Brit."

"Why? I'm not eight anymore."

I pushed my plate away and examined the young woman, who at this moment looked like her pouty eight year-old self. "Robbi ran the gauntlet of the family for me. All your uncles. My dad. She let the family get to know her before we moved in together almost a year after we started dating. What's the rush?"

"Times have changed," she said, finishing her beer. "We don't have to hide or pretend to be 'roommates' anymore." The air quotes were sharp gestures. "Either you and Robbi come or you don't. I'm beginning not to give a fuck."

"Not true. I know that and so do you. Now stop dancing around the question and answer me. What's the rush?"

"Look, DJ, if you think Georgi's after my money, forget it. She's loaded and it's not in a trust fund. Money's just not an issue."

"Then what is?" I braced myself for the explosion, but it didn't come. She looked down at her hands that were clenched. I thought I saw tears before she blinked rapidly. "I want to be supportive, kiddo. Robbi already is. But something just feels...wrong to me. You love your studies, you've had plans to become the next Indiana Jones for years. Why abandon them now?"

"I can't talk about this anymore, I've got class in twenty minutes." She rose in one fluid motion, as the young are wont to do. "Don't badger me. Please."

I watched her as she turned and rapidly threaded her way through the tables to the door. She didn't look back. As apt a description of Brit as I could come up with. I called Kate with a few more questions that had just occurred to me.

Robbi nearly killed me when I got home and told her what had gone down. "Jesus, you want to alienate her from what's left of her family?"

"I love the kid and I don't want to see her hurt," I said. Sounded thin to me once the words were spoken. "She's not telling us the truth about the whole situation."

Robbi sat at the kitchen table, folded her hands together. "One enchanted evening, that describes us. Our eyes met across a crowded room and we've been together ever since. We were damn lucky. What if I hadn't wanted to hear the poet who read that night? Or you hadn't closed your case yet?

So many damn 'ifs,' DJ. A lifetime of tiny links that if the first one hadn't appeared, we wouldn't be bound together now. Why should you deny Brit that chain?"

I grabbed a beer from the fridge, sat down too. The table was battered, had been with us since those days on Eastlake Terrace. Top was tiger oak, someone had told me, its tight grain not impervious to movers, but a hell of a lot more durable than the table's pine legs. Durability, that's what I wanted for Brit. She had so much more living to do, so many places to see, so many people to enter her life. I didn't want to see her like these old table legs, scarred and barely functional.

"Where are you, DJ?"

I looked up and into Robbi's dark eyes. "Thinking about this table."

"It's history with us? How it stands like a metaphor for our life together?"

"How I don't want Brit's heart to look like these legs in a couple of years."

She drew in a deep breath and let it out slowly. "You can't protect her heart and you know that. Dig away on the Salazar girl, but don't ever forget that Brit has to live her own life. And follow her own heart. You cannot fend off life for her, even if you knew how." She pushed herself up. "Call her and apologize for thinking you're a superhero. Even if I think you are."

I did call, but I didn't apologize. I asked her to bring Georgi to Thanksgiving dinner.

"Love to, but we're already scheduled. Going to her family's place."

"Next year, then." Let her think about the future, more than the next time in bed.

Brit was quiet for a few moments. "Yeah, sure. Putting it on my calendar right now," she said in a super-chipper voice. "Gotta go."

Oh, man. Had I screwed up everything with her? Brit had always trusted me, though I'd been open about questioning some of her decisions. This was the biggest decision she'd ever make and she was closing me out.

Robbi called me from the kitchen for help. While I loved having people over for turkey day, I truly hated all the fuss it caused and Robbi's lists. She took such joy in crossing off an item that I'd done.

"I have an item to add to your list," I said as I walked into the kitchen. "We'll have to get word out that we're not going to be home for Christmas dinner."

She stopped chopping. "We're going? You're not going to boycott?"

"You know I'm a Riordan to my DNA. I'll do everything I can to discover what's up with Georgi girl, but I can't say no to something so important in Brit's life."

"Crusty on the outside, mushy on the inside—just the way these are going to be if you don't give me a hand." She handed me the chef's knife and directed me to a pile of veggies. Our dinner would be half-Italian, half-Irish celebration of an American tradition with friends. Crazy and fun. As soon as Thanksgiving dinner was cleaned up, dispersed to participants and the new day dawned, Robbi would have another list for me.

Outwardly, I was a bit of a Scrooge when it came to the Christmas season, but inside I loved every minute of the preparations we did together. Taking the day to go all the way out to an Aurora tree farm to cut down our tree, with a stop for a late lunch at a pub with a welcoming fireplace. Leaving our fresh-cut tree on the back porch until the seventeenth, when Italians started celebrating Christmas and didn't stop until the Epiphany. Unwrapping each ornament to trim the tree, each with its memories and story. I wondered how many more years we could keep the tradition we'd built up over our time together. The hip that had stopped a bullet bothered me in cold weather and Robbi wasn't so spry anymore either.

Lousy way to think, but getting older did that to me. Wondering if we could celebrate the same way? With the same people? How many more years did we have?

Robbi looked up at my heavy sigh. "Just be grateful for all the Christmases we've had together and don't go all moody. Chop, DJ."

"Are you serious about getting married?" I asked.

"Damn serious. It's legal and who knows how many good years we have left. I don't want to be rolled down the aisle in a wheelchair. Unless you're still having commitment issues?"

I snorted. I'd gotten over whatever commitment issues I'd had that night at No Exit, and Robbi knew it. From the time I'd sat down, I knew this was the woman I wanted to share my life with. So why couldn't I accept Brit's engagement?

"Then let's go down and get the license tomorrow and get hitched next week," I said.

"Are you serious?"

"Absolutely."

"Well, first you'd better propose—I don't expect a rock like Brit's. Then get the rings. And we'll have to decide where we'll have a little reception for family and friends. I'm not cooking for something like that."

"Shit, Robbi. I was thinking get license, get married. Not receptions or caterers or having to dress up." I chopped vigorously. "And if this is something you want so badly, why don't you propose to me?"

She put down her cleaver, walked around the island and got down on one knee. Stiffly. "Will you marry me, Deirdre Jean Riordan?"

I sucked in my breath as she took her mother's engagement ring from an apron pocket. "You led me on. What all do you have planned?"

"Nothing, if you don't give me an answer," she said, her grin threatening to break into a smile.

"Yes, I'll marry you." I pulled her up and she put the ring on my finger. We kissed and it took my breath away just like the first time we kissed in the tiny foyer of Robbi's building on our third date. If only Brit was half as lucky.

It began to snow again as I was finishing up with the fairy lights outside. I limped down the ladder, favoring my damn hip, when my cell rang. I waited until I had both feet on the ground to pull it out of my jacket pocket. "Kate? You have some news on Georgi girl?"

"Yeah. I'd like to come over. I can be there in forty minutes or so."

"Sure. Fine. See you then."

Robbi let go of the ladder. "I think next year we forget these lights and just put the big candle in the front window for travelers." She looked at me. "What's wrong?"

"Kate's coming over to give me the report on Georgi."

"She's coming here? That doesn't mean good news, does it?"

"Probably not." I stamped my feet on the walk I'd cleared this morning. "Let's get a good fire going and make something hot and alcoholic. And Robbi, what about Kate and Shea for our witnesses?"

"I already asked them. So many of our old friends are gone, DJ," she said, her breath haloing her head in the cold air. "It should've been Roberta or—"

I put a finger to her mouth. "They'll be with us anyway. If Kate's good enough to take over my business, she's good enough to stand up for us. I'm so glad you're in charge of all of this." I lowered the top half of the extension ladder and picked it up. "How about hot buttered rum?"

She nodded as she went in the front door and I carried the ladder back to the garage. I knew something had been hinky with Brit's rush to the altar. I ran through a list of possibilities, each worse than the last. Whatever it was, I wanted a stiff drink first.

I lit the fire and settled on the couch while Robbi fixed the drinks. We waited until Kate's Escape pulled in the drive and I went to open the door, dread slowing my steps. I opened the door to Kate's fist.

"Sorry," she said. "I didn't want to try the knocker with the wreath over it."

She came in, left her boots by the door and hung her parka on the coat tree. Robbi gave her a mug as she sat in a wing chair. She sniffed. "Rum?"

Robbi nodded. "Are you going back to work? Would you rather have something non-alcoholic?"

"This is just what the doctor ordered." She took a sip, then slipped a file folder from her messenger bag. "You want to read it now, or should I just summarize?"

"Summary's fine. If I have any questions, I can read the whole thing later."

Kate opened the file. "Her financials are superb, doesn't spend much although she's worth millions—and it's all free and clear. Inherited from her grandmother. As I said, she lives modestly. Has a condo on Lake Shore Drive with the mortgage paid off. Good student, graduated a year and a half ago from the University of Chicago in English. Enrolled in the graduate journalism program at Northwestern, but asked for a leave of absence for this spring semester."

"Brit said they wanted to travel for awhile, so that makes sense," I said, fingering the scar on my temple.

"Maybe," Kate said. "But Georgi started seeing a doctor in the fall on a regular basis. An oncologist, DJ."

"She has cancer?" Robbi asked.

"I didn't know if you wanted me to proceed, so I didn't dig for specific answers. I will, if you want me to."

I shook my head. "I shouldn't have had you do this in the first place."

Kate shifted in the chair, re-crossed her legs. "I thought your request was sensible, DJ. You've been looking after Brit since her dear mother walked away. You became a safe harbor for her. You still are."

"Kate's right," Robbi said. "And I think Kate should find out the prognosis if she can. If there's little time left, we should do everything we can to make them happy. Don't you think?"

"Maybe we should do that regardless of the prognosis."

When Kate left, Robbi sat down next to me on the couch. "You're going to go all mopey now. Blame yourself that you didn't jump head first into Brit's bridal bliss. Guilt makes you morose, DJ. I do not want a morose wife." She lifted my chin and kissed me. "You've done your best for Brit since Nan kicked her out."

"Nan blamed me that Brit came out queer."

Robbi took my hands. "Nan's social position went down the toilet when her husband—your brother—went over to the dark side. She blamed your whole family, as if a family full of cops *had* to turn out one crook. Nan always was full of bullshit and you know it. Now stop wallowing."

I smiled at her because nobody could read me like Robbi. "So what are we having for dinner?"

"Let's go out," she said releasing my hands. "We haven't done that in a long time and all the talk of our past is making me nostalgic."

"We used to go out more, didn't we? Why don't we?"

"Because you've become way too fond of lying around in your sweats. Now go change."

Robbi decided we'd get married on the seventeenth so that we could start celebrating Christmas in a big way. Every year. I pulled my old tuxedo out of the guest room closet, but Robbi nixed the idea. "This isn't the *image* of marriage, it *is* marriage."

After thirty-five years together, I should've known. Anything but a tux because neither of us had dreamed of a princess wedding when we were young. She'd also banned a sweatshirt and jeans. She was a woman with taste and I'd surrendered to it long ago.

We'd traipsed through the snow to the judge's chambers, the judge who was also our next door neighbor. He looked so damn officious in his robes and the impressive, paneled office only amplified the feeling. I began to understand what Robbi had meant. This was the real thing. It hit me like a line drive when she slipped a gold band on my ring finger and I could barely find my voice.

When the brief ceremony was over, the judge hugged us both. "Thank God, my neighbors are no longer living in sin!" He grinned and started Kate and Shea on the paperwork. We walked out legal and officially hitched. I'd never dreamed. Ever.

The four of us walked to a close-by restaurant for a fancy lunch. Shea examined the rings that an artist friend of Robbi's had made. "These are gorgeous, kind of a continuous Celtic Eternity Knot. Who's the artist?"

While Robbi and Shea talked design, Kate leaned over to me. "Georgi had a brain tumor. They think they got it all out and have been doing targeted chemo. But there's no guarantees."

"I still feel like the biggest shit. What was it the nuns used to call a hypocrite? Whitened sepulcher. That's how I feel."

Kate rubbed my shoulder. "Hey, this is your wedding day and Brit's is coming up soon. Give her your support now, that's all that's important, DJ."

"Speaking of Brit's wedding, we might not make it," Robbi said. "Have you seen the weather forecast for next week?"

"Been too involved in the here and now," I said, squeezing her hand.

She squeezed back and smiled the most contented smile I'd ever seen on her face. We gazed at each other and I finally understood how much this meant to her.

She sighed. "Blizzard, and it may last several days. I thought last winter was supposed to be the one of the century, but it looks as if we're stuck in the polar zone."

"I wouldn't want to be stranded in a blizzard with anyone but you."

By the time Thursday night rolled around, I called Brit. "It looks like we're going to be socked in with the storm. Why don't you and Georgi go down and get your Illinois license tomorrow? Just in case."

"But we've got everything planned—"

"I realize that. It's something rare and beautiful that you want to remember."

"Yeah, not some quickie downtown. It should be romantic, with candles and a roaring fire in the fireplace and snow outside."

"Sometimes life hands us a detour." I waited for her response, but all I heard was a sharp intake of breath. "How about you get the legalities done tomorrow for Illinois, but if we can fly out, then you don't have a worry in the world about the wedding."

"And if we can't?"

"Get married here. Judge lives next door. Robbi and I will cook a feast and if it's really bad out, you can start your honeymoon in our guest room."

"Wow." Brit let the silence grow. "Let me talk to Georgi. A Plan B's a good idea. Thank you, DJ. Thank you so much."

She called back about ten minutes later. Plan B was in action.

Robbi was so sure of the approaching storm, she went out and bought enough food to feast the wedding party for a week. While she was in the kitchen prepping, it was my job to transform our living room into a bridal grotto. Sure. I hightailed it to Home Depot and snagged the only garden arch they had left in midwinter, a dozen boxes of fairy lights and assorted big red bows. We had greenery on the back porch. I wondered what I'd realize I'd forgotten when I started work. I went back inside and picked up a box of staples for my staple gun. Then I had another thought and added a box of old-fashioned, plain ball ornaments. Two red, two green, two white, two silver. I'd let Robbi choose which ones we'd use.

The storm toyed with us, slowing down, then lashing us with slender, icy fingers like a lover promising more. Brit and Georgi arrived on Monday afternoon, afraid they wouldn't be able to get out in the morning. Robbi put them both to work cooking while I took their bags upstairs to the guest room. I noticed Robbi had been busy up here, making a cozy nest for two lovebirds. I shook my head. This almost hadn't happened because of me and my stubborn Riordan attitude.

I finished my work in the living room, inhaling wonderful scents of Christmas cookies coming from the kitchen. I tacked the last bow on and tested the lights. As good as I could do, but I thought it looked rather spiffy. Better than spiffy. I'd get Robbi's opinion when the kids went to bed tonight.

"You've created a real memory for them," Robbi said later when it was dark out and my work provided the only light. "The light's like love—all glittery, but still soft. Christmas will always hold a special place in their hearts, no matter how long those hearts beat. This definitely joins the cosmic dance, DJ."

"Glad you like it." I put an arm around her waist and pulled her close. "Please tell me we're not going to celebrate the feast of the seven fishes tomorrow night."

She smacked my shoulder and looked like she was keeping Mona Lisa's secret.

The judge arrived at seven on Christmas Eve, struggling through the drifts between our houses and carrying his robes encased in a cleaner's bag. He took off his boots and slipped into a pair of loafers, hung his parka and put on his robes. "Everybody ready?"

"Chomping at the bit."

I watched the two young women exchanging their vows and got all teary. I kept blinking, but it didn't seem to help. Robbi reached her hand to me as we stood on either side of Brit and Georgi. I took it and held on for dear life.

After the paperwork was finished and the judge had left, I asked our newlyweds to return to the arbor I'd created. "The first Christmas Robbi and I were together, she made two special ornaments for our tree." I pointed to the top our tree. "Though it took me a couple of years to make one myself, it's become a tradition we've kept every year. Each ball tells a story of that year, of how our love grew—"

"Those two commemorate our Big Fight," Robbi said with a grin. She pointed to two half-way down the tree.

"Yeah, but we made it through and that's the important part." I reached up to where I'd hung two ornaments and handed one to Robbi. "We made these to start your life together." I handed mine to Brit while Robbi handed hers to Georgi. As they looked at the pumpkin I'd painted and the more intricate holiday-themed one Robbi had made, they both began to sniffle.

"Hey, this is supposed to be joyous," I said. I lifted a flute of champagne. "So this is our toast to you. We wish you a tall tree full of wonderful memories."

The glasses clinked and there was hugging all around. Robbi announced dinner and as we walked to the dining room, Brit pulled me aside.

"You know, don't you?" she asked.

I nodded. "An iffy prognosis and—"

"Is that what it took to change your mind?" Brit asked with a jut of her chin. "That Georgi may die?"

"No." I turned her to me. "I kept remembering Christmases Past, all of them with Robbi. She was terrified every day I went to work, afraid I'd never come home. Finally she told me what she felt—and a decision she'd made: to love every moment we shared, let go of the little stuff. She realized none of us know how many moments we have to go." I hugged Brit, and whispered in her ear. "I couldn't deny you your chance to know the same feelings, the same joy, even the same uncertainty. Merry Christmas, kiddo."

Slaying the Ghost

(of Christmas Past)

NIKKI BUSCH

Last Christmas
was tense and raw.
A chill of indecision rattled my bones.
Tenuous,
we'd split,
or
hadn't.
In a holding pattern,
you left me hanging ,
curled up like my own misshapen Christmas ornament—
a ball of confusion,
poised to shatter
along with my heart.
This Christmas
you are here.
Mine.
A glorious gift shining by my side…
Your small, strong hands
wrap me gently in sparkling paper.
I am still fragile,
so handle with care.

About The Authors

JOAN ARLING

Joan Arling is a little hard to localize: She lives on German bread, French wine, Irish beer, and Dutch tobacco.

When she can afford it, she also likes whiskies from the southern coast of Islay. She's been a truck driver, a teacher, a drug courier, a rock musician. Her favourite pastimes are mistreating her guitar and spoiling her best friend's three tabbies.

Oh yes, reading and writing, too.

So far, she has published two short stories and one novella.

E-mail: JoanArling@gmx.net

JOVE BELLE

Jove Belle lives in Vancouver, Washington with her family. Her books include The Job, Uncommon Romance, Love and Devotion, Indelible, Chaps, Split the Aces, and Edge of Darkness.

Website: http://www.jovebelle.com

ERZABET BISHOP

Erzabet Bishop is the author of *Sigil Fire*, "Written on Skin" (a *Sigil Fire* series short), *Fetish Fair*, *Temptation Resorts:*

Marnie's Tale (upcoming), *Temptation Resorts: Jess's Adventures* (upcoming), *Pomegranate* (upcoming) and multiple books in the *Erotic Pagan Series*. She is a contributing author to *Club Rook*, *Hungry for More*, *A Christmas to Remember*, *Forbidden Fruit*, *Sci Spanks*, *Sweat*, *When the Clock Strikes Thirteen*, *Bossy*, *Can't Get Enough*, *Slave Girls*, *The Big Book of Submission*, *Gratis II*, *Anything She Wants*, *Coming Together: Girl on Girl* and more.

She was a dual finalist for the GCLS awards in 2014. Erzabet lives in Texas with her husband, furry children and can often be found lurking in local bookstores.

Website: erzabetwrites.wix.com/erzabetbishop
Facebook: www.facebook.com/erzabetbishopauthor
Twitter: @erzabetbishop

NIKKI BUSCH

Nikki Busch began writing song lyrics in her teens and progressed to writing poetry and short stories while attending Rutgers University, where she earned her bachelor of arts degree in English. Her poems have been published in the anthologies *Delectable Daisies: Sappho's Corner Poetry Anthology*, Volume 4, *Our Wonderful Country*, *Caret*, and *i.e.*

Nikki worked as an advertising copywriter for thirty years before becoming an editor and publicist. She provides editing services for Ylva Publishing. She lives in Warren County, New Jersey with her wife, and is currently completing a graduate-level certificate program at the University of California-San Diego. She is a member of the Golden Crown Literary Society and Editorial Freelancers Association.

Website: www.nikkibuschediting.com
Facebook: www.facebook.com/NikkiBuschEditing
Twitter: @NikkiBuschEdit
E-mail: NBwritethink@gmail.com

JEAN COPELAND

Jean Copeland is an English teacher and writer whose fiction and essays have appeared in *A Family by Any Other Name*, *WIPs Journal*, *T/Our Magazine*, *Sharkreef.org*, *Connecticut Review*, *Texas Told 'Em*, *P.S. What I Didn't Say*, *Off the Rocks*, *Best Lesbian Love Stories*, *Harrington Lesbian Literary Quarterly*, *The First Line*, and *Prickofthespindle.com*. Her debut novel, *The Revelation of Beatrice Darby*, will be published by Bold Strokes Books in 2015

T.M. CROKE

T.M. Croke lives in Newfoundland, Canada, and hold degrees in English and Classics. She's always had a love of writing, but it was only a secret passion. Her voracious writing habit led to the creation of a weekly writing group, which inspired her to step out of her comfort zone and share her expansive portfolio of original lesbian fiction.

When not writing, she spends her time playing hockey, hiking with her dog, Karma, and reading. She is currently working on a full-length novel.

E-mail: tmcroke@gmail.com

CHERI CRYSTAL

Cheri Crystal is a healthcare professional by day and writes erotic romances by night. She is a native New Yorker who was born in Brooklyn and raised on Long Island. Recently, Cheri has crossed the pond to live in the United Kingdom with her loving wife. A day doesn't go by that she doesn't miss her three kids, technically adults, but thanks to Skype and lots of visits with her family, she enjoys living in England's southwest coast. Cheri began writing fiction in 2003 after reviewing for Lambda Book Report, Just About Write, Independent Gay Writer, and other e-zines. She is the author of Attractions of the Heart, a 2010 Golden Crown Literary

Winner for lesbian erotica. In her spare time, she enjoys swimming, hiking, viewing wildlife, cooking, jigsaw puzzles, and spending quality time with family and friends.

Website: www.chericrystal.com
Facebook: www.facebook.com/chericrystal

FLETCHER DELANCEY

Fletcher DeLancey is an Oregon expatriate who moved to Portugal to be with the love of her life. Now happily married for five years, Fletcher lives in the beautiful, sunny Algarve, where she devotes her spare time to learning the local birds and plants, and trying every regional Portuguese dish she can get her hands on. (There are many. It's going to take a while.)

The rest of the time, she teaches Pilates, gardens, bakes extremely good brownies, rides her road bike on narrow country lanes...and writes.

She is best known for her five-book *Star Trek: Voyager epic, The Past Imperfect Series,* and for her science fiction novel *Without A Front.* Currently, she is working on a prequel to *Without A Front* and as an editor for Ylva Publishing.

Website: fletcherdelancey.com
Blog: oregonexpat.wordpress.com
E-mail: fletcher@mailhaven.com

R.G. EMANUELLE

R.G. Emanuelle is from New York City and spent more than 20 years in publishing. She is co-editor of *Skulls and Crossbones: Tales of Women Pirates*, as well as *All You Can Eat: A Buffet of Lesbian Erotica and Romance* and *Unwrap These Presents,* both from Ylva Publishing. Her short stories can be found in numerous anthologies, including the 2014 Goldie nominee *When the Clock Strikes Thirteen.*

When she was a child, a neighbor called her a vampire because she only came out after dark, so it's fitting that her first novel, *Twice Bitten*, is about creatures of the night. Her 2013 romantic novella, *Add Spice to Taste,* stars a love-burned chef, but she is always summoned back by the things that go bump in the night.

Blog: www.rgemanuelle.com
Facebook: facebook.com/RGEmanuelle
Twitter: @Rgemanuelle

EVE FRANCIS

Eve Francis's short stories have appeared in *Wilde Magazine*, *The Fieldstone Review*, *Iris New Fiction*, *MicroHorror*, and *The Human Echoes Podcast*. Romance and horror are her favourite genres to write in because everyone has felt love or fear in some form or another. She lives in Canada, where she often sleeps late, spends too much time online, and repeatedly watches old horror movies and *Orange Is The New Black.*

Website: evefrancis.wordpress.com
Tumblr: paintitback.tumblr.com

S. M. HARDING

S. M. Harding has had two dozen short stories published in various crime fiction publications, both on-line magazines and in print anthologies and magazines. Two of the most recent include *A Snake in the Grass* in *Spinetingler* and *Scarecrow Field* in *Indiana Crime Review. Spirit of Christmas Past, Christmas Future* is forthcoming from Ylva Publishing. The novel *I Will Meet You There* will be published by Bella Books in Spring of 2015. She teaches classes at the Writers' Center of Indiana and participated in panels for their annual Gathering of Writers, also at Indy Author's Fair, Magna Cum Murder and various local libraries. She edited and contributed an essay to *Writing Murder*, a collection of essays by Midwestern authors about writing crime fiction.

Blog: storytellersfire.wordpress.com
Facebook: facebook.com/100004961079442

LOIS CLOAREC HART

Born and raised in British Columbia, Canada, Lois Cloarec Hart grew up as an avid reader but didn't begin writing until much later in life. Several years after joining the Canadian Armed Forces, she received a degree from Royal Military College and on graduation switched occupations from air traffic control to military intelligence. Lois married a CAF fighter pilot while in college, and went on to spend another five years as an Intelligence Officer before leaving the military to care for her husband, who was ill with chronic progressive Multiple Sclerosis and passed away in 2001. She began writing while caring for her husband in his final years and had her first book, *Coming Home*, published in 2001. It was through that initial publishing process that Lois met her wife-to-be. She now commutes annually between her northern home in Calgary and her wife's southern home in Atlanta.

Website: www.loiscloarechart.com

JAE

Jae grew up amidst the vineyards of southern Germany. She spent her childhood with her nose buried in a book, earning her the nickname "professor." The writing bug bit her at the age of eleven. For the last eight years, she has been writing mostly in English.

She used to work as a psychologist but gave up her day job in December 2013 to become a full-time writer and a part-time editor. When she's not writing, she likes to spend her time reading, indulging her ice cream and office supply addiction, and watching way too many crime shows.

Website: jae-fiction.com
Facebook: facebook.com/JaeAuthor
Blog: jae-fiction.com/blog
E-mail: jae_s1978@yahoo.de

CATHERINE LANE

Catherine Lane started to write fiction on a dare from her wife. She's thrilled to be a published author, even though she had to admit her wife was right. They live happily in Southern California with their son and a very mischievous pound puppy.

Catherine spends most of her time these days working, mothering, or writing. But when she finds herself at loose ends, she enjoys experimenting with recipes in the kitchen, paddling on long stretches of flat water, and browsing the stacks at libraries and bookstores. Oh, and trying unsuccessfully to outwit her dog.

She has published several short stories and is currently working on a novella.

Facebook: facebook.com/profile.php?id=100004577749399

CLARE LYDON

Clare Lydon penned her first novel at primary school and it scored 9.5/10. She's still not sure what she was docked half a point for. A lack of lesbians perhaps? It's not something anyone could accuse her of these days.

Clare's debut novel, London Calling, was released in February 2014 and became an Amazon No.1 best-seller overnight. A tale of one woman's search for love in modern-day London, the book is littered with ladygays, a vat of tequila and a colourful array of Converse. Her second novel, The Long Weekend, is due out in November 2014.

Clare's a Virgo, a Spurs fan, a karaoke queen and a Curly Wurly devotee. She's also never owned a cat and runs screaming from anything DIY. She lives with her wife in London.

Website: www.clarelydon.co.uk

LEE LYNCH

Lee Lynch's most recent book is *An American Queer*. It, *The Raid and Beggar of Love*, are published by Bold Strokes Books. She is the namesake and first recipient of The Lee Lynch Classic Award for The Swashbuckler. She's been honored with the Golden Crown Literary Society Trailblazer Award, the Alice B. Reader Award, induction into the Saints and Sinners Literary Hall of Fame, the James Duggins Mid-Career Award, and, for Beggar of Love, the Lesbian Fiction Readers Choice Award, the Ann Bannon Popular Choice Award, and Book of the Year Award from ForeWord Reviews.

Website: www.boldstrokesbooks.com/author-lee-lynch.html

ANDI MARQUETTE

Andi Marquette is an editor and award-winning author of mysteries, science fiction, and romance. Her latest novels are *Day of the Dead*, the Goldie finalist *The Edge of Rebellion*, and *From the Hat Down*. She is also the co-editor of the anthology *All You Can Eat: A Buffet of Lesbian Romance and Erotica*.

Website: andimarquette.com

PATRICIA PENN

When Patricia was a teen, her school's job qualification test said that she should be a surgeon since she has a big ego, and she doesn't like other people. Later, she read a theory about how all authors secretly are social outcasts anyway, and decided that the pen suited her even better than the scalpel. She currently also sells her soul to a day job in marketing in Frankfurt, Germany. She lives with her dog in a small town near Frankfurt, and has given long-distance relationships a new meaning with her girlfriend, who lives in Massachusetts.

CINDY RIZZO

Cindy Rizzo lives in New York City with her wife, Jennifer, and their two cats. She has worked in philanthropy for many years and has a long history of involvement in the LGBT community. Cindy is the author of *Exception to the Rule*, a lesbian romance and winner of the GCLS Debut Fiction award. Her second book, *Love Is Enough*, was released in September 2014. Earlier writing includes essays in the anthologies, *Lesbians Raising Sons* and *Homefronts: Controversies in Non-Traditional Parenting*. She was the co-editor of a fiction anthology, *All the Ways Home*, published in 1995 (New Victoria) in which her story "Herring Cove" was included. She serves on the boards of Congregation Beth Simchat Torah in New York and Funders for LGBT Issues. She and her wife have two grown sons, a wonderful daughter-in-law, and a baby granddaughter.

L.T. SMITH

L.T. is a late bloomer when it comes to writing and didn't begin until 2005 with her first novel *Hearts and Flowers Border* (first published in 2006).

She soon caught the bug and has written numerous tales, usually with a comical slant to reflect, as she calls it, 'My warped view of the dramatic.'

Although she loves to write, L.T. loves to read, too—being an English teacher seems to demand it. Most of her free time is spent with her furry little men—two fluffy balls of trouble who keep her active and her apologies flowing.

Facebook: facebook.com/pages/LT-Smith/535475523205666
Blog: ltsmithfiction.wordpress.com
E-mail: fingersmith@hotmail.co.uk

ASHLEY STEVENS

Ashley has been spinning yarns for as long as she can remember. Originally trained in sociology, she made an honest attempt to function in the real world. However, it has since become clear that her calling is definitely a literary one as she does not play well with others. She is now a student at Georgia Regents University in Augusta, Georgia, where she is studying English with a concentration in creative writing. Ashley has lived in the Augusta area for over 20 years but has plans to run away and live on the beach. She shares her life with her two beasties (aka her children) and one spoiled Catahoula Leopard Dog.

DEVIN SUMARNO

Devin lives a life full of contrasts and contradictions. She loves short verses and big dramas. Her voice couldn't decide whether to be a tenor's or a soprano's. She's too shy to say hello to a stranger but enjoys reciting monologues onstage.

Being half German and half Indonesian at least makes her a complete Hapa. Constantly being less than complete made her believe in diversity on the one hand and not taking herself too seriously on the other. She tries to close gaps because she sees no spaces between the letters of LGBTIQ.

Devin tells tales from the borderlines she lives at. She has a tendency to walk on the darker sides of life and literature but always tries to brighten them—with odd humor and idealistic naivety.

Come and visit Devin—she appreciates the company:

Website: devinsumarno.wordpress.com
Facebook: facebook.com/devinsumarno
Micro fiction blog: devinsumarno.blogspot.de
E-mail: devin.sumarno@aol.com

WENDY TEMPLE

A passionate Scot, Wendy grew up in East Edinburgh. As a child it was her dream to live on the historic Royal Mile, which she did for a number of years before returning to the seaside a few years ago.

With an academic background in Community Education; Healthcare & Physical Education, she has held numerous jobs in these fields and is a passionate advocate of keeping access to further education & healthcare free for all and lessons in physical education available to all schoolchildren.

A sports fanatic, Wendy played hockey & volleyball competitively & five-a-side football for leisure. Her hobbies include watching lots of sport, reading & writing; genealogy & history.

Wendy started writing fanfiction in 2005 to impress a woman…

Website: facebook.com/profile.php?id=100006125834803
E-mail: weebod@mac.com

Other books from Ylva Publishing

www.ylva-publishing.com

Still Life

L.T. SMITH

ISBN: 978-3-95533-257-0
Length: 352 pages

After breaking off her relationship with a female lothario, Jess Taylor decides she doesn't want to expose herself to another cheating partner. Staying at home, alone, suits her just fine. Her idea of a good night is an early one—preferably with a good book. Well, until her best friend, Sophie Harrison, decides it's time Jess rejoined the human race.

Trying to pull Jess from her self-imposed prison, Sophie signs them both up for a Still Life art class at the local college. Sophie knows the beautiful art teacher, Diana Sullivan, could be the woman her best friend needs to move on with her life.

But, in reality, could art bring these two women together? Could it be strong enough to make a masterpiece in just twelve sessions? And, more importantly, can Jess overcome her fear of being used once again?

Only time will tell.

Under a Falling Star

JAE

ISBN: 978-3-95533-238-9
Length: 354 pages

Falling stars are supposed to be a lucky sign, but not for Austen. Her new job as a secretary in an international games company isn't off to a good start. Her first assignment—decorating the Christmas tree in the lobby—results in a trip to the ER after Dee, the company's second-in-command, gets hit by the star-shaped tree topper.

Dee blames her instant attraction to Austen on her head wound, not the magic of the falling star. She's determined not to act on it, especially since Austen has no idea that Dee is practically her boss.

Barring Complications

BLYTHE RIPPON

ISBN: 978-3-95533-191-7
Length: 374 pages

It's an open secret that the newest justice on the Supreme Court is a lesbian. So when the Court decides to hear a case about gay marriage, Justice Victoria Willoughby must navigate the press, sway at least one of her conservative colleagues, and confront her own fraught feelings about coming out.

Just when she decides she's up to the challenge, she learns that the very brilliant, very out Genevieve Fornier will be lead counsel on the case.

Genevieve isn't sure which is causing her more sleepless nights: the prospect of losing the case, or the thought of who will be sitting on the bench when she argues it.

Bitter Fruit

LOIS CLOAREC HART

ISBN: 978-3-95533-216-7
Length: 244 pages

FUELLED BY BOOZE AND BOREDOM, Jac Lanier accepts an unusual wager from her best friend. Victoria, for reasons of her own, impulsively challenges Jac to seduce Lauren, her co-worker and a young woman Jac's never met. Under the terms of their bet, Jac has exactly one month to get Lauren into bed or she has to pay up. Though Lauren is straight and engaged, Jac begins her campaign confident that she'll win the bet. But Jac's forgotten that if you sow an onion seed, you won't harvest a peach. When her plan goes awry, will she reap the bitter fruit of her deception? Or will Lauren turn the tables on the thoughtless gamblers?

Mac vs. PC

FLETCHER DELANCEY

ISBN: 978-3-95533-187-0
Length: 148 pages

As a computer technician at the university, Anna Petrowski knows she has one thing in common with doctors and lawyers, and it's not the salary. It's that everyone thinks her advice comes free, even on weekends. That's why she keeps a strict observance of her Saturday routine: a scone, a caramel mocha, and nobody bothering her. So when she meets a new campus hire at the Bean Grinder who needs computer help yet doesn't ask for it, she's intrigued enough to offer. It's the beginning of a beautiful friendship and possibly something more.

But Elizabeth Markel is a little higher up the university food chain than she's let on, and the truth brings out buried prejudices that Anna didn't know she had.

People and computers have one thing in common: they're both capable of self-sabotage. The difference is that computers are easier to fix.

All You Can Eat

ED. R.G. EMANUELLE, ANDI MARQUETTE

ISBN: 978-3-95533-224-2
Length: 260 pages

Chef R.G. Emanuelle and sous chef Andi Marquette locked themselves in the kitchen to create a menu that would explore the sensuous qualities of food and illustrate how the act of preparing and eating it can engage many more senses than simply taste and smell. They gathered a great group of cooks who put together an array of dishes, and they present to you here a menu that ranges from sweet and romantic to sultry and seductive, from relationships enjoying a first taste to those that have moved beyond the entrée.

Each story also ends with a recipe. Some of these require cooking implements while others are whimsical accompaniments that don't require cooking at all—at least not in the traditional sense. After all, food serves as more than sustenance—it's a trigger for love, laughter, sex, pleasure, and carnal and sensory satisfaction. Whatever your palate prefers, you're sure to find something tasty here.

The menu includes dishes by Ashley Bartlett, Historia, Jae, Rebekah Weatherspoon, Cheyenne Blue, Karis Walsh, Victoria Oldham, Cheri Crystal, Andi Marquette, Jove Belle, R.G. Emanuelle, Sacchi Green, and Yvonne Heidt.

Sigil Fire

ERZABET BISHOP

ISBN: 978-3-95533-206-8
Length: 131 pages

Sonia is a succubus with one goal: stay off Hell's radar. But when succubi start to die, including her sometimes lover, Jeannie, she's drawn into the battle between good and evil.

Fae is a blood witch turned vampire, running a tattoo parlor and trading her craft for blood. She notices that something isn't right on the streets of her city. The denizens of Hell are restless. With the aid of her nest mate Perry and his partner Charley, she races against time before the next victim falls. The killer has a target in his sights, and Sonia might not live to see the dawn.

Coming from Ylva Publishing

www.ylva-publishing.com

Good Enough to Eat

JAE & ALISON GREY

Robin's New Year's resolution to change her eating habits is as unusual as she is. Unlike millions of other women, she isn't tempted by chocolate or junk food. She's a vampire, determined to fight her craving for a pint of O negative.

When she goes to an AA meeting, hoping for advice on fighting her addiction, she meets Alana, a woman who battles her own demons.

Despite their determination not to get involved, the attraction is undeniable.

Is it just bloodlust that makes Robin think Alana looks good enough to eat, or is it something more? Will it even matter once Alana finds out who Robin really is?

The Caphenon

FLETCHER DELANCEY

ON A SUMMER NIGHT LIKE any other, an emergency call sounds in the quarters of Andira Tal, Lancer of Alsea. The news is shocking: not only is there other intelligent life in the universe, but it's landing on the planet right now.

Tal leads the first responding team and ends up rescuing aliens who have a frightening story to tell. They protected Alsea from a terrible fate—but the reprieve is only temporary.

Captain Ekayta Serrano of the Fleet ship Caphenon serves the Protectorate, a confederation of worlds with a common political philosophy. She has just sacrificed her ship to save Alsea, yet political maneuvering may mean she did it all for nothing.

Alsea is now a prize to be bought and sold by galactic forces far more powerful than a tiny backwater planet. But Lancer Tal is not one to accept a fate imposed by aliens, and she'll do whatever it takes to save her world.

Driving Me Mad

L.T. SMITH

For Rebecca Gibson, her journey to a work convention will be one she'll never forget. After driving around for four hours, Rebecca stops to ask for directions at an isolated house on the outskirts of Kirk Langley, Derbyshire.

Her initial meeting with the house's attractive owner, Annabel Howell, seems strange and unsettling, but at her hostess's insistence, Rebecca spends the night.

Plagued by nightmares, Rebecca senses that her dream world has blended with what she believes is reality. When she leaves the next day, her life has changed.

Can Rebecca solve a mystery that has been haunting a family for over sixty years? Will she find love along the way?

Or will the events drive her mad?

Unwrap These Presents
Edited by Astrid Ohletz and R.G. Emanuelle

ISBN: 978-3-95533-277-8

Also available as e-book.

Published by Ylva Publishing, legal entity of Ylva Verlag, e.Kfr.

Ylva Verlag, e.Kfr.
Owner: Astrid Ohletz
Am Kirschgarten 2
65830 Kriftel
Germany

www.ylva-publishing.com

First edition: November 2014

Credits
Edited by Nikki Busch, Day Petersen, Glenda Poulter, Michelle Aguilar, Sandra Gerth, Andi Marquette, R.G. Emanuelle, Astrid Ohletz, Julie Klein, Blu, Debra Doyle, Alissa McGowan, Fletcher DeLancey

Cover Design and Formatting by Streetlight Graphics

CPSIA information can be obtained at www.ICGtesting.com
Printed in the USA
LVOW07s0254091214

417937LV00001B/33/P

Twenty-three authors of lesbian fiction contrib
that give you snow, presents, plenty of food,
nicely wrapped curvy women under the tree.

All profits of this anthology will be donated to
Trust in the UK and the Ali Forney Center
Both organizations provide housing for homeless

Authors:
Andi Marquette, Ashley Stevens, Catherine Lane, Cheri Crystal, Cindy Rizzo, Clare Lydon, Devin Sumarno, Erzabet Bishop, Eve Francis, Fletcher DeLancey, Jae, Jean Copeland, Joan Arling, Jove Belle, L.T. Smith, Lee Lynch, Lois Cloarec Hart, Nikki Busch, Patricia Penn, R.G. Emanuelle, S. M. Harding, T.M. Croke, Wendy Temple

ISBN 978-3-95533-277-8
9 783955 332778

www.ylva-publishing.com